I0563463

THE UNRAVELING OF COVENS

HS SULLIVAN

Copyright © 2025 H.S. Sullivan

All rights reserved.

This is a work of fiction. Names, characters, businesses and business names, events, and incidents are products of the author's imagination. Any resemblance to actual persons, living or dead, or actual events is purely coincidental.

No part of this book may be reproduced or used in any manner without the prior written permission of the copyright owner, except for the use of brief quotations in a book review.

Without limiting the author's and publisher's exclusive rights, any unauthorized use of this publication to train generative artificial intelligence (AI) technologies is expressly prohibited.

Edited by Brit Corley at This Bitch Reads Media IG: @thisbitchreads_

Hardcover: 979-8-9901349-4-2

Paperback: 979-8-9901349-3-5

Ebook: 979-8-9901349-5-9

Cover photo: Wolf Quillin (roses), Brita Seifert (burning rose)

Cover design: HVS

hssullivan.com

Printed by Crocketts Point Press

Also by HS Sullivan

Daughters of Legianne

For all of those that feel like they don't have a place in this world. You belong.

AUTHOR NOTE

This book contains themes of violence, addiction, physical and emotional traumas, intolerance to sexual orientation, gender, and identity, and politics.

There is on page violence which includes, death, murder, blood, and gore.

Off page reference to self-mutilation, murder, sexual assault, and violence.

This book contains explicit intimacy scenes.

Please exercise care for yourself and your boundaries as you read if you choose to continue.

PRONUNCIATION GUIDE

People
    Róisín - Row-sheen
    Madigan - Mad-ah-gan
    Lina - Lee-na
    Aoife - Ee-fah
    Brenna - Bren-nah
    Shasta - Shass-tah
    Nanette - Nah-net
    Lucius - Lew-shuss
    Matthew - Math-yoo
    Lily - Lih-lee
    Ione - Eye-ohn
    Jessamyn - Jess-AH-min
    Rastead - Rah-steed
    Dionomis - Dee-oh-no-miss
    Marsenna - Mar-sen-nah
    Runa - Roo-nah
    Aja - A-jah
    Anelle - Ah-nell
    Cicile - Siss-EE-l

Fatome - Fah-toe-m

Places/Things
    Legianne - Lee-jhaa-ahn
    Molennius - Ma-lay-nee-us
    Ely - Ee-lie
    Roidon - Roy-dawn
    Alleyette - Ah-lay-ett
    Aunellion - Awn-ell-ee-awn
    Shianshani - Shee-awn-sh-awn-ee
    Talista - Tah-liss-tah
    Briigie - Br-EE-j-EE
    Trifoa - Trih-foe-ah
    Baijiola - Buy-jee-oh-la
    Nianti - Nee-awn-tee
    Locaw - Low-cah
    Nautilanis - Naw-tih-law-niss
    Granier - Gr-ah-n-ee-r

"Life is not easy for any of us, but what of that? We must have perseverance and above all confidence in ourselves. We must believe that we are gifted for something and that this thing, at whatever cost, must be attained."

–Marie Curie

PROLOGUE

THE SENSATION that crawled along his spine and raised the hairs on his neck urged him to turn back down the hall to his rooms with as much fervor as the heart that pounded in his chest did.

Marcelo Dionomis had never liked to consider himself a smart man. At least not publicly. He lacked the grit he would need to change the public's opinion of the spoiled, idiot prince they believed him to be.

It allowed him to force them to think him incapable, so that when the time came, they would back his younger brother, Anthony, as king when their father stepped down.

If there was anything Marcelo wanted less, it was to bear the weight of that Goddess awful crown upon his head and rule Shianshani.

No, outside of the ruse, he was far from unintelligent.

Which is why the keening he heard from his father's library had drawn Marcelo close when he had returned from his evening with Nolani.

It wasn't natural. There was a wrongness to that high pitch slipping beneath the crack of the heavy wooden door of the library.

It was what Marcelo imagined death to sound of.

Marcelo crept closer; his feet silent upon the stone floor of the foyer.

A low snarl halted his movement. He stood frozen, waiting for the door to be opened. Waiting to be caught. He readied any excuse for being there, letting the words he knew his father would buy from his sorry excuse of a son rest on the tip of his tongue.

When the door stayed bolted, Marcelo's shoulders sagged with relief.

It took just three steps to reach the door. Slowly, he lifted a hand to the handle, praying that it would not creak as he nudged it open a crack.

No longer muffled by the door, the sounds became deafening, quickly overwhelming him. The urge to close the door and retreat to his rooms lit like a fire at his feet.

Instead, he pressed on, focusing on what the inch-wide crack had revealed to him.

A young woman sprawled on her back on his father's desk. Her gown ripped open down the front, exposing her breasts.

Marcelo's stomach seized.

It wasn't that his father was having an affair. No, King Rastead Dionomis had never been faithful to the queen for even a day of their marriage. Their union had been for the political gain of both families, and to ensure a good royal bloodline with their offspring.

It was the blood that covered the woman. The blood on the king's hand as it palmed her breast.

So much blood. Marcelo blinked, trying to focus, but his head swam as it grew lighter, his vision hazing.

The king's head whipped up with a deep growl and Marcelo had to swallow down his gasp at what he saw in the side profile of his father.

The rows and rows of snarled, jagged teeth. They were pointed and set in an extended jaw that dripped rivers of dark red blood. The eye on the left side of his face was large, solid black. Depthless.

The king licked the flat of his tongue along his bloodied hand. His grin was wicked as he looked down at the young woman.

"Larissa, my love." The king's voice was thick and guttural. "I had no idea you were so...delicious."

Then he dropped his head down to one of her breasts, mouth

opening wide, and sunk his teeth into her flesh. The sounds that followed made the bile rise from Marcelo's stomach. With a hand over his mouth, he ran.

CHAPTER 1

L ILY WALLINGSFORD stopped in the middle of the pathway in her sister's garden.

Ione moved from flower to flower, soothing them, bringing the wilting, drooping ones back to life. Her golden locks tamed into a long braid that stretched down her back, glinting in the light from Roidon's suns overhead. The corner of her mouth tipped up into a soft smile. A smile mirroring their late mother's.

"Are you going to stand there all day, or are you going to come help me?" Ione called over to her. Her attention never moved away from her beloved flowers.

Lily willed her feet forward. She knew Ione would ask how things went, and the lack of progress they were all making on *everything* had triggered a part of Lily that she hadn't known existed. That piece of her that ignited red and hot with anger.

"Grandmother stopped by." Ione finally looked at Lily.

She swallowed hard and licked her lips, her mouth suddenly a desert. "And?"

Ione waved a hand dismissively. "And nothing." She reached out and put her hands on Lily's shoulders. "I meant what I said that day I took you away from her. This is your home now. You don't have to go back to that. *Ever.* Do you understand?"

Unable to find her voice, Lily could only nod.

After the night Matthew disappeared and Nanette had learned of the bond between him and Lily, everything had exploded when they returned to Roidon. Nanette had first been furious that Shasta Fiero, the Coven leader of Molennius, had known before her. But the black powder that spewed from her as she shouted angrily at Lily ignited when Lily found the courage to admit that she was going to accept the bond, and Matthew, once they had brought him home. Nanette hadn't wanted to hear that Lily was confident in the man Matthew was. That he would find a compromise, so neither of them would have to forfeit their roles as heir to their Covens.

Lily had thought she'd been prepared for it. She felt it when they were trapped in Shasta's home. It had shot down the line that Nanette held as leader of their Coven, then doubled down their familial line in angry bursts. A bomb ticking, ticking, ticking.

"I'm going to have to talk to her eventually," Lily said.

"Let eventually be some other day. Right now, she's working with the boy on occasion, and you're doing whatever it is with Ro that you two are doing." Ione brushed a thumb over a white lily that had browning edges. Slowly, the brow faded away, the petals lifting with a sigh.

Ione had arrived in a blur in the middle of the argument. No words had been exchanged, just a cold, measured look from Ione, before she shifted Lily with her to her home on the other side of the capital. Then Lily had slipped off with Róisín, first to Baijiola, then to Trifoa.

"The boy? Caid's a grown man, Ione. And what do you mean by on occasion?" Had Róisín said something, and she had missed it? It was possible. At times, Lily was swept away, losing herself in the few moments she and Matthew had shared before. She felt the roots of guilt over her selfishness grow deeper.

Ione paused and looked up from the flower she had bent over. "He's been noticeably absent, that's all."

"Are you spying, Ione?" Lily lifted a brow.

She flashed a quick grin. Her cornflower blue eyes flashing with mischief. "Maybe."

"Ione," Lily said, drawing her name out.

"What? What is grandmother going to do about it? Tell me I'm a disgrace? Tell me I won't be leading our Coven someday?"

Lily sobered. Despite Ione being nearly a century older, it was Lily who had been named heir of Roidon. It'd been clear from the start once their mother had passed; Ione never had a chance. She not only was Moira's mirror image, but she had Moira's same fiery, independent personality.

Ione clucked her tongue and moved down the pathway. "Have you and Ro made any progress?"

Lily stepped to the edge of the path and leaned over a dahlia, frowning at its tightly balled bud. "Still trying to figure out the best foot forward. Róisín wants to see how the Covens are in this post...whatever that night was. We don't know how Troy is compared to Henry, nor who stepped into the role after Frederick died. We've been able to gather that no one really knows. Some say that *both* Runa and Jessamyn have taken the leader's title. It's so overwhelming. We don't know what we're doing, what we really need to do, or *why* we need to do it. I need—" She let out a frustrated noise. "I don't know what I need, but it's certainly more than this."

Ione placed a hand over Lily's that held the dahlia stem. "You're going to crush it. I can feel that energy trying to leak out of you."

"Sorry." Lily straightened. "It's been hard. I have no idea what I'm doing right now." Her confession was a whisper. "I've never done something like this before."

Ione moved closer, her mouth turning down slightly for a moment. "And Matthew?"

Lily's heart gave two quick, hard beats before it stuttered in her chest and slipped closer to her stomach where the acid bubbled, reaching to burn it. "Nothing."

Her magic reached down her line and grasped for a bond that hadn't yet had the chance to snap into place before Matthew had gone missing. "And before you even ask, no, I haven't told Róisín."

"Lily..." Ione closed her eyes and sighed. "Tell her. At least talk it out."

Lily squared her shoulders. "We'll get there when the time is right. Right now, it couldn't be the furthest from that."

Ione frowned. "So, you're gonna risk waiting until it's too late?"

"If that's how it works out, that's what the Sisters have fated for us." Lily's shoulders dropped.

Ione crossed her arms over her chest. "Sometimes, you're too trusting."

"You weren't there, Ione. That night we—" Lily wrapped her arms around her middle. "So much happened."

"Yeah, well, it's pretty stupid if you ask me to keep going on and pretend like nothing has changed," Ione said.

"We're not."

Ione snorted and shook her head. "You all are, and the quicker you admit it, the better. Otherwise, the time is going to run out, and then we're *all* fucked."

CHAPTER 2

E VERYTHING *HAD* changed. Then time seemed to stop.

Róisín McKenna dug her toes deeper into the burgundy sand of Trifoa. Her turquoise eyes stayed on the horizon where the surf rolled in toward her. The light pink waters of the Oceano di Luce foaming as they lapped at the sand near where she sat. One stuttered frame at a time was how life seemed to move. Even the sounds of the birds calling overhead were disjointed.

Pressing her toes further into the sand, she tried to press that new anxious feeling that had buzzed beneath her skin deeper. It was here, in the quiet moments with no other people around, that her heart beat the loudest. Each breath she took sounded like the winds of a hurricane pounding in her ears. Her vision struggled to focus.

It had been one month since Róisín had killed her grandmother.

That wasn't what chased her with every step. It wasn't what almost reached out and grabbed her right now, in this moment, when she tried to lose herself in a once lost memory with her mother on this very beach a century before.

It wasn't how easy it had been to wield her death magic and kill not one, but two people with it.

Nor that her best friend remained lost somewhere in the realms.

Róisín pressed her lips together and drew in a shaking breath, her eyes burning with tears.

Something was off. Something was wrong.

With each passing day, her stomach grew heavier, dread dropping rock after rock into her core.

Her anxiety must have been shouting, because when the waves finally reached her, soaking through the shorts she wore, Caid's magic reached through their tether and wrapped around her, beckoning her home.

Closing her eyes, she centered herself, breathing in steadying breaths. Then she reached within, deep within, and grasped what little of her magic she had left. Tears sprang to her eyes, and before the first sob could break free, she did the only thing she could still do with her magic. She shifted home.

CHAPTER 3

Róisín and Caid had been living at her remade childhood home in Northern Ireland. They had agreed that even with the threat of Madigan gone; they were still facing too many unknowns in their world to risk the safety of Caid's younger sister, Lina, who was now very pregnant with twins.

Relief slowly settled into her bones when she arrived at the cottage that sat cozily in a vibrant, verdant glen. It always felt like a warm hug welcoming her.

The shower water immediately shut off, and Caid appeared in the bathroom door. His features were soft and open at first until he saw her. Then the lines appeared between his brows and around his mouth. His normally hazel eyes darkened to a deep brown, with flares of dark green, as his magic rose inside him.

Hers sparked in response. Just a small, electric little thing. But it was enough. Her limbs loosened. Her heart moved from her throat to her chest, where it could beat without constraint. And she could finally draw in a full breath, soothing her aching lungs.

He was her Polaris. Her home.

"What happened?" His voice was low and rumbling.

Róisín did nothing to hide the appreciative look she cast over his naked body while he toweled off his curling, wet, sand colored hair. His own eyes remained on her, waiting. She had seen many the naked bodies of men, and women, before. None like his.

Kincaid McGrath took up space, and there wasn't any other way to describe it. Not only his height of six and a half feet, nor his broad chest and shoulders muscled from his years in construction, carrying heavy materials. His thighs, Róisín often compared to heavy tree trunks when he used his legs to maneuver her around whenever they sparred in Lucius's training room. Her eyes traced along the muscled lines of them, the sand-colored hair there. Her eyes had just begun to move northward when he wrapped the towel around his waist.

"What'd you do that for?" She pushed out her bottom lip.

"I asked you a question, and you're clearly distracted." He flashed her a mischievous grin, then moved across the room to her. He wrapped her in his arms and bent his head to kiss her.

She hummed, leaning against his solid frame and into the kiss.

"I missed you." The words were hot against her mouth.

She buried her face in his chest. His heart had a steady, calming beat there. "Can we run away?"

"You don't have to ask *me* that. I just need to convince you to change *your* answer."

"Let's do it. Let's just vanish. Just..." She tried to burrow deeper into his chest. "Go."

He brought his fingers to her chin, tipping her head up to look at him. His mouth turned down into a frown. "What happened?"

Róisín sighed, shoulders slumping. "Nothing. That's the thing. *Nothing* has happened. I feel like I'm wasting so much time, and before long, time will be out. It would have been fan-freaking-tastic if I got more than 'unite the Covens.'" She changed the tone of her voice, trying to mimic the low, lyrical tone the Goddess had that night in the Dead Forest.

Slowly, Caid's eyebrows rose.

"I mean, with Madigan, it was clear. By any means necessary, he had to go. Easy!" She threw her hands up and spun around, stomping her feet as she neared the bed. When she dropped onto the mattress, her breath came out in a heavy whoosh.

"Isn't this sort of"—he tipped his head from one side to the other—"an exploratory or investigative thing? Gauge moods, test waters, whatever it was you and Lucius said?" He followed her across the room. "Have you talked to Lily about it?"

Róisín laughed lightly. "I can see it even wearing on her. She's been quieter than she usually is, which sucks, because I'd like to get to know her better. Especially given she'll be family."

"Come here." He gestured her closer with his hands. Once she rose and stood in front of him, he reached out and brushed a strand of auburn hair from her face before pressing a kiss to the tip of her nose, then her forehead.

Róisín let herself fall forward and into him, letting his body be her anchor. Exhaustion tugged at her, threatening to pull her skin from her bones. If her mind would just slow down, if the dreams would just... stop. That's all she needed. Those quiet moments when the clarity could wash over her. She had that before, with Madigan. Those were the moments that also gave her the confidence she had needed to face the task before her.

She felt stretched thin. Near to breaking.

"Why don't you take a break?" Caid's voice broke through her thoughts and growing panic.

"That's all it feels like I'm doing. Taking one really long break." She frowned up at him. "I don't know what I'm doing." Her admission came in a shaking whisper.

He cupped her face in his hands. "It's safe to say that *none* of us do. We haven't exactly been left with a manual for this."

Róisín gave him a faint smile.

"Look, I'm still new to all of this, so I won't offer you words of advice because it'll just be platitudes or whatever." His thumbs stroked softly along her cheeks. "But I will say this: you doubt yourself too much. You did it with Madigan and look at that outcome."

"I—"

"No. I know exactly what you're going to do, and I won't hear it. Got it?" His eyes danced over her face. When she nodded slightly, his hands moved to her hair, to the back of her head, making her look up at him again. "Stop. You'll figure it out. You always do."

"And you have *way* too much faith in me," she muttered.

"Because I've seen what you're capable of when you push that part of your brain away that tells you that you suck."

She tipped her head to one side and made a popping sound with her lips. "Oh, really?"

He gave her a casual shrug in response.

Róisín wanted to believe him, but those voices that niggled in the back of her mind wouldn't let her free of their chains. They yanked at them now, telling her she would never get the Covens to come together as one completely. And they wouldn't find Matthew.

Caid's arms banded around her, hugging her tightly. "We'll find him."

"How can you be so sure?"

"Lucius and Shasta have been working around the clock, and they're wicked fucking smart. Ow!" He shouted when she pinched a spot on his side. "What the hell was that for?"

"Nothing." His chest muffled her voice where she hid her face and her smile.

"I can feel you smiling, you know."

She hummed. "Can we..." She glanced over her shoulder at the bed.

Caid arched an eyebrow at her.

"Not that." She rolled her eyes, pushing his chest playfully. "Not yet anyway. I just need to not think about all this crap and take a nap or something."

He scooped her into his arms, and she laid her head against his chest as he walked toward the bed. Before he lowered her to the soft blankets, her eyelids had already fluttered closed.

Chapter 4

MATTHEW MCARTHUR rested the golden eyed toddler with strawberry blond hair at his hip. When she had been born, he had been relieved that she hadn't had his dark red hair. As he looked down at her now, the carbon copy of her mother, he could only smile.

Samira may not look like him, and couldn't talk yet, but he could tell more and more with each day that went by that she at least had a dash of his... What did his own mother call it? *Zest*.

There was a commotion in the kitchen where he heard Lily and Nanette speaking clipped sentences to one another. He wondered if he should go in and check if they needed help. Remembering the last time he had been caught in the middle of one of their squabbles, he hesitated to take that risk again.

"Ah, there she is." Lucius beamed, coming into the living room. "The birthday girl!"

Samira reached for him, squealing in delight.

"Careful." Matthew warned as he handed her to him. "She's biting."

"It's a good thing your mother gave me this." Lucius produced a frozen teether, making Samira's eyes light with excitement.

"Get the Hells out of my kitchen, Grandmother." Lily's voice scolded sharply.

"I'm going to..." Matthew nodded toward the kitchen doorway.

Lucius chuckled and lowered himself and Samira onto the sofa. "You're a far braver man than I."

Matthew hummed absently.

"Maybe you can talk some sense into her. She's doing far too much. It's only her first birthday." Nanette squeezed by him.

He waited until she had joined Lucius in the other room before stepping into the kitchen and surveying the damage. Two cakes sat on the island of their sunny kitchen. Lily had said one was for Samira to squish and smash to her heart's content, the other was for everyone to eat.

"Cupcakes?" Matthew asked when he saw the two trays on the cooling rack.

"Muffins. Róisín gave me that recipe for those amazing breakfast muffins she made a few weeks ago. I had everything out already, so I figured." Her shoulders rose and fell in a jerking shrug. "Everyone's starting to arrive?"

"Dad just got here. I'm sure Shasta will be here soon. She's always early too. Róisín—" He huffed a laugh. "Those two kids will have her late for everything until the end of time."

Lily's hand went to her swollen stomach. "They say that the first ones are always so easy. When you add that second one in, they warn that it's chaos."

"I'm not worried about it." He crossed to her and spun her to face him. "We've got this. We make a good team." He gently kissed her flour covered nose. Like a well-loved blanket, calmness settled over him and he brought her closer, soaking in the moment.

"Matthew." Her tone may have been firm, but her eyes, so much like Samira's, laughed at him.

"Hm? Can't I kiss my wife?" He kissed her nose again, then each cheek. He nuzzled her neck, inhaling the smell of flour and citrus, before pressing a soft kiss to her shoulder.

"You can kiss me any time you'd like." She smoothed her hands over his chest, rising to her toes to brush a kiss over his mouth. "However, I can *feel* you." She chuckled and glanced down. "I need to get this all cleaned up, then get the rest of the party set up before everyone gets here. You know how my cousins and sister are."

He rolled his eyes. Once they had come to that place in their relationship when she was ready for their bodies to come together, it had felt like he couldn't get enough. He had never wanted someone so completely before, mind, body, and soul. "Let's make a deal. I'll clean all of this up, and you go out and get the table set up the way you want it for the photos you want. This way, you won't have to see whatever abomination I create in those photos."

She leaned into him and hummed. "That sounds absolutely perfect. I love you."

He cupped her face and took her mouth with his for a slow kiss. "I love you, too. Now, let's get this party started."

Something damp brushed over Matthew's cracked lips, and he let out a breath that was more of a whimper. With effort, he got his hand to his mouth, his blistered fingers brushing the rough skin of his face. The fog in the field in Aunellion had grown denser. Its heaviness settled over him and saturated him. When his tongue darted out to lap up the moisture on his lips, he let out a moan.

When he had thought about his death, it hadn't been this. He hadn't thought he would waste away, dying slowly while his mind moved him through false realities that felt more real than the life he lived before he had shifted there with Mildred.

Lily...

Their child had felt so real when he held her in his arms. Her smell was sweet like fresh spring flowers, like Lily.

There was a faint sound to his left, a rasping breath.

"I..." Mildred sucked in air. "... the pit destroys your soul."

"Fuck off," he muttered. "You'll get there before I do."

Silence fell over them again. He licked his lips one more time before he blinked up at the fog overhead. It was thick, like winter soup, and it seemed to breathe, to reach for him. His body had grown so weak that breathing felt like a chore. His breaths came far between one another, and he kept them as shallow as he could.

He couldn't help but wonder how much longer it would be before he finally took his last.

CHAPTER 5

THE ALLEYETTE castle was tumbling down around Róisín. Her heart hammered against her chest, and she fought for air as she called out for Caid. Chunks of jagged rock fell from the ceiling, narrowly missing her. Digging for courage, she pushed herself to keep moving deeper into the castle.

She tugged on their connection again but felt nothing in return. Frantically, she continued to pull, until she was met with the frayed end of their line. What it meant trying to claw through her, rip through her heart. Shoving it down and pressing on, she used her magic to shield herself from the rain of debris that continued trying to pelt her.

Mildred stepped from the hallway and stood before her. Her face twisted into a sharp sneer. "Your lover boy is gone. You'll have nothing at the end of this, you know. The Goddess gave you empty promises. You'll lose it all, just as it was meant to be."

Róisín jerked awake, gasping for air.

Caid's arms were around her, his breath warm at her shoulder. "I'm right here." His voice was rough from sleep. "I'm right here. It was a dream."

Rolling, she burrowed herself against him. She drew in a long breath, taking in the scent of him, using it to ground herself. "Mildred is still alive."

His body tensed around her.

"Trifoa hasn't called upon its Coven heir. Beatrice still hasn't," Róisín said against his chest. "The other realms... Troy has taken leadership in Baijiola. There are rumors that both Jessamyn and Runa had stepped into power with the Shianshani Covens, but we've yet to have that confirmation." She drew in a shaking breath, closing her eyes. "We had Frederick's body, and you saw Henry—" She shuddered at the memory of the charred outline of a body on the judgment chamber wall. "We at least know it's one or both Lunestran siblings at the head."

Caid stroked a hand in circles over her back. "With Trifoa, that no one had stepped up, that really means that she could still be?"

Róisín pushed herself up into a sitting position, tucking her legs beneath her. She tugged at her bottom lip for a moment before dragging her index finger back and forth over it, lost in her thoughts.

"When a Coven leader dies, their magic and the power it holds are passed on. The ascension to leadership occurs after. Through the connection with the other Coven members, that person is then recognized as the head of the Coven. There's no way to stop it or avoid it." She shook her head.

"Is that what happened when..."

"It was awful." She couldn't stop the way her body convulsed as she recalled the moment she inherited her entire Coven's worth of magic. "I think it was more intense because there was no one else and it was a Coven's worth of magic that just slammed into me. It was almost a month before I could get out of bed again."

"Do you want to talk about it? The dream?" Caid asked, his voice soft.

She pulled her gaze from where she had been staring distantly and looked at him. That panic, the fear she had felt in her dream, that she had felt that day she'd pushed through the doors of the castle, feeling their connection fading. Without a word, she threw her arms around him, pulling him to her and crushing her mouth to his.

His hands went to her hips, maneuvering her so that she was astride him. When she shifted so that she aligned with him, his fingers flexed, gripping her flesh. He rocked himself up and from his throat came a deep sound that was more growl than moan.

"I can't wait." Her words were a whisper in the air between them. "Not tonight." She clung to him desperately. Her want, her need, bursting into flames inside of her.

He brought his hands to her back, then rolled them over, tucking her beneath him. She tipped her head up, her turquoise eyes holding his hazel ones. She opened, leaving herself completely exposed to him so that he would see her desperation to chase away the clinging edges of her dream. Then she reached between them and took his cock in her hands. She stroked him once, twice, before bringing him to her entrance.

A low rumble of pleasure vibrated from his chest as he eased himself into her. He pressed kisses along her neck, nipped at her chin, stilling with a satisfied sigh when he was fully seated inside of her. Lifting her legs, she wrapped them around his back, bringing him in deeper.

Slowly, he drew out, his eyes remaining locked on hers. Then he thrust into her, making her cry out his name and grip his biceps. He drew out again. This time she met his thrust, her hips coming up to meet him.

"Fuck, I can't hold on long," he ground out.

Róisín's became alight with the coming orgasm. Unable to find words for him, she could only moan and writhe her body in response. Her stomach tensed and her walls tightened. Arching her back, she pressed her face into the pillows and screamed as the world around her exploded with light when she came.

Caid's thrusts became faster, harder. A moment later, with a low growl vibrating from his chest and throat, his release came. He caught himself on his forearms, just over her, and panted heavily.

"Sorry."

She let her fingers brush over his back and pressed a kiss to his shoulder. "For?"

"That was quick." He leaned his body to one side, collapsing next to her.

She hummed and rolled, slinging a leg over his hip. "It's not like I didn't come too."

He half-shrugged and nuzzled her neck.

"Caid, I'm scared."

He pulled back to look at her.

"I keep having this dream about Mildred. I don't know if it's because of what happened with Matthew, paired with being on Trifoa or not. She's there that day in the castle. It's falling down around me. I can't feel you. No matter how hard I pull, *I can't feel you.* Mildred tells me I'll lose it all. I'll have nothing when this is done, just as the Sisters said, despite what the Goddess has said."

His index finger traced her jaw until he reached her chin. Hooking it, he turned her face to his. "What were the exact words the Goddess said to you that night in Roidon?"

"My mother had been let to live with my father in the afterworld." She blinked away the tears that had built. "And I was to unite the covens."

The Seer drifts...

She drew in a breath, holding it, trying to suffocate the words that had been haunting her.

"Madigan is gone. Aoife is gone. The others are too. Well, maybe not Mildred, but the others should be able to help us figure that out. There's nothing left, Róisín." His lips brushed over the tip of her nose, then her forehead. "This is it. This is just our life now. I know the past year has been on-edge, for all of you. *You* especially. But this?" He tucked her against his side. "It's trying to crawl under your skin. You can't let it. It'll eat you alive."

"I wish I had that sense of surety you have."

His body tensed ever so briefly next to her before he relaxed again. "Let me let you in on a secret. I have absolutely no fucking idea what I'm doing. I thought I did, but life happily showed me otherwise."

Róisín tapped one of her fingers against his chest lightly. Dark edges crept in, trying once again to shut out the light she desperately searched for. *Not right now, please, not right now.* "Guess we're figuring shit out together, huh?"

He grunted before rolling them over and showering her face, neck, and body with kisses, sending her into a fit of giggles.

CHAPTER 6

THE SMOKY darkness that had circled Caid after his magic had awoken grew legs after that night in Alleyette. Now, he could hear the slap of its feet rushing toward him in the shower. It had him cornered. Or so it thought. He squeezed his eyes shut and counted slowly to ten as he drew in a breath.

Suffocating. He was suffocating. His lungs expanded, yet no air entered.

The steam from the hot water pressed against him, stealing his breath, weighing down his chest. Holding him down. Giving the darkness a chance to reach for him.

He released his breath and pressed his hands against the shower wall. The scalding hot water turned his skin red as it pelted his back. Caid hung his head, letting it drop between his shoulders, and flexed his fingers. When he felt grooves in the tile, he jerked back, eyes shooting open.

"What the fuck?" He dropped his hands quickly, taking a staggering step back.

Lines from his index, middle, and ring fingers on each hand marred the gray tiles.

His heart, the sound of wind and thunder, hammered in his ears. His breath quickened.

"Caid?" Róisín called from the other side of the door. "Are you alright?"

His chest heaved with his pants and he tried to gather himself. Was he alright?

"Caid?"

"Yeah." Shaking his head, he tried to free himself from the feeling. He wiped a hand over his face, reminding himself that he was alright. There was no other option but for him to be. There wasn't any other choice. Róisín needed him. Lina needed him. "I'm good."

"You sure?" The door opened, and he saw her shadow moving on the other side of the curtain.

The thunder in his ears grew louder. His lungs tightened, making his chest burn.

Róisín's head popped around the curtain. Her eyes were bright. Like the Caribbean under a summer sun, sparkling. It had taken two days for the dullness that had been in them when she had come home from Trifoa to fade. "I heard you shout something."

He lifted his left arm and pointed at his elbow. "The funny bone isn't so funny."

She snorted. Her eyes roamed over his body, from his head to his toes and back. The mischief on her face painted clear. "Need me to kiss it and make it better?"

"We're already late meeting Shasta because *you* let *me* kiss it and make it better."

Róisín hummed and licked her lips. "Good point. I don't like it, but it's a good point."

"I'll be out in a second and then we can go." Somewhere inside of him scolded him for being foolish.

Instead of closing the curtain, she stayed with her attention on him. Her brow furrowed and her eyes searched his. The only sign she let on that she knew something was going on with him. That she had said nothing to him, hadn't asked him, was an indication that she was giving him the space to work it out and come to her when he was ready.

"Let me take care of you..." she had said to him that night. The question was, would he ever be ready? When he was, if he was, what would it mean for them and their future?

CHAPTER 7

MARCELO STOOD, spine straight, chin high, in the large oval entertainment hall of the Dionomis Castle. The high society of Shianshani, both humans and witches, adorned in their finest, danced around the room, surrounded by walls of jade and a golden domed ceiling from which a twelve-tier crystal chandelier hung.

"Prince Dionomis." A sweet-faced brunette approached and curtsied to Marcelo. "Wonderful to see you here this evening."

Marcelo clenched his jaw at the retort that fought to rise from his throat. Lady Freya wasn't at fault for her and his mother's schemes. She was just doing what duty had demanded of her.

At twenty-four, his family expected him to be married and have at least one heir added to the Dionomis line. Much to his father's disappointment, he remained unwed and as far as the public or his father's concern, Marcelo also remained unattached. His mother was just trying to keep the peace and pacify his father. Yet, it still didn't stop that chafing feeling that rode his nerves.

"Pleasure, Lady Freya." He tipped his head in greeting.

"Mother said you and Anthony have just returned from the jungles.

Do tell me, did you catch sight of the elusive Mornash? I hear they're quite beautiful."

He hummed, studying her. "They are quite beautiful, indeed. However, their *smallest* teeth are nearly thirty centimeters. Gorgeous cats, but deadly."

She tapped her chin in thought. "I should still love to see one someday."

Marcelo's brow rose. "Perhaps a visit to the sanctuary can fulfill that desire."

"Why, Prince Dionomis"—her lips curved in delight—"are you proposing a date?"

"Ah, Celo, there you are!" Anthony nearly shouted the words, coming up next to him. His eyes dipped down to Freya's toes and crawled back up the length of her body. "Freya."

"Lord Anthony." She curtsied. "Prince Dionomis and I were—"

"I need you." Anthony gripped Marcelo's arm. "Immediately."

Marcelo offered her a shrug in apology. "Good evening, Lady Freya."

"I'll hold you to that sanctuary visit, Prince," she called after him.

"What? What's going on?" Marcelo asked when they had made it to the other side of the grand room.

"When was the last time that you spoke with Father?" Anthony's eyes were everywhere, on everyone but Marcelo.

"Ant, what's wrong?" Worry surged like a tidal wave inside of him. He could not shake the scene that he'd discovered weeks before. It had chased and nipped at his heels, laughing at him and the helplessness he felt.

"He—" Anthony swallowed visibly before taking a moment, pressing his lips together. "He's been asking curious questions about Cassius. I know he confides in you, does he... Does he know?"

"He hasn't said a word to me about Cassius. How do you know about the questions?" Marcelo asked.

"*The entire staff is talking about it.*" Anthony's answer was both exasperated and dramatic. "Where in the Hells have you... oh. She's back from university, isn't she?"

As if on cue, Nolani Fatome entered the room. Anthony and Marcelo's eyes tracked her movements as her lithe frame carried her through the crowd. Her bright smile flashed in greeting to those she passed by. Her deep chestnut hair shone under the massive chandelier and made her coffee-colored skin seem to glow.

"You're staring," Anthony whispered next to him.

"Of course I'm staring. She's fucking gorgeous," Marcelo muttered.

"Go to her. She's looking for you, you know she is. But please, see if you can find out if Father knows about..."

Marcelo turned to his younger brother and saw the worry lines etched around his face. It was clear that they were brothers. Both had wheat blond hair and eyes like ice on an overcast day. They had their father's high cheekbones and square jaw. His height had passed on to them as well. The brothers stood at six-foot-two-inches. However, Marcelo's body was strong and lean, whereas Anthony was broad. And Marcelo could keep his emotions from his face. Anthony could not.

"When you're king, you can change all of this." Anthony had dropped his voice should anyone be trying to eavesdrop. "You can fix all of this, this *shit*."

"I don't want it, and you know that," Marcelo said.

"He won't give it to me. We both know that. He knows what I am. It revolts him. We can't forget the laws against it, Celo. No matter how many meetings I attend, how many wars I fight in, or what political games I play—he'll never choose me."

And that fact, Marcelo knew, broke Anthony's heart and cracked his soul. Anthony had been born to lead. He had a kindness and a fairness to him that their people, human and witch kind, rightfully deserved.

At the thought of what he had seen in Rastead's library, Marcelo shuddered.

"Marcelo," a smooth, honeyed voice, like music to his ears, said over his shoulder.

He turned and faced Nolani. "Evening, Lady Fatome." He dipped his head.

"You boys look quite dapper this evening." She looked from him to Anthony before dropping her voice low. "Cassius said he'll be at the far end of the courtyard garden."

Anthony's eyes widened, and Marcelo could hear his intake of breath before his shoulders sagged. "Thank you." He planted a loud, smacking kiss on her cheek before darting off.

"When do we get to slip away?" She let her arm brush against Marcelo's, her eyes, the colors of a tiger's eye rock he had seen once on a trip to the realm of Earth, scanned the room.

King Dionomis entered the room with the queen on his arm. Rastead's coal black suit decorated over the left side of his chest with the family's crest of the Locaw bird. Its blunt, pointed beak was open in mid-screech. Large talons held Nautilanis, the ancestral sword of the Dionomis bloodline.

"Right now." The bite in Marcelo's tone made Nolani shiver, and he winced. "I'm sorry. Right now, please," he said more softly.

"Are you sure?" Her eyes followed the king and queen as they crossed the room. They both knew that Rastead was searching for Marcelo.

He slipped his hand into hers and tugged her through the servant entrance two steps to their left.

"Marcelo, wait." She squeezed his hand. "Let me take these off. If we're sprinting, I can't do it in these ridiculous things."

Marcelo halted.

"What is it? What happened?"

"I... We need to... shit." He stooped and swept her in his arms. "Not here. I can't tell you here."

CHAPTER 8

JESSAMYN LUNESTRAN stood in the shadows and watched as the oldest prince lifted the eldest Fatome daughter into his arms and sprinted through the lower level doors. Castle staff working quickly to clear his way, lest he trample them.

"Shit." Runa Lunestran's voice was low and deep next to her.

"He knows." Jessamyn nodded.

Runa's maroon eyes scanned their surroundings, his mouth in a tight line.

"It's alright." Jessamyn turned to him and placed one of her ebony hands upon his chest. "To the others, he just looks like a lust lorn child taking his sweetheart off to a rendezvous. I'm going to make my rounds. Meet me in my suite in twenty."

Runa's nostrils flared for a moment as he exhaled long and heavily. Then, with a curt nod, he spun on a heel and disappeared into the fray of staff.

Jessamyn took a moment to herself to smooth her features. She tucked a piece of her emerald hair behind her ear and patted the tight braids along the side of her head. Closing her eyes, she swallowed hard, counted to ten, then shoved through the heavy wooden doors that led to the entertainment hall.

"Ah, there she is," Queen Marsenna said. Her bright red lips parted in a wide smile, revealing her perfect white teeth.

Jessamyn dipped into a low curtsy before the queen, then shifted to face King Rastead and curtsied again. "Your Highness."

Rastead nodded to her and immediately disregarded her presence. His eyes darted around the room, searching for someone.

Marsenna leaned in close to her. "Did he get out of here?"

"Just moments ago," Jessamyn confirmed softly. "He had Lady Fatome with him."

Marsenna brightened. "Good."

"Where's Marcelo?" Rastead returned his attention to them, his eyes dark on Jessamyn.

"Apologies, Your Highness, I've only just arrived. I was held up doing"—she glanced at Marsenna, who was indulging in her glass of champagne—"some research on the matter you presented this morning."

The heaviness that had visibly weighed his shoulders down released, and his posture relaxed. "Any news?"

She struggled with the urge to lift a curious eyebrow. Was that hope that she heard in the Wicked King's tone? With fresh interest, she studied him closely. Something was different, something was... off about the man who stood before her. He shifted his weight from foot to foot, eyes constantly moving. Almost like he was...*uncomfortable.*

This new king in the Dionomis line, Rastead the ninth, had thrived on these gatherings, holding them often, and practically dancing around the room in delight as he socialized and flaunted the Dionomis wealth.

To see him suddenly looking like he wanted to disappear into one of the intricately woven tapestries along the wall had her itching to get back to her suites and to her brother's journals.

"Unfortunately, not yet, Your Highness. If you would let me bring some of my Coven members in, I could find what you're looking for sooner."

"No!" he shouted, startling both her and Marsenna, who dropped her champagne glass when she jumped. "Dammit. Find someone to clean this fucking mess up."

He turned with an angry growl and stomped his way into the crowd of people.

"Don't worry about him." Marsenna waved a dismissive hand. "Or this. I know you don't want to be here, sweetheart. Take this as your opportunity to high tail it. When you see that brother of yours, thank him for the help earlier today."

Jessamyn had to stifle her laughter at the way Marsenna wiggled her eyebrows.

"One perk of vigorous men working in the summer," Marsenna added over her shoulder before dipping into the crowd.

Jessamyn waited thirty seconds before making her exit from the room and shifting to her suites.

"That wasn't twenty minutes." Runa had his large frame sprawled across one of her sofas so that one leg was over the back, while the other was almost slipping off the edge, his foot hovered near the floor.

She lifted a brow and shook her head. "Why don't you just"—she swept an arm out—"make yourself at home, darling brother of mine?"

"Meh." He shifted so that he was sitting upright. "Let me guess, Marsenna is already drunk and Rastead is plotting the best ways to thrash Marcelo?"

She walked over to her wardrobe, opening it and depositing her cloak. She hated the formal attire that the court demanded and needed to be free of it. When she stripped down naked, Runa let out a loud groan behind her. "Oh, shut up." She growled and rolled her eyes. "You've seen it all plenty before."

"That was then." He made a show of slapping a hand over his face just as she turned to him.

"Do you—" She cleared her throat, clearing away the emotion that quickly pressed there, trying to wrap its fingers around her windpipe. "Do you ever miss it?"

Runa spread his fingers, doing his best to glare at her in the space he created. "Miss what?"

"You know." She gestured to her naked frame.

Dropping his hand, he shrugged. "To be honest? I don't even remember what it was like. I was kept so sheltered until we went to the well source." He tipped his head to one side. "No one remembers Runaani Lunestran." His voice cracked when he said his former name. "I've always been Runa. So, it..." He turned his hands over and shifted them back and forth. "It's like Runanni never existed."

Frederick had never forgotten. And even though Frederick was gone, her muscles tightened, readying to protect Runa from Frederick's viciousness. Jessamyn tried to shake off the feeling. It would do them no good to let Frederick have any power over them in his death.

"For that, I'll always be grateful to have the parents we had. What they did gave me the chance at this life. Gave me the ability to be who I was meant to always be."

Runa may not remember his years before. Jessamyn did. She studied her younger brother. The heart that was always soft for him danced in her chest, remembering. How broken and bruised he had been in those years before. What he had experienced as he tried to live in his light. The man sprawled on her sofa showed almost no trace of that person. She wondered if he ever felt the shadows move through him that she sometimes saw in his eyes.

Now, Runa radiated comfort and peace. His energy pulsing in soft yellows, greens, and purples. They were nearly a century apart in age, but of all her siblings, they had been the closest. She had been his protector when Frederick would decide, repeatedly, that Runa was a disgrace to their coven.

"He's gone," Runa said softly.

She blinked away the sting burning her eyes and nodded. "I know. It'll take time, but I know."

Runa clapped his hands together and sprung to his feet. "Let's change the topic." He joined her at the wardrobe, and after a moment of rifling through the hanging clothes, pulled out a pair of deep blue sweatpants and a faded gray sweatshirt. He pressed the clothes into her arms. "But first, I'm done talking to you naked."

After dressing, she took a seat on the sofa, directly across from him and the oval wooden coffee table.

"Do you think Anthony knows?" Runa asked.

"If Marcelo has learned about the king, then it's only a matter of time before Anthony and Cassius do." She looked over to the clock ticking softly on the wall, then back to him. "By now, Nolani already knows."

"The question now is, what do we do?"

Jessamyn rubbed her hand over her face and groaned. "I received notice this morning. Róisín McKenna is planning to come visit. She has requested a meeting with Rastead and I."

"With current developments, are we changing the plan?"

She drummed her fingers on her knees. Marcelo and the others certainly knowing complicated things, but she had spent the last several decades laying the foundation for her plans. No, nothing could get in her way, not now. Risks were always present, so what were a few more in having the humans know now?

"I know what I was told. I know what I've seen. We stick to the plan. We *have* to."

Runa grumbled something under his breath.

"I can find a new captain for our army."

His eyebrows became dark slashing lines as he drew them down over his eyes that glared at her. "That's not what I meant, and you know it. It was just easier when there weren't any humans involved."

"Our king is human, Runa, and he's at the very center of this whole damned thing."

CHAPTER 9

Róisín rolled her bottom lip between her fingers as she trudged her way down the stairs toward the kitchen. Worry was a living, breathing being that hovered over her shoulder. It prodded her to turn around and go back into the bathroom and demand answers from Caid. She had felt it in the air around him in recent weeks. Felt it in the way it sometimes burned like acid sliding along their tether, threatening to melt it.

It pounded at her door again.

Something is wrong. Something isn't right.

But here, in their home, it was different. It wasn't what she felt out there among other people. That pressing and pulsing was different, bigger, more confusing. This? This had her heart racing, skipping, throwing itself against her chest in desperation.

Something was happening with Caid, and it terrified her. Not only that, but he was so obviously trying to deal with it in a very Kincaid McGrath type of way. On his own.

It was slipping through her fingers and she didn't even know what it was.

The soft knock at their front door as she rounded the hallway toward the kitchen had her pausing. They were already late for meeting

35

Shasta in Ely where she had been staying. Another person in Róisín's life who was far from alright. Shasta had become quiet, distant even after that night. She and Lucius worked day and night, scouring books in Alleyette's libraries and were now in the archives in Ely's capital city, Cascadia. Despite weeks of searching, they were still no closer to a way of locating Matthew.

Róisín's hand hovered at the doorknob. There had yet to be another knock. Had she imagined it? So much clamored around inside her mind that she wouldn't be surprised if she had.

"Open up. I can practically hear you breathing through the door."

Róisín yanked open the door and lifted a brow at Shasta. "What are you doing here? We were supposed to come to you."

"Is that really the question to ask?" Shasta gave Róisín a rare smirk. Or at least, considered rare as of late. Shasta's overall demeanor had been somber, not just distant. "I feel as though you should thank me for using the door and knocking first, judging by your..." She let out a soft snort before grinning widely. "*Appearance.*"

"The good thing about you coming to the door, *Auntie Shass*, is that I can slam—"

Movement behind Shasta had Róisín gasping, then choking out a sob. *No. It can't... how?* She blinked her tear-filled eyes, trying to clear them so she could see. Be sure. She struggled to find her voice as she stared at the tall, blue eyed, auburn haired man next to her mother. "Daddy?"

Stephen stretched his arms out wide, grinning at her, his face wet from the tears streaming down his face. "My *calon bach.*"

Without hesitation, she launched herself at him, wrapping her arms tightly around him. The smell of cedar and lemon slid around her in a comforting embrace. "Daddy," she whispered.

"I've missed you so much." His breath brushed against the top of her head as he spoke. "So, so much."

The heavy thud of something hitting the floor behind them had her jerking her head around to the doorway. Caid stood wide eyed, panting as though he had just sprinted a marathon.

Brenna, who had been standing next to Shasta, nodded to him. "Good afternoon, Kincaid. Apologies for the lack of notice, but..." She turned back to Róisín and Stephen. Her eyes emerald eyes glittered with tears as she smiled.

"How?" Róisín asked, her voice barely a whisper, afraid if she spoke too loudly, her father would disappear.

"It was tricky. Some trial and error." Brenna shrugged. "But we got it figured out. That's what matters."

Róisín took her father's face between her hands. His beard pricked her skin just as it had when she was a child. He was there. Her father was there. "I'm incredibly rude. Daddy"—she motioned toward Caid—"this is Caid. Caid, my—" She brought a hand to her chest, trying to calm her breathing and her heart. "My father, Stephen."

Caid stepped forward, hand extended. "Pleasure to meet you, sir."

Róisín watched the way her father's knuckles whitened as he squeezed Caid's hand in his and had to fight back a smile. A moment she dreamed of one hundred times over, her father meeting someone she loved, only to wake with her heart in pieces knowing that Stephen was gone and the humans, unlike the witches, didn't get to cross the veil. To have him there with her... Her heart stuttered.

"I've heard a lot about you," Stephen said. His gaze slid down to Brenna.

"Uh." Caid's throat bobbed with his hard swallow.

"Why don't we go inside," Shasta said. "We can scrap our earlier plans and worry about that later. I'm hungry."

Brenna stepped up to her and hooked her arm through Shasta's. "That sounds wonderful. We have about an hour before the veil calls us back." The duo moved toward the door and Brenna halted, tipping her head back. "Since when did we have two floors?"

Róisín's cheeks heated. "I may have taken a liberty or two when I recreated it after Madigan found it."

A shadow crossed Brenna's face and her jaw flexed with the clenching of her jaw. "You did well, my little rose. It's beautiful."

Róisín stood, her feet rooted, watching Shasta and Brenna walk into the house, followed by her *father*.

"Are you okay?" Caid's voice was quiet next to her.

"It's—" She blinked, the thickness of her emotions clogging her senses. "He's here, Caid. My father, who is *human*, is *here*. I never thought I'd see him again."

Caid brought her against his chest, his arms wrapping tightly around her. "Anything's possible."

She pulled back to look up at him. So many words lingered on her tongue, ready to be spoken. Questions ready to be asked. Promises to be made to the man looking down at her like she was all that mattered in his world. Instead of asking them, trusting that space and time were the best for them, for him, she rose to her toes and brushed a kiss over his lips. Linking their hands together, she led him into the house where her family waited.

CHAPTER 10

S HOUTING DREW Lily from her room and sent her racing down the stairs of Ione's home. Not the murmurs that had pulled her from sleep. Nor the electric energy of magic simmering in the air.

"Get out of my house, *Grandmother*." Ione's voice lifted into a shout, her shoulders high and square. Her eyes were no longer blue, instead they swirled with the yellows, greens, and purples of her magic.

"You cannot keep her from me. I am this Coven's leader and she is their heir!" Nanette screamed back.

"I don't give a shit—"

"Enough!" Lily shouted from the steps behind them.

"Lily—"

"No, Ione, I've got this. It's okay," Lily said.

"Are you sure?"

Lily looked from her to Nanette, feeling the anger radiating off her in waves. She swallowed hard. "Maybe don't go far. Please?"

Ione moved closer, taking one of her hands and squeezing it lightly. "She can't hurt you," she whispered.

"I can hear you," Nanette said.

"That was the point." Ione glanced over her shoulder. "I'll be in the kitchen."

Lily nodded, then brought her attention back to their grandmother. Her salt and pepper hair in an untidy bun atop her head. Amber and red danced in her irises like flames. The whites were bloodshot.

"This is no way for an heir to behave." Nanette's barely contained magic seethed just under her skin in flashes of white and red lights.

"I wouldn't need to behave this way if you could just accept the fact that Matthew and I are bound."

"Being bound means nothing. You can deny the bond, and we can move on with our lives. There is absolutely no need to disrupt your Coven this way, Lily."

Lily's hands fisted at her sides. She counted to five, then back from five before she answered, "I will not risk disrupting *everything* by going against the Fates. Not taking the bond will have far more damning consequences for us all."

And she had begun to fall in love with Matthew. The weeks they had spent together in the libraries and archives researching ways to help Róisín, it had happened slowly. He had, like a marinade, seeped into her skin, into her heart. At first, it had scared her. Falling in love gave him too much power to hurt her.

That was the one thing that Lily did her best to do, shield herself from hurting. It had happened when her mother died. That pain was like no other, and she made the silent vow that never again would she feel that way.

Then Matthew came into her life. The thought of never hearing the deep, smooth timber of his voice, or being surrounded by his wood-smoke scent again made her chest hurt.

"You would put other Covens before your people?" Nanette asked.

Lily studied her grandmother, the woman she had once looked up to and respected. Held to a high regard because there wasn't anything Nanette wouldn't do to keep her Coven safe. Even if it meant befriending someone as awful as Aoife.

Now Lily realized no one was immune to Nanette's will. "Yes, I would. If putting my Coven first meant bringing harm to all our people? I absolutely would." A warmth spread across her chest. If they didn't find Matthew, if she couldn't... *No,* her heart shouted at her. They *would* find Matthew. Their bond would be tied, and they would move forward together. What forward looked like for them, they would navigate when they were together again.

Nanette stood quietly, her face stone as she stared at her. "You are not the leader I thought you would be. I regret the day I named you my heir."

Lily snorted and shook her head. "You only think that because I'm not selfish."

Nanette shook her head. "You'll learn. Hopefully, it will not be too late when that happens. When that day comes, I will be there. To tell you I told you so, and to pick up the pieces."

Before Lily could respond, she was gone.

Ione entered the room moments later. "Are you good?"

"I can't believe I told her off." Lily blinked at the empty space before her.

"Everyone needs to hear that they should go fuck themselves once in a while." Ione shrugged. "What next?"

"I..." In the heat of the moment, she had forgotten the timeline that she and Róisín had mapped out before parting ways in Trifoa. "I need to research Shianshani more. They have certain customs and traditions for their guests."

"Alright." Ione cracked her knuckles. "I'm at your service. Whatever you need, I'm your girl."

The warmth in her chest grew. "I love you."

Ione flashed a wide grin at her. "Of course you do. I'm amazing."

CHAPTER 11

Róisín and her father sat in the garden behind the cottage in one chair. When he had grinned at her, that wide, face-splitting smile she remembered from childhood, and patted his lap, there was zero hesitation from her. She lowered into his lap and wrapped her arms around his neck, laying her head on his shoulder.

Brenna and Shasta had cornered Caid in the house, insisting that he help them bake whatever it was Shasta had decided she needed to make at that very moment. Róisín had known that it was their way of giving her and her father a quiet moment before the veil pulled them back. She had seen the way her mother's form had begun to fade around its edges just before she ushered the pair outside and closed the door behind them.

Now, she nuzzled her nose against her father's neck and drew in a long breath, savoring the smell of him. It had been over a century since she had last had a moment like this. There wasn't anything that was going to stop her from soaking it in wholly.

"Do you, by any chance, have a book?"

She hummed and closed her eyes. A second later, Stephen's body shook with laughter, the book *The Wind in the Willows* in his hands.

"This was your favorite." His voice was soft, but it rumbled from his chest against her body.

"Still is." She shifted so that she was curled tighter against him. "Will you read it before you go?"

He pressed a kiss on her head, then cracked the book open and read. Listening to the cadence of his Welsh accent, Róisín's eyes fluttered closed. The soft timber of his voice soothed her like a song she knew the chords to but had forgotten the lyrics.

The nights he would stretch out in her small bed, reading the same book to her came to mind along with many other memories of him that were still somehow locked away tightly when the others had filtered free.

When he finished, he closed the book and set it next to them. "You've grown just a wee bit since I last saw you. But you look just the same. So much like your mother."

"But taller."

"Quite a bit taller." His laughter was a rumble beneath her ear. "That comes from my side of the family. Tall and sturdy are the McKennas."

"Did they know? About her?"

He patted her knee and grew quiet. "We never outright told them, but I think my mother and Gran both knew. In their own way, they knew. They loved and adored Bren. They had us off and wed before I even dredged up the courage to find my tongue and ask her hand."

"Caid's sister and brother-in-law know about me. Lina was the first human after—" She swallowed hard.

"After?" He prompted after a moment. "Someone hurt you, didn't they?"

"It's complicated." She shifted her weight. "And it's only that way because I made it so. I carried it deeper than I should have and let it affect things I shouldn't have."

"But you learned your lesson, did you not?"

Róisín thought about the first person, the first human she had given her heart to. How it had broken when Alexandria left after learning about Róisín's magic. The way she drew herself inward, letting no one in, never trusting. Until she had met Lina, then Caid. The siblings had brought her out of herself, helped her stretch her aching limbs. Held her heart with care when she gave it to them.

"The question then is, why haven't you accepted his proposal?" Stephen broke through her thoughts.

She straightened, pulling away from his warmth and smell. "You didn't."

"Now, now." He took her hand in his and shook his head. "Yes, I had a fatherly-like chat with the lad. It's expected, after all. Or at least, from the way he was watching me, he expected it. So, I gave it to him."

"Daddy," she whined.

"Oh, hush now. It wasn't anything like that, and you're dodging my question, my *calon bach*." He tapped a finger against her nose, making a tsking noise with his tongue.

"It's complicated."

He pursed his lips. "Life usually gets complicated."

"No, it's—" She lurched to her feet, restlessness quickly overtaking her. "I don't know."

"Perhaps it's best to start with what you know."

"It's selfish." It wasn't the full answer she wanted to give him, but Shasta had pulled her aside shortly after their arrival to tell her that Brenna knew nothing of the Goddess's words to Róisín, nor that Matthew was missing. There was nothing that Brenna could do from the afterworld, and Shasta hadn't wanted to worry her or Stephen.

"Says whom?"

Aoife, she had wanted to tell him. At that moment, she realized just how deep under her skin her grandmother and her words still were. All the times that Aoife scolded her for being selfish over silly little things. Taking a day or two to spend with Matthew, her wants to have a garden for vegetables and fruits at Aoife's home in Wurbray, the capital city in Legianne, their Coven's home realm. She knew now that it was any time that she had displayed her own desire, or a slight show of independence, Aoife considered it selfishness because it wasn't to her wants or desires of control.

"Life is far too short, even for those who get to live in an abundance of years, not to be selfish." He rose and stood next to her. "I know that you two are bonded, and while I never got to experience that with your mother, she told me how much it meant to your people to find the person you connected with in that way. That's what marriage is for us human folk. To you, the bond being tied is your way of showing him your his. To him, marriage is his way of showing you he is yours."

She turned to him, but before she could say more, the back door slid open and Brenna stepped onto the patio. Her expression was bright, a soft smile turning her lips upward. "It's time."

No, not yet. I need more time.

Róisín could tell by how much her mother's figure had faded since she had ushered Róisín outside to her father that she had fought against the call to give them more time. Tears instantly filled her eyes.

"No worries, my little rose." Brenna held open her arms, waving her fingers for Róisín to come for a hug. "We can return in a while. It's different now."

If you only knew how different things were, Róisín's heart gave one heavy thump in her chest. She wrapped her arms around Brenna, letting the lavender smell of her envelop her. "Thank you," she whispered into her hair. "For everything. Not just today, getting to see daddy again."

Brenna smoothed Róisín's autumn-colored hair from her face, letting her fingers stroke along her damp cheeks as she did. "I would do it all over again. When the time comes for you to have children, you'll understand why I did not hesitate, why I made the choices I made for you, for us."

She realized that Caid and Shasta had joined them outside, and that Caid's posture was tense as he stood several steps away from Shasta, watching her closely.

Had he noticed how her hands had shaken as she hung the coats upon the rack too?

Róisín had worried Shasta had learned news of Matthew, and that news wasn't good. Unfortunately, as Stephen moved toward Róisín for one last hug before they left, she knew that they would have to wait to find out what was troubling Shasta.

LATER THAT NIGHT, RÓISÍN LAY IN BED, SHIFTING restlessly. Worry had squeezed its way into their bed, wrapping its arms around her, holding her like a lover would. Her body was icy from it. Her muscles were sore from holding tight against shivering. Caid would feel it and ask questions. Her emotions were still too charged from her mother and father's visit. She wasn't ready to answer anything he asked.

And in the empty spaces of time that she had been home, her mind and heart were given the room again to comprehend what they faced. Not only with what she needed to do with the Covens, but Matthew. She missed him so much that she'd worn a hole in the corner of her heart where she had always held space for him.

Caid pulled her against him and pressed a kiss to the top of her head. "You good?"

She rolled and buried her face against the side of his chest. "We could have a court marriage."

Caid's hand, which had been stroking soothingly over her shoulder, froze.

"My father, he asked me why I hadn't given you an answer if I loved you, if we were bonded. Time's short, even for us." She pushed up to her knees abruptly. "Things may be quiet now, at least with the Covens. But... What if it doesn't stay that way? What if things change? What if what we have faced so far is easy compared to what's coming?"

In the light of the full moon that spilled through the windows, she watched as his face shifted. His eyebrows came together, drawing down over his eyes slightly. She felt the heat of his eyes on her as he studied her.

"What are you saying, Róisín?"

"I'm saying yes, Caid. I'm being damned selfish for once, and I want this. I want us. I want to call you mine." Urgency washing over her, she shifted over him. Using her mouth, she pressed feather light kisses along his torso, up his chest. "We have our bond." She used the flat of her tongue along his neck, satisfaction filling her at the sound of the rumble that vibrated from his throat. "But husband has a certain..." She nipped his chin. Feeling her arousal pooling between her thighs, she took one of his hands, moving it there. She was near enough that even in the dim light, she could watch how his pupils blew wide, and his nostrils flared. She brushed her lips over his then grinned. "See?"

He released another rumbling sound, this time more animalistic, and stroked his fingers gently along her center.

"I don't want all the pomp." Ecstasy jolted through her, making her body tremble, then tighten. "I wish my parents could be there, but I don't think there's a way to reach them in the afterworld. I think that's all by chance. Could we get Lina and Thomas?"

Her eyes fluttered closed and she let out a loud moan, her peak rising with the teasing of his fingers.

"We could," he said at length.

"Should we bring them, oh..." Her words ended with a low moan when Caid slipped two of his fingers inside of her.

"You're so fucking wet." His voice was filled with awe. He used his thumb to circle her clit. She rocked against his hand, whimpering and panting softly.

"Wedding planning makes me hot, I guess."

"Next, it'll be washing the dishes that fire you up."

An electric spark caught fire inside of her. She hummed her pleasure before a small chuckle escaped.

"Jesus, Róisín." He shook his head.

"I'm all for the domestic and mundane with you." Róisín rolled and circled her hips. The motion paired with the slow draw of his fingers was enough to send her plummeting over the edge. Her fingers dug into the skin at his chest as she clenched, crying out his name when her orgasm exploded through her. He continued stroking her, slow, almost lazily, until she completely came down from the high of the orgasm. Then he flipped her onto her back.

"I could build a clothing line for out back," he said.

"Mm." She smoothed her hands over his chest. "Keep talking."

"But you'd have to promise me to hang the wash out wearing nothing but what you've got on right now." He lowered his head and took one of her nipples in his mouth, sucking it once, releasing it with a loud pop.

She dug her hands into his hair, fisting it and arching her back to him. "What about when we have kids?"

"We'll send them to Shasta on laundry day..."

Unable to stop herself, she burst into laughter. Moving her hands to cup the back of his head, she pulled him up to her and kissed him fiercely. "How long have you been planning all of this?"

Without hesitation, he answered, "Since packing up my tools the day we finished the work at your house and I realized not seeing you every day wasn't what I wanted. I wanted to wake up to you every morning, fall to sleep with you in my arms every night, forever."

"Oh, Caid," she said with soft adoration, tears pricking her eyes. "I love you."

CHAPTER 12

S HASTA'S BODY was slick with sweat. Her glistening skin hummed with pleasure as she writhed against the soft body that was home to her.

Evelyn's honey-colored eyes, rimmed in amethyst, lifted and Shasta could feel the way the gaze heated her skin as it moved over her body.

"You have...to stay... Please...don't go," Shasta said around her heavy pants.

Evelyn stroked her fingers in and out of her and lowered her head to one of Shasta's nipples. The edges of her had begun to fray, the veil calling her back.

Evelyn's death day had been two weeks before, and she had not come as she always had on her anniversary, causing a falling sensation to overcome Shasta. She tumbled down, down, down toward an abyss, unable to grab hold of anything to stop her plummet.

"I'm here, love." Evelyn took a nipple between her teeth, nipping it lightly, causing Shasta to cry out and rock her hips against Evelyn's hand. "I'm here."

When Evelyn had finally come, a dark shadow trailed behind her. Something ominous following from the afterworld.

"Things are changing there," had been all Evelyn said before she collapsed into Shasta's arms, clinging tightly to her.

It had been left at that. Whatever had held Evelyn in the afterworld could wait. They both needed each other's touch, their soft-spoken odes of love. They had been apart too long. Their need too strong.

When Shasta couldn't take anymore of Evelyn's broken sobs, when it had felt as though she would tear in two at Evelyn's pain, she coaxed the first orgasm from her. Now, Evelyn stroked, tasted, squeezed and Shasta's body was in a state of euphoria.

Shasta moaned, hands gripping at the sheets, heart racing. "Ev, oh…" Ecstasy exploded inside of her. Evelyn brought her closer, slowing her stroking, watching Shasta rock against her hand and ride the wave of her orgasm. Shasta wrapped her limbs around her, sealing her mouth over hers. When the buzzing dimmed, and she could find her breath again, she brushed her nose against Evelyn's. "I miss you so much."

"Burn it down," Evelyn said.

Shasta drew back, her brows pinching together.

"The house, Sha, burn it down and start over."

"But…"

Evelyn shook her head and stroked a hand through Shasta's raven colored hair. "They can't take the memories of us away. They can't taint it, what we had, because it's here." She placed a hand over Shasta's heart. "The same place you carry me still. Burn it. Roast some of those sticky marshmallows you, Brenna, and Róisín love so much. Celebrate what we created, what we had and then build new."

Shasta cupped her face, her thumbs stroking over the cinnamon-colored skin of Evelyn's cheeks. "Are you sure?"

"I hate seeing you so broken," she said.

"I'm not—"

"You are. You feel betrayed by the house, and rightfully so. We built it as our haven, and in the time of most need, it wasn't that. The only way forward is to start fresh."

"I don't know if I'm strong enough to let it go."

Evelyn rolled onto her back, wrapping her arms around her. "You are the strongest person I've ever met. Witch or human."

"With two hundred years on me, I take that as a compliment." Shasta tried to keep her tone light, joking.

"As it should be. Look at all you accomplished as the Coven leader. You ushered us into centuries of calm. We'll never live in unity like they do in Shianshani, but you've created a space for witches where we feel heard, we feel seen, and, most importantly, we feel safe."

You're only being named my heir because there isn't anyone else. You'll never be fit to lead... Shasta pressed her lips together as her mother's words flooded her mind.

"She was a cruel, cold bitch, and selfish."

Of course, Evelyn would know where Shasta's thoughts had gone. She had been there to witness some of the darkest moments.

"She was right. I wasn't ready. I'm still not. Look at what's happened, Ev. Matthew is missing. Nanette won't answer any time I've reached out to her. Bren's gone, and our house tried to lock me in when Róisín needed me the most."

Evelyn's chest rose and fell slowly. Shasta knew it was only a reflex. Evelyn's body was so steeped in the habit of breathing that it happened without thought. The first time Evelyn had come to the living side of the veil, they had so much they needed to learn. How long they had, how to connect their bodies, how to exist in the new season of their relationship.

"You can't keep blaming yourself, Sha." Evelyn pressed a kiss to the top of her head. "Or keep letting that guilt build. You hold so much of it. It is only a matter of time before it will bury you alive."

Shasta rolled on top of her. "At least we'd be together all the time, then."

A dark shadow moved across Evelyn's eyes. "She found me. Brenna. She's with Stephen."

"I know." Shasta stroked a chestnut colored finger down Evelyn's neck, delighting in the way Evelyn tipped her head back, stretching. "She was able to bring Stephen to see Róisín."

"Something isn't right, Sha. Something felt off, hovering around her and wrapped around him. I think she..." She moaned when Shasta stroked along her folds. "I think Brenna could feel it too."

Shasta pressed a finger into Evelyn, stroked once, then added a second finger and used her thumb stroke over her clit. She watched Evelyn's eyes glaze over. "Did you tell her?"

It took several moments for Evelyn to reply. Her body writhing and hips pumping against Shasta's hand, her own hands moving over Shasta's body, squeezing her breasts, gripping at her hips to hold her closer.

"I told her everything."

Shasta pressed in deeper, letting out a groan at the way Evelyn's warmth pulsed around her fingers. Shasta lifted a leg over Evelyn, straddling her.

"She's going to help me." Evelyn's words came out more like soft gasps, her body tightening around Shasta.

At the statement, Shasta halted her movements. Her heart beat further and further up her chest, reaching for her throat. Pressing her lips together, she studied Evelyn. Her fading edges and the defiance despite it, flashing in her eyes and in the way her mouth set into a hard line.

"Be careful," Shasta whispered. "We don't know what we're going to uncover, and I can't lose you again."

"And I can't lose you," Evelyn said.

"You'll always have me, completely. You'll always have me." Shasta bent over her body and took her mouth with hers, feasting on the taste of her lips, her tongue. Their bodies rolled against each other, Evelyn's hands finding Shasta's entrance again. Together, they blocked out their fears and tumbled into the abyss.

Chapter 13

Róisín let the warm Maine sun soak through her skin, heating her frozen bones. A feeling she had yet to shake from that night, walking out of the Seer's house as they broke apart and drifted like ash. A chill set so deeply that it had become a part of her.

"What happens now?" David asked around nibbles of a purple clove flower.

Greens Glen had sprung back to vibrant, bold life in the days after Madigan's death. It had been almost blinding to Róisín when she had shifted into her backyard there, slipping out of the cottage after a twenty-minute back and forth with Caid on how he should continue his training with Brent even while she was between her realm travels. He was to meet her there when he finished so that they could finish packing up his house and get it on the market. Lina had promised she would handle everything with the realtor so that they didn't have to keep bouncing between their duties and selling a house.

Now that "Stewart Munson" was gone and Munson Technologies defunct, Lina claimed to have time on her hands between town meetings and preparing for the twins.

Róisín blew out a breath and stretched her legs out. Lowering herself so that she sprawled on the soft green grass, she blinked up at the blue sky and puffy clouds that passed over. Autumn was slowly settling over the town. She could feel everything around her preparing to go into a deep slumber.

"Lily and I plan to visit Shianshani. I hope that after, we'll know how to approach what the Goddess is asking. But..." She sighed heavily. "How am I supposed to figure out how to bring us all together, let alone actually do it, if none of the Coven leaders will speak to me?"

"Perhaps it just takes time. Everything is so new to the realms that lost their leaders. Troy is barely a century past, a babe, by all standards."

Róisín gave him a side-eyed glance. "It's stopped no one from tasking me, only thirteen years older, with saving us *all*. And let's not forget this new...whatever thing this is." She made a face of disgust.

David fell silent.

"David, can I ask you something? Not just, no." She shook her head. "Never mind."

"Something troubles you." He made to move closer to her but stopped and cast a look over his shoulder toward the woods.

She rolled onto her side so that they were eye to eye. "If I ask you something, how honestly can you answer me?"

Another look behind him. "That depends on the question," he whispered.

"Who do you really work for?"

His whiskers twitched once, twice, his eyes growing larger. "That is not a question I can speak aloud, as it has two answers. However"—he took one of his ears between his paws, stroking it slowly—"you can look inside."

Róisín drew in a sharp breath.

"Lucius has taught you, I trust you."

"Are you sure?" she whispered. Lucius had helped her learn some of her magic of mind, yes, however, she considered herself still in the very primitive stages of that learning. She had seen the way Lucius had winced when she practiced.

"I would not have offered you this if I was not."

"Okay." She pushed herself into a sitting position and cupped her hands in front of her so that he could hop into her palms. "I'm sorry if it stings a little. Lucius may have taught me, but I'm still clumsy with it."

He shifted one of his paws forward to her wrist, a reassurance. "It'll be okay. Ask your questions."

"Who do you really work for?" She repeated her initial question, this time shielded by the walls of their minds.

"I work first for Sister Future," he answered.

Her nose wrinkled as her brows drew together. *"First? What does that even mean?"*

His nose wiggled as he sniffed the air, and she rubbed her thumbs across his side. Just a woman on a late summer day with her bunny.

"My spirit is her charge. There are many of us across the realms."

"What is it you do for her? All of you?"

"We're tasked with guiding fate as the loom dictates to Sister Future by"—his ear twisted back, then forward—*"setting the table or bringing the ingredients to make dinner to the same place."*

Róisín lifted her eyes and surveyed the tree line. *"When you say first, does that mean you work for someone else, too?"*

Please don't say my mother, I can't bear anymore of my family's secrets, I can't.

"I am a charge of the Goddess second."

His answer filled Róisín with relief.

The wind kicked up, rustling the leaves of the surrounding trees. Despite her relief, a chill skittered along her spine, making her shiver. She clutched David to her chest and braced herself for his next answer.

"Who... Who sent you to me?"

"Sister Future."

Róisín's body jerked violently in shock, almost causing her to drop him. Just as another rock slammed down onto the others that had been collecting in her stomach in recent weeks, she felt Caid's presence nearby and his slight tug on their tether.

"Your human is here," David said aloud.

She tipped her head down at him. "You know he's not human."

David's reply was casual as he hopped from her hands to the grass. "Oh, I always knew."

"Wait!" Róisín scrambled to her feet and hurried after him. David had known Caid wasn't human? Had Sister Future known? Nearing the house, it felt like the ground beneath her feet was shifting.

What was going on?

CHAPTER 14

C AID PULLED his head back, dodging the broken end of Brent's staff as it passed by his face. He spun, lifting his arm to use the handle of the battle ax in his hand to block Brent's second blow. The head of the ax lay discarded on the floor of the training room.

Sweat coated him, making his shirt and pants stick to his skin. The muscles in his arm screamed in protest at the contact of the next blow he blocked.

Yet, it wasn't enough. None of it was enough.

It will never be enough, a quiet voice taunted from within.

It almost distracted him. His body instinctively leaned to the left, his right hand flying upward, fingers wrapping around the staff before it hit his side.

"You've much improved," Brent said. He spun the staff expertly and took a step back. He bowed to Caid, signaling the end of their training.

"Not enough." Caid waved a hand toward him. Brent's black hair was still in a neatly tied bun atop his head. His shirt buttoned to his neck, and his chest rising and falling evenly. Caid knew his hair was a disheveled mess. He could see the strands that had brushed just over his eyebrows. His shirt was soaked and his chest heaved with breaths that rasped from his burning lungs.

"It will come." Brent bent to pick up the ax head. "Your stamina, that composure, all of it. But it is not a lie or a placation. You have improved incredibly since our first session a few weeks ago. How is your work with Nanette going?"

Ice settled in Caid's veins. When the chaos had segued and calm returned, his solo work with Nanette had begun. But something had felt off. His gut pulsed with warning, and he couldn't shake the feeling of constant alert his magic had around her.

Then, Róisín had learned that Lily had moved out and was living with her older sister, Ione. Róisín hadn't known the details of what caused the move, but it had been enough to make Róisín appear to be weary of Nanette, someone she had seemed close to. It was enough to drive him to stop going to their training all together.

"You need to train your magic, Kincaid." Brent's voice broke through his thoughts. "If not with her, another elemental."

Caid rubbed his hand over his face. "I'll figure something out." He walked over to the weapons table and set the ax handle down. "I need to get to Earth. Róisín and I have an appointment." He had made it three steps to the door before Brent was in front of him. He lifted a hand and placed it against Caid's chest.

"It's festering without proper training," Brent said. His spring grass colored eyes steady on him. "Something else, as well. But the fester, it's growing. You feel a pressure along your spine and in your head, don't you?"

Caid could only nod. He wasn't ready to voice the whole of it yet. How the darkness tried to consume him almost every waking moment. How it pounded harder at the door he tried to keep it behind when he wasn't near Róisín, or when he wasn't in Earth's realm.

"You cannot physically exhaust it out of you. By training it, and using it, you learn to calm it, move with it, exist with it. It's a part of you, and right now, you're letting it have too much room to dominate. Our magic isn't meant to be that."

Caid held his arms out. "Then what do I do?"

"Perhaps we should have you train with Ione instead," Brent said. "Her skill with the elements is quite incredible."

The awe was clear in Brent's voice. Caid tipped his head to one side, curious. "Then why was Lily named the heir if she's that good?"

Brent's nostrils flared slightly. "That would be a question for Nanette, I'm afraid."

Caid lifted an eyebrow as Brent stepped back, dropping his hand. Something told him Brent knew exactly why Ione wasn't the heir to the Roidon Coven.

"If not Ione, Lucius or Shasta could guide you."

"They're sort of busy trying to find Matthew so we can get him back, if you haven't noticed."

At the sharpness of Caid's tone, Brent chuckled. "You're far more like her than either of you realize." He smirked and moved away.

"What?"

Brent set the broken staff and the ax head on the table, his shoulders shaking with his quiet laughter. "And because I know exactly what Róisín is like, no matter how much she tries to hide it, you should probably go to her before she yanks on your bond tether and brings you to her herself."

Relieved to be dismissed from the discomfort the shift in their conversation had brought, Caid reached out his senses until he felt the familiar, steady beat of Róisín's heart, and shifted to her.

Róisín, however, wasn't waiting for him. When he arrived in the kitchen of her Maine home, he saw her through the patio doors, sprawled on her back on the grass. Her left arm extended upward, she drew circles with her index finger. Her mouth moved occasionally as she spoke. David sat next to her, ears twitching, listening.

For a moment, he felt brought back to that day when David had spoken to him and everything had changed. How the world ceased to exist as Caid had known it, catapulting him into uncertainty.

He rubbed at the middle of his chest, the place where he had felt the most of that darkness pressing at him. Here, at home, it ebbed a little. Let him breathe.

The front door of the house clicked closed, and he heard the quiet footsteps approaching.

"I don't like this whole not driving thing you two do now," Lina said.

He turned to her and lifted a brow. "Yet you still somehow know when we're here."

"You, yes." She nodded. "It's probably some stupid sibling bond thing. Or hell, who knows, maybe it's witchy shit. But I can never tell when she's here." She nodded toward the backyard. "She just, poof"—she popped her hands up, splaying her fingers—"shows up."

Caid couldn't stop the way his mind drifted back to the day Róisín had shifted into his shower, naked. Heat gathered in his belly.

Lina snorted, drawing his attention back to her. She shook her head. "You two are so gone for each other."

"At least we're not trying to inhale one another's faces like you and Thomas."

She placed a hand on her chest and let her mouth fall open, feigning shock. "We most certainly do not do that. We never have." The laughter dancing in her hazel eyes said otherwise. "Anyway." She waved a hand in the air in a sweeping motion. "Why are you two here? I thought we agreed on your place?"

He turned back to the patio doors. Róisín was sitting now, David in her hands, their noses almost touching. Something about the tense way Róisín held her shoulders had his senses go on alert.

Lina waved a hand before his face. "Hello, Earth to Caid?"

"Sorry. There's just…" He let out a heavy sigh. "A *lot* going on."

"Is everything okay? Have you all found Matthew yet?"

He and Róisín had agreed to tell Lina the bare minimum of what had happened that night. She knew Madigan was no longer a threat, and that Matthew had gone missing. The others' deaths, what Róisín's Goddess was asking of her, Lina knew nothing about. Shasta had suggested they wait to see what happened once everyone had come together before saying any more, and Caid and Róisín had agreed. The less stress and worry Lina had to face, the better.

"Shasta and Lucius are still trying to work it out, where he could have gone. Some type of locator thing or whatever." He rubbed at the back of his neck, at the nagging sensation that built there. He had been holding his own in the council judgment chambers, despite not having his magic for long. Yet, he couldn't fight that feeling that if he had learned more, there could have been something he could've done to stop Mildred. Then Matthew wouldn't have done what he did.

He had confided that much in Róisín. The 'should have' and 'could have' moments that gripped him like a plague woke him at all hours of the night. He took care of people, that's what he did best, fixed things. Yet, at that moment, he hadn't been able to do anything for Matthew.

Róisín had told him it wasn't his fault, that Matthew had made his own choice. Caid had wanted to believe her and had tried.

"It's too bad the Winchester brothers weren't real. I bet they would know how to help you out," Lina said. "Hey." She rested her hand on his shoulder. "Are you sure you're okay? I know I ask you every time I see you." She motioned with her other hand to his face. "Something there. And you look like hell."

"Thanks." He rolled his eyes. "I'm fine, just tired." The lie singed his tongue. "Training magic is like running a marathon every day."

"Ew." She scrunched her face up and cringed. "Maybe I don't want magic."

From the corner of his eye, he saw Róisín spring to her feet and hurry toward the door. He nudged Lina out of the way and opened the door, meeting her at the threshold.

"What's wrong?" he asked, looking down at David, then back to Róisín.

"What?" She halted and blinked at him. "Lina, hi! Wait, did we say meet here? I thought we...?"

"Oh, no, no, I felt this oaf somehow the second his big feet landed their Chippewas in Greens Glen. So, I rushed right over." Lina shuffled around Caid so that she could wrap her arms around Róisín. "I've missed you."

"It's only been a few weeks," Róisín said. "Not any different from when I lived here."

"I know, it's just—" She planted a smacking kiss on Róisín's cheek. "It *feels* different somehow."

He stood, watching the way Róisín melted into Lina's embrace, her face softening and a smile curving her lips. His attention dropped back to David. "David."

"Kincaid. I trust you're well?"

Damn rabbit. Now I know something's up. He had learned quickly the more formal David was, the more he concealed. "Depends on the day."

David's nose twitched, whiskers dancing.

Feeling Róisín's eyes on him, he shifted. "What?"

She lifted a brow. "*Later*," she spoke to him with her mind.

"I'm holding you to that," he said aloud, still not sure how to communicate back the same way.

"Hm, what?" Lina stooped to pick up David. "I have strawberries in my car."

"Always my favorite human," David said.

"I guess I'll meet you two at the house, since you can do that teleporting wooshy-woosh thing," Lina called over her shoulder. "And you two clearly need a moment."

"We do?" Róisín's brows pinched together.

Before he could overthink it, he scooped her up and tossed her over his shoulder. Then, spinning on his heels, he marched for the stairs.

"Caid?"

"We'll talk later. Ah—" he said when she tried to interrupt. "Trust me. Something's up between you and the bunny, but right now..." He flipped her onto the bed, her breath coming out in a whoosh when she landed. He crawled over her, propping himself up on one elbow, and smoothed the hair from her face before smiling down at her. "Hi."

Her eyes lit, the turquoise color shining, and a smile split her face. "Hi."

He pressed a soft kiss to her lips and felt the grimy sludge inside of him settle and recede.

"How was training?" she asked, her voice soft as her eyes searched his.

"Brent kicked my ass, as usual." He kissed her again. "But I broke his stick."

"Uh-oh." Her eyes widened. "You broke one of the weapons?"

Caid had begun to lower his lips to her jaw but paused. "You mean to tell me you and Matthew never broke anything?"

"Oh, Hells, we broke so many things over the hundred odd years. I'm surprised Brent has anything left."

"Then why do you say 'uh-oh' to me doing it?" He stroked his nose along her neck, breathing in the honey and lavender smell of her. The sludge just hovering at the edge now, nearly gone.

"That just means he's going to stop taking it easy on you," she said.

Caid popped his head up. "You mean to tell me he was going easy on me?" He expected the sludge to seep back in and the dark threatening to choke him again. Both remained away and quiet.

Róisín's laughter shook them both. "Oh, Kincaid James McGrath." She said his name like a sigh. "You're in for it next time."

"Well, damn."

She stroked her fingers along his face, then down his arm. "Will you tell me about it yet?"

His throat tightened. He should have known. She caught on to him well from the start, and knew his tells before they had even come together.

"Let me take care of you..." Her words echoed back to him, and he squeezed his eyes closed.

"I..."

"Caid." She lifted a hand to his face with a hand, her thumb stroking over his cheek lightly. "There's something going on, and it scares me. Not just with the realms, or my people, but us, you."

He dropped his forehead to rest on hers. "I'm sorry."

"No. Don't you dare apologize. Just tell me what's going on so we can figure it out together. You're the one that likes that word 'together' so much."

"Yet you still shut me out the moment we faced Madigan and Aoife."

"I didn't shut you out."

He moved so that he was sitting up and shook his head. "You shut me out, Róisín. Like you—" He shifted his hands back and forth as he searched for the words. "Somehow, you sealed our bond right off. Everything I tried echoed right back to me. I don't want your apologies either," he said when she opened her mouth to speak.

"I wasn't going to apologize." Her voice held a sharp bite to it. "I was going to tell you that you're a stubborn idiot. And because I know you're a stubborn idiot, instead of waiting for you to let me help, I took control of the situation. I'm not sorry for what I did that night. *Any of it.*" Her eyes grew wide, and her face suddenly paled.

"What?" His heart kicked his chest.

"Goddess." She lifted a hand to her chest and gasped. "Shit, that felt good."

Caid sat quietly, watching. Waiting.

"I've been holding that in for *weeks*. Not just that I don't feel bad about what I did between us, but that I, well, I played the devil against the devil, and I *won*. I showed my grandmother that I wasn't a game piece to play with, and I showed Madigan that I *was* ready to use my magic against him. I'm not sorry for any of it, because if I hadn't done it, we wouldn't be here right now. And I... I can't fathom what that would be like, how much it would hurt to not be here right now, with you. What?" She blinked up at him. "Why are you looking at me like that?"

When her brows knit together, he realized he was grinning at her.

She made to scoot away from him.

"Oh, no you don't." He moved toward her, like a cat ready to pounce on its prey. "I remember when I first met you. You were shy, a little timid." He stopped advancing once he had her backed against the headboard. "You doubted yourself."

"I did not."

"How many times did you tell yourself you couldn't do it? What you needed to do with Madigan when the time came?"

"More times than I want to admit," she whispered.

"And how many times did you beat yourself up over your relationship with Aoife?"

She closed her eyes, a tear spilled onto her cheek.

"Everyone else may have bought the act." He thumbed away the tear. "But you couldn't fool me."

"The night you were waiting for me..."

"That was me finally finding *my* courage. Shaking off the things that chased me so I could be there for you."

"Now?"

"Now? Maybe I need you to use that courage you found, so you're there for me." He said the words as quietly as he could and felt exposed as soon as they left his lips.

Her eyes shot open, dancing with a deep Atlantic blue and pale turquoise. He felt something light spark in his chest seeing them. For weeks, he hadn't seen them anything other than the turquoise color they were when her magic wasn't present since she hadn't been able to shift home with him.

"I'll always be there for you, always. But Caid, you have to tell me what's going on."

"Not yet." He shook his head. "Not right now. First, we're going to mess this bed up. Next, we're going to go get the rest of my shit at the house to bring to the cottage."

"Then you'll tell me?"

"I'll try."

CHAPTER 15

T HE STACK of books landing with a thud on the table before him snapped Lucius McArthur out of the daze that he had fallen into. He used a thumb and forefinger to rub his steel-gray eyes, then looked over the stack to where Shasta's honey-colored eyes stared, unblinking, at him.

She shook her head and put her hands on her hips. "When was the last time you slept?"

"I, ah..." He heaved a sigh. "An hour last night? Maybe?"

"Oh, Lucius." She frowned and moved around the table, dropping into the chair next to him. Wrapping her arms around him from the side, she pressed her face into the side of his arm. "You big dummy. You're of no use in this state. Go upstairs and sleep. I can work here solo for a bit while you rest."

"I can't, Matthew." His voice cracked on his last word.

"Needs you whole and rested."

She was right; he knew she was. Yet, he could never, would never, admit it to her. They had grown close, like siblings over the centuries.

There had been a hammering pain in his chest that followed him from the moment he had seen Matthew's last seconds in Caid's memories. When things were the quietest around Lucius, that pain became more. It was no longer just a feeling, but it had sound. One that flooded his senses, driving him to stay awake, to scour the books on the shelves in the libraries in Alleyette, in Ely.

The more time passed, the longer they stood far from any sort of answer to something, the more pain beat him, the more it deafened him.

He patted Shasta's hand wrapped around his shoulder. "Ev come?"

"Don't think changing the subject is going to keep you down here with me." She straightened and turned to him. "But, yes, she did."

"And?" He leaned back, waiting.

"No explanation as to why she was late." She shrugged her shoulders before reaching for the book at the top of the stack.

He studied her for a moment, watching as she busied herself scanning the pages of the book. That was how he caught the glints of the amber and soft green dance through the honey color of her eyes. The flare of her magic. She was lying, but he would not press. Their history told him that in time, the truth would come.

"She wants me to burn the house down." Shasta slammed the book closed and tossed it on the table. "She wants me to burn our house down. Start fresh."

Lucius heard the unspoken words. "And you don't want to?"

"Of course not. That house is full of memories. Ours. We built it together."

"Then why are you still here, Shasta?" His voice was soft.

She blinked rapidly and shook her head.

"Shasta." He moved his chair closer and took her gently by the chin. "You say you're here because of me, that you're taking care of me, helping me. While I appreciate it, perhaps it's time we're honest. I think I know the truth, but I want to hear you say it."

Her eyes closed, her lips pressing tightly together. Finally, her voice uneven, she said, "I can't go back to it. I can't shake that feeling of betrayal. Our magic was used against me like that. When I was needed most, I couldn't... I was trapped."

"Why do you not want to take Ev's suggestion?"

Shasta snorted through a soft sob. "Ah, how quickly you forget Ev. It was *not* a suggestion. She told me. Flat out."

"Question still stands."

"It's the last thing I have from us," she whispered.

"Shasta." He pulled her from the chair and against his chest in a tight hug. "You have so much more than a house with Ev. That will carry on with you regardless of where you are, what you live in, what you do. She's not telling you to forget her."

"No, she's asking me to move on."

He stroked a hand over her hair. "No, she's letting you know it's okay to live your life."

Silence fell over them for a long moment.

"You're disgustingly wise, Lucius, you know that?" Shasta said finally.

"One of us has to be."

She shifted and licked her lips. "Well, you *are* the oldest of us all. So, it makes sense for it to be you."

"Excuse me, Lucius?" Brent popped his head into the library. "Lily is here to see you. Do you want me to bring her here, or?"

Lucius and Shasta looked quickly at one another. Lucius's brows knotted, Shasta's high on her forehead.

Lucius cleared his throat. "Here is fine."

Brent nodded and ducked out.

"Do you think something's happened?" Shasta asked.

He could only shrug. Deep down, he hoped that somehow, some-way, Lily had found a way. Despite that hammering at the back of his skull that scolded him for that hope, he reached out toward the beacon.

Lily came into the library, followed by her sister, Ione. Shasta made a clicking sound and let out a low whistle. Ione was known to stay close to Roidon, often secluded at her home.

"Hi," Lily greeted them in her quiet voice.

Shasta moved to her, wrapping her in a motherly embrace. "Hi, sweetheart. Ione." She gave her a soft smile before moving to hug her as well. "It's been a long time."

"Too long." Ione hugged Shasta back.

"I—" Lily's eyes darted between him and Shasta. "I feel like I should be forthcoming with you both. I've already told Róisín about moving in with Ione. You two should know as well."

"Okay." Lucius dipped his head slightly. "Come, sit down." He waved to the chairs. "You and Róisín will leave for Shianshani soon?"

"Yes. Three more days." Lily folded her hands in front of her.

"We should all meet before you two leave," Shasta said. "It feels like so much hinges on things going right with Jessamyn, given the lack of reception in Baijiola and Trifoa. Maybe Shianshani will be our spearhead for something of a plan."

Lily nodded in agreement.

"Lily?" Lucius looked at her. "What's going on?"

"I'm not accepting my position as Coven heir for Roidon," she blurted, then cursed quietly. Ione placed one of her hands over Lily's folded ones.

The muscles around Lucius's spine tensed. Shasta sucked in a quiet gasp.

"What—"Shasta quickly looked from him, to Ione, then Lily. "What happened?"

Lily opened her mouth to speak, but then closed it, looking at Ione. Ione nodded, a look of understanding in her eyes.

"It was not long after they returned from Alleyette. If I could hear the shouting, feel that energy from their magic from my home, I know I'm not the only one in the capital that did," Ione said. "I didn't think twice. I shifted in, grabbed her"—she nodded toward Lily—"and shifted out. Once we were home, Lily told me everything."

"Everything?" Lucius ran a hand through his dark hair, then leaned forward.

"Everything," Lily whispered. "From that first moment I felt the tether, already feeling...more, for Matthew. Right to when we were trapped in your house," she said to Shasta. "I hope that's okay?"

"You need someone you can lean on and trust right now," Lucius said. "Your sister is that person."

"I want to help," Ione said. "I'm not the researcher Lily is, but I know all the old languages. I can help look through books to help you find what you need to find Matthew. Or I can go with Lily and Róisín to Shianshani. Anything. I just can no longer be in Roidon." She swallowed hard, her throat bobbing. "*We* can't go back to Roidon."

Lucius caught Shasta's eye. She gave him a slight dip of her head, permission.

"*You need to go to Nanette. There's something happening, or something has happened to drive them away from their home like this. It feels like there's more. Find out what's going on,*" he instructed, using his magic of mind to communicate with her.

"Of course." Lucius rose from his chair. "All the help we can get, for the better. Let's get everyone together so we can connect before we scatter again. Ione, you're more than welcome to take one of the guest rooms upstairs."

"Thank you." Ione rose with Lily.

Lily stepped closer to him, an uncertain look on her face. Holding his arms out, he waved her closer with his fingers. She crashed against him, her body nearly collapsing once his arms came around her.

"We'll get everything back to rights." He pressed a kiss to the top of her head. "Whatever that looks like in the end that gives both you and Matthew comfort, we'll get there."

"Thank you," she said against his chest.

Rubbing a soothing circle over her back, he looked at Shasta, seeing his feelings of concern and worry mirrored in her expression.

Nanette had once been close with Aoife. The possibility that everything that Nanette had done to help them against Madigan could have been to aid Aoife's quest, to aid something else entirely that Nanette had wanted, was possible.

CHAPTER 16

R ÓISÍN'S CHEEKS hurt from grinning so much. She let out a hearty laugh, as faint pulses hit the palms she had on either side of Lina's swelling stomach.

"What's it feel like *inside*, though?"

"Like they want to use my kidneys or lungs for a game of football." Lina winced slightly. "Like that right there? Is that necessary? That's my bladder, for heaven's sake."

"Are you two going to just stand there all day, or?" Caid asked from where he was stacking another box in the living room of his house.

"I'm not allowed to lift heavy things anymore," Lina said. "Helen's orders. And I need Róisín to assist me."

"Assist you in what? Supervising?"

"Of course." She nodded.

With a groan, he cursed under his breath and disappeared into his bedroom.

Lina turned back to Róisín. "I know you can't tell me what's going on. No." She lifted a hand to stop Róisín from interrupting. "Don't you dare tell me it's nothing. I've known that man over there"—she jabbed her thumb toward the bedroom—"for almost thirty-six years. He's shoving something deep down right now. You." She pointed at Róisín.

"You are so on edge, I, a mere mortal, can feel it. I don't need to know what's going on. I need to know that you two are okay, despite whatever it all is."

Róisín chewed on her bottom lip, and nodded, her heart beating slow, heavy thuds against her ribs. Something was going on with Caid, and earlier at the house had been what she had felt was the end of the line waiting for him to come to her. He clearly wouldn't, so she would need to hammer on that door he was trying to hold closed, until he opened for her and let her in.

As for her, she wasn't sure how to voice her growing doubts, her questions, her suspicions. Everything had once seemed so sure around her, even when she had doubted herself, her abilities. Her world had had enough constants that it felt sturdy. Now, the foundation was shaking and threatening what she had believed, what she had trusted.

The Seer drifts...

"I guess you could say I'm questioning my religion," Róisín said at last.

"Witches have religion?" Lina blinked, then shook her head. "Oh, wow. I'm sorry, that was really fucking rude of me. Of course you have religion. Isn't it paganism or something?"

"Sort of? I only know a little about paganism. Our religion from the outer realms is a little different."

"Okay." She motioned toward the sofa. "I don't know how much help I can be. We grew up in a house that recognized zero religion, so I don't know how this works."

Róisín offered her a smile. "It's okay. I don't even really know how this works. I just feel something here." She placed a hand over her stomach. "And it's causing me to, I guess you could say, look at things through a different lens."

"Well, I don't know what all happened, but it was serious, right?"

Róisín thought of Madigan, of Aoife. *Matthew.*

"So, I think your feelings are valid right now. I've seen on news specials and documentaries how people who experience life-changing events look at things differently afterward. Sort of like how someone who almost dies starts to believe in God. Or even people who've lost loved ones no longer believe their God exists."

Róisín hoped Lina couldn't hear the way she sucked in her breath sharply, a knee jerk reaction to her last statement.

"The Goddess gave you empty promises..." Mildred's words slammed into her, full speed, threatening to knock the wind from her.

Her parents coming to the cottage should have been proof enough that the Goddess was right and that Mildred was wrong.

Yet something still settled heavily inside of her.

"Hey." Lina reached forward and took her hands in hers. "Don't let it cloud your sunny days, okay? I know it's easier said than done, but the more power you give it, the more it takes from you. You're worthy of a happy life, filled with warm and sunny days. You and my brother both."

Worthy. Was she truly worthy? She remembered what her mother had said about the Goddess planning to have her sent to the darkness after she defeated Madigan. Now, the Goddess had her bringing all the Covens together. What happened to her then? Had Brenna done enough in her effort to keep her safe?

Or was she only worthy when there was something she could provide her people?

Caid walked into the living room at that moment, his attention zeroing in on her in an instant. His eyes darkened and his expression hardened. Róisín's stomach tightened, and she wanted to flee.

Lina's phone chirping from the table broke the tension. Leaning forward, her eyes scanned the text on the screen.

"Dammit." She pushed to her feet with a huff. "I need to go take care of some town shit." She went to Caid first. "Put that down and stop scowling. Give me a hug." He hesitated before putting the box next to the growing stacks. Then he righted himself and took Lina in his arms. The pair swayed in their little back-and-forth dance as they always did, and Lina giggled.

"I love you, assface." Lina's voice was muffled against his neck.

"I love you too, shithead." Caid pressed two loud, smacking kisses on each of her cheeks.

Róisín watched Caid's body soften. The tension leaving his muscles. She did that. Everything circled back to her. Whatever it was he was holding onto, the way his body tightened, his face hardened. It was connected to her. Did he regret meeting her?

Lina released Caid and came to her next. She put her arms on Róisín's shoulders, her voice low when she said, "Put it in a can and kick it down the street, okay?"

Róisín didn't trust her voice with the sudden flood of fresh doubt swimming within. Instead, she held Lina, not wanting to let go, wanting to go back to how everything had been before, when she wasn't being pulled in so many directions and away from the people she loved the most. "I love you," she whispered into her hair.

"I love you too. Don't forget that. No matter what, I love you." She kissed her cheek. "He does too. Never doubt that."

She had to fight away the tears that threatened as they separated.

"Don't be strangers, you two," Lina said. "I get the feeling the visits will be spaced out a bit more for a while but come when you can. Okay?"

Róisín and Caid nodded.

"Don't you dare." Caid's words cut through the room the moment the door clicked closed and Lina was gone. His voice was dark and rough.

Róisín turned to him. Her heart thundered up her throat, making it hard to breathe. A tingle raced over her skin, and a rushing wind roared in her ears. She licked her lips, trying to keep herself upright despite the onslaught on her body at the moment.

He took long strides across the room to her. "Don't you dare," he said again. "Don't think I can't feel that."

"Feel—" She swallowed, trying to push the sudden dryness from her throat. "Feel what?"

He took her chin between his thumb and forefinger, tipping her head up to look at him. "The only regret that I have with you is not telling you how I felt sooner, so that I could be there for you when you were here alone."

Her eyes closed when he rested his forehead against hers. "But look at everything that's happened to you since you did."

"Like falling in love with you?" He took a step forward, forcing her back a step. "Realizing that I wasn't broken, that I just hadn't found my person yet?" Another step. "Or that I'm allowed to want, and have *more*?" Another step. "And let's not forget about this door to a whole new world that's opened for me." He tugged on their tether at the same moment her back hit the wall he'd moved them toward.

"Don't think that I don't see the way you tense so much that I don't know how you don't explode into pieces." She drew in an unsteady breath. "Or the how the lighthearted side of you has slowly faded away." She felt the sting of tears at the back of her eyes. "Then there's that feeling, that energy that pulses around you in heavy, hot waves. I don't know what it is, but just feeling it... it's..."

"It's dark," he whispered, his mouth closer to hers. "Your mother was wrong, Róisín. I don't think any of my magic is in the light."

"Wh-what do you mean?"

"Since the moment it woke inside of me, it's only gotten heavier, thicker, and darker."

Her heart stopped, and the air left her lungs. Her grip on everything slipped, and she was falling, falling, falling. "Why didn't you tell me sooner? Even at the house before we came here?"

He backed away from her and shoved his hands into his hair, then flung his arms wide. "What would I say? Where would I even start? I remember exactly what your mother said. The way she said that it would save you. And she was wrong. So *fucking wrong*." He had been shouting but lowered his voice. His next question came out hoarse and broken. "What does that mean for you in the end?"

No, he couldn't be right. She refused to believe it. He was good; he was pure of heart. The way he took care of Lina. His friendship with Wyatt. The way he had fought, without question, at Matthew's side.

"There has to be an explanation for what is happening to you," she said.

He shook his head. "I think we need to face the truth, Róisín."

"But..." She reached, finding strength somewhere deep inside to make her voice firm. "No. You're wrong. You are *wrong*."

"Róisín." He rubbed a hand over his face and sighed.

"Caid." The first hot tear splashed onto her cheek.

"Maybe it's just not what your Fates had in the cards for us and we need to accept that." He took her face between her hands, his fingers cradling the base of her skull. "That's my way of saying I'm not spending whatever time we've got left fighting."

When he took her mouth with his, her stomach sank, her throat grew tighter, and an overwhelming sense of helplessness flooded her. Had this been what it had felt like for him when she had come to him to say goodbye the day that she had felt Madigan creeping in and trailing her?

Caid brought an arm around her, bringing her in closer, and her heart shattered into millions of unrepairable pieces.

CHAPTER 17

S HASTA STOOD before the large, vibrant orange doors of
Nanette's home in Roidon. She had waited until she and Lucius
had settled Ione and Lily in the manor before making up an
excuse to leave alone.

Before she could lift her hand to knock, the door flew open, and
Nanette, her salt and pepper colored hair wild around her face, greeted
her with narrowed eyes.

"Oh, Nanette." Shasta could not keep the sadness from her tone as
she took in the woman's appearance before her. "What has happened to
you?"

The lines around Nanette's mouth deepened as her lips pinched
together. "I'm sure you know by now. Ione's poisoned her thoughts
enough to have her running right to you all with nightmare tales about
me, I'm sure." Nanette's face hardened, her eyes a storm of dark golds,
reds, and browns.

Shasta frowned. She had understood Lucius's concerns and had
shared them. However, her gut told her this was something else. Something less nefarious, and something more heartbreaking.

"Neither of them has told us anything. Lily is going with Róisín,
and Ione offered her help to find Matthew. That's neither here, nor

there." She shook her head. "I'm here because I'm worried about *you*, Nanette. I hope there's enough trust between us, you'll tell me what is going on."

She made a noise between a groan and a closed-mouth scream before spinning on her heel and stalking back into the house, leaving the door open, but giving no verbal invitation for Shasta to come in.

Nanette stopped at a table in the foyer and picked up a glass of amber liquid. She scowled at it before tossing it back. Her expression pinched when she turned back to Shasta.

"Nanette, your girls are scared of you right now. You can't push them away like this."

"Pah." Nanette spat the word. "Like you could ever understand. You and your queer ways. No children, how could you know what it's like?"

Shasta wanted to react with anger. The words Nanette spewed at her were coming from a place of hurt, not anger. And they stung. But it was then that she realized Nanette's actions were her lashing out against Matthew's bond with Lily.

"She can still be heir, you know," Shasta said quietly, speaking about Ione.

"No. They'll never accept her. That's why I chose Lily. There would be unrest among our Coven and I've worked so hard to keep Roidon peaceful. To keep us off the humans' radar. Unrest among the Coven would cause tension with the humans." Her voice dropped to a whisper. "All they want is a chance at us, Shasta. Just one."

Shasta crossed her arms over her chest. "This is why you're so angry about the bond."

"She needs to think about our people. Selfish twat." Nanette snatched the empty glass back up from where she had set it on the table and stomped to the kitchen at the back of the house.

Shasta followed her wordlessly.

"I gave up everything for this Coven," Nanette said, more to the cabinet door than to Shasta. "My husband, my daughter. Everything."

"You still have Lily and Ione."

Nanette spun to face her. "Do you know my council is voting at this very moment on whether I'm fit to remain leader? *Me*. My family is at the core of this Goddess damned Coven, and now my people want to unseat me."

"Have you..." Shasta stared at her. Her mind was like a ship trying to navigate a storming sea. What did she say? What did she do? "Have you told them what happened? What the Goddess wants?"

"I made that mistake, yes. My choice is to deny the Goddess and the Sisters to keep everything my family has worked for, or lose what's left. Whether we land safely or fall, we'll do it as Roidonians."

Shasta found herself speechless. Roidon had always thrived on autonomy from the other realms. The only place the Coven worked with the others was at the council table in Alleyette, backing only ideas and policy that didn't interfere with that autonomy. Nanette had always supported it. Yet, in the after, Shasta had been sure that Nanette had recognized the importance of working as one.

"You're choosing your coven?"

"I have no choice, Shasta. Lily has made it clear she chooses Matthew. They barely know one another, but she is throwing it away for him."

"Nanette." Shasta moved further into the kitchen. "Bring this back to the beginning. Make this make sense for me. Because as of right now, I'm seeing exactly why Ione and Lily came to us, scared."

"Roidon cannot join the other Covens," Nanette said. "It would go against our very core of who we are. We remain on the outside. Because of that, because I would dare to defy the Goddess, Lily has chosen to leave. Which leaves me heirless. Hence the vote to remove me and vote for someone new to lead us." She braided her hair in angry, jerking movements. Her eyes remained steady on Shasta. "I cannot name Ione my heir, or they'll kill her. They threatened once, after Moira passed on. I cannot allow it, even just someone to even *think* of threatening her again."

Shasta felt her stomach drop to her feet. "Why did you never say anything?"

"What would I say?"

"The truth? Instead of letting that girl believe you didn't choose her because she's a mirror image of her mother?"

"Because one hurts differently than the other. I can't have her hating herself because of who she chooses to love. It's easier for her to hate me over a lie."

Shasta reeled, trying to capture everything Nanette was saying. "Instead, you'll punish Lily?"

"Regardless of what I do, I lose, Shasta."

They fell quiet. Shasta watched as Nanette topped off her glass for the third time since she had arrived there.

"What happens now?" Shasta asked, her voice barely a whisper.

"I scare my girls away to save my Coven, only to watch my Coven crumble when whatever is coming comes." She poured the contents of the glass down her throat. "You should go. You're wasting time here. The others need you. Find Matthew. Do what you can with the other Covens."

Shasta blinked away her tears and nodded. Turning, she made her way back toward the front door. Stopping in the doorway, she looked back at Nanette. "We'll keep them safe."

Nanette lifted her glass in salute to her. "You better."

CHAPTER 18

MATTHEW LOOKED over his shoulder at the lanky boy, who followed him around like a lost puppy dog, desperate for attention. Jackson was his name, and he had been full of thousands of questions from the moment he had seen Matthew.

They had been on Earth for three days this time. The last time, it had just been Jackson's mother, Marion, they'd seen. Clarissa, Matthew's mother, had been working with Marion on something that seemed important. Matthew had questioned Clarissa when they'd left the first time she'd brought him. Had asked why he had needed to come.

"They're family." Clarissa had told him with a soft, sunny smile that lit up her brilliant green eyes.

That had been all, and he still didn't understand.

"Bark! Bark!" Jackson shrieked from behind him. "How'd you get so tall?"

"I got older." Matthew shrugged. They assigned him to keep Jackson occupied while his mother had a private moment with Marion.

"Can we sit down? My legs are tired." He punctuated his complaint with a loud huff.

Matthew scanned the trail they'd been walking along, noticing a fallen tree up ahead. "Just up here, kiddo."

"I'm not a kiddo." Jackson's tone was defiant.

"You just barked at me. I don't care how old you are, *kiddo*." Matthew chuckled, shaking his head.

After they settled on the log, Jackson looked up at Matthew, face hopeful. "Your mom is going to really help my mom? My family?"

"I think so," Matthew said with honesty. He didn't know what his mother was doing; however, he knew that shew as smart, capable, and determined. He believed whatever it was, she could do it.

"I hope she can. I really don't want to take my dad's job," Jackson said. Sadness laced his words, making him suddenly sound many years older.

Matthew looked down at him, studying him carefully. There was something different about the Burke family. Their energy, their scent. It was almost witchlike, yet not.

He leaned close to Jackson, lowering his voice. "Can I let you in on a secret?"

Jackson's wide and deep copper-colored eyes gleamed up at him. Lifting a hand, he drew it along his closed mouth, as though he were zipping a zipper.

"I don't want my dad's job either."

His eyebrows shot up. "You don't?"

"I say I do. I know he's proud of me for training for it, getting ready for it. He's got faith that I'll do a good job. I want to think I'll do an okay job, but that's a lot of people to be in charge of. It's a super big responsibility."

"My dad says his job is a big responsibility, too. Do our dads do the same work?"

That's a great question.

"You still...over there...MacArthur?" Mildred's thin voice broke through his hallucination. "Or are you...pretty little dreams with Róisín?"

Somehow, Matthew gathered the strength to roll, rising to his knees. Moving on all fours, he felt around until a hand brushed against Mildred's prone body.

"She'll turn..." Mildred rasped. "She'll turn and you'll all be done for."

"I really hoped you'd die on your own, you fucking bitch," Matthew bit out.

"You don't...balls," she gasped out. How she was still alive, Matthew didn't know. She'd been broken the moment they had shifted, Matthew's weight falling atop her. For what felt like endless weeks, she had struggled for air next to him. She either had the genuine belief that she would be saved somehow, or she lacked that much faith in her daughter taking leadership of Trifoa.

"I bet you also didn't think I'd have the balls to do this, did you?"

"I dare—" She hacked out a harsh cough. "You."

"Proof you know nothing about me. I've yet to back down from a dare." With his jaw set, he wrapped his fingers around her throat and squeezed.

CHAPTER 19

DAUGHTER OF the Goddess, Sister Future, sat before her loom. Her violet eyes scanned the dancing, twisting threads. The colors moved up, down, twined together, then broke apart. Some trailed alongside one another. Others broke off, abruptly disappearing.

Her fingers trailed along the line of a deep burgundy line. If it had been just a hair higher, or lower, it would stand out amongst the lighter, pale colors of the threads. Instead, it blended with the amethyst, forest green, bark brown, and gray threads it moved with. It made the burgundy thread almost imperceptible.

Róisín's thread, Future knew. There had been a maroon thread above it when Brenna had been among the living side of the veil.

Movement from her left drew her attention away from the motion of the threads. Sister Past scraped her bench across the stone floor of their cottage, moving closer to her loom.

"The Wallingsford lines have separated," Past said.

She turned to look at Future, who offered a shrug. For Future, it was the loom that sat before her that mattered. She truly cared not what her sisters saw in theirs. Not anymore.

Something that the trio already knew, having seen the lines break apart on Future's loom, then days later, on Present's.

Future's eyes flicked over her loom. "They're together again on mine," she said.

Together, they turned to Sister Present. She sat on the edge of her stool, eyes darting frantically up and down her own loom. She pinched her bottom lip between her thumb and forefinger.

Finally, she looked at them, her eyes wild. "I can't—" She shook her head. "I can't keep up with the changes."

Past frowned, looking back at her loom. "Should we call Mother?"

A thin black thread appearing below Róisín's pulled Future's attention from her sisters. Her stomach sank and then twisted painfully, causing her vision to blur. "No," she whispered.

It couldn't be.

Everything had been falling into step as it was supposed to. The work she had done, what she had risked...

"Future?" Present was next to her now. "Should we call upon Mother?" she asked when Future dragged her eyes from the loom.

"No, I think we should wait. The Wallingsfords are not a concern of hers. The lines are together again here." She pointed to the ochre, amber, and gold lines.

"What about—" Present looked over her shoulder to her loom and its frantic movements. Some threads had knotted, jutting outward.

"It'll be okay. This isn't the first time a lot has been happening in our current time. I think we need to keep note of those Mother has asked us to, and should their lines change, then we call her." Future itched to go back to her loom, her attention undivided.

"Are you sure?" Past's voice was tight with her nerves.

"How are their lines?" Future motioned for Present to return to her seat.

Hesitant, Present rose from Future's stool and went back to hers. Leaning in closer to her loom, she lifted a finger, tracing the lines of a dozen different threads. "Everything is fine."

"Okay," she said with a decisive nod. "Then we're okay."

Past eyed her warily, but seemed to accept the answer, turning back to her dancing threads.

Once Present seemed completely settled back in front of hers, Future spun around, leaning so that she was almost nose to canvas.

No, she hadn't been seeing things. The black thread was there, so very thin and tucked just so, next to the burgundy thread.

It shouldn't be there. Present had neatly snipped the line, ending its journey. Future and Past had sat at their own looms, watching. The black thread ended, and days later, that end reflected on Past's loom. Once Past performed the ritual and sent the soul to the beyond, it sealed the sisters' action for eternity. Future shifted closer to the edge of her seat, her eyes scanning Present's loom.

The Sisters had only interpreted their own looms in the beginning. It was Future that watched her sisters, studied them, learning how their looms were moving when they voiced what they saw.

She searched and searched, squinting, letting her magic amplify her sight. But no, the black thread on Present's loom was not there. Looking to Past's next, she saw the same absence.

Turning back to her own loom, she watched the black thread dip under the burgundy thread and teased briefly along the green and golden thread.

No.

Stifling a gasp, she looked at the windows. The fading light showed that it was nearly dinner time. They would eat, and then retire to their rooms with their looms where they would rest but keep the threads close should something bothersome happen and they needed to take action.

Then I can go.

CHAPTER 20

MARCELO WATCHED his mother at the end of the table, head bent close to Jessamyn's, as they were deep in conversation about something. He wondered how his father felt about their relationship. The High Mage of the court was supposed to be the king's right hand, and Frederick had held that title well.

Perhaps too well. Marcelo shuddered. Frederick had been cold, filled with malice right to the brim, and worn with a twisted sense of pride. Had he known what had become of the king? Had he stumbled across Rastead as he feasted on another?

Marcelo's eyes found Anthony's across the table. His brother's attention flitted between hard stares at their father, and questioning looks Cassius's way as he stood at attention near the dining hall's massive glass doors.

If the table hadn't been so wide, he could have reached with his foot and kicked his brother. If he was concerned about their father finding out about their relationship, he should do a better job of concealing it.

The thought brought him to Nolani. They only had a few short weeks together before she needed to return to the university. Before he would need to go back to making excuses for his need to travel. It was easier, their relationship, when she was away where the walls didn't have eyes.

"Isn't that right, Celo?" Marsenna asked.

"Hm?" Marcelo blinked and shook Nolani from his mind.

Marsenna laughed softly, giving Jessamyn a knowing look.

"He's daydreaming, Your Highness." Jessamyn offered him a smile.

"He has always been my daydreamer," she said. Before she turned back to Jessamyn, she gave him a wink, leaving him confused what part of their conversation he had missed.

Anthony's voice was low. "We need to talk. After."

Marcelo tipped an eyebrow up. "If it's about what you asked the other evening, the answer is still no. And perhaps you should stop making eyes at him if you don't want Father to know."

Anthony's eyes darted down the table to where Rastead was angrily spearing a piece of near-raw meat. "I saw," he began, louder than he had clearly intended by the way his eyes widened at the sound of his voice. Leaning over the table, he dropped his voice. "I saw something."

Every muscle in Marcelo's body tensed.

"So, I repeat, brother, we need to talk."

"Would you two just stop that incessant chattering?" Rastead's voice boomed.

Everyone in the room flinched at the sound before composing themselves and giving the king their attention.

"Now." Rastead looked pointedly at Jessamyn. "What is it you were saying to my lovely wife?"

Something about the way Rastead had said 'wife' made Marcelo's skin feel like his skin had grown legs and begun crawling away from his body.

Jessamyn rolled her eyes, a blatant sign of her disinterest in her king. Marcelo envied the Lunestran backbone they all had.

"I was telling the queen there has been rising talks among the Coven of the visit from the last Legianne witch. Although we may not be able to call her that anymore."

"No?" Rastead's attention was rapt, causing Marcelo's curiosity to rise.

"She is bringing a guest with her, and we've heard reports that there has been a defect from the Roidon Coven to Legianne," Jessamyn said.

"Who is it?" Marsenna asked, reaching for her wine. The jewels that covered her hand and wrist glittered in the lights overhead. Marcelo had noticed she had been wearing more and more of them from her collection as of late. Just as he had noticed Runa spending more and more time in her gardens. If his father was going to dally with others, why not his mother, too?

"Nanette Wallingsford's granddaughter." Jessamyn glanced around the silent table. "The younger one."

"The heir? That makes little sense." Marsenna bit her lip and shifted in her seat. "Rastead? Do we need to be concerned, is there unrest in Roidon?"

Rastead quickly turned toward the guards at the door. "Intel, immediately." Each syllable of his words snapped in the air, making the guards flinch as though they had teeth.

Without taking a drink of the wine, Marsenna set her glass back on the table. "When is she to arrive?"

"We received her notice a week ago. Her arrival is slated for later this week," Jessamyn said.

"Why was I not notified of this?" Rastead slammed his fist against the table, making the cutlery clatter.

Jessamyn cleared her throat, and if Marcelo didn't know any better, judging by the slight smirk and glimmer in her eyes, he would say she was amused by the king's reaction. "You did, Your Highness. It was in our briefing the morning I received the request. Róisín McKenna would like an audience with us both when she arrives."

The sound that vibrated out of Rastead's throat was far from human, yet no one in the room reacted outwardly with anything other than sharp intakes of breath.

"You lie." Rastead's voice was venomous.

The unease building over the new tension in the room made the air heavy, oppressive. They had opened court to Coven leaders from other realms before making the reaction from Rastead feel out of place and concerning.

"Don't you dare leave this room," Rastead barked at Anthony when he slid his chair back from the table.

"I need to take a piss," Anthony said.

Rastead's nostrils flared. Suddenly, he began blinking rapidly and rubbed his hand down his face. "Apologies, son. You both may leave." He waved a hand toward the door. "But I want to see you both in my office first thing in the morning. By then we should know news from Roidon and if we need to take further action."

Not waiting to see if he would change his mind, Marcelo and Anthony both practically leapt to their feet and darted toward the door.

"What the fuck was that?" Anthony asked once they were in the hall.

Marcelo shook his head, casting a weary glance over his shoulder.

Once they had cleared the wing completely, Anthony gripped Marcelo's arm. "We found a body just before dinner."

"What?" Marcelo whisper shouted. "Why didn't you say anything before?"

"There wasn't any time."

Marcelo bit back a groan. "Who was it? Where were they found? What happened?"

Anthony held up his hands to stop the barrage of questions. "Staff. Nina from laundry. She was found in the back half of the orchards outside of the walls. Celo." His throat bobbed and his next words were hoarse. "She had marks all over her body and she was drained."

"Drained?" He recalled the night outside of the library, what he had seen through the crack in the door. His stomach churned knowing what Anthony was going to say next.

"Somehow she had no blood left in her, at all." He drew a hand down his pale face.

"What were the marks?"

"Like something tried to make a meal of her."

Marcelo's brain tried to organize his thoughts. "Where's the body now?"

"We left her there. We thought first to move her, to bring her to the forensics investigator outside, but... Celo, what the fuck is going on?"

"I have no idea. I wish I did. Now, we add in whatever that reaction was to the Legianne Coven arriving in a few days." Defeat tugged at Marcelo's shoulders, causing them to droop and round. "Shit. I guess, first, take me to the body. We can work out what's going on with Lady McKenna along the way."

It had been like Rastead had heard Legianne and Róisín McKenna's name, and the reaction was uncontrollable. Was it tied to whatever was going on?

He had heard rumors that talked of the immense power Róisín had, as she was the last witch of her Coven. Could she help them? Marcelo's list of questions was growing longer and longer with each passing day, while the knot in his stomach grew tighter and tighter.

CHAPTER 21

Lucius sat at the island of his kitchen, staring blankly at the wall of cupboards ahead. He had been awaiting word from Shasta once she had gone to Roidon to speak with Nanette. The longer he sat without that word, the more the acid in his stomach bubbled and rose. Now, it was prodding at his chest with its burns.

Róisín's abrupt arrival on the other side of the island startled him.

"Shit," he heard her mutter before she spun to face him, eyes wide.

Waiting for her explanation, he leaned back so that he sat upright on his stool.

"I guess now's as good a time as any to—" She cleared her throat and gave him a sheepish smile. "Finally tell you I've lost the power to my magic." When he said nothing after a long moment, she held her hands palm up with a small shrug. "Surprise?"

The small bits that held his world together the past few weeks crumbled, causing the bottom to drop out and that world to tumble down.

"There will be sacrifices."

Clarissa's words had haunted him, chased at his heels, nipping every chance they had. They caused him to fly out of bed, blind with fear the moment sleep pulled him down.

What sacrifices? Who would have to make them? Matthew had

already made his, yet Clarissa had insisted he would be okay. With each hour that ticked by on the clocks, Lucius doubted more and more that it was possible.

The only thing that kept him anchored was that Matthew's magic had yet to come to him. And it would, regardless of where Matthew was, when that time came. Lucius drove himself to the books, to the scrolls, day after day, racing to get him back before that could happen.

Róisín standing before him, arms around herself as though she were trying to give herself comfort and support. She had been the one that he had carried the other half of his worry for. She had given them the glossier version of what had happened at the Seer's home, but he had seen Frederick's shared vision, and he'd seen the way her eyes had dulled after Roidon. The way she would drift away, her mind going somewhere else.

Finally finding his voice, he said, "But you've shifted here."

She gestured toward the front of the manor. "I was supposed to come to your door and knock as a polite witch would do."

"You're here just the same, and that's what is important." He walked around the counter and pulled her into a tight hug. "Because it means that you haven't lost all of your power."

"It's the only bit of it that's come back," she said. "At first, I couldn't do anything. After this long, I can't. This is all I can do."

And she was going to the other realms, knowing should someone wish to, they could harm her because she was defenseless. Needing to busy himself, he opened the freezer and pulled out a tub of ice cream.

"Mint chocolate chip?" Róisín asked, sounding hopeful.

"The only kind I keep." He smiled at her over his shoulder before taking down two bowls, then retrieving spoons.

They had shared many bowls of her beloved mint chocolate chip ice cream over the kitchen island in her little more than a century of life. While her father had been alive, the moments had been few, but after, she came to him often. He knew he could never replace Stephen or his influence. However, he also knew that he could be the father figure she had needed and that he had wanted to be for her.

"Start from the beginning." He set a bowl in front of the stool next to the one he had sat on.

She rubbed at the back of her neck, tipping her head to one side and pressing her lips together. "Okay." She gave a firm nod. "I can't fix this if I don't talk about it."

"Exactly. And going to Shianshani when we don't know what the situation with the Coven is..."

"Shit, Lucius, what do I do?" She slumped on her stool, her features pulling down into a full faced frown. "Once the reality of everything hit, I was exhausted in a way that I'd never been before. Not with that guy that night with Alexandria, or when I'd helped Caid that day we fell, and I was gushing blood at the same time." She winced when his spoon clanked harshly against his bowl. "Sorry, that was a bit too much detail."

"No." He waved his other hand dismissively. "It's alright. You're here and okay now."

Róisín lay her head against his shoulder. "Have you and Shasta made any progress with Matthew?"

He paused his spoon in mid-air and looked down at her. "Don't deflect, sweetheart. First this."

Sighing, she straightened. "I didn't notice it at first. I slept for a few days, but still felt this bone deep drain. Caid and I talked about going back to Earth for a bit before I started trying to figure out this Coven thing." She frowned down at her bowl. "When we went to return to Earth, he shifted, but I stayed behind."

"Did you feel as though something were holding you back?"

"No, that's the thing. Nothing held me, or there wasn't a wall trying to stop me. There was just... absolutely nothing there, Lucius. I was completely empty."

Lucius dug his spoon into the ice cream and ate the bite, considering her words, trying to work out what it could mean. "Then?"

"Well, naturally, Caid came back, pissed off at me like I'd done it intentionally. He seriously thought I was trying to run from him or shoo him away." Disbelief was rich in her voice.

He kept his chuckle in but couldn't stop the smile from spreading across his face.

"Don't." She pointed her spoon at him. "Don't you dare. I know, just like I know, he was absolutely justified in shouting at me about it. I made some mistakes. But I had perfectly valid reasons. Thank the Goddess that man has the patience of Earth's Saints."

Lucius couldn't hold back the laughter now. "Oh, sweetheart. You have no idea how much I've needed this visit from you. Regardless of the situation with your magic, or larger at hand."

Róisín gave him a soft smile, and he felt his chest warm with the love he held for her. They'd weathered many storms, and he needed to remind himself that this was all that this was. A rather massive storm compared to the others, but a storm. And they would weather it. He would do whatever needed to be done to be sure of it.

"There will be sacrifices."

He shook the echoes of Clarissa's voice from his mind. "What happened next?"

"I cried like a baby. Turned into an ooey, gooey, puddling darn mess. I'm talking snot nose, blotchy, and puffy face." She wrinkled her nose and stuck out her tongue like she had tasted something gross.

"I take it that didn't scare him away."

"Oh, there's not a thing in the world that will scare him away." She fell silent, eyes shining with the unshed tears that sprung forth.

There was something she was leaving unspoken. One thing at a time. Sort out her magic, preferably before she left for Shianshani, then hope she opened up to him about the other so they could fix that as well.

She cleared her throat and lifted her shoulders. "Anyway. I tried again a few times. But still nothing. Then, I remembered how my magic would rise to meet his whenever he reached through our line. We tried that"—she lifted her hands and shrugged—"and absolutely nothing. He said it felt empty. I was there. He could feel the other end of our line connected to me and I to him, but that was it."

"There has to be an explanation as to what has happened," he said. There had to be. "How long before you could manage a shift again?"

She tapped a finger on her chin. "It was literally just a few days before Lily and I were to leave for Baijiola. It was another week before I could do it and did not want to sleep for an entire day."

"Now?"

"I still get tired." She nodded to the other side of the island. "And, as you can see, my aim isn't so good. I know Caid doesn't mind wherever I pop up, but it's pretty rude to waltz into someone else's home like that."

"You're always welcome here, sweetheart." He rubbed her back. "Any time."

"Is there a way, I mean, can we fix this?"

He collected their bowls and spoons, then placed them in the sink. "I believe we can. As I said, there has to be an explanation. A reason. Once we figure out what happened and why, we should be able to do something."

She slid off her stool. "Before I leave for Shianshani?"

"That may be a stretch." He gave her honesty because she deserved that. "But not impossible. Especially having Ione here to help us. It's an extra brain and an extra set of eyes at our disposal."

"Ione?" Her brow knotted together.

"Ah, yes, a...well..." He shrugged. "Come on, she and Lily are in the library. Better they explain it, as it's their story, not mine to share."

CHAPTER 22

Jessamyn pushed into her suite and immediately stripped her head wrap off.

"Before you take anything else off, can you let me report the latest?" Runa asked from where he sat near her bookshelves.

"Why are you sitting in the dark?"

"A body was found in the orchard." He ignored her question.

"When?"

He rose and stretched his arms over his head. "From what the princelings discussed just after dinner, it was discovered sometime just before you all gathered. And before you reprimand me, they had their chat in the hall."

"A hall you just happened down?" She waved a hand, and a low light illuminated the room. When she saw Runa's face, she gasped. "What happened?"

"Hm? Oh." He put a hand on his swollen eye. "That."

"Yes, that. How on earth do you forget about a swollen eye?" Jessamyn stopped walking when she was in front of him. He winced when her fingers brushed along the open cut that was oozing slightly. "Hold still," she whispered. Her magic moved along her arm to her fingertips.

"Leave the bruise at least, please. It'll raise suspicion."

"What—no." She shook her head. When he aimed his dark eyes at her, she sighed. "Fine."

The cut knit itself closed, and the swelling around the eye lessened until, finally, his eye could open. She saw then that the white around his iris was flooded red. He had been in plenty of fights before, had been in battle for Talista. She knew that this was not a normal blow to cause this sort of damage. "The vessels of your eye, they're..."

"It's not just the body we have to worry about."

She reached up again to heal the vessels, but he snatched her wrist, his grip tight.

Runa spoke through clenched teeth. "He's made *more*."

Her brow furrowed. "Frederick?"

He shook his head. "*The king.*"

"But how? It was Frederick's magic that... It's not possible, Runa."

"The thing I came across going out to the orchard says otherwise." His voice was ominous. "Do we think it's wise to allow Legianne to come when we're in the middle of this? How would it look should something happen to her, Jes? We don't need any more attention or ire from the other Covens. Not now, not in the middle of this. Our plan will fail."

She rubbed at her temples and felt the threads of her carefully laid plans beginning to slip through her fingers. Before they could escape her, she latched onto them and pulled them back to her, clutching them to her chest.

"If anything"—she turned away from him to stalk over to her desk —"this could work in our favor." She rounded the desk and placed her palms on the cool wooden surface, lifting her eyes to him.

Shock exploded across his face, his eyebrows shooting upward, lopsided from the damage that remained on the one side of his face. "Excuse me?"

Jessamyn glanced down at the calendar she had on the corner of her desk. "I've got three days until their arrival. I want you to stay on Rastead's guards, to be there when their intel comes back about Roidon. I don't think it's a threat. If anything, I think Nanette's grandchildren are more like their mother than Nanette wishes and there's been the beginnings of the fall of the Wallingsfords at the head of the table. *But* I want to know what they uncover."

"I can do that." He dipped his head in a slight nod. "What else?"

She chewed on her bottom lip and sat in her chair. "I don't know yet. Protocol will have Róisín and I meeting first."

"His reaction at dinner..."

"That could be a part of..." She gestured toward the battered journal that had been their brothers. "We need to keep an eye on him. I want to know what she is doing, why she has been to other realms. If she's a threat to our plans."

"If she is?"

Jessamyn squared her shoulders. "Then we adjust our sails, little brother. We've waited too long for this moment. Don't think for one second that I don't have backup plans should we find ourselves facing any interference of any kind."

Runa rocked back onto his heels and let out a low whistle. "And this is why you lead us, My Lady." He bent into a mock bow, making her laugh.

"Get out of here." She waved him away. "Go be a good little spy and bring me what I want."

He saluted her, then spun away, disappearing into the hall.

Once the door clicked shut, she pulled open a drawer and reached behind it. Taking the small book and pendant that she had hidden there, she then set them before her on the desk. Stroking a thumb over the piece of jewelry that had been given to her over a century before, when the truth had been revealed to her. She felt the magic of the witch that had given it to her hum against her skin.

"She's coming," she said to the glinting jewels. "As you said she would. I hope you are right and that this is the end, because I cannot bear another moment of this."

The jewels flashed brightly when one of her rose-colored tears splashed on them and a warm, comforting sensation settled over her, as though assuring her. She flipped open the book, scanned two pages of notes she had written hastily on that day. Then she pressed her lips to the pendant and stashed them back in their hiding place. Rising, she went to her wardrobe, stripping down naked. With a sigh, she cleared her mind and found her way into her bedroom, falling asleep the moment she lay on the soft covers.

CHAPTER 23

Things felt as though they were in constant motion and she couldn't stop to catch her breath. Róisín wanted to stomp her feet and scream, throw a tantrum, cry, or break down and lock herself in a room until everything was over.

While she had felt lighter after confiding in Lucius about her issues with her magic, finding out that Lily and Ione had fled Roidon had unnerved her. To exacerbate everything, Caid had been a quiet wall since their return to Ireland from Maine.

Standing in the hallway of the cottage where they all gathered now, her fingers flexed at her sides, as though she were trying to grip something, trying to hold on.

In the living room, Ione and Lily sat with their heads together, a book spread over their legs. Their words were a quiet rush in a language Róisín didn't recognize. Caid had disappeared somewhere outside, mumbling something about them needing more wood for the wood stove. Lucius and Shasta were in the kitchen. *Their* words were harsh and clipped as they argued about something in whispers.

To Róisín, it was an accurate visual representation of just how separated they had become since coming together against Madigan.

They couldn't help it. They were being pulled in a multitude of directions. She with figuring out the Covens while quietly trying to battle the voices inside of her head that were trying to stop her. Lucius was trying to find Matthew. Ione and Lily now separated from their Coven. Caid's confession about his magic. Shasta's distance.

It's a mess. A fucking mess.

"...problem Lucius, how do we let Róisín know?" Shasta's words made their way to Róisín's ears.

Turning away from Ione and Lily, she stepped into the doorway of the kitchen. "Let Róisín know what?"

Shasta's eyes widened. "Oh, that I'm, um, training Caid."

"What?" Lucius and Róisín asked in unison.

"You heard me." Her tone was sharp. "*Someone* has to. At least with the magic. Nanette's clearly tapped out of group duties. Physical ability is one thing. He has that, but he needs both."

Róisín eyed her with suspicion. What was Shasta not telling her? What was Lucius withholding? His reaction clarified that it was not what he and Shasta had been discussing. Shasta had just returned from Roidon, and it was safe to assume that the trip was to speak with Nanette after the sisters had arrived in Ely.

"You know, just in case the reason we have to, after we..." Shasta brought her hands together.

"Can't hurt," Lucius said finally.

"Excellent." Shasta beamed. "I'll go let him know."

"What was that all about?" Róisín asked, watching Shasta dart through the raindrops toward where Caid was swinging an ax. Instead of the wood breaking into smaller, log-like pieces, they were splintering from the force of each of his blows, creating something that more resembled a pile of wood shavings. They really needed a moment to catch their breaths and talk.

"Your guess is as good as mine." Lucius scratched his jaw. "We'll give them a second, then we'll talk about Shianshani?"

She shrugged. "I guess."

They stood at the kitchen window and watched Shasta's hands move animatedly while she spoke to Caid.

"Things good with you two?" Lucius asked.

"Yeah. I think he still struggles a bit with the whole magic thing.

Not mine," she added quickly. "His." In the days that had passed since his confession to her, she had tried to show him he was wrong. Yet, Mildred had come again last night, her voice a warm breath in her ear, making the recurring dream feel more real than ever before.

Her stomach had been a sloshing, rolling mess all day. What if her mother had been wrong? She wished there was a way to call her mother to her side of the veil. She had so many new questions to ask her.

Caid set the ax down and put his hand into Shasta's extended hand, shaking it. Something about his face seemed more relaxed, less pensive than it had been when he had gone outside.

"I guess that's our cue." Lucius turned toward the living room.

When Caid stepped into the house, his eyes landed on hers. "Good?" She mouthed to him. He gave her a slight nod before ducking into the bathroom off to the side.

"I've been able to gather the clothing we'll need for court." Lily's voice drew Róisín back to the new conversation in the room.

"You'll also have to stick to your story as long as you're within the walls," Shasta said.

"Well, that's easy enough, given, you know..." Lily shrugged.

"With her hostility toward me, I think all the realms will easily believe it," Shasta added.

"Hostile, how?" Róisín hoped she could somehow figure out what Shasta had really meant about telling her.

"She was drunk for starters," Shasta said. "Apparently, she's an angry drunk. Nanette is, how do I say this kindly?" She sighed and sat on the armrest of the sofa Ione and Lily sat on.

"A control freak?" Ione said.

"You said it, not me." Shasta winked at her. "But yes, she's always had her hands on everything and run it all. Right now, things are spiraling a bit and she's reacting. By tossing me out of her house."

Róisín shifted her attention to where Lucius sat in one of the over-stuffed red loveseats. Deep lines bracketed his mouth, and his eyes were pinched. Yes, there was definitely more happening. Something was being kept from her.

After a moment, Lucius cleared his expression and sat forward. "Alright, so it's believable that Lily defected from Roidon. Only Róisín has been to Shianshani, and you were never inside the wall of Talista when you were there, correct?"

Róisín nodded. "I spent most of my time in the rainforest in the Briegii province. They had accommodations for me there while I worked, so I never needed to head to the capital."

"We really need to tread carefully here. What do you know about it?" Lucius asked.

"It's sort of confusing. The whole what's law within the wall, but it being different outside," Lily said.

Róisín hummed her agreement. "Not just that but keeping track of what's allowed in versus what's not. Like no cars, phones, or *blue jeans* within the wall? What in the Hells is up with that?"

"Say what?" Caid asked from next to her. She almost jumped at the sound of his voice so close, not knowing he had finally joined them.

"The capital of Shianshani, Talista, is basically a walled city." Shasta brought her arms in front of her, holding them in a circle, fingers touching. "And within the wall is, well, heck, how do I explain it?" She looked to Lucius for help.

"It's as though there's two very drastic time periods the Shianshani people live in. And they can cross that timeline several times a day if they wish," he said. "Within the wall, where the king and queen live, is comparable to the fifteen hundreds time period here on Earth. A full court where women are to wear dresses of a certain style, the lower classes are workers denoted by their style of dress. Absolutely no technology allowed within the walls, etcetera."

"Yeah, all that." Róisín turned back to Caid.

He stood with his mouth open, remaining that way for a second before finally blinking and closing his mouth. "Outside of the wall?"

"Very much like life is now." Róisín said. "Cars, public transport, modern attire, a democratic political system. Shianshani is actually pretty progressive in that aspect. It's the one realm where witches can live openly with the humans."

"Wait." Caid held up a hand. "How does that work, then? Does the king only rule inside the wall?"

"That's actually a good question." Róisín turned back to Lucius, knowing he could explain. The more she knew about going into the realm, especially given the situation with her magic, the better.

Lucius lifted his hands. "They have their version of a political system"—he waved one hand—"and the current king, Rastead Dionomis, rules the realm, yes." He waved his other. "It's sort of like the United Kingdom here."

"He's just a figurehead then?" Róisín asked.

"Not exactly," Lucius said. "The political parties outside the wall are still held to his rule. If he wishes to overrule a vote, he can and has done so in the past."

"What's the deal with life inside the wall, and why does that sound like prison when we say in the wall and outside of the wall?" The burst of energy pulsing off Caid was enough to have Róisín wanting to take a step away from him. Before she could move, his pinky latched onto hers, holding her in place. She took a deep breath and instead of moving away from the heat of him, she moved closer, lacing their fingers together.

"The Dionomis family likes their life of opulence. Somewhere along the way, they felt that would be threatened as life changed and things progressed. The wall wasn't erected until—" Lucius moved his fingers as though he were counting. "Ninety years ago?"

"Wait." Ione lifted her hands to stop the conversation. "You mean to tell me that this has happened with our—" Her eyes darted to Caid. "I mean, *most* of our lifetimes?"

Lucius nodded.

"What about before?" she asked.

"The laws were a bit looser and bound by the city limits," he said.

Now it was Róisín who lifted a hand to pause things. "The wall is really the entire city?"

"Most of it. The heart of it," Lucius said.

"This is going to be fun." Róisín released a disgruntled huff.

"We're going to screw this up so badly." Lily rolled her bottom lip between her index finger and thumb.

"No, you won't." Shasta rose from her seat. "You two have established a rhythm together from Trifoa and Baijiola. Habits being around one another day in and day out there. That's going to be key here."

"You'll meet with Jessamyn first," Lucius said. "We know little about her. If she's like Frederick, or not." His face hardened for a moment, the lines deepening around his eyes and mouth again, before he rubbed a hand over his face to clear whatever thought had crossed his mind away. "Be careful, both of you. Lean on what you've established as a pair in the other realms, and follow the rules to a *T*. If something happens, leave. Come home immediately. With Troy turning you away, and Beatrice still only an heir, we're not in a place to move forward on the Goddess's request yet. Discovery, not action."

Róisín didn't miss that Lucius hadn't looked at Lily when he had spoken his last words. That he had held his attention on her. She knew the unspoken words, and that he was telling her not to run into a burning building, figuratively or not.

"Alright." Shasta clapped her hands together. "That settles it for now. You." She pointed to Caid. "I'll be here first thing Saturday morning. Don't hide from me. I'm going to get a drink and go to bed. Tomorrow, I'll be in the library, Ione. We need to make a list of the books we've been through already." Shasta made her rounds around the room, giving hugs to everyone, before shifting away.

Lily and Ione followed after Róisín and Lily agreed on a departure time for the following day. When it was Lucius's turn to leave, he stepped up to Róisín and cupped her face in his hands.

"I wish you'd come to me sooner about your magic," he said. "We could have maybe found a way before you left. *Be careful*," he added with a fatherly firmness. "Jessamyn and King Dionomis will not be like the others. They *will* want to see you, meet with you. Tread carefully, say little. Okay?"

"Okay." She threw her arms around him, hugging him tightly.

"Check in two days from now. Hopefully by then, I'll have something. Either for your magic or for Matthew." He pressed a kiss to the top of her head before releasing her. He clasped his hand with Caid's next. "Good luck with Shasta. You'll need it."

Caid's reply was gruff. "Thanks."

Then Lucius was gone.

"Let me come with you," Caid said when they were alone. "After all that." He gestured toward the living room where everyone had been sitting. "I can't." He shook his head. "Not alone."

"I won't be alone. I'll have Lily. She's an incredibly smart and powerful witch. We'll be okay, *I'll* be okay." She tried to assure him, to assure herself. "You need to stay with Shasta, work with your magic more. Maybe it'll help."

His eyes darkened. The greens, browns, and yellows of the hazel being edged out by black. "Or maybe it'll just prove that I was right."

"If it does? We'll figure it out. If my mother was wrong—" Her breath hitched and her throat tightened. "We'll figure it out."

"Not if it means your Goddess gets to lock you away in the darkness."

She brought her arms around his waist and buried her face in his chest. His heart thundered against his chest, and she rose to her tiptoes to press a kiss to the spot where it raced.

"We'll figure it out," she repeated.

CHAPTER 24

LILY TRAILED behind Róisín through the sprawling Talistan market. They arrived in Shianshani that morning, and staff from both King Dionomis's court and members of the Coven had gathered to show them to their suite within the guest quarters of the castle.

Unlike the bright and airy castle in Alleyette where the council gathered for meetings, judgment hearings, research, or sanctuary, the Shianshani castle was dark and looming. Its blackened stone walls seemingly reaching for their carriage that had brought them from the gates of the wall as they neared.

They checked their dresses and their hair and then made their way through the courtyard to the markets. While their visit had been approved, they were limited to what they could do and who they could talk with until Róisín had met with both the king and Jessamyn, then were introduced in the court to the people of Shianshani.

"The well-to-do citizens of Shianshani." Róisín had corrected with a roll of her eyes once their escorts had left them alone in their suites.

Now, in the sweltering heat of the Shianshani summer, they busied themselves with a false interest in the trinkets that lined the stalls they passed by. In truth, they had just wanted to be free of the castle walls. The city wall, while intimidating, felt less threatening

Róisín had complained several times already about how having the sun bear down on them with such a vicious heat so near Christmastime was blasphemy. Lily, for whom summer was almost never-ending in Roidon, wondered what a snowy Christmas would be like. While she had only celebrated the Earth realm's holiday a handful of times with others, she knew at that moment she would barter a few of her limbs for reprieve from the heat.

"This is absolutely ridiculous," Lily said under her breath from beside Róisín. She peeled the sleeve of her shirt from her sweating forearm, then waved the fabric at Róisín when she turned. "Is this really necessary?"

Róisín stopped and picked up a bookmark made from a thin, carved piece of wood. "I don't make the rules." She used her other hand to fan her face. Her cheeks had quickly turned pink from the heat, and now the hair that had escaped her crown of braids was matted to her forehead and neck. "But I agree. If so much wasn't riding on all of this, I'd say let's get the hell out of here. It's close enough to winter in Maine. I bet there's snow and I'm dying to go build a snow person. Then hug it. *Naked*."

Lily covered her mouth to stifle her chuckle. She felt guilty for enjoying this time she got to spend with Róisín, getting to truly know her and become closer. Under the circumstances, her joy felt wrong. Like she was betraying the others.

"I don't know about naked for me." Lily flicked her hands back and forth, eyes tracking the movement of the frilly ruffles at the end of the sleeve. "Ruffles, Róisín, fucking *ruffles*."

Róisín laughed and put the bookmark back on the stall table. "At least your boobs are covered."

Because Róisín was the Coven leader of Legianne, her societal status was considered higher than Lily's, and therefore their dresses were nearly exact opposites of one another.

Lily's was made of flowing layers of silk over a velvet bodice. The sleeves were solely velvet, with ruffles at the wrists and along the base of a high neck. Róisín's dress was made of velvet and suede, its bodice hugging tightly with half-sleeves and a deep V in the front.

"I'll never complain about my life again once we're out of here. Talk about humbling." Lily released a dramatic sigh, making the pair burst into laughter.

Róisín picked up another bookmark and waved it at her, opening her mouth to speak, but was interrupted by an approaching male.

"Excuse me." He lifted his hands, nodding to them. "Apologies if I startled you."

"It's fine, we were just lost in..." Róisín glanced down at the bookmark she held in her hand. "Bookmarks."

A snort snuck out of Lily before she quickly covered the sound with a cough.

He gave them a small smile. "I should have made my presence more known. I try to not make it a habit to sneak up on people."

"Is this your stall?" Lily asked.

"Oh, no." The young man shook his head. "I happened to see you both enter the market." He turned to Róisín, giving her a slight nod. "And you look much like the description I have heard of the Lady Róisín McKenna, the last Legianne witch."

Róisín looked at Lily from the corner of her eye, an eyebrow rising.

"Are you by chance?" The hope in his voice was as clear as the sky overhead.

"I am." She dipped her head. "This is Lily. She has come to my Coven from Roidon."

"It's truly a pleasure." He extended his hand to Lily. "What an honor it must be to train under such a powerful witch."

"It has its moments," Lily said. She gave Róisín a quick wink, causing her to roll her eyes.

"Ah, my manners." He frowned briefly, then bowed his head. "Marcelo Dionomis."

Lily's sharp intake of breath was a knee-jerk reaction. Róisín's eyes briefly flared on her, and she shook her head almost imperceptibly.

What was the Prince of Shianshani doing in the common market?

The sharp jab in her side had her quickly clearing her head. Róisín was eying her expectantly. Lily hastily offered a curtsy in greeting.

"To what do we owe the honor, Prince Dionomis?" Róisín asked.

He visibly cringed at the use of his formal title. "Please, Marcelo. I —" He glanced over his shoulder before stepping closer to the stall table. He slipped a small piece of paper from his sleeve and discreetly tucked it among the bookmarks. His voice was so low when he spoke again that Lily almost didn't hear his words. "Please, meet me at this location tonight, at ten o'clock. It's about my father."

As quickly as he had appeared, he was gone, slipping through the milling market goers.

"That was...rather odd." Lily tracked his movements.

Róisín hummed, her head swiveling around the stall and the surrounding ones. After a moment, she took up the stack of bookmarks before them. Then she made her way to the end of the stall. "Are you the owner?"

The man looked up briefly from the book he was reading. "I am."

"We'd like all these," Róisín said.

"How many ya got?" He asked, turning the page.

Róisín did a quick count. "Eleven."

Another page turned. "That'll be ninety."

Once they paid for the bookmarks, they moved with the crowd toward the park to the left of the market.

Lily looped an arm through Róisín's, bringing them closer, and kept her voice low when she spoke. "What do you think this is about?"

"He seemed nervous, the prince," Róisín said. "Didn't he?"

"He was fidgety." Lily nodded. "And he looked over his shoulder a few times. I can't tell if he was looking to see if he was being watched, or if someone was with him and he was communicating with them somehow."

Róisín hummed again.

"What could he have meant about his father?"

"Here." Róisín tugged her toward a small table with two seats. She dumped the bookmarks, which numbered twice the amount she told the stall keeper. "Oops." She winced. "He was overcharging anyway. Ninety cintras is nearly a thousand mill marks," Róisín explained, converting the Shianshani currency to the Roidon one.

Lily blinked at the wooden pieces on the table. "Holy crap. That's ridiculous."

"Which is why I don't feel bad my numbers were off." Róisín simultaneously dropped into the chair and slid the small piece of paper from the stack. Keeping the paper in one palm, she turned one bookmark over in her hands under the guise of studying the design. She lifted her eyes to Lily. "Nothing can ever be just one thing. Straightforward. This is getting old, really quickly."

"What do you mean?" Lily leaned forward.

Róisín slid the paper to her. "Something tells me that this trip just got far harder than it already was."

Discreetly, Lily scanned the hastily scrawled words. The urgency seen in the sharp lines of the letters, the way they dipped and rose across the paper. She noted that please had been written seven times in the brief note.

"Shit," she muttered.

CHAPTER 25

"WE CAN stand here all day long. Ione's considerably better with the books than I, so it's not like I'm in a time crunch here."

Caid didn't bother to hold in the growl that loosed from his throat as Shasta stared him down. She had been at the door to the cottage, pounding and shouting, first thing that morning. He was already awake, unable to sleep after a violent dream about Róisín woke him.

Her glee about becoming his teacher gave him a headache almost instantly. But it was her probing questions that had raised the hackles.

"You stopped going to Nanette. Why?" As she asked him the question, she swirled her fingers into a dance, around and around. A soft breeze kicked up around them, lifting her hair. She chuckled quietly, more to herself. Dropping her hand, she turned back to him. "You felt it, didn't you? Her change?"

He felt the wall he had tried to hold between them waver and fought the urge to give her a nod. He was being an asshole, and he knew it. She was there to help him, and he certainly needed the help she was offering, but she too seemed different, off. Not quite like it had been with Nanette. His gut remained quiet, or at least as quiet as it could be, around Shasta. She had always been soft-spoken and optimistic, but this almost air-headed, overly cheery woman standing before him was new.

She sighed loudly and shook her head. "Alright. Different approach. Where do you feel your magic is at its strongest?"

That was an easier question to answer. "What do you mean?"

"You've used your magic here, in Molennius, Alleyette, Roidon, and Ely, correct?"

He gave her a nod.

"Okay. Now, think about all those times. Which was the place that it felt the strongest? I know it was quite magnificent when we began in Molennius, but I've not been privy to it elsewhere."

"Here," was all he could say. He wanted to add that everything was quieter, calmer here in Earth's realm. Not just stronger.

"Hm." She crossed her arms over her chest and studied him. "I wonder if... No. But maybe? *Could* you be?" She tipped her head to one side.

He shoved his hands into the front pockets of his jeans and rocked back on his heels. "Care to include me in this thought process?"

"Ah, like it just took me"—she squinted up at the sky as though she were tracking the morning sun—"nearly forty minutes to get you to more than grunt at me? You're a brick wall, Kincaid McGrath."

He shrugged. "Not so great at small talk."

"Alright, then don't small talk with me. You're the strong and silent type, I get it. But I've seen you with Róisín. I've had you at my kitchen island many times to share a meal with, so I know you've got some wonderful layers to you. I'm not asking you to spill your guts to me and tell me your entire life story." She shook her head. "Because opening up like that takes time and a whole new level of trust. We'll get there, perhaps, but right now, what I need from you is to trust me as Róisín's family and work with me. Not against me. Can you give me that?"

He took in a slow breath, and let it out, shoulders falling, defeated. She was right. Brent had been right; he needed to work with someone on his magic. "Fine."

"Excellent!" She hopped and clapped her hands, beaming at him. Definitely not the Shasta he had come to know. "First things first though, what do you know of your family history?"

"Same thing I told Nanette, nothing. My grandfather was an orphan or something. Came from Tennessee with my grandmother and my father."

She scratched her chin. "Mom's side?"

"Uh, pretty much that her family came over on the Nina, or the Pinta. Shit, maybe the Mayflower?"

She snorted a laugh, then pressed her lips together. "Ah, you're dead serious."

"They'd been in Massachusetts for a really long time, then they moved through New England. Most of them to Western Maine. Why?"

"You said your magic feels the strongest here, which means that your lineage stems from this realm. I know your history books leave the implication that there were many witches here at one time, but there have been very few here in the past millennia. One Coven, a tiny one at that." She walked over to the patio Róisín had made behind the house and sat in a chair. With her elbows on her knees, she put her head between her hands and rubbed at her forehead aggressively.

After a moment, he followed, sitting across from her. Noting the deep lines between her brows, he offered her an olive branch. "Sometimes I have to talk things out to put my thoughts in order. Speak it all out loud, then organize it."

She lifted her head and blinked at him.

"You think knowing which Coven I'm tied to will help? I know when—" His voice broke, and he cleared his throat, not wanting to say anything about that day in the ravine, not wanting to stir the heavy emotions that came with the memories. "Nanette seemed to think it was important."

"It could be, but it also may not be. You're not just a witch with late awakening magic. You're a *bonded* witch—and to Róisín no less." She settled back and leveled her stare at him. "Alright, so your mom's side was settlers. A traceable history. Given Earth's reception of witches, I think that can give us cause to cross maternal lines off the list."

Caid drew a finger through the air in front of him. "Done."

The tension that had held her body upright and stiff before dropped, and she visibly relaxed. Caid relaxed some as well. He could do this. He *needed* to do this.

"I have a really wild idea. I don't know if it'll work, but...I get the feeling that you may just be willing to try it."

"That depends...."

"Earth's lost Coven, one of the very first Covens in our history, was the Jordbrand family. They saved many witches from the hunts over the centuries, but eventually they all disappeared." She held up her hand when he opened his mouth to speak. "We each have these places in our realms, where our Covens were established, sort of sources of power for our magic. Unfortunately, I don't have a clue where Earth's is."

"That seems like a valuable piece of information, though."

"It is. However..." She wrinkled her nose and pursed her lips. "We don't have much by way of archives for Earth, or the Jordbrand family."

He bounced a knee, and something hot wrapped around his chest, settling a heavy weight there. "Not much? Like a book or two? There's got to be something in one of them. Granted, you'll have to be a translator, because I saw the books Róisín carried with her back in Maine. Aside from English, I know enough French to ask directions. And that's only because we were close to the Canadian border."

"No, Kincaid, by not much, I mean nothing. We have nothing documented on the page. What we know of Earth and its Coven is all oral."

The way Shasta had said it, the way her shock and disbelief had been clear, had his magic frantically rising within and reaching for his bond with Róisín. Almost immediately, she gave a small, reassuring tug back. It wasn't enough, though. This revelation only added more layers, more questions. More doubt. More worrying that he had been right, Róisín's mother was wrong about him.

"Why?" he asked when he could manage the simple word.

"I wish I had that answer." She rose. "I wish I had answers to a lot of things. Yours, even your unspoken ones that I can see in your eyes, the ones I know Róisín has yet to figure out how to ask. But I don't."

He caught the way she grimaced before she turned away. The sludge, like it had woken from an afternoon nap, yawned inside of him, then stretched. He clenched his jaw and pushed it back down. Standing, he ran a hand through his hair. "Where do we go from here?"

Shasta turned back to him. "Well, first we go to Washington, D.C."

"What? Why there?"

"If I remember right, it's the largest library in this realm. Which also means that they'll have a few—" She coughed lightly and lowered her voice conspiratorially. "Secret spots that may just hold the information we're looking for."

"And just what kind of information are we looking for?"

"Anything and everything we can find about your Coven."

SIX HOURS LATER, CAID FOUND HIMSELF ON A SIDEWALK IN Stockholm, Sweden. He had been convinced that not only were they going on a wild goose chase for information, but that Shasta hadn't been right about any hidden books in the Library of Congress. *The Library of Congress* of all places.

He'd been quickly proven wrong. Tucked behind one of the shelf walls there had been an entire room, filled to the brim with well-worn books of cloth and leather. Shelves and shelves full of books about the history of the paranormal and supernatural on Earth. However, unlike Róisín's books, Caid could read nearly all the ones they had pulled down and skimmed through.

For once, he had felt useful. Even if it had been self-serving.

The books about the Jordbrand Coven had referred to Sweden, including a small island off the coast. Shasta had deduced that it would be the best place for them to start.

Now he waited, taking in the lines of the bright, historical buildings that surrounded them, while Shasta spoke in hushed tones with a stooped, elderly man who had been sweeping the steps of what appeared to be an apartment building.

In Swedish, she thanked the man and stepped next to Caid. "It's quite a marvelous place, isn't it? How are you feeling?"

"Jittery." He flinched at the honesty in his answer.

"Okay." She looped her arm through his. "Anything else?"

"Really, really fucking hot."

Something that sounded like a strangled snort escaped her. "That's a little self-centered for a typically humble young man."

"No, like inside, I'm on *fire*."

"Oh?" She stopped walking and looked up at him.

"And a pressure," he continued, pointing to the base of his skull. "Here."

Her eyes shot wide open. "Shit. Hold on to your hat, kiddo." She shoved him into an alleyway.

"What—"

"Quiet! You'll draw attention to us," she whisper shouted at him before gripping his arms. "Come on."

Moments later, they were surrounded by trees. "The woods? We didn't have to come to Sweden for the woods."

"Blåkulla Island," Shasta corrected. "Ancestral roots and whatever." She waved a hand at him when he only stared blankly at her. "Hopefully, at least."

"Okay, and?"

"How are things feeling right now?"

"Like..." Caid doubled over, a raging storm growing inside of him, thrashing around, pressing for release. He put his hands on his knees, panting. The pressure became unbearable. The heat was consuming him, sweat rolling along his spine.

"Reach for your magic," she instructed.

Before he could, it exploded through him on its own. "Jesus." He gasped, then sucked in a breath. "I can't." He clenched his jaw, trying to hold it in. "I can't control it."

"This is going to get very interesting," she mused with a chuckle when he turned to her wide-eyed.

CHAPTER 26

"FOLLOW HER." Jessamyn's tone was low and dark. She and Runa stood in the shadows of the alleyway across from the stalls Róisín and Lily browsed.

"You meet with the king in less than an hour."

Despite the dark that hid them, Jessamyn could make out his tight features. The way his mouth pinched, the deep lines bracketing it and the lines that scored the space between his brows.

"And I can handle him." When he made no move to follow the two women, she rested a hand on his forearm. "I didn't survive nearly three centuries under Frederick's thumb by luck or even the Fates. You have to trust me, Runa."

His throat bobbed with his swallow. "Be careful." And with a nod, he was gone.

JESSAMYN TOOK CARE WITH HER DRESS AND HAIR IN HER preparation to meet with Rastead. She donned her cloak, smoothing the edges away so that the front of her dress with the Locaw and Nautilanis

119

crest were visible. When she opened the door that led to the main hall from her rooms, she was greeted by Anelle, a sergeant in her army.

"Runa shifted this to my desk moments ago." Anelle thrust a folded slip of paper into Jessamyn's hand. "Their stops, overheard snippets, etcetera."

"He still tracks?" Jessamyn asked.

Anelle gave a slight dip of her head.

"Excellent. Keep me posted. Has Aja been able to get me what I need?"

Aja, Anelle's twin brother, appeared at that moment. He handed her a deep blue vase. The contents hidden inside made it heavier than it appeared.

"What you'll need for the king is inside." His voice a deep rumble, always reminding Jessamyn of a slow rolling thunderstorm. "I'll remain posted outside as we agreed."

Jessamyn looked from Anelle to Aja. It hadn't only been in the twins that she had seen the shift over the past weeks since Frederick's death. Yes, the onyx skinned, red-eyed twins had been the first she'd seen lower their shoulders, lengthen their strides to slow their pace. One by one, she noticed it in others.

Relief. It hadn't only been she and Runa suffering under Frederick's rule. She had known. She had plotted, had planned. Seeing her people taking full breaths, hearing their laughter come naturally, it only reminded her of what she needed to do for them. What she needed to do to keep them safe. There was still more to do. She wasn't finished, yet.

"We'll return in an hour," Jessamyn said to Anelle.

Aja was the first to step away, moving down the hall toward the king's wings of the castle. Jessamyn gripped the vase between her hands, digging deep within herself to find that shell to hide herself behind. Once she had hold of it, she pulled it up and over herself. The coldness she had needed for these next minutes seeped into her marrow.

"I know it's not who you are, but..." Anelle shivered watching her face and posture change. "We're with you, Jes. Every step of the way, no matter what needs to be done."

Jessamyn wanted to smile at her, wanted to hug her and promise her the world. They had grown together, trained in the Coven army together. Fought Talistan battles together through those years. Instead, she gave Anelle a tight nod and followed Aja.

"Word on the body found?" Jessamyn kept a low voice as they moved through the castle.

"Marks on the young woman's feet, along with slight cuts on her legs and arms, indicate that she was running through the orchard. This was definitely a hunt," Aja said. "Nothing like what the king has his guards dispose of."

Jessamyn ran her tongue over her teeth, processing the information. "This doesn't make any sense, Aja. Frederick's curse was specific to the Dionomis line. Unless..."

"We're looking into it," he said. "Ten and Cicile are working through the lists of births that have happened since the curse was settled into place."

She gathered herself, lifting her shoulders and chin, the show of a regal, powerful High Mage, readying to enter the king's wing. But her steps were abruptly halted. Confused, she looked down and saw that Aja had her forearm in his grip.

"Be careful, Jes." His red eyes were soft on hers. "Runa told me what happened the other night at dinner. How quickly his temper changed. This king is different from the others with the curse, and I don't like it."

She reached up, placing a hand on his cheek. "I haven't waited this long to let things fall apart now."

"But what if you fall apart?"

Rising to her toes, she brushed a kiss over the corner of his mouth. "I know my fate, Aja. That will come regardless of what happens with this plan. Tonight is not my night."

Before he could say more, she walked down the hall and pushed into the king's quarters.

Rastead greeted her from his small dining table. "Lady Lunestran."

The table was like a toy in the middle of the spacious room, filled with trinkets and lush golden hued oversized sofas. The candles at the center of the table flickered, casting eerie shadows across his smooth face.

Jessamyn tightened her muscles so that he did not see the way she shivered.

A young boy approached her, his hands extended, expectantly. She placed the vase in his hands, feeling the weight of its contents and their meaning drop from her body as she did so. Until she saw the way the young boy's eyes were clouded but glassy, unseeing almost. His movements as he walked back toward Rastead were stilted.

"Ah, it's fresh." Rastead's delighted tone filled the room.

"Of course," she said. Slowly, she exhaled the breath she had been holding.

"Lady McKenna has arrived, I heard. Sit." He waved to a chair at the other end of the table. "Join me."

Once she had settled, trying to keep her eyes from the young boy and not think of the unease prickling along the base of her skull, she nodded. "Yes. She and Lady Wallingsford arrived this morning. I've been told they enjoyed our market and parks this afternoon."

"Excellent." The smile was wide that he flashed her before picking up the goblet the young boy had just finished filling. He raised it in a quiet toast to her before drinking it in its entirety. "Oh." He licked the thick, red liquid from his lips. "That is delicious."

"I am pleased you found it to be to your liking," Jessamyn said.

"Any luck with your research?" He speared a chunk of raw meat with his fork, then put it in his mouth.

"Unfortunately, no, Your Highness." As far as lies went, this was the only one that never tasted bitter when she spoke it. They were certain they had the book in which Frederick and Aoife had used. They only needed someone who could read it. Ten had been working her way through the list of all the Coven's linguists. However, Rastead didn't need to know that. "Is that, is..." She fought the urge to lean over the table. "Are you eating Locaw?"

"Would you like a bite?" Rastead held out a piece to her. "It's amazing. I cannot believe we've never thought to consume it before."

Bile rose in the back of her mouth. The Locaw was a revered and endangered bird. And was illegal to hunt. "No, thank you."

"Like your brother, then? A forager, not a hunter?"

"I guess you could call it that." She breathed through her nose, letting her throat work slowly as she swallowed. Her eyes watered with the acidic taste that grazed the back of her tongue. Her composure was crumbling. Her walls leaning in, threatening to crush her.

"Lady McKenna is expected in my sitting room tomorrow morning," he said.

"Excuse me?" She straightened. The young boy had returned to the room, Jessamyn only at that moment realizing that he had left. The collar of his shirt was now buttoned high on his neck this time, his movements slower, like he was attempting to move through thick mud. "That's not proper protocol for court."

He waved a dismissive hand. "I'm the king, I make the rules."

Deciding against the voice in her head that told her proceeding was a bad idea, she folded her hands before her and adjusted her train of thought. "What is it about Lady McKenna that intrigues you so, Your Highness?"

He mumbled incoherently around a mouthful of Locaw. "Perhaps it is just that she fascinates me."

The way his jaw ticked, his eyes shifted, and lips pulled tighter, she knew the beast was trying to break free. This had been the first time she had seen him unable to compose himself in the presence of others.

"Do you wish her to be one of your mistresses?" She gripped the arms of the chair she sat in, her magic simmering just below, ready. She would not use it. No, not yet at least, but it wanted her to know it was ready when she needed it.

A snarl slipped through his lips and his head snapped up. "And if I do?"

"If you want to keep order in your court, it would be wise to be very discreet should she agree to enter a courtship with you, Your Highness." She met his stare unflinchingly. "Not only would it create discord among our realm's Coven with you having an affair with one from another realm." She gestured to the room around them. "Your own court would be very disapproving paired with the fact that King Rastead the Second placed the law that made it illegal for humans and witches to come together intimately."

His features twitched again.

Jessamyn's curiosity grew deeper, creating the perfect hole for a seed of unease to drop and grow roots. *I need just a little longer.* "Have you met Lady McKenna before, Your Highness?"

"No, of course not." He shoved his plate forward, trying to appear disinterested, but the lie was clear. The way his voice pitched higher. His tongue flitting out between his lips, licking the bottom one. "The Legianne Coven has not come to Shianshani in my lifetime. How could I have met Lady McKenna?"

"I apologize. I just got the impression that you had." She shrugged casually. Jessamyn also knew that the Legianne Coven *had* been within his lifetime. Not just Aoife, but Róisín as well. Their jungles of the northern provinces were saved and thriving because of her magic of life. "And given you were willing to break court protocol to meet with her before the Coven met and welcomed her..."

His eyes were hard on her when he faced her. "I'm the king. I make the rules."

"Of course, Your Highness." She rose, needing to get back to her suite. Needing to find Runa. The threads of her plan trying to break free of her grasp, yet again. "I'll make sure to address my invitation to the Coven for later in the day to not interfere with your time."

He dipped his head. "Thank you for the"—his eyes dropped to the goblet—"treat, Lady Lunestran. We will meet tomorrow evening. Perhaps I may find it in me to allow further help with your research."

"That would be wonderful, Your Highness." She dipped into a shallow curtsy, hanging her head low. When she rose, the young boy was at her side, holding out a hand for hers. She placed her larger hand into his smaller, much colder one, and allowed him to lead her toward the door. It was when his arm extended to the knob, she saw the beginning of blood beginning to seep through the fabric at his shoulder.

"What is it?" Aja was at her side when she stepped into the hall.

"We need to meet. All of us. *Now*," she said.

"Come." He gripped her hand and shifted them back to their Coven's wing.

"Interesting information about Róisín," Runa said when they arrived in the front room of her suite. When he saw her ashen face and Aja's tight expression, he tossed the pen he had been toying with on the table before him and jumped to his feet. "What happened?"

"Something has happened to the king," she breathed. Her eyes looked from him to Aja, then around the room at Anelle, Ten, and Cicile.

"You kill him? I told you that'd be the solution—"

"No, Runa." She spun to face him squarely, her voice sharp like daggers. "The king is... I don't know." She blinked quickly when she realized she didn't know—*was* he dead? "But it's not him."

She felt Aja approach her, the wall of his muscle at her backside. The heat from his magic simmered and radiated from him.

"You're not making sense," Runa said.

"Because it doesn't make any *sense*. The king isn't the king. Our king. Something has happened, and he's someone else." She lifted her hands in the air, frustrated that she couldn't find the words she needed to explain.

"But he looks like Rastead," Anelle said.

"It's like a skin? No. It is the king's body, the curse is still there. I can feel Frederick's magic. It's as though the rest of him is someone else." She felt her heart begin to gallop and thrash in her chest like a wild stallion that had been lassoed.

"Like a possession?" Cicile suggested.

"If that's even possible. Where's Frederick's first book?" She frantically scanned the table where she had set it before she and Runa had gone down to the markets earlier.

"Here." Cicile picked it up from the side table.

"That's not all." Jessamyn clutched the book tightly in her hands. "He really has found a way to change others. Turn them into what he is."

"I told you," Runa said at the same time the others said, "Fuck."

CHAPTER 27

MARCELO PACED the courtyard in the shadows of the Talistan Church's steeple. Under the full moons, the shadow cast by the intimidating structure kept both him and Nolani hidden. He could sense how Nolani's eyes tracked him from where she sat on a bench. He knew what she saw, a man who had lost his mind. Even he had wondered if he had.

He had agreed with the others to put their trust, a lot of trust at that, in someone that none of them had ever met. It had been Nolani, the only one of them who had interactions with witches from other realms, that had suggested it.

"Not all witches are wicked like Frederick was," she had said.

"What about that one that caused all the discord among them, Madigan Milsenett?" Marcelo had asked.

"Every people has bad seeds. Look at humans over history."

After circling the topic several times, they had agreed that trying was better than not doing anything. Standing idly by was not an option.

"We may not get another chance," Nolani said.

He tugged at his coat, which had fallen askew from his restless movements and tried to smooth down his hair. Nolani hummed the song that had been playing from the cafe's outdoor speakers the day they had met. The tune stopped Marcelo in his tracks.

"I knew that would work." She smiled at him, her teeth flashing white in the dim light. "Calm down. You're making *me* nervous."

"What if she doesn't come?"

"She'll be here. It's early yet."

He huffed a breath before lowering his chin to his chest and ambling over to her, sitting on the bench. He reached for her hand and wove their fingers together, gripping tightly. The warmth of her touch soothed his nerves. His shoulders that had worked themselves up around his ears lowered as he relaxed. "How long do I get you for this time?"

"I'm home until the end of next month. Father wants me to consider going for the extra three years once I've completed this coming year." She used her free hand to push a stray lock of hair from his face.

"And?"

"If we, if he has to—" He could hear her swallow. "Will you take the crown?"

Marcelo closed his eyes. The weight of what they were facing was heavy for both of them. What would it mean for him as the next in line? He had still not convinced Rastead that Anthony was the better suited leader. The king adamant his kingdom would not be ruled by a man who lay intimately with another man. If Rastead had to die to save the kingdom, Marcelo was king, even if only temporarily.

"We could get married, force their hand," he whispered. He lifted their joined hands, brushing a kiss over her knuckles.

She leaned into him. "They could force you to divorce just as easily. The lengths my family has to go to in order to keep us concealed to keep our place at court." She shook her head. "Someone would dig and discover us. We'd lose everything."

"Then we run away."

"What about Anthony? Cassius?"

Marcelo sighed heavily. Before he could say more, there were soft footsteps near the rear gate. "She came."

"See? You worry for nothing sometimes." She rose with him, but before she could turn to face their visitor at the gate, Marcelo stopped her. He lay his forehead against hers and cradled her head in his hands. "Marcelo..."

"I love you, Nolani. We'll find a way. I refuse to live this life without you at my side. Okay?"

She let out a shaky breath and nodded.

"Do you trust me?"

"Always." She rose to her toes and kissed him softly. "Always. I love you."

CHAPTER 28

Róisín studied Marcelo carefully. Approaching, she had made note of the exit points in the courtyard, where the shadows fell, and the chief points where danger may lurk. She knew in the market that Marcelo appeared nervous about being caught talking to her. Just as she also knew that it could have been an act.

They hadn't been there long enough for her to get a handle on exactly how the human royal court and the Shianshani Coven worked, separately or in tandem. She was to meet with the king in the morning, and with Jessamyn that afternoon. Not the way Lucius had said the meetings would work, but they had wanted to meet with her. That was what mattered most.

Where they went from there, Róisín didn't know.

She noted that Marcelo and the woman stood off the pathway around the main garden, where the shadows were darkest. Where they would be away from even the best eyes one could have in the dark. When the energy shifted around her, her eyes honed on Marcelo's guest.

"You're a witch," Róisín said.

"I am," the woman said. "Nolani Fatome." She offered her hand. "Pleasure to meet you." She dipped her head into a slight bow.

A small well of relief filled inside of her at the ever so faint flicker of her magic rising to greet Nolani's when she took her hand in greeting.

"Um." Marcelo lifted his hand and rubbed at the back of his neck. "If you could keep her magic close to your chest. We would appreciate it."

"My family are members of the Shianshani court," Nolani said, as though it explained the need for secrecy.

Chewing on her cheek for a moment, she nodded and said, "Your secret is safe with me." Making the mental note to find out why, before she turned to face Marcelo. "You wished to speak in private?"

He let out a loud sigh. "It's going to take a minute to find a proper way to explain this, so please, bear with me if I ramble some. I've only recently discovered this. I'm still trying to process it."

"Start from the beginning," Nolani said. "That night."

"I was in the halls of our family wing and something pulled me toward my father's suite, his library in particular. As I got closer, I..." Even in the dark, Róisín could see the color drain from his face. His skin became so pale that it reflected the light from the moons overhead. "There was this noise. Like—" His teeth snapped together loudly. "But not quite. A biting and squishing would be more apt."

Róisín felt her pulse leap. *It's the dark of the courtyard. It's like a campfire story. Everything is fine.*

"I was able to open the door a crack. My father had one of the castle employees with him." He stopped, taking a ragged breath. "He was—" His voice became thick. "It was Larissa. The daughter of our cook."

See? An affair. He walked in on his father having an affair.

"Tell her what he was doing," Nolani said softly when silence fell over them.

Marcelo cleared his throat. "He was eating her."

Róisín's brows shot up. *Okay, graphic affair details.* "You brought me to a dark courtyard to tell me that your father is unfaithful?"

"I could have done that this morning in the market. It's no secret my father takes lovers outside of the chamber he shares with my mother. No." He fell quiet for a moment. "He was literally consuming her. He had blood all over his face and hands, and his *teeth*, so many fucking teeth."

The laughing voice in her head had fallen silent. As did everything around them. "What else did you notice?" She struggled to ask, unsure if she was prepared for the answer.

"His jaw was long, kind of"—he motioned around his face with his hands—"extended. Two rows of teeth on the top and more on the bottom. They were all pointed, like knife points. And jagged. His eyes were enormous and completely black, and his entire face was... It wasn't his, he was transformed somehow." Marcelo's voice had dropped lower, becoming breathier and filled with disbelief. "I only saw him from the side. But it was enough."

"Have you ever heard of anything like this?" Nolani asked.

"I..." Róisín pressed her lips together, holding back the urge to vomit. Her stomach became more unsettled than it had been when she arrived. "No. Not at all."

"Are we safe?" Marcelo asked. "How can we protect the people of Shianshani when it's our own king?"

Róisín willed her thoughts to catch up to the moment so she could formulate a response that could help put them at ease, but her mind raced. Had this been what the Goddess had meant when she had said that the threads for both worlds had changed? The Dionomis family was human. The witches coexisted with the humans here in the open, even witches from other realms.

"I'm to meet with him first thing tomorrow. Maybe I can get a feel for anything lingering, following him around. Magic leaves a scent when it's in use or being used." She noticed the pained look on Nolani's face. "If you haven't trained with your Coven leader, it would be easy to miss it."

Nolani quickly looked at Marcelo. "The Coven, would they know? My family, they... They do little, and when they do, it's at home."

"I—" He dropped his head, his chin falling against his chest. "You can't anymore. I don't care about your family, but *you*, please don't."

"Okay. I can do that." She leaned into him, and for a moment, Róisín saw a version of her and Caid. Before she could reach for him, he tugged on the tether. It was a quick tug, and she returned it, adding a little warmth trickling down their line.

"I'm going to be straightforward here, as I'm not quite up to speed on how things are done here. Can I ask why I've been asked to keep your magic a secret? Why could I sense Marcelo's heart almost coming to a complete stop, and now it's trying to run from his chest?"

Nolani and Marcelo's heads turned to face each other before looking back at her.

"If we're trusting her with the discovery of my father," Marcelo said.

Nolani straightened her shoulders. "While witches and humans intermingle here in Shianshani, we may not hold positions of power. My family, over three centuries ago, fled Aunellion and settled here. They learned rather quickly that their ambition to create a better life for witches, even in a realm that had human acceptance of them, would continuously be met with a glass ceiling of sorts. They changed their names, stopped practicing, and over time, integrated Shianshani politics. My father's parents were the first to be formally accepted into court."

Róisín didn't dare to ask the consequences of being found out. Especially with what she knew of Frederick and had heard of the kings.

"Should they be found out, they will lose everything. Not just their status and possessions, but the Coven will strip them of their magic and exile them," Marcelo said.

"Well, shit." Róisín brought a hand to her chest. "I have a brilliant researcher with me here for my visit. If it's okay with you, I'd like to ask her if there's a way we can mask that signature. I can't." She shook her head. "I can't leave here knowing that's the risk you face. I thought..."

"Many witches do," she said. "That's why we have so many refugees come. Then they arrive and learn it's not all sunshine and rainbows, as the expression goes. One of the earliest things non-Shianshani Coven members learn when they arrive in the realm is how to tailor their faces to appear as though they age. Some sons and daughters of families are the same witches that settled here decades or centuries before. Just with a different face."

Róisín's heart cracked, pieces of it falling down her chest, toward her stomach. She had walked into one grand mess upon her arrival in Shianshani.

CHAPTER 29

FUTURE STOOD facing the heavy steel door, waiting. The thumping and scratching noises from the other side were loud enough that the rooms lining the hall began to clamor. The cloaked figure that stood just behind Future stepped forward.

"She didn't cooperate the first time." Their voice was a rasping wind at Future's ear.

Future clenched her jaw. "That's why she'll be offered less this time."

"What makes you so sure that you need *her*?" Their hood fell forward more with the motion of their harsh nod toward the door.

"Because she is tied to it all." Future rolled her head from side to side and stepped forward. "Open!"

With a screech, the door swung open and out stepped a large, gray-skinned creature with tall, with twisting horns upon its head, spikes jutting from its shoulders, and clawed hands. It dropped its obsidian eyes down to Future.

Its deep voice rumbled, causing the ground beneath her feet to vibrate. "She's ready."

"Thank you." She gave it a curt nod and entered the room.

"What do you want?"

Future eyed the woman chained to the floor of the room. Her auburn hair was a knotted mess around her face. Kneeling before her, she reached out and put a finger under her chin, tipping it up. Smoothing the hair from the woman's face, she revealed bloodshot, angry maroon eyes. "You failed me, Aoife."

Aoife's laugh came out broken and rough. "It was your fault for trusting me to begin with."

"I told you," the cloaked figure said from where they stood in the doorway.

Aoife's eyes widened. "How? You can't... You don't..."

A corner of Future's mouth tipped up. "She does, Aoife. A little more every single day thank to your granddaughter."

"No." She shook her head frantically.

Future playfully tapped Aoife's nose with her index finger. "Now maybe you'll do as I instruct."

Aoife spat in her face, then burst into laughter that quickly became a coughing fit. Future let her laugh for a moment, then her magic rose and reached out as it had been begging to do the moment they stepped into the room.

Aoife gasped, her eyes bulging.

"You're just a child, Aoife." Future's voice was dark and other-worldly as she spoke. Who she truly was grasping for a way out. To be seen. "And I cannot allow this to continue."

"Nor can I," the cloaked figure said.

"You have no power here," Aoife gasped out. "Not anymore."

"Change is coming, Aoife." Future released Aoife with such force. Her head rocked back into the stone wall behind her. Rising, she faced the cloaked figure.

"Are you sure?" they asked Future.

Future squeezed her eyes closed, felt the burning begin at the back of her eyes and over the bridge of her nose. No, it was not the road she wanted to travel. They both knew it. Yet... "If it's what I have to do."

She could feel the eyes beneath the hood studying her, scrutinizing. "You are strong and brave, Future. It is you that has gotten us this far." Their pale, freckled hand reached from the cloak and rested on Future's shoulder. "Be careful. I will wait outside."

Future felt a piece of herself shatter the moment the door closed and locked. However, that black thread had appeared in her loom, and left her no other choice. She couldn't leave this to simmer.

Turning back to Aoife, she let her glamour fall, revealing her true form. It was then that Aoife visibly recognized that she had made a mistake. Her breaths quickened as she saw who stood before her. The ugliness of the thin, straggling hair and jagged teeth. The mottled, paper thin, wrinkled skin and hollowed eyes with flames that danced and swirled within.

"By the time I'm done, I *will* have your complacency." Future stepped forward just as a scream broke free from Aoife, echoing around the room.

CHAPTER 30

"IT'S LIKE a library in here." Shasta broke the silence that had fallen over Lucius and Ione.

Lucius lifted his head from the notes he'd been taking from a book. "Well, Miss Fiero, it is a library."

She clucked her tongue before rolling her eyes and dropping with a huff into a chair across from him.

Lucius looked at the doorway, expecting Caid to not be far behind. "Where's Kincaid?"

"At home, sleeping like a baby." She tugged a book closer and flipped it open.

"I take it you had luck then?"

"That boy is sealed tighter than a submarine ready for dive. But yes, I got him to open the hatch a bit and let me in."

Ione's attention bounced between them from where she sat at the head of the table.

"And?" Lucius lifted a brow, waiting.

Shasta grinned. "You'll never guess where I'm *pretty* sure his Coven lines lay."

He made a circular motion with his hand. "We live for some time, Shasta, but not forever."

"He's a Jordbrand witch."

Ione coughed.

Lucius found his body moving forward on its own accord. It was impossible. The Jordbrand Coven had long ceased to exist. If there had been even traces of it in any human lines, he or Clarissa would have surely discovered it with all their visits to Earth. "Are you sure?"

"He said his magic felt the strongest on Earth, so I had a suspicion." She lifted a hand, her finger running along a line of words in her book. "Ugh, I thought I had something there. Anyway! We went to the Library of Congress, dug through some books and traced the Jordbrand back to Sweden. A, what does he call it? A 'blinky' trip later, and I'm pretty sure the fact that he lit up like a Christmas tree with his magic means that I hit that nail right on the head."

Ione was still quiet, but her eyes had grown wide, unblinking, as she stared at Shasta. Lucius had to admit, the bouncy, peppy raven-haired women across the table was not quite the Shasta they all knew. Between Evelyn's late visit, what she had told Shasta to do, and the admission from Nanette that Roidon would not be joining the other Covens, Lucius had a growing suspicion of what was happening when Shasta was alone. He had seen it with her before when Clarissa's sickness had taken over her body in her last days.

"We were there for a few hours," Shasta said. "And it tapped him out, so I told him he could have a day to sleep it off. We should hear from Róisín soon, and I know he'll want to be clearheaded when we do."

"That's reasonable enough," Lucius said. "What do we do going forward?"

"To be honest? I don't have a clue, Lucius." She looked down the table to Ione. "Is there a way to communicate with those on the other side of the veil?"

Ione chewed the corner of her bottom lip. "Maybe? I seem to remember grandmother trying after my mother passed away. I can slip back to Roidon and poke around her library."

"Would it be safe for you to do that?" Shasta asked.

"If she's drinking and dealing with our council..." Ione ran her tongue over her teeth. "I could probably walk in and right by her without her even seeing me."

Shasta licked her lips and was quiet for a moment. "Okay. If you think you can. That Kincaid is from the Jordbrand Coven, and he is bonded with Róisín." She stared, unblinking at Lucius.

Lucius's mind began churning and spinning, while at the same time the things he still clung to his chest whispered around him.

"Wait." Ione sat back abruptly, almost like she had been struck. "Róisín is a Byrne descendant."

"She is," Lucius said. "What are you thinking, Ione?"

"I—" Her mouth opened and closed for the rest of her words, but they didn't come. "The two oldest Covens in our history. Well, I mean, what we know of it."

Lucius hummed. "That we have no documentation of the Jordbrand history is troublesome. We don't know how much is certain and how much is rumor."

"Oh, the library on Earth had walls of books about the Jordbrand," Shasta chimed in.

Lucius looked at her expectantly.

"Give me a second," she said before shifting away.

"Where is she..." Ione asked.

"Probably to go pilfer some books from a government library," Lucius said. He sighed and pinched the bridge of his nose. That had been all the proof he had needed. Shasta was drinking her feelings away, just as Nanette was.

What a mess.

Ione rose and went to where Lucius had Brent bring in a whiteboard so they could begin tracking notes better, and the books they had already looked through in their search for a way to locate Matthew.

On one side of the blank half, she wrote Róisín's name. The other, she wrote Kincaid. In the middle, she listed the Covens of the realms and their established dates. Then, she annotated each with how they had been founded.

"The only two founded solely by a family, Byrne." She pointed. "And Jordbrand. The rest of us are sort of mutts from whatever wherever. We just all sort of lived long enough near one of the well sources and overtime, developed magic in our bodies."

Lucius gave her an appreciative nod. A sharp pang hit his heart at the thought of what she had been denied just because of who she was.

"Given our lack of inclusion of the Jordbrand, and the Goddess no longer recognizing them." She turned to Lucius, her brows furrowed. "Begs the question, who made the bond?"

"That—" He stood and walked over to the board, studying all her notes. "Is a really good question."

"Oh, my Goddess." Shasta appeared back in the library, breathless with an armful of books. "I cannot believe I didn't think of it before. I'm so fucking sorry, Lucius."

"What?"

"Loading up with these." She dropped the books onto the table with a thud. "I was digging through my memories of when Brenna was trying to do all the, you know." She sucked in a sharp breath and waved her hands around. "With locating the McGrath family, warding any potential bond... Lucius, what if the spell we used to find the McGrath family can locate Matthew?"

Lucius's heart skipped in his chest, and his vision went fuzzy as his breath left him.

"I need Bren's books, but, if I remember right, you need one person from the bonded's bloodline for the spell, which would be Lily, or—" She glanced at Ione.

"I could do it. This way, if it doesn't work, Lily won't have her hopes up. Sorry, Lucius." She winced. "I didn't mean that insensitively."

"It's okay." He put a hand on her shoulder. "You're looking out for her, which is exactly what she needs right now. But I think having both Lily and I performing it could be better. Am I right?"

"I hate saying it, but you probably are." Shasta sighed. "It would strengthen it."

"Do you want me to let Lily know?" Ione asked.

Lucius had wanted to say yes, bring her to them at that very moment. He wanted to bring his son home and focus on the rest of what was happening. However, he knew that getting Matthew home was only a part of it. Much larger things were at play. That much was clear in their discovery about Caid.

"When do you train Kincaid again?" he asked Shasta.

"I told him to expect me tomorrow morning. We need to go to Maine to Lina," she said. "I'll explain that part later," she added when he frowned. "I'll retrieve what Róisín had for Bren's books, so we'll have the spell and the notes."

"Then we rendezvous here, hopefully timing it with the girls' first visit back from Shianshani," Lucius said. "Sound good to you both?"

"Glorious," Shasta said.

He was going to have to pull her aside before she left for Earth and talk to her. The Shasta he had known for centuries would be devastated at her actions once the dust of all of this settled. He needed to get her back to herself before she became lost. Before he could say anything to her, Lily appeared, panting, eyes wild.

"She's not here?" Her tone was laced with terror.

"Róisín? No." Lucius edged around the table. "Lily, what's happened? Where is Róisín?"

"She—" Lily looked around the room, eyes wide and glassy. "She met with the king this morning. I was in the halls and saw Prince Marcelo. We had just stopped to talk when she shifted in front of us, paler than a sheet. She said, 'he's back, he's back.' Then she grabbed my arm, and we both shifted. Except... I came here, and she's...."

Lucius struggled to catch his own breath. Everything around him shifted inward, closing in on him, suffocating him.

"Who did she mean by him?" Ione's muffled voice asked from somewhere beyond.

Lucius stumbled back a step, finding the edge of the table and gripping it for support.

"I-I'm not sure. She just kept saying he was back."

A moment later, everything went black as Lucius lost consciousness.

CHAPTER 31

Róisín dressed in the Shianshani court robes of smooth deep blue and red velvets that Lily and Ione had found for them to bring. Lily helped her brush out and braid her hair, pinning it in a twisting crown atop her head. As the pair readied Róisín for the meeting with the king, Róisín filled Lily in on what Marcelo had said, and the discovery of the truth about Shianshani's witches.

Lily's face had twisted in disgust. "Given that this is news to us, my guess is that there are also consequences for speaking out about it as well."

"Everything is just so, ugh." Róisín tightened the sash at her waist with a frustrated yank. "If Frederick wasn't already, wherever he is, I'd put him there myself."

"I'd happily help. Then we could go after the king for allowing it. I've heard that the last several kings in the Dionomis line have been as atrocious as Frederick," Lily said. "The Wicked King most, if not all, have been called."

Róisín took the slippers Lily offered her. "Do you think Frederick was behind that?"

"No, Frederick was ambitious, but he was ignorant. I'm pretty sure they've just been asshole humans."

Lily swore and insulted Frederick with such a sweetness that it had caused Róisín to laugh. "I'm curious about Jessamyn. The card that came this morning was a request from both her and her *brother*. They also requested that I bring you."

Lily's mouth fell open. "That's not protocol. Not according to what Ione and I read."

"Neither is this." She swept her hands down, motioning to her attire. "The king is supposed to come *after* the Coven when it comes to our people."

Lily crossed her arms over her stomach and shifted her weight from one foot to the other. "Be careful, okay? Even without what the prince has said, something just seems really off here. I can feel it in the air throughout the castle."

Róisín had felt it, too. Something snaking along, creeping into every space it could fit. It was slimy and reeking of decay. She blew out a breath and pat her hair, her eyes locking on Lily's as she stood behind her in the mirror. "We get through this, then we slip home to the others. Okay? A lot has happened since we got here. We'll take a breather."

Lily's eyes glistened with her unshed tears.

"Lucius seemed to think they were close. We'll find him, Lily. He's coming home."

"I hope you're right," Lily whispered. Her chin quivered. "We hadn't even had a chance yet."

Róisín was careful not to disturb their work as she turned and took Lily in her arms. "You'll have it."

A tall, broad, and devastatingly handsome guard arrived at their suite to escort her to the king's wing. Introducing himself as Cassius, he offered his elbow to Róisín politely once she stepped into the hall. The only other words he spoke were the announcement of her arrival when they came to the doors of the king's greeting room.

The moment her foot crested the threshold, she felt the wrongness of it. Here was the epicenter of what was crawling around the castle halls. This was where its heartbeat and it breathed. Her back muscles tightened as whatever it was slipped over her spine.

"Come." A deep rasp beckoned from the head of the room. "Join me, *my love*."

Róisín's heart stopped, and she closed her eyes.

No.

It was impossible.

She was dreaming. She had to be.

Everything sounded like thunder then. The wood scraping across stone, the soft tapping of booted footsteps approaching her. The air before her shifted as a hand ghosted her cheek and she fought back the urge to shiver. "Open those beautiful eyes, Róisín. You have no idea how I've longed to see them again."

She drew in a slow breath and forced her eyes open.

"You left me behind," King Rastead Dionomis said softly.

"I..." She couldn't breathe. She couldn't swallow. The room around her began to blur.

"I understand why you did what you did. Your magic is untrained, through no fault of your own. I was an unlucky bystander." He lifted a hand, reaching for her again, but stopped. He pulled the hand back, letting his hand fall to his side. "You are *stunning*, my love."

"How?" Her voice cracked on the single word. She wrinkled her brow and forced herself to keep her feet rooted instead of fleeing. Nothing was making sense.

He shrugged, then stalked a circle around her. His eyes grazed over every inch of her body, hungrily. Memories from that day in the ravine and Roidon crept along the edges of her mind.

"I never trusted Aoife," he said finally.

He *sounded* like Madigan, yet he looked... Beneath a golden crown filled with rubies and diamonds, he had cropped blond hair. His eyes were a faded gray, ringed with a brilliant topaz. He was tall, to where she had to tip her head almost completely back to look at him. As Madigan, he had been an average build, but as the king who stood before her, he was built like a machine.

"Even when she and I were one, there was something there." He stepped back and licked his lips. "I had a goal, something I was to attain at any cost. Failure was never an option, so I played several hands. On one, it united Aoife and I, the power of our magic. Pity she never quite figured how to use mine." He motioned to the stand near them on the wall. "Would you like a drink, my love?"

She somehow shook her head with her attention remaining fixed on him. He lifted a crystal decanter of dark brown liquid and tipped some into a small glass. Swirling the liquid for a moment, the pupils of his eyes grew large as he watched her. Then he tossed the contents back, letting out a satisfied sigh, and placed the glass next to the decanter.

"Where was I? Ah, another hand kept my own much larger and ultimate plan in play. And this one?" He smiled wickedly at her before he smoothed his hands down her arms until he reached her hands. Linking their fingers, he brought her hands to his lips, brushing kisses over the backs of each. "Was the failsafe for it all should things go awry. I slipped in a few generations ago cloaked as the Dionomis that had just married and had no heirs yet. Before ending the future queen's ability to have more children, I sired a few heirs of my own. It was a path for me to have a warm body, ready and waiting should my time end in another life."

Róisín could only blink at him, her mind racing. Madigan was still alive. Madigan was there, and he stood before her. What was more, was that he seemed to truly believe she hadn't meant to kill him.

"Why Shianshani?" she finally managed.

"Below its shining surface, Shianshani is much like Aunellion. And because of that, it's"—he tipped his head to one side, grinning—"pliable."

He needn't need to speak the words, but the hungry way in which he was studying her meant he found her to be equally pliable. Her short, quick breaths and ache in her throat were reminders of the toll playing the role of *pliant* in Roidon had taken on her.

You don't have to do this again, a quiet voice said from deep within.

What were her other options, though? Or was this a part of what the Goddess wanted from her? Madigan her foe, over and over, until the day he was the one to win, and Róisín locked into the depths of the darkness?

"However, both Frederick and Aoife had several plans in play of their own as well." Madigan sucked his teeth. "There's Aoife's dirty little secret with you." He eyed her appreciatively. "Although that didn't quite go as she had planned. Unfortunately, what she and Frederick have done together seems to have gone off without a hitch." Bitterness laced every word.

"Wh-what was their plan?" Róisín's throat had become like sandpaper, and she could not swallow the lump that was growing there, making it hard for her to breathe.

"*They* cursed the Dionomis line. Every single heir." His tone was dark as he spoke.

"Every?" she asked and thought of Marcelo.

"Every male heir." He clasped his hands behind his back, then spun around and walked back to his throne. "Upon the turn of their twenty-fifth year, they awake with this...this thirst unlike any other."

Blood. Marcelo had said he had seen his father's face covered in blood.

"Just drink more water," she said.

"Oh, Róisín, my love." He laughed loudly, the sound deep, booming around the sparsely filled room. "So young, so naïve." He lowered himself onto the throne, resting one ankle atop the opposite knee, and studied her. "That's how I know what happened in Roidon was an accident. I cannot hold against you that no one taught you how to truly harness your magic's power."

What did she do now? What was she supposed to do? Her mind was a jumbled mess of thoughts, of worries. She should have found her footing by now, yet she still stumbled. Now, she had stumbled to the edge of something and was left teetering.

She couldn't fall. She had too much to lose now. Finding that steadiness Caid always brought to her, she clutched it tightly. Somehow, she managed to find her voice. "I'm sorry for that." She let her chin fall to her chest.

He was back in front of her again, his fingers beneath her chin, raising her face to his. "Never apologize for others' wrongdoings, my love. *Never.*"

She cleared her throat, words on the tip of her tongue, but his mouth closed with such ferocity, she heard his teeth snap together. The joints bulged from the sides of his face and his eyes narrowed into slits, black bleeding into the whites. Suddenly, his nostrils flared. He stepped away from her, reaching behind him for the throne. With visible effort, he forced himself down, gripping the armrests of the throne. Barely a second later, the sound of wood groaning and splintering from his grip filled the room. "Róisín, you need to leave." The veins along his temple pressed outward as he ground out the directive. "Now."

The change in his demeanor and tone lifted her magic inside of her body. A reflex in the face of danger. The part of her that hadn't become terrified felt relieved over its response. Madigan's eyes changed again, rounding, sinking inward as his cheekbones flared outward. This had been what Marcelo had been talking about.

"Róisín." His tone was guttural and thick now.

"Shit." She slammed her way through the doors and began running down the hall. It was after the first corner she saw Lily talking with Marcelo. "He's back." She gripped her arms. Her heart hammered in her throat, causing her words to sound more like a gasp as she spoke. "He's back." Then she shifted Lily and her away.

CHAPTER 32

———————————

CAID WAS trapped in a nightmare. They had been on frequent rotation since the day in the ravine. Each leaving him helpless and Róisín slipping from his reach.

He was in a chair on Róisín's back patio in Maine, a glass of beer at his side. The trees in the yard were shedding their leaves for the autumn season, and in the light wind, there was a flurry of reds, yellows, oranges, and browns floating to the ground. The scene should have been peaceful, relaxing. Instead, he was filled with rage and terror.

"Caid!" Róisín's voice called frantically from within the woods, just as it had been doing for the last several minutes. Each time she called out, her voice sounded farther away.

Once again, he tried to rise. And once again, the chair only held him tighter.

"Caid!"

Where was David? Surely there was something he could do to help free Caid, right?

"Caid!"

With a roar, he struggled against the chair's hold on him. Its legs rooting through the cracks of the patio stones. Wood wrapping tighter around his chest, nearly suffocating him.

Then, a weight crashed against him. Freed, he jolted awake. His arms gripped what had fallen against him.

"Caid." Róisín's voice was hoarse and broken, as though she had truly been shouting. "Caid." Her arms wrapped around him, her fingers digging into his skin as she grasped tighter.

Alert, and heart racing, he held her against his chest, then reached over and snapped on the lamp next to the bed. Later, he would ask about her attire, but at that moment, he used his hands and eyes to check her for injuries.

Her body stiffened, and she blinked. "Where's Lily?"

"What?"

"Lily, where is she? She was supposed to come with me." She leapt from the bed and darted from the room.

Caid quickly tossed the blankets back and raced after her.

"Lily!" She spun in a circle in the hallway upstairs, then took the stairs down, two at a time. "Lily! Dammit, there has to be a way to fucking loophole this stupid tether shit with other Covens." She screamed in frustration, her fingers diving into her hair. When they snagged on the jeweled pins, she screamed again and began pulling them from her hair, throwing them to the floor. With her hair tumbling around her face, she clenched her fists at her sides, her body tensing so tightly, she trembled. "Fuck!"

Helplessness washed over him seeing her in this frenzied state. She lifted her hands to her hair, tugging, and he spurred into action. He took her wrists in his hands and brought her arms around his neck. Then he wrapped his arms around her, holding her tightly against him. "She's probably with the others and they'll be here in a minute."

"Caid." His name, muffled, came out as part sob, part hiccup. "He's back. He's, somehow, he's come back."

In the calm of the moment, the smell reached him finally. That familiar scent of smoke and decay. He recognized it immediately. In the ravine, at the Seer's house. It had covered Róisín, muting her smell of lavender and honey when she'd found him under the floor in Alleyette.

Madigan.

"Did he do anything to you?" He pulled back, pushing her hair away from her face, eyes scanning her. Inside, something awoke with an angry, raging rumble.

"No, he—" She shook her head and squeezed her eyes closed, forcing the tears to spill over her cheeks. "He sent me away. He's—"

"There you are!" Lily's voice broke in. "What was *that*, Róisín?"

Lucius, Shasta, and Ione weren't far behind, appearing only a moment later. Lucius's face was so pale, his skin was nearly translucent. Ione and Shasta flanked him in what looked to be as support for him. When his eyes landed on Róisín, Caid saw the way his entire body sagged, as though relieved.

"How did you get separated?" Ione asked. "Lily said you shifted you two away."

"I got to Ely, and you weren't there." Desperation tightening Lily's voice and lifting her tone higher as she spoke.

"I don't know what happened. You were supposed to come with me. Maybe it was because I wasn't thinking of *where*, but just that we needed to go." Róisín leaned her body against Caid.

"You're together now, that's what matters most," Shasta said. She wrapped an arm around Lucius's waist and helped him to a seat. "More importantly, *why* did you two come home so abruptly?"

Róisín flinched, and Caid heard her make a quiet gagging sound. "Madigan's still alive. Or has come back from the dead. I don't know, but he's in Talista. In King Dionomis's body."

Lily pulled her bottom lip between her teeth. "But that's not all."

Silence fell over them, expecting Lily to elaborate. When she said nothing, Lucius finally spoke, "What do you mean, that's not all?"

"He's—" Róisín shuddered. "He's become a literal monster." Her hand covered her mouth, and she hurried to the bathroom by the kitchen.

Caid didn't hesitate to follow her, closing the door behind him once he entered. She stumbled, almost falling against the porcelain sink stand. He caught her by the waist and walked with her to the toilet. As she lowered next to it, he went with her, sitting on the edge of the bathtub. He took her hair in his hands, pulling it away from her face. His jaw tightened, molars grinding when she heaved.

"I saw it in his eyes." She panted the words into the toilet bowl.

"And his face." Her body wretched violently. "The *king's* face, it...it began to change."

He pressed his lips together, holding in the angry words he wanted to scream and shout. He lowered himself to the floor and pulled her into his lap. Seeing its opportunity rise, the sludge crept along his insides. His magic hummed loudly, pressing against him, wanting release.

"You can't go back."

"I have to, Caid. I don't know how he's here, but he is. And that means I failed."

"Let us find the one that you seek," a deep, hissing voice said in his ear.

His head spun in the direction it came from, but all that was there were the towel holders and the small shelf lined with some of Róisín's trinkets.

"I have to find a way. I have to..." Róisín wiped at her face. "Caid?"

"And destroy," the voice was closer now.

Róisín's brow pinched, and she frowned. "Caid, are you okay?"

"Destroy," it said, *inside* of him this time. Sharp nails clawed along his lungs and his heart, reaching for his throat.

He clenched his teeth together, trying to fight whatever it was down. "Then let me come with you."

"I can't." She shook her head. "No. Especially with him—" The shudder that rolled through her body stole the rest of her words.

Caid took her face in his hands. "Look at you, Róisín, you're a fucking mess. You came shifting in at a mach-ten, talking about Madigan and monsters. You don't have your power back, it's not safe."

"It's not safe for me anywhere as long as he's still alive, Caid. He thinks Aoife was controlling me, making sure I didn't know how to use my magic well. That's only partly true. But he really thinks I killed him by accident. Except it wasn't. And I *didn't* kill him." She let out a snort, then cackled. "This is where I lose my mind." Her eyes grew wide, and she snorted a laugh again. "He's nearly, no, he really *is* obsessed with me. The way he acted, the way he spoke to me. He's going to...again, he's going to." Her hand shot to her mouth, fresh tears spilling from her eyes. Turning away from him, she crawled back to the toilet.

"We need to get your power back. Figure out how. You can't be there defenseless."

"Deeeeeestroyyyyyy..."

Caid shook his head, trying to clear the voice from where it had pushed roots into his mind.

"Lily is with me. I haven't met Jessamyn yet. I was supposed to—" She dropped her head onto her forearm that rested on the toilet seat. "I fucked this up, leaving the way I did. Shit."

"Hey." He fought to keep his voice soft and level. "You reacted to what you saw. You said the prince knew?"

Her chin quivered, and her nod was slow.

"What are the odds the Coven knows, too?"

"High? There's also the chance that the Coven is the reason he's a monster," she said. "He said it was Aoife and Frederick that did it."

"Destroyyyyyyyyyy." Like a tongue caressing affectionately, the words lapped along his skin. A whispered promise.

"This changes everything."

She lifted her eyes to him, and it took every ounce of strength he had to hold himself still. To not grab her and run. To make sure she was safe wherever they landed, so he could go to Shianshani and end Madigan himself. Something had shifted with his magic when he and Shasta were in Sweden. The power of it throbbed inside of him and he could feel that power. The rest of it had grown even quieter. Until that moment. When the thought of what he wanted to do if he was given the opportunity to stand before Madigan crossed his mind, the sludge inside of him stretched and hummed in delight.

"What do I do?" she asked.

He closed his eyes and took a few slow breaths to steady himself. When he opened them, he stroked his knuckles over her cheek and said, "We'll figure it out. Together."

She let her weight fall against him again, curling her body. "Can we stay in here for just a minute? I need to, before I go out and tell everyone what he said."

"We can take all the time you need." If he had it his way, they would stay locked away from the world forever.

CHAPTER 33

J ESSAMYN'S CLOAK and dress danced behind her like curtains caught in the wind through a window as she stormed down the castle halls. Runa and Aja jogged behind her in their efforts to keep up.

Ignoring the guards posted outside of Rastead's library, she shoved through the doors. Rastead's head whipped up from where he had been licking the exposed breast of a young woman sprawled across one of the low sofas.

"What did you do to her?" Jessamyn's voice was loud in the room, her rage clear.

Rastead blinked down at the woman, whose eyes bounced nervously between him and Jessamyn.

"Nothing, yet." He flashed Jessamyn a cat-like grin. "I've only just gotten started, haven't I, Lady Tynan?"

The young woman dipped her head slightly and cleared her throat. "Y-yes, Your Highness."

"Not her. Which"—she waved her hands in an *up* motion—"fix your dress and get the fuck out of here before I tell Lord Tynan what his lady has been doing." Jessamyn watched, her anger ebbing just a little, as frustration flitted across Rastead's face when Lady

Tynan jumped to her feet and straightened her disheveled appearance.

"Lady Lunestran," Lady Tynan said. She dipped into a shallow curtsy in front of her before she slipped out of the room.

Rastead rose to his feet. "I'll just snack on her later, you know."

Jessamyn let her magic dance along her arms to her fingertips. Three centuries she had stayed quiet, stayed small. For the last two, she played it as safely as she could, waiting for the time to be right for her plan to be put into place. If the past few days had shown her one thing, it was time. Time to show not just Shianshani, but all the realms, just who Jessamyn Lunestran was.

Snakes slithered along the floor toward Rastead. He tried to kick them away, but they were too fast, skirting his foot. She let her magic push into the room; the walls becoming waves of black smoke, rolling further and further into the room.

The spoils of generations of Dimonis trophy hunts lining the walls began to draw in her magic. Flaring to life, their eyes glimmered with fire, mouths opening, searching for food. A low roar sounded from one. Angry that the predator had become the hunted. It wanted vengeance and Jessamyn was ready to give it.

"I will only ask you one more time before I put an end to all of this," she said through clenched teeth. "What did you do to her?"

Rastead backed up, crashing into his desk. He let out a shout of pain, and his face distorted.

Good, let the monster out to play.

The words he spoke were garbled as his jaw changed, the rows of pointed teeth glinting in what little light was still left in the room. "It would be wonderful if you could tell me *who* Lady Lunestran."

"Lady McKenna."

Suddenly, she was looking at the king's human face again. "What do you mean? What has happened to Lady McKenna? Where is she?"

Was that fear she heard shaking his voice?

"Lady Lunestran," he said more firmly. "Tell me what has happened immediately."

Jessamyn moved closer to him, watching the snakes move up his legs, twisting and tightening. "Or what?"

"You may have magic, Lady Lunestran, but you've yet to see me when my beast has taken complete control. All of this..." He looked around the room. "And whatever other tricks you may have up your sleeve, would only be a game for it. Are you sure you're ready for that kind of battle?"

She was. She was ready to end everything at that very moment. However, she couldn't find herself in the dungeons, leaving the others in her Coven to face the punishment for what she had done. And she *would* end up in the dungeons with the warded cells, because she wouldn't leave her people behind to suffer for her actions.

"Prince Marcelo came to my study today, Your Highness. Lady McKenna left abruptly, visibly *terrified*, after your meeting today with her. He also said she took Lady Wallingsford with her. I have had my Coven guards search all of Talista, and my contacts throughout Shianshani have checked in—it is true. She is nowhere to be found in Shianshani." She had been advancing toward him as she spoke, and now she stopped when they were toe to toe. "I'll ask again, *what did you do to her?*"

The features of his face sagged. "I couldn't stop it." He drew a hand over his face. "I began to change in her presence. When I told her to flee, I had assumed she would just return to the guest wing and her suite. Not truly flee." He sounded more like a small child caught wrongdoing than a monster or the Wicked King.

Jessamyn leaned in so that her nose brushed his. "You had better hope she returns so I can fix this, or else, to be quite blunt, we are fucked. I will not have the chance to break the curse my brother put on you. The other Covens will come and that will be the end of you."

His lips tipped up, and a soft laugh broke free. "You would rather enjoy seeing that, wouldn't you, Lady Lunestran?"

"No." She took a step back and called her magic back to her. The room brightened. "Because if anyone is going to end you, Your Highness, it *will* be me."

With that, she left him.

Runa and Aja were on her the moment she entered the halls, their questions coming at her in rapid speed, making her head throb. She halted, the pair almost running into her. She sliced a hand through the air and shouted at them, "Stop! The both of you."

Both men exchanged a wide-eyed look.

She pressed an index finger to her forehead where the throbbing was the heaviest. "He, thankfully, did nothing to Róisín. However, he began to change in front of her. Which is why she left in the manner she did."

"What now?" asked Aja quietly.

"Have Marcelo come to my study tomorrow afternoon. Too much has changed for my plan to work as it was."

One of Runa's brows tipped up. "Does that mean?"

"That I have no idea what I'm doing anymore? Yes." Instead of letting them ask more questions, she shifted into her bedroom. Collapsing on her bed, she gasped, unable to catch her breath. Out of control, everything had spiraled out of her control.

And the last time that had happened, she had been forced to watch as Frederick took Diana's head.

CHAPTER 34

LILY SAT on the steps of the front porch at Róisín and Caid's cottage. Ione beside her, head resting on her shoulder. They had let the silence wrap around them as the weight of the conversation moments ago settled heavily over them all.

Madigan was still alive. Somehow.

There may be a way to find Matthew.

The way hope and terror twisted in slow circles to a soundless waltz inside of her now as she stared across the expanse of green that stretched before them.

"Do you think it'll work?" Ione broke the quiet with her whispered words.

"Which thing?"

Ione lifted her hand and rested her hand on Lily's thigh, giving her a light squeeze. "All of it. But mostly, what Shasta thinks will work with the bond."

Lily chewed on her bottom lip aggressively, only releasing it when she felt the tang of copper hit her tongue. "Maybe? I mean, I don't know what the spell entails and if it only worked for locating Caid's family because of Brenna's magic."

"I don't think it depends on where the magic lies. That would be incredibly limiting."

Lily shifted to face her. "Spell work usually is, though. We can't forget that."

Ione's shoulders sagged, and she frowned.

"Let's say, for argument's sake, it works. I'm able to locate him, and somehow, we can get that bond to snap into place—will it be enough to get him back?"

"Lily." She moved closer, dropping her voice even lower. "What are you saying?"

Tears filled her eyes, and her breath hitched. The suspicion had been building. Starting as a shadow that trailed her heels wherever she went. With each day, it became a living thing that held her hand, walking with each step she took. She had gone to Róisín several times, wanting to voice her worry, but she was scared that once she said the words, it would no longer be suspicion, but become truth.

"Lily." Ione took one of Lily's hands between both of hers. "What do you know?"

"I—" She pressed her lips together. "I don't know. It's just something that I've been thinking about."

Ione only stared back at her expectantly.

She blew out a breath. "First, he and Lucius have a Coven tether. Lucius said that he had checked in with Matthew when he and Clarissa crossed over the veil to our side and Matthew pulled back. Róisín said she'd gotten a tug back from him as well when she reached for everyone."

"Okay, what does that mean?"

"Well, with Róisín's connection to all of them, it's like a muted version of a Coven tie. What we found to connect everyone together to push our power to Madigan, it only gave us that." She couldn't help but wish it had been more, because then maybe he wouldn't have survived.

And neither would have Róisín.

She hadn't been there that day, when Róisín had died, but she had seen everyone's haunted expressions after. The way the air around all of them seemed so heavy, it made them round over, move slower.

And Caid... His pain had been palpable. The energy it created poured from him and screamed at everyone with it.

"So, it would make sense that she would only be able to sort of check-in," Lily said. "It would be easy enough to know if one of them *didn't* tug back that something was possibly wrong. There's also a chance that there's a range limit on her tether to them as well. We didn't exactly have time to test it out before everything went..."

"Sideways," Ione said.

"Exactly. However, Lucius, their tether, is *strong*. Yet, when we were in Molennius, he could not locate Matthew as he should have been able. Just as now, although he can still reach all the way down their tether and still faintly feel Matthew there, he cannot locate him."

"Shit. Shit, *shit*." Ione shook her head. "No. It's not possible."

"It's the only explanation that makes sense."

"But *Aunellion*?" She nearly shouted. "No one can get there, Lily. I know you've got the hots for him and think he's the best thing since toast, but..."

"I think the expression is sliced bread."

Ione's face hardened. "It doesn't make a difference what the expression is. That's not the point."

"Look, I have feelings for him, yes. I hope to get the chance to explore them, *with him*, and see if we can build something that is deeper and more important than the bond. But this is me being the book nerd you've always teased me for being."

"Wait, have you read something?"

"Not directly, no." She pursed her lips. "But because I have read so much, especially when we were looking for ways to deal with Madigan, I know enough to know that, yeah, it's supposedly 'off the map' for us now, but it's not impossible."

"Alright," Ione drew out the word. She put her hands on the porch behind her and leaned back. "Which means the question now is, what do we do?"

"Róisín and I go back to Shianshani. Lucius is right. Being forthcoming with Jessamyn about *why* we left is the best foot forward. We can only hope that our honesty spurs her to be honest."

Ione snorted. "She's a Lunestran, and we all know that the Lunestrans aren't known for kindness or honesty."

Lily winced. "Every day this just becomes more and more of a mess for all of us." She glanced over her shoulder back at the house. Lucius and Shasta sat in the living room, she knew, having heard their quiet chatter and his stern whispered words about how Shasta needed to stop doing something before she regretted it. She had wanted to listen a little longer, but when Róisín had tugged Caid away from the room, Ione had grabbed Lily's hand and dragged her outside.

"You all have a lot going on," Ione said.

"You do too. I'm not the only one that left Roidon."

"Think you'll ever go back?"

Lily stretched her legs out before her, then placed her hands behind her, mirroring Ione's position. "I think I knew I was leaving the moment grandmother found out that Matthew and I were bonded. Ione." Lily tipped her head so that it was angled enough for her to see her. "You'll be there, right?"

"For what?"

"When the time comes to find Matthew. The others, they've all become like family to me, but..." She bit the side of her bottom lip.

"Of course I'll be there. Whenever you need me, I'll always be there. And Lily?"

"Hm?"

"You really need to let Róisín know you know about her magic. You two can't keep acting like everything's okay and going at it from your two different sides."

Lily let out a heavy breath. Ione was right. While she and Róisín had become closer and found that they worked well together, their brains always trending along the same thought paths, they had also been shouldering their individual worries alone.

CHAPTER 35

MARCELO WATCHED Anthony settle into the plush, red suede wingback chair facing Marcelo's teak desk. He let out a soft sigh as he sank into the cushion, then propped his feet up on the chair next to him.

"You get all the good stuff." He practically moaned the words as his body relaxed.

"I'd much rather you be the oldest, you know," Marcelo said. "I was made more for fighting than leading."

Anthony hummed, sinking lower.

"Is Anthony not here yet?" Nolani asked from the doorway. "Oh, you're napping."

"I am not." Anthony's response was muffled, as his body had been swallowed so wholly by the chair, his chin pressed atop his chest. Pushing up, he dropped his feet to the floor to free the other chair for her. "Although, I'd much rather be. What of Cassius?"

"He's a few moments behind." She offered him a sweet smile as she lowered into the seat. "When shall we expect the grand engagement party?"

Marcelo swallowed the cough that had surged in his throat, causing him to make a strangled noise instead.

"Not until this one"—Anthony jabbed a thumb in his direction—"becomes king of this shit hole realm and strips the law that says Cassius and I are *disallowed* to be together openly."

"Apologies for being late." Cassius burst through the doors. "I got waylaid by Margaret on the way up."

"Margaret?" Marcelo's brows knotted. "The head laundress?"

Cassius dropped heavily onto the footstool between Anthony and Nolani. "She's down two girls, Marcelo. Alice and Emily, the twins."

Marcelo pressed his lips together, an effort to hold in the curses he wanted to shout.

"That's eleven women since I've returned home," Nolani said.

"Thirty-six this month," Anthony added with a whisper.

"Father is locked down in his wing yet again," Marcelo said grimly.

Nolani reached across the desk, taking one of his hands in hers. "What of Lady McKenna?"

The room spun slightly as Marcelo felt all the blood drain and pool in his feet.

Anthony pushed himself up in his chair, dragging it closer to Marcelo's desk. "What is it, Celo?"

"I've met with Jessamyn this afternoon." He swallowed deeply. "I, it's, there's..."

Nolani rose and went to him, sitting on the armrest of his chair and placing a supportive arm around his shoulders. "Let's start with why she requested you. She's more known for keeping to herself, interacting mostly with Marsenna. Even now, as the High Mage, she limits her interactions with Rastead. So, to meet with one of our princes—" She frowned.

"It was about my father. About the monster he's become," Marcelo spoke quietly, looking at each of them as he did. "It's a curse, she said. Frederick, with the help of Aoife, placed it on my father's line a few generations ago."

Anthony lifted a hand like he was a schoolboy before a teacher. Marcelo nodded to him. "If that's the case, why is Father the first one we've known of? Surely with the others, they did the same."

"Frederick had some kind of control over them. Jessamyn deduces he used the curse as some type of leverage whenever he wanted something," Marcelo said.

"So..." Cassius waved his palms back and forth. "Like blackmail?"

"Not so much that as it was control," Marcelo said.

"But that doesn't make any sense, because your father is *out* of control," Nolani pointed out.

Marcelo dragged a hand over his face. "That apparently is a recent development. Things seemed 'as usual' until a little more than a few month ago."

"What changed?" Anthony asked.

Suddenly feeling restless, Marcelo gently scooted Nolani from his chair and paced in front of his windows that faced the training courtyard. He watched the king's guards spar with swords and their fists for a moment before turning away.

"Jessamyn isn't sure. She had noticed he was acting out of character. *Nicer*, she said, and he sought her skills, hoping to break the curse. The outburst at dinner and breaking of guest protocol with Lady McKenna was the final tip off for her."

Nolani crossed her arms over her chest, her jaw flexed as she clenched it. "I love you, Marcelo Dionomis, but you really need to stop walking us around this bush. What does Jessamyn think has happened to your father?"

"Aside from the curse," Cassius said.

"Yes." She tipped her head toward him. "Aside from."

"He's no longer our father."

Cassius and Anthony jumped to their feet, simultaneously shouting, "What?!"

Marcelo gave them all a slow nod. "She's not sure what has happened. Cicile called it an essence, or spirit. Something about how Rastead's spirit has been pushed free of his body and another occupies it."

"But who?" Nolani pressed.

"That is what they're trying to figure out. The only logic that they've been able to come up with is that it is a spirit that knows Lady McKenna," Marcelo said. "It would explain the reaction at dinner."

Anthony put his hands on his hips, shifting his weight from one foot to the other. "And possibly the way she abruptly left?"

"Yes." Marcelo nodded. "He told Jessamyn he felt himself changing into whatever, the monster, the animal, he becomes and told Lady McKenna to leave to protect her."

"Well, fuck," Cassius said, almost breathlessly, as he let his large frame fall back into his chair.

Nolani crossed the room so that she was standing next to Marcelo. "What do we do now?"

"I don't really know," Marcelo said. He had known little about how to even approach handling what he had seen that night in the library, but this...this changed everything. They were human. What could they do?

Anthony stalked over to the low stand where Marcelo kept his glasses and liquor. His movements jerked as he lifted a bottle of pale amber liquid, and forgoing a glass, downed the bottle. Wiping his mouth with the back of his hand, he asked, "Do we know where Lady McKenna and Lady Wallingsford went?"

"The Coven has searched everywhere. They are no longer in Shianshani. That is all we know right now," Marcelo said.

"Shit," Anthony muttered.

"Do we have any way of tracking her?" Cassius turned an expectant gaze to Nolani.

"I wouldn't even know where to begin." She shrugged. "My parents aren't exactly plugged in anymore."

"And even if we did, there's too much risk," Marcelo said. "Absolutely no magic from Nolani right now."

Cassius and Anthony glanced from him to Nolani.

"We learned when speaking with Lady McKenna that magic leaves behind a scent trail of sorts." Nolani reached a hand out and laced her fingers with Marcelo's, giving him a light squeeze.

Anthony's mouth dropped open. "Oh. Oh, shit. I didn't know."

"Neither did we." Marcelo rubbed at his temple with his free hand. "Until we find a way to hide that scent, Nolani won't be using any of her magic. The risk far outweighs the benefit."

Silence fell over the group as they absorbed the change in their world around them. It had been terrifying before, faced with the unknown that it had started as. But now, now that they knew what was going on, the well of terror suddenly had become bottomless.

Anthony was the first to break the silence. "When did he go under lockdown?"

Marcelo ran his hands through his hair, then rubbed them over his face, letting out a deep breath. "Not more than seven hours after the last was lifted," he said from behind his hands.

"Shit," the trio replied in unison.

"What next?" Nolani asked.

"Honestly?" Unable to contain it, a chuckle bubbled out of Marcelo. "How in the hells do we stop an actual, in the flesh, monster?"

CHAPTER 36

S HASTA STOOD before her house, one million millipedes
marching along her skin pulling at the tiny hairs as they went.
Her insides were having some sort of fire dance celebration by
the way everything felt as though it were roasting, and feet stomping all
over.

"Why didn't you tell me Kincaid was Jordbrand," she said when the
air shifted next to her. She clenched her body, afraid she would fall apart
if she moved too freely and turned to face Brenna.

Her best friend stood with her mouth opening and closing like a
fish out of water. Her lashes fluttered over her emerald eyes. "Wh-
what?"

She took a step closer and put her hands on her hips. The urge to
hug her was strong, but she also needed to remember that she was mad
at Brenna. Yes, she had made a promise to keep the secrets, yet she
hadn't expected that there had been so many more that Brenna had held
to her chest. "Don't act stupid, Bren. You knew. A heads up would have
been nice."

"What's happening?" Evelyn appeared next to her. "Sha?" She
reached a hand out, gingerly touching Shasta's shoulder.

The breath Shasta took made her entire body shake. To have her there, to know the slip of paper that Ione had retrieved from Nanette's house had the correct words upon them to call through the veil. That it worked. Could this be their answer? The way they fought against whatever was happening in the afterworld? Despite wanting to turn and melt into Evelyn, Shasta stayed with her attention on Brenna, waiting.

"Shasta." Brenna shook her head, sending her flame red hair spilling over her shoulders. "I-I didn't know. The Jordbrand family, they were... are *gone*."

Evelyn lifted a hand to her mouth, stifling a gasp. "Are you sure he is?"

Shasta let her chin fall to her chest. "One hundred percent sure. I'll dig through to trace his family line on his father's side once we're settled with"—she motioned toward the house—"and everything else." She pinched the bridge of her nose. "But what I saw when I took him to Sweden, this island that was tied to the Jordbrand, Blåkulla Island I believe it was called...that was all the proof I needed."

"We have nothing on them, though." Evelyn's eyes darted from her to Brenna.

Brenna shrugged. "It wasn't me."

"No. Going on a hunch, we went to one of the libraries in the States. Found the honey pot, so to speak. Book after book referred to the island, so I figured it was worth a shot."

"And his sister?" Brenna asked.

"That's where I'm going once I take care of this." Shasta shifted around so that she was facing the house again. "I'm curious to see if taking her there will wake her magic if she has any. Where's Stephen?"

Brenna's laugh was full and hearty. "Doing what he does best, spying."

"Say what?" Shasta's eyes blew wide, and she reeled back around. "What's going on?"

Brenna looked over Shasta's shoulder at Evelyn. "Evelyn's not the only one that's struggled to come through the veil. We've found others. Every story is the same. There's something that holds them back, almost like they're tethered to the afterworld. If they can break free of that, they're finding themselves facing a wall of some type."

"Is that? Why didn't you tell me?" Shasta asked Evelyn.

"I didn't want to worry you until I had more information," she said.

"But you two are here, now," Shasta said.

"To be honest, I'm surprised we could make it," Evelyn said. She had stepped close enough that the back of her hand brushed against Shasta's, and their fingers reached for one another at the same time.

Brenna stepped up to her shoulder on her other side. "The two of us crossing at the same time was probably enough to break down whatever has been put into place."

"I don't like this," Evelyn whispered.

"Neither do I." Shasta said, giving her hand a firm squeeze. "The timing of all of this. *All* at once."

Brenna and Evelyn hummed their agreement.

"Stephen will find out. At least get us a thread to follow," Brenna said. The words were assuring, but the tone they were spoken with sounded laced with doubt and fear.

"Well." Shasta huffed. "Those two things are crossed off the topics of discussion. What are we going to talk about next while we burn this fucker down?"

Evelyn snorted, then slapped a hand over her mouth. Her eyes were glittering with mirth when she turned to Shasta. "I'm sorry. You said that with so much passion, though, I couldn't stop myself."

"Said what with passion? Fucker?" Shasta stressed the last word.

"I think it was more how you said *burn this fucker down*," Brenna said.

Shasta tried to fight the smile that wanted to split her face.

"Do you have marshmallows?" Brenna had leaned closer to whisper to her.

"I'm sure I can wrangle some up for us before we light it up," Shasta said.

She grinned. "Perfect."

Twenty minutes later, the trio sat in chairs that they had dragged out of the house. They had to keep shuffling them back as the fire burned hotter and hotter. Fingers sticky from the marshmallows Brenna had located in the pantry. Their faces were flushed from the heat and tear-stained from the memories that brought forth the kind of laughter that made tears and aching stomachs.

For just one moment, the weight of the tumbling world fell from Shasta's shoulders. For just one moment, that small spark of hope that everything just may be alright was given the chance to ignite in her chest.

CHAPTER 37

Róisín stood at the window of their suite in the castle, watching the people within the wall mill around the markets either buying goods or sightseeing. Knowing now that the wall and its rules had been put into place in her lifetime, she wondered how those of the Shianshani Coven felt about it. The backwards shift of their progress at the heart of the realm.

Then again, after what Marcelo and Nolani had told her that night about just how little witches were truly free to exist in the realm, she had to believe that the Coven only followed to keep what little freedom they had there.

"We're being honest with Jessamyn when we go?" Lily came to stand beside her.

"At this point, yes. There's nothing left to lose. Right?" To Róisín it felt like it was all left hanging by the thinnest thread, nearly invisible.

She rubbed her fingers along the base of her neck. A habit Róisín noticed she had when she was nervous. "Like, *everything*, everything, or just that the king is Madigan, part?"

Róisín let out a sharp exhale and turned from the window.

Lily lifted her arms and spread them out. "We're in a realm surrounded by *her* witches, for starters. I don't know about you, but I was terrified of Frederick. Which means I'm terrified of Jessamyn already."

"Lily, it all circles back to the Covens and bringing us together. Maybe this is our..." She searched for an appropriate word. "Two birds." She raised her hands, extending the index finger on each, then brought her hands together. "One stone."

"And if it goes south?" She rubbed at her neck harder, making her skin turn red.

"Then we run," Róisín said, her tone firm. "Shift out of there. Go to Ely, or my house. Just get the Hells out of there. *Then* we catch our breath and figure it out."

"Shit," Lily whispered. "If you think this is the way forward..."

Róisín burst into laughter. It was loud and had her bending over to catch her breath. Standing, she dabbed at her damp eyes. "Is this the right choice? Hells if I know, Lily. I'm flying by the seat of my pants right now. I've never been in such uncharted waters. Not even before, with Madigan."

"Or without your power," Lily added quietly.

Róisín's heart jumped into her throat, and for a moment, she couldn't breathe. "What?" The word was a strangled sound from her mouth.

"I've—" Lily's eyes dropped to her feet. One foot moved, scuffing the stone floor. "I've known since we arrived in Baijiola. Why didn't you tell me?"

The room around Róisín spun, and she blindly reached for the arm of the chair she stood next to. "I thought I could fix it before anyone noticed."

"I can bet Caid noticed. That's why he's been more protective of you than usual. Why he keeps pressing you to let him come with us."

Róisín nodded.

"We shouldn't be here, Róisín. Not like this."

"I have to, Lily." The tears burned in her eyes, and she squeezed them closed, trying to hold them back, trying to keep her walls up.

"You don't *have* to do anything, Róisín. You can stay at home with Caid. Rest. You owe the Goddess nothing."

Róisín let out a watery laugh. "Oh, Goddess, you sound exactly like

Matthew right now. Not that long ago he stood in my kitchen, saying pretty much the same thing."

"He's right." Lily sat next to her and took her hands in her own. "That night took a lot from us, and a lot out of us. You far more than the rest with what you had to do. The power that it took to use your magic that way."

"And I still failed. Not only that, but she said—"

"I know what she said. And right now, do you know what I say to that? Not right now." Defiance flared on Lily's face, narrowing her eyes and pinching her mouth. She had seen many sides to Lily in the past few weeks, her humor, her compassion, her quick thinking, but this was new.

"We can't just walk away from *this*, though." The urgency that had ridden her spine since the discovery of Madigan pressed in tighter now.

Resignation settled over Lily, pulling her shoulders down, rounding them. "One thing at a time. Okay?"

"Two," Róisín whispered.

Lily had started to rise but stopped. "What?"

"Two things. No." She shook her head and held up a hand when Lily began to interrupt. "Madigan, and Matthew. We can't forget Matthew."

"Oh." Lily's cheeks bloomed pink. "He's pretty hard to forget."

Róisín couldn't stop the laughter from exploding out of her again. "Alright." She rose and held out her hand to Lily. "The plan remains the same, though. But if anything feels off or wrong, run. Got it?"

Lily clasped Róisín's hand tightly. "Got it."

CHAPTER 38

C AID STRETCHED his legs out and brought the beer he had
stolen from Lina's refrigerator to his mouth when he heard
her patio door squeak open. Taking a long pull from the
bottle, he winced at the taste of it, forgetting that Thomas, Lina's
husband, preferred lighter beers.

Lina came to a stop next to him. "You have one of those things for a
reason."

"What is this shit?" He held up the bottle, ignoring her question.

"Looks like beer to me." She rolled her eyes and grabbed the cell
phone that was on the armrest of the chair. "Did you forget how these
work already?"

He shrugged a shoulder and took another drink. "The last time I
was here, you said you knew I was without me using that." He gestured
toward the device she still clutched.

"Sure, but a heads up you were here, or going to be here, would be
nice."

"Thomas home?" He looked over his shoulder back at the house.
"You two have"—he wiggled his eyebrows up and down—"plans?"

"I am not talking about my currently non-existent sex life with my
brother." She dropped into the seat next to him as he began coughing.

"You just did." He side-eyed her while he pounded his chest where his last mouthful of beer seemed to have lodged itself. When he saw the frown she wore on her face, he cleared his throat. "Everything good?"

"It is." She blew out a breath between tight lips, creating a trumpeting noise. "And, it's not. We wanted this. *I* wanted this." She motioned to the small swell of her stomach. "But shit, Caid, this is *hard*."

And he had left her with no one.

"Nope, cut it out right now." She pointed a finger at him, her face set in a deep scowl.

"Cut what out?"

"That! Right there." She made a circle with her finger. "Lights on, lights off. You're *brooding*. Cut it out. I'd have been more pissed at you if you'd stayed here because of me than I was when you left."

"Ah." He tipped the mouth of the beer bottle, pointing it toward her. "So you are pissed at me for leaving."

"*Was* pissed. Past tense, asshole. At first, yes. Because I'm selfish and I've had you here for my entire life. But no." She shook her head. "I realized how foolish I was to even think about being mad at you for having your own life, having your own things."

"It was Thomas, wasn't it?"

A sound between a sigh and a groan released from her mouth. "Yes. That man, damn him. He's my sanity. He saw me moping those first few days and did that dad talk thing he does. After another day or so, I saw the light, so to speak. Then, I couldn't help but wonder if it was because of me you stayed for as long as you did."

He downed the rest of the beer, then placed the empty bottle on the table next to him. "I stayed because I wanted to, Leen. You were just the bonus here."

"But Kate—"

"Kate and I didn't fit," he said. "We wanted two different things. We were two different people."

"You let her go because she wanted you to choose," Lina whispered.

He was quiet for a moment, studying the way she kept her eyes downcast and drew her index finger along her bottom lip. "But Róisín didn't."

She lifted her gaze, but only blinked at him in response.

"That's what I mean, Leen. Kate wanted me to choose her, every single time and for everything. Róisín has let me be who I've always been, right from that first moment. She knows what this place means to me, what you mean to me. And she doesn't push me to make the choices."

Lina gave him a small smile, but he could still see the doubt on her face.

"She loves you too," he said softly. "Why do you think she's keeping her house here?"

"Will you tell me what's going on? Maybe not with everything, but with you?"

"I..." He couldn't tell her the whole of it. He didn't want to put words to any of it outside of what he had told Róisín. There were minutes that grabbed hold of him every day since telling her he feared even what little he had said had been too much. A distraction for her, that's what it was, this...*thing* inside of him. Right now, with the loss of the power to her magic, a distraction could be dangerous.

"Caid." Lina's voice was tender.

"It's just this whole magic thing. Everything has changed, and so fast. *Too* fast. I'm just trying to adjust and adapt, while also being of some kind of use to the others."

"It's okay to take a minute to settle into this thing, Caid. When will you realize you don't need to be everything for everyone? That it's okay to need others sometimes. To let them help you, you know."

He rubbed a hand over his face, and that was when he noticed David hopping along the back garden. Lina followed his light of sight and gave a light chuckle.

"He keeps me company. Helen's great and all, but she's always business about the babies. She's terrible at conversation," she said.

"And a pompous rabbit, is?"

She gasped and pressed her hand to her chest. "Lower your voice, Kincaid James McGrath. He'll *hear* you."

"Good." Smugness had his lips curving into a grin. *Let the fluffy asshole hear me.* Róisín still hadn't told him what she and David had been talking about that day in the backyard of her house there. His confession to her that day had overshadowed it. But he hadn't been able to shake the look on her face when she had run across the yard to catch up with David. The fear in her eyes.

"I thought you liked David?"

He had, and if he were to be honest, he still did. There was so much going on, and with everyone scattered, he was more angry at how helpless he felt than at the conversation he didn't know the topic of.

David saw they were outside and began to approach them.

"Be nice, or I'll cook *you* for stew tonight," she said in a low voice.

"I'll make that palm tree right there, that is definitely *not* fake, hold you to give me a head start on my escape."

Lina's attention shifted to the palm trees in the yard. "I have no idea what you're talking about. Those are most definitely fake."

"Mm." He shook his head, fighting back the laughter that was building. He'd needed this time with Lina, alone. He hadn't realized just how badly, until that moment. "I know damned well that it was my fiancée that grew those for you."

The chair Lina was sitting in scraped over the patio loudly, the sound assaulting his ears and making him cringe.

"Your fiancée? You two are—"

"Please tell me you kids are not fighting." Shasta's voice came from behind them.

Lina let out a squeal, a mix of obvious frustration and excitement.

"She's not doing that blinky thing," Caid said.

"Blinky thing?" Lina's head swiveled back to him. "What the hell is that?"

"That thing we do, you know the..." He fisted his hands, then sprung them open. "Poof!"

Shasta snorted and looked skyward. "It's called shifting."

"Whatever. She's not doing it while she's pregnant."

"Given we can't shift with humans, she's going on a plane," Shasta said.

"Um." Lina rose, waving a hand at them. "Excuse me, but could you two tell me why I'm getting on a plane? Can I fly? Where's Helen?"

Shasta lifted Caid's bottle and frowned. "Helen's currently in Molennius handling a lumber delivery for me. And she said absolutely yes, you can still hop on a plane. We just need to keep you rested and hydrated. Got another one of these?"

Caid had remembered the way she had acted at the cottage. A little off-center, giggly. Then everything clicked. Shasta had been drinking. And given her behavior as of late, he had to guess a lot. He stood and swiped the bottle from her. "I grabbed the last one."

"Damn," she whispered.

Lina's eyes bounced between them. "When are you two going to tell me where I'm going?"

"Some island in the middle of nowhere," Caid said as Shasta said, "Sweden."

"What?" Lina pressed her hands to her cheeks. "Why?"

"Are they Jordbrand?" David asked, having finally arrived where the trio were standing.

"Yup," Shasta said, emphasizing the end of the word with a loud popping sound. "This one here"—she jabbed a thumb in Caid's direction—"exploded with power almost the moment we arrived. Wait." She squinted at David. "How did you know the tie to Sweden for the Jordbrand family?"

Caid really wanted a moment alone with David now. First Róisín, now this. Shasta had said the Covens had nothing written on Earth's Coven. The history had been a spoken one in the other realms. Yet, David somehow knew.

"I'm a great many centuries old," David said, as though that were enough of an explanation.

"So, we're taking a field trip to this island, to what?" Lina held her hands palm up. "See if I have magic too?"

"While it's okay to play the wait-and-see, why not explore the chance that we can poke it with a figurative stick and wake it up early," Shasta said.

Lina's face lit up with excitement. "Give me five minutes to pack and we can go."

Caid waited until she was in the house before facing Shasta. "I'm flying with her."

"I figured as much. I'll be at the airport to pick you two up. With a car," she said. "We'll have to charter a boat or something to get there."

"And if she has magic?"

"Helen's here with her. She's not only a midwife for us in Molennius, but she's also an amazing teacher. I can't think of a better person to be here with your sister."

Caid heard the confidence in Shasta's voice, and it settled the acid bubbling in his stomach. He gave Shasta a nod, then looked down at David. "Perhaps David here can fill us in on what he knows about our Coven while we wait for Lina."

Shasta looked at David as well. "That's not a bad idea. The books were helpful, but you may know something more," she said to David.

David's whiskers twitched and Caid swore he saw the rabbit's black eyes grow larger.

"I only know that the Jordbrand family was Earth's true Coven, but it's been nearly a millennium since there was any known trace of them, or Earthborn magic, here in this realm." David said.

Caid ground his teeth together. Inside of him there was a knock that echoed from his mind, right to his core, like something pounding at a door. He hesitated, then heard it again. Slowly, he reached in and opened the door.

Lies. It was the same voice from the night Róisín had come home after discovering Madigan. The sound of the single word slithered along his insides, humming.

David sat on his haunches, his attention on Caid. That was all he needed to know that the voice, regardless of what it was, or where it had come from, was telling him the truth.

David was lying.

CHAPTER 39

Lucius reached out and adjusted Matthew's index finger further down the fishing line on his rod, nearly dropping his own into the creek below the bridge they had been perched on for the last two hours.

"You have more control of the line to bring your catch in," Lucius said.

"We've been here for two hours and have yet to catch anything," Matthew grumbled. He reeled his line in completely, then recast.

Shrieking barks peppered the air, drawing their attention to the small boy leaping from rock to rock directly below them.

"He's quite a wild one," Matthew said.

"Not all that different from a young boy I once knew." Lucius's mouth curved with a soft smile.

"I didn't run around barking and digging holes with my hands, making constant...*noise.*"

Lucius chuckled. He pulled the white bobber at the end of his line back and forth, then gave it a small tug before letting it settle again in the water. "You were plenty noisy, Matthew. Quite feral as well. Especially when Róisín was around. Speaking of—"

The groan Matthew released was almost comical to Lucius. "Don't. Please, Goddess, don't. Mom's already bagged on me about it."

Lucius shifted to look at him and saw the tight frown he wore. "Did it not go well in Shianshani?"

Matthew made a popping noise with his mouth, then blew a raspberry-like sound through his lips. "Well..." He released his line and rubbed at the back of his neck. "It didn't go good or bad, I guess."

"She punched you."

"Ha. She definitely did. No hey, hi, how are you? Or I missed you." He rolled his eyes. "Just a straight fist to the face."

"And?" Lucius waved his free hand, encouraging him to continue.

"Then there were lots of tears"—his throat bobbed—"from both of us. And we promised to never speak of it again. It was a mistake and in the past."

"That doesn't sound all that bad."

"That part wasn't." He bit the corner of his bottom lip, falling silent, his eyes watching the boy scale the creek bank. "It'll never be the way it was before. And that's my fault. I shouldn't have been an idiot and taken off like I did. Or stayed away as long as I did."

"Some lessons we learn the hard way. Give it time, things will even out between you two again. Jackson, mind the rocks, you'll cut your feet there," Lucius called out to the boy.

"I've got it, Uncle Lucius," Jackson said. "I've been climbing these since I was a baby. At least that's what momma says." He hopped over the last rock, landing on the top of the bank. He let out a whoop, his small fist pumping in the air.

"He's filthy," Matthew said.

"Just building a bit of character. That's all." Lucius reeled his line back in. It was time to head back to the house. Clarissa and Marion would surely be done by now. And Clarissa would need to get back home to Ely and rest. She was fading faster and faster with each passing day. His heart pinched in his chest and he struggled to keep in his gasp. Moving on in life without her was becoming more real. He wasn't ready. He wasn't sure that he would ever be ready.

Matthew lay his pole between them. "How does Mom know the Burkes?"

Lucius's hand froze midair. "They're family to her."

"That's what she said." He tipped his head toward where Jackson was swinging a stick like a sword. "He calls you uncle."

Pushing to his feet, he reached a hand down to help Matthew up. "You know how your mother was with Brenna?"

Matthew let Lucius pull him to his feet. "But Róisín doesn't call you uncle."

He shrugged his shoulders. He had asked Clarissa if she had been sure when she had suggested to bring Matthew with them on their recent trips to Montana in Earth's realm. She stood firm in the choice. She had said that Matthew needed to know the Burkes. Needed to have a relationship with them.

His shoulder was harshly jolted forward. A familiar voice was faint in his ear. "Lucius, wake up."

Awareness slammed into him, forcing him upright in his library. Blinking, he cleared away the dream's haze. Ione stood next to him, open book in her hand, and her face wet with tears.

"Shasta was right," she whispered. "It'll work. We can find Matthew with this spell."

He wasn't sure if it was the dream that still fogged the edges of his surroundings, or a sudden, prodding urgency that woke when Ione had shaken him awake, but he knew one thing for certain—when they got Matthew home, it was time. No more hiding.

Chapter 40

J ESSAMYN STOOD before her desk in the front room of her suites. Ten and Cicile sat to her left on a small sofa. They had been working through the books she had found in Frederick's rooms after his death to learn more about the curse that had been placed on Rastead and the Dionomis line so they could work on a way to reverse it. They were Shianshani's most intelligent linguists and historians. And they were a part of Jessamyn's group of most trusted of the Coven.

Anelle stood near the floor-to-ceiling, wall spanning bookshelf. Her eyes trained on the door, waiting for her brother. Aja and Cassius had been tasked with making sure Róisín and Lily made it to the Coven's wing, and to Jessamyn, without incident.

Marcelo and Anthony sat across from Ten and Cicile. Marcelo thumb and forefinger kept squeezing the space of this thigh just above his knee. Anthony's eyes darted between watching his brother's movement and the door.

"You going to fill me in on what exactly is going to unfold here in a few seconds when the ladies walk through that door?" Runa came to stand next to her. "Or is this going to be like all the other times? You plan, and I only get clued in when shit goes off the realm or you need me?"

Jessamyn pinched the bridge of her nose. "I can't tell you what will unfold here, because I'm just...rolling with it."

"That helps with my confidence," he mumbled. "What exactly do you plan on telling them?"

"Everything, Runa. We know Rastead isn't Rastead anymore, and that somehow he knows Róisín. Which means we now need each other."

"I don't know if I like that. We don't know her, and we don't trust her."

She turned to him. Was it a risk she was taking? Yes. However, not only did she not see another workable option presented to them, something festering deep in her gut told her to do this. That this would be what brought them to their next step. "This leap we're taking will be big, but we have to trust ourselves, Runa. Trust what I have been told and have seen. That what we have built here, what's settled into place since Frederick, will be enough."

"If she's on his side?" He crossed his arms over his chest.

The door clicked open and Aja stepped in, catching her attention. His sharp nod meant that Róisín and Lily were in the hall with Cassius. "We do whatever we need to do, Runa. That part will never, ever change. Our people are more than worthy of freedom—at whatever cost."

Aja cleared his throat, earning the attention of everyone in the room. "Róisín McKenna, and Lily Wallingsford," he announced, moving aside so they could enter the room. Cassius trailed in after them.

"Welcome." Jessamyn stepped forward and bent slightly in a half-bow. "I apologize for what happened yesterday that had you fleeing. It would seem that our king is not himself, literally."

Róisín returned Jessamyn's bow. "Thank you. And no, he's not. He's Madigan Milsenett. Somehow."

Runa began to cough and hit his palm against his chest hard enough that Jessamyn heard the thump. "Excuse my rudeness, but I could have sworn I heard you say that King Rastead is possessed by Madigan Milsenett, whom rumors claim that you killed months ago."

"Because that's exactly what I said." Róisín's tone was steady, yet Jessamyn detected a hint of testiness in it. No nonsense, just what Jessamyn liked. She kept her shoulders high and held Runa's gaze. "And I did. Unfortunately for all of us, he had some sort of plan, or failsafe, set into place."

Jessamyn let the noise in the room rise, taking the moment of chaos to gather her senses. To calm the heart that pounded all over inside and loosen the lungs squeezed so tightly, she wasn't sure how they hadn't popped yet. A pulse beat in the outside corner of her left eye. The flutter it caused quickly became a nuisance.

"Enough!" She clapped her hands together, effectively silencing the entire room, then turned to face Róisín. "Are you absolutely sure?"

"I knew the moment I walked into the room for our meeting yesterday. Something felt off, wrong when I stepped in. Then he spoke." Her body visibly shook, and she drained of all color. Lily moved closer to her. "And then he—" She cleared her throat; her voice had wavered slightly. "He told me what he had done, and what had happened with his bloodline."

Marcelo shot upright. "His bloodline?" He exchanged an uneasy look with Anthony.

Róisín looked around the room at each of them. Her hands were clasped so tightly before her that her knuckles were white. Her chest expanded with a heavy intake of breath. "I don't know why he chose the Dionomis line. He only said that your realm is much like his."

Cicile had begun frantically flipping through the stack of books that sat on the table before them and Ten. Jessamyn watched their movements for a moment, her brain in tumult. "What did he do? Did he explain how?"

Róisín looked over her shoulder to where Lily was standing, silent. When the blonde gave her a slight nod, Róisín appeared to relax. "I think it's probably best that I begin at the start of this. Not when Madigan severed his connection with the Covens, but when Madigan's brother, Bernard, married my grandmother, Aoife."

Runa hissed out a breath next to her. "Shit."

"I know." Róisín frowned. "How do you think I felt when I started uncovering how fucked up my family really is? The secrets they kept?"

"I'd have burned shit." The honesty of his opinion was harsh, but so very Runa.

"If there was anything left to burn, I would have," she said quietly.

Jessamyn lifted her hand to halt the wandering of the conversation. As much as she felt sympathy for the witch standing before her, she needed answers. She needed to know how her realm was involved, and just how much her people would be harmed by this. "Start with Madigan having a brother," Jessamyn said. "Because that is news to *all* of us."

Róisín began with a story about her mother's travel chest, and how it had taken her decades to open it up. Only doing so because she felt as though there may be something in there to help her face Madigan.

From there, Róisín's story spiraled into twists that, from the sound of gasps and curses around the room—no one had expected.

It hadn't been that Aoife and Madigan were bonded, nor that Bernard had actually been an adopted brother of his. That had caused the biggest reaction. No. It had been when Róisín had said that the Seer, *their* Seer for all the witches around the realms, in Roidon had been Madigan's birth parent that had everyone on their feet and talking at once.

"How?" Anthony asked from where he had moved to stand next to Cassius.

Runa scoffed. "Well, I'm sure you know about the birds and the bees—"

"No, I mean how in the Hells did we *not* know? That's a big, *big* thing." Jessamyn could practically feel Anthony's body vibrating from anxiousness where she stood.

"Did he tell you anything about that?" Jessamyn asked Róisín.

She shook her head. "No. He said very little to them that night. He said and asked nothing about them yesterday. It seems that he, too, wishes to keep that part quiet."

"There has to be a reason," Aja said. The response earned a nod from Anelle.

"What exactly happened yesterday?" Jessamyn needed this meeting to be over. She had a summoning she needed to perform. There were answers she needed. Anger she needed to express over being left in the dark over such important information.

The room quickly fell quiet. All eyes were back on Róisín. Lily moved closer to her, gripping the hand of Róisín's that hung at her side between both of hers. It seemed to be the bolster of support that Róisín needed.

As Róisín recounted the entire meeting with Madigan the day before, Jessamyn watched the faces of those in the room with them. Only her most trusted surrounded her, but she knew anything could be possible. She knew the tells of all of them, even the princes. Her chest loosened when she recognized the same shock and fear she felt among their expressions.

"Which is where we come in," Jessamyn said when Róisín finished. "We knew *of* this curse." Jessamyn and Aja had lost Diana because of this curse. "However, we didn't know the what or the how of it." She gestured toward Ten and Cicile. "This is Ten Tretap, and Cicile Nulessa, our Coven linguist and historian. Ten has been working on translations, as that's where she's strongest." Ten gave Róisín and Lily a small wave. "Cicile is a master historian, and they have been looking across all the realms, trying to locate the source of the curse. At this point, we only know Frederick found it *somewhere*, then had it translated from one of the long dead languages."

"It appears to be a blend of all of our founding languages, so that presents a challenge even for the most knowledgeable linguist." Ten shrugged.

Lily shifted so that she was more in view. "Have you made any progress?" She dragged her index finger along her chin as she studied Ten.

"Absolutely none since we've been able to get our hands on these." Ten waved a hand to the books.

Róisín blinked twice before her eyes widened at Ten, then she spun to face Lily. "Do you think?" she began, but then dropped her voice. "What about Matthew?"

"She could do both," Lily whispered. "She was serious about wanting to help."

Jessamyn cleared her throat and both women's heads snapped toward her.

"My, um, my sister Ione, she's left our Coven as well and has been working to help us locate Matthew McArthur after his disappearance from Alleyette. She was sort of a rebel—"

Róisín snorted. "Was?"

Lily glanced at her sidelong. "And made it a point to learn every language *other* than the few our grandmother wished of her to learn. It's made her incredibly fluent in the older languages of the realms, both human and witch."

Ten looked at Jessamyn, the question in her eyes, the need for approval from her before asking. Jessamyn dipped her head slightly.

"Would she be willing to come here?" Ten asked.

"If it would be okay for her to split her time between the places so she can continue to help Lucius, I'm absolutely sure she would."

"Fantastic." Ten grinned. "We'll connect after this meeting to set something up so she and I can meet and create a plan of action."

Lily gave Ten a shy smile before she turned to Cicile. "I'm also a historian myself. I'm more than happy to offer my help with that. If that's okay, I mean."

"The more eyes, the better," Cicile said. "Right?"

Jessamyn could only chuckle at Cicile's words. Ten's cousin, but they couldn't have been more different. Cicile was the type to ask for forgiveness after and not permission. The sharp jab at her side had her turning her head, finding Runa looking at her expectantly. It was at that moment, she realized she missed a key piece of this puzzle.

Before she could ask, Runa was staring down Róisín once again. "What's Madigan's connection with *you*? I'm not talking about the half-uncle, unrelated uncle or whatever. I'm talking about what has made him such a loose cannon about you?"

The composure that Róisín held before crumbled. The color drained from her face and her eyes quickly filled with tears, shining in the room's light. "He... he..."

Lily stepped closer to Róisín and wrapped an arm around her waist in silent support.

"He thralled me. Then violated my mind and my body. Then I

killed him and my grandmother." Róisín's voice had become hard and cold.

The room had been stunned into silence. It was Jessamyn that found her voice first. "It's not safe for you here, Róisín. You're a target for him. I know he began to change in front of you yesterday. The kings before had controlled it, kept the beast and its cravings at bay, so to speak. That was my first tipoff that something wasn't right. He has managed some control, but he still visibly fights for it. That it tried to release itself in front of you, and again in front of me later that day, is alarming." She looked around the room once more at them all, taking a moment to catch her breath in an attempt to urge her heart from her throat. "For us all."

"Is he human?" Lily asked.

"Yes. Outside of what the curse had done, he is human. His magic from his life as a witch has, thankfully, not continued with him into this one," Jessamyn said.

"Is there a way it can?" she asked.

Jessamyn sought out Anelle who shrugged, then to Cicile, who mirrored the action. "We don't know. Which adds a layer to this. It's clear that we need to all work together on this. If I cannot guarantee even the safety of my people, I cannot guarantee yours." She lifted her gaze from Róisín, to Lily. "Or yours."

"Risk isn't anything new to us," Róisín said. "It's best if we stay closer, where we're needed right now."

Jessamyn could only sigh. She knew she would respond the same way, so she couldn't deny this to Róisín or Lily. "Okay. However, if he learns that you have returned and requests your presence, you will not do so without guard. Aja, Runa, and Cassius will be with you both whenever you need to go somewhere while you remain in our realm."

Róisín stepped around Lily, her arm extended. "I wish we could have met under better circumstances," she said.

"As do I." Jessamyn took Róisín's hand. "We'll come together again, all of us." She looked at Marcelo, Anthony, waiting for their acknowledgment before continuing, "Tomorrow, and get the foundation of a plan in place. Agreed?"

A variation of yeses echoed around the room. Then, one by one, everyone filed out. Anelle taking Aja's place in seeing Róisín and Lily back to their suites.

When Jessamyn and Aja were alone, his voice was a quiet rumble when he said, "I know you felt that too."

She squeezed her eyes closed. "And yet, she still chose to stay. Aja. I commend her for it, for that determination and strength she displays." She sighed and let her body fall against his, needing someone to hold her up when all she had wanted to do was fall to the ground. "What in the Hells are we going to do? This changes *everything*."

His strong arms banded around her, holding her tightly. "It does, but we can still do this. We can still be free."

"You sound so sure. How?"

"Because if there's one of our Coven who believes that we can truly be free, and has the means to do it, it's you, Jes."

She had wanted to reply. She had the retort in her throat. Instead, she soaked in his surety and focused on Róisín. "Now, the question is, how do we keep a powerless witch safe while facing this monster?"

CHAPTER 41

L ILY WALKED alongside Róisín in the quiet courtyard that was hidden on the Coven's side of the castle. Aja had informed them it was shielded from the humans when Róisín had asked where they could go when they needed air that would still give them some level of safety.

It had given Lily a sense of relief to see Róisín pulling back instead of continuing to charge forward. Would she heed Jessamyn's words that it was clearly not safe for her to remain in the realm? Lily doubted that. She had seen it in the way Róisín carried her shoulders, high, but slightly rounded. The burden of the Goddess's request, what had happened that night, and now facing the fact that Madigan was still among them, all of it rested atop of those shoulders.

Lily couldn't fathom how heavy the weight of it all felt and didn't know how to lessen it for her friend. She could quietly admit to herself that it had all been so much easier when she was tucked into the stacks of the Alleyette library, away from the more intense parts of everything. Being an active participant, as she had been these past few weeks, had been the biggest challenge she had ever faced.

"I wanted to say thank you." Róisín's voice cut into her thoughts.

"For?" Lily looked up from where she had been watching the stones beneath their feet as they walked along the winding pathway. Runa and Cassius trailed behind them; Aja paced ahead.

"Coming with me each of these times. I don't know if I'd still be able to keep going if I had to do this alone."

The rough, hoarse sound of Róisín's voice had Lily drawing in a slow, steadying breath.

Lily stopped and faced her. "Róisín, we've always been at your side. Even when we couldn't physically be there. You've never been alone."

Róisín gave her a small smile before she glanced back to where Runa and Cassius stood with their heads on a swivel, eyes scanning. The pair were like night and day. Runa's skin was a deep, beautiful ebony, whereas Cassius's was a smooth ivory. Runa's bald head caught the sunlight, glistening like a beacon in the sun. Cassius's dark mop of short curls seemed to absorb the sun, rather than reflect. Aja had stopped moving with them as well. His muscle flexed beneath his onyx-colored skin when he crossed his arms over his chest, tipping up an expectant brow when he looked at them.

"You don't have to be. Any of you," Róisín said. "This is my mess, Lily."

"No, this is Madigan's mess. Fredericks's mess." She let out a harsh exhale through her nose. "*Aoife's* mess. And you, us? *We* are clean-up crew."

"She's right, you know." Aja's voice felt more like a low roar across the short distance that they stood apart. He was a man of few words, but when he spoke, you felt the voice in the wall of a man, rather than heard it.

"It still feels like my responsibility. It always will. Given her words and what was said to my mother," Róisín said.

"No." Lily said the word more forcefully than intended, making them both wince. "You can't let it. It's not yours."

She brought a hand to her chest, trying to steady her heart. After a moment, with her hand still at her heart, she let the lid blow off her contained anxious rage. Let every thought that had kept her awake, aside from Matthew being lost, spill forth. "It's not your responsibility. Róisín, don't you ever wonder why she's let this happen? Why something so damning to all our people? Why is it you she's put in this position?"

Róisín gasped at her words, but Lily pressed on. "For someone so all-seeing and mighty, why? Why is it only *you* that can fix this? Why couldn't we *all* have been set on Madigan? And why can't we work on the rest? I've been going through our books and can't help but feel we're missing something."

The men had moved closer to them, creating a wall of privacy around their conversation.

"She's our creator." Runa's snort was quiet, but Lily still had heard it behind her. She waited, and when he said nothing, she brought her attention back to Róisín. "The most powerful of us *all*. She has the Sisters, who know everything, see everything."

"I, shit." Róisín's reply wavered. "I *have* thought—"

The courtyard broke into shouts as the men went on the defensive.

Lily became airborne, crashing into the hedge to the left of the pathway. Her shoulder screamed at her in protest when the branches dug into her skin. The hedge quickly gave way to her weight, sending her slamming to the ground. Her ribs burst into a searing pain that made her eyes water.

Róisín shouted, and Lily saw her leap into action. Her leg flew high as she spun in a circle, connecting with the head of one of the newcomers.

Scrambling to her feet and racing back to Róisín's side, Lily finally saw who had entered the courtyard. There were five of them, and from behind, they all looked like normal Shianshani guards to the king. She could not hold back the air shattering scream when one of them advanced on her and she saw its face.

Everyone had been calling Madigan an animal, a monster. This? This was something entirely different. Something otherworldly. The eyes were large black orbs. They reflected nothing, nor did they move. The skin was stretched thin, their blue veins webbing over their cheeks, across a nose that tipped up sharply, exposing the cartilage behind. Its jaw was inhumanly long. At that moment, it snapped at her with its seemingly endless rows of sharp, glinting teeth.

Falling on her ass, her magic quickly rose inside, throwing up a wall of wind between them. The guard smashed against it. Stepping back, it stared at her for a long moment, then threw its shoulder against the wall.

Panic clawed at her insides. She knew magic, and that was all. Unlike the others, she had never been called to physical training.

"Your place is with the books," Nanette had told her.

What had she been thinking, coming with Róisín when she was so utterly helpless in moments like this? Had it been false courage? Or had it been an excuse for her to hide away from the pain and grief that plagued her over Matthew's disappearance? To give herself a distraction so that she could remain numb? No matter the truth of it, she was not only damning herself not being able to fend for herself, but she was putting Róisín at risk.

Just beyond, she saw Róisín dodge an incoming blow, ramming one of her shoulders into the gut of the guard that had advanced on her and flipping them over her back. They needed to get out of there, and with Róisín's lack of power...

Gritting her teeth, Lily struggled to keep her shield up. She lifted one of her hands, pressing it forward to help. Then, she urged the ground beneath the feet of the guard, still pommeling the wall, up. The smooth rock of the pathway shifted, the guard lost their footing and stumbled. At that moment, the break in the path had been enough for the twisting, twining roots that crisscrossed the courtyard from the hedges, to spring up and grab hold of the guard's legs.

Letting the wind go, Lily pushed to her knees, and her elemental magic completely encompassed her body in a rush. Then she pressed it outward. A second later, the guard was locked inside of a cage of roots.

"Get them out of here, now!" Jessamyn's voice called from across the courtyard. Two guards had halted her, trapping her in a battle of magic and strength before she had reached them.

Runa's response was tight when he called back. "If you can't see, sister, we're fucking *trying*."

Lily needed to move, to get to Róisín, who was still fighting off the guard that had tried to grab her. And she was losing. The guard had pushed her back, back, back, toward the hedge on the far side. Right to where she saw two more had appeared and were waiting, having pushed the branches of the hedge apart, making a hole for escape.

She put every ounce of energy she had left into her voice, hoping she could lift it up over the shouts and roars of the others. Over the thunder from magic erupting around her. "Aja!"

His head shot up, and he looked around. He saw where Lily was pointing and was instantly shifting away. A moment later, with Róisín tucked against his side, he was next to Lily, and he shifted the three of them away.

Jessamyn was waiting for them when they arrived wherever Aja had taken them. There wasn't any roof to the stone-walled and floored area, and only one door that Lily could see.

"What—" Róisín hunched over, heaving. "What in the Hells was that? What were they saying?"

Saying? Lily had heard nothing other than an assault of noise and gnashing teeth.

"It was Founder Shiini," Aja said.

Lily looked from him to where Jessamyn stood with her lips pressed into a tight line. "What—"

Jessamyn dropped her head, her shoulders rounding forward. "I tried." The defeat rang clear in her words. "I tried, but if I can't even keep you safe for just *one* day." She was looking at Róisín when she spoke. "I can't. We need to find another way and do it with you where you can be safe. You remain here, powerless like this, *he will win*, Róisín. Against you, against all of us."

Anger flashed bright in Róisín's eyes, and a small swirl of color gathered around her irises.

"Lily." Jessamyn's voice was soft.

Without a word, Lily nodded and moved to Róisín's side.

"I need to take care of this here, and then I will find you both," Jessamyn said.

Lily brought one of her arms around Róisín's waist, pulling one of Róisín's arms around her neck for support. "Thank you. Both of you."

"No, fucking Hells, Lily, let me—" Róisín tried to push away from her, but Lily shifted them away before she could free herself.

CHAPTER 42

S HASTA PINCHED the bridge of her nose, a closed mouth scream of frustration echoing through her head. If she could go back to that morning and slap herself across her face, she would.

What had she been thinking? Not only taking a woman pregnant with *twins* and plopping her onto a plane for several hours but having that pregnant woman's brother travel with her.

What an idiot.

She had been an only child, most of her friends had been only children—Brenna, Clarissa, Nanette. Lucius had an awful relationship with his brother, and Evelyn was the youngest of eleven in her family. Her siblings had long gone and been out of the house by the time she had come.

Seeing the McGrath siblings in action had been something new and foreign. And it was *terrifying*.

"Gah! You're such a fucking pain in the ass." Lina threw her hands up in the air and spun away from him. "I cannot wait until you have kids of your own so you can see just how much of an asshat you are!"

He blew air through his tight lips, making a trumpeting noise. Then, as though suddenly remembering Shasta was there, he turned his sights on her.

"Oh." She breathed in sharply. On the exhale, she said, "no."

"Didn't think this through too well, did you, *Mom*?" He asked.

That was another thing she had certainly not been expecting. Every time she tried to interject and calm the situation before her, *both* siblings had taken to calling her mom. Their shouts at her, *Mom*, to butt out of it had been what had ignited the headache currently rioting against her temples.

"No." She licked her lips. Hells, she needed a drink. "I definitely didn't think this through at all."

Lina had been frazzled and worked up the moment she had come into the airport lobby. From the looks of Caid's shirt and hair, Shasta had wondered if Lina had used him as a punching bag during the flight.

He insisted, and continued to insist, he had said nothing to set her off.

Five minutes ago, Lina's spiraling anger had been given a root, then grew wild. Caid had innocently asked if they had names picked out yet.

Shasta drew a hand down over her face. "Why don't we get back on the boat and head back to shore? We'll stay the night in a hotel and then get you both back on a flight to Maine?"

Lina's eyes flared wide and Caid took a cautious step back.

They had been on Blåkulla Island for the better part of five hours already, and there hadn't even been a blip of magic to arise within Lina. Shasta held her breath and let her senses reach. They stretched and probed, but still nothing.

"No," Lina said. "I want to go home. Now. I'm over this shit. Completely over it. I clearly don't have magic." She held her arms out wide. "We've been here long enough that something should have happened by now, right?" She looked over at Shasta. "You said it was instant with him." She jabbed her thumb in Caid's direction.

"It was," Shasta said with a nod. "And no, I think this makes it clear that despite him having it, you somehow don't. I'm sure Nanette could explain the why of that." If Nanette ever talked to any of them again. Her heart gave a painful, heavy beat in her chest.

"Great. I'm gonna die in a few decades, and he's going to, what, live forever?"

"I thought you didn't want this?" Caid asked, eyebrows high on his forehead. "When Róisín and I told you a few weeks ago, you almost had a meltdown over you and Thomas."

"I did. I don't." She groaned loudly. "I don't know what the hell I want. I'm scared about all of this. You two are obviously deep in some shit, but no one will tell me what is going on. Even David is acting weird!"

"Leen—"

"We were supposed to grow old together. Raise our families together. Instead, you'll get to watch my kids' families grow up and have families. You'll know my great-grandbabies. Hell! You'll know my *great great* great-grandbabies! And I'll be hanging with the worms in the dirt. Just little old skeleton me, and the worms. While you're up here with our family. For centuries—" Her voice broke.

Caid and Shasta exchanged a look. He was clearly as lost as she was. The childless woman, and the man, unsure of the best way to support Lina amid this onslaught of hormones that were pumping through her.

Cautiously, Caid approached her. "I'm sorry," he said softly.

"Don't be sorry, you big oaf." She slapped him on the chest. "Sorry. I told you this was really fucking hard. I have no control over my emotions, and this is a really, really shitty time to not have that control." She buried her face in her hands and cried.

Shasta wanted to scoop her into her arms and rock and soothe her. She took a small step toward them but stopped. This wasn't her family. It wasn't her place. Instead, she pressed her lips together and watched Caid do what he did best, handle things.

She wondered, at that moment, just how much he could handle. Would he have a breaking point? Would he ever reach out for help before that time came? Or would he let it consume him?

"Look, I don't have answers, Leen. I wish I did." He slipped his arms around her shoulders and slowly brought her against his chest. "I wish I had a grasp on it all so I *could* tell you what's going on, but even I don't really know. All I can tell you is, nothing is any different from it was yesterday, last week, last month, or last year. Okay? You and I will never change. You'll always be my bratty little sister, and I'll always be your obnoxious, sometimes overbearing, big brother."

"Sometimes?" came her muffled response against his chest.

Laughter rumbled out of him, and Shasta felt the anxiousness over the situation ease.

"But I really don't want to stay the night here. I want *my* bed. Can we go home now?"

When he turned his attention to Shasta, she gave him a slight nod.

"That we can manage." He stroked a hand over her hair and down her back.

She stepped away from him, her fingers wiping at her wet eyes. "Ugh." She groaned and made a face of disgust. "Never get pregnant. It fucks with you so bad."

"Given I sort of, uh, can't do that...wait." He spun to Shasta. "Can I?"

Shasta barked out a laugh. "Oh, Goddess, no. Magic doesn't work *that* way."

"Anyway." He put his hands on Lina's shoulders. "It'll be worth it, though. When you've got them in your arms, it'll be worth it."

Shasta's heart puddled and oozed away from its resting place in her chest. *Oh, Bren, this boy...*

Lina smiled through her tears. "It really will. I can't wait. You're going to be an amazing uncle. Róisín will be an awesome aunt. Okay." She blew out a quick breath, then nodded. "Let's get the hell home."

"Has anyone ever told you that you're good with people?" Shasta asked after they shifted into the kitchen of the cottage in Ireland.

Caid shrugged. "Sort of comes with the territory of being a parent-less kid with a sister, I guess."

"And a businessman," she said.

"If you could call it that. I mean, the jobs sort of came to me after Wyatt's dad, Ed, retired. Oh." His face fell. "Shit."

"What?" Shasta's magic felt around them, stretching out along the glen for a threat.

"I..." He covered his mouth with a hand, then drew it down to his chin. "Shit," he repeated. "I can't believe I never thought about that.

Telling Wyatt. I mean, do I tell him? What do I tell him? At some point, he's going to realize that I'm probably not coming back."

"Well, what did you tell him when you two came here?"

"I told him Róisín had a work trip. I needed a vacation, so I was going with. Call me if things went south, and I'd handle it. It's still my business, he's still my employee, I couldn't leave him to handle it all."

Shasta tapped her chin. "Got a beer?"

"Not for you."

His response was so gentle, but the words were quick, sending Shasta rocking back onto her heels.

"Took me a little to get it figured out. Why you were acting so weird. It wasn't until you came to Lina's and picked up my empty that it clicked."

"And?"

"You can't condemn Nanette for being drunk when you're drunk, too."

She huffed a laugh. Feeling the burning at the corners of her eyes, she tried to blink the coming tears away. "I wasn't drunk when I went to see her."

Caid slowly raised a brow. "Really? You're going to handle this like a toddler? I expected more from you, Shasta."

Shasta suddenly felt very small.

"So, no. I don't have a beer for you. We can sit." He motioned to the small table that sat in front of a large bay window. "Talk it out. We all went through some shit that night. Maybe it's time for me to get it off my chest, too."

She saw the egg of his own vulnerability he was offering her in exchange for her offering her own. And damned him, he was right. She needed to get it off her chest. She needed to stop losing herself to the hazy mist of a buzz every day.

"Okay—"

"We found it!" Ione shouted, appearing in the kitchen, waving a book over her head.

A moment later, Lucius was walking into the kitchen. "Doors, Ione. We knock on other's doors when we arrive. We don't just *shift* into their homes."

"Bah." She waved a dismissive hand. "This is too exciting to knock on a door, wait for someone to answer and invite—"

"You standing here babbling is wasting as much time as knocking on someone's door," Shasta said. "What'd you two find?"

"The books you brought me from Brenna." Ione set it on the table and spun it around so the letters read upright for Shasta. "The one you used to find him." She pointed to Caid. "Will work to not only find Matthew but nudge the bond into place. And if we have a bond..."

"We can bring him home," Shasta finished.

A yelp, punctuated by a thud, sounded in the living room. Before Shasta could process the tangle of limbs she was seeing on the floor, Caid was leaping over the kitchen table and Lucius was rushing forward.

As they gently separated the heap, Shasta couldn't breathe. Suddenly, anything and everything could wait. Róisín's face was cut, bruised, and swollen. Her elegant dress in tatters. Lily only slightly fared better, mostly dirty, with a few cuts and bruises.

"I'll get damp cloths." Ione raced from the kitchen.

"Bedrooms," Lucius said. "Let's get them up to the bedrooms. Get cleaned up, then we can talk."

Caid swept Róisín up into his arms. When she hissed in pain, he laid a gentle kiss on her forehead and apologized. Then Lucius led Lily carefully up the stairs behind them.

"I'll... I'll help Ione," Shasta said to no one. She was alone in the kitchen now. It would be so easy for her to sneak a quick drink. Just one. Soothe the way her body vibrated, the way her heart raced, and her lungs burned for the air it couldn't seem to find.

"I expected more from you, Shasta." The disappointment in his words would have cut deep regardless, but they slashed to her core after the way he had been affectionately calling her mom only hours before. The siblings may have been bickering, but she had heard it in both their tones when they tossed the word her way every time she had tried to intervene.

No. No more. She forced herself to move toward the bathroom where Ione had gone.

CHAPTER 43

MARCELO DID his best impression of aloofness he could as he sprawled in his chair across from Anthony while they played a game of chess. His brain had chattered at him nonstop for the past four days. Words he couldn't understand. Just constant noise. His head throbbed with it.

Jessamyn had gotten Lady McKenna off-realm, although she had told no one where. He could only assume it was because the situation had turned far more dire than any of them had truly realized it to be.

Marcelo spoke from the corner of his mouth. "You're too stiff. Relax, or someone will notice."

Anthony's shoulders slumped as he released a deep sigh. "I cannot help it."

"If we're to eavesdrop on any of the conversations, we cannot appear overly interested in our surroundings." Marcelo moved his knight to a square, then pulled his attention from the board. "Relax."

"What exactly *are* we out here to learn?" Anthony moved his knight, then frowned, recognizing the poor choice in his move.

"Hells if I know." Marcelo swiped Anthony's knight and placed his own on the square.

Anthony leaned closer to the table under the guise of studying the pieces on the board. His voice low, he asked, "Do you... Do you think he's completely gone?"

Marcelo tracked Anthony's move while scratching his jaw. For the first time, he had skipped shaves, and stubble was peppering his jawline. He contemplated letting it fill in after the way Nolani had continued stroking her fingers along his face earlier that morning while they lay in bed.

"To be honest?" He nudged one of his pawns. "Yes. Only because listening to the others, the ones *with* magic, and their doubt, leads me to believe that once he is gone, if we can accomplish that, that's it."

"You're king," Anthony said.

"And I can make *you* king when I am."

"That's not how that works and you know it." Anthony drummed his fingers on the table next to their board.

"If I'm king, I can do whatever I want, so, yes. If I have to don the crown for a day to put things into their proper places, so be it." He sat back in his chair. "Then I'll renounce my title, naming you in place. Nolani and I can—" He sprung to his feet, Anthony instinctively following suit. "What's happened?"

"Quickly." Nolani grabbed hold of Marcelo's arm. "Come with me."

Anthony moved to follow, but she shook her head at him.

"We'll be back in a moment." Her words were slightly above a whisper. Marcelo could only let himself be dragged along behind her. He almost tripped over his feet when she instructed, "Squeeze my ass cheek."

"What?"

"You heard me." She shot him a glare over her shoulder. "Make this look as though we're sneaking off into the bushes for a tryst. Squeeze. My. Ass."

"Remember you told me to do this." He gathered his feet beneath him to catch up to her, and with a grin, gave her left cheek a firm squeeze, followed by a quick swat. "That do it?"

She feigned laughter and coyness, but shock flared in her eyes, brightening them and lifting her brows slightly. "That'll do."

When they neared the hedge, she disappeared, leaving him standing just off the stone pathway, bewildered. "Nolani?" he whisper shouted.

"Shut up, you buffoon." She poked her head out of a spot in the hedge, waving her fingers at him, beckoning.

He moved closer and saw the space between the branches had been hollowed. From the ends of the branches, he could tell that it had been done some time long before. "How long has this been here? Better question"—he thumbed a smoothly cut end—"how in Talista have I just learned this little hideout was here?"

"Would you shush?!" Nolani said.

"Nolani, what's—"

She pressed her small hand over his mouth, shaking her head.

That was when he heard it. The pitching and rolling sounds of Founder Shiini, the first language of the humans around the realm. Rastead stood before a well-decorated member of the Royal Shianshani Guard. Several stripes and badges from service lined the breast pocket and sleeves of the guard's service dress jacket.

"I may no longer have my magic, Linden, but I can hear your thoughts." Rastead's voice was soft, but the danger was like fire in his tone.

Marcelo felt Nolani coil against him. Quietly, he brought his arm around her protectively. What he would do should they get caught, he didn't know. Jessamyn's brother and lead Coven command had been battered and bruised after the surprise attack in the Coven's courtyard. If *they* had struggled against whatever these beings were, what good would his skills be?

"That's *my* queen you've laid your hands upon," Rastead continued.

Through the branches, they saw Rastead pacing along a row of men dressed in the colors of the Guard. Service dress the colors of black, blue and red. The Locaw bird and Nautilanis over the left breasts of each. His hands were clasped behind his back, shoulders and head high, emanating power with his stature.

He stopped pacing, looking out over those that had gathered before him. His voice lifted higher. "You've all been warned of what will happen." His head turned slightly as he took in the guards standing in the first row. Seven of them, legs shoulder width apart, right hand over their heart, left hand behind their back.

"Hells, Nolani." Marcelo fought the clawing that was at his throat, trying to steal his voice. "Behind them."

She gasped, her fingers digging into where she clutched his arm.

Behind the seven stood at least one dozen rows of fifteen men in each. Were they all like the king?

"I apologize, sire." The guard named Linden hinged at the hips in a bow. "I beg forgiveness for my transgression."

"When you all signed on for my special operations unit, you knew the rules. Just as you know…" Rastead stepped closer to Linden, looking down his nose at him. "Rules change."

Marcelo held his breath, waiting for what was to come. Nolani's body tensed under his hold.

"And when those rules change—" Rastead's voice had become lower, snarling. Nolani buried her face in Marcelo's chest, but he couldn't pull his attention away. He had to see, to know what they were facing. If only to tell Jessamyn as much as possible to help in the effort to end this.

"Sire—"

"You broke a rule, Linden. You were given a grand privilege in this unit, yet you spit on it like a foolish child." Rastead turned in a way that had him standing profile to where Marcelo and Nolani were hidden.

The pressure and pain from the way Marcelo had his jaw clenched tightly were the only things keeping him grounded from running. Rastead licked along the bottom rows of his teeth, then grinned.

The sight of it was pure horror. A thing of nightmares to witness. Marcelo didn't dare to imagine how grotesque it was face on. He found himself suddenly grateful for the poor lighting his father had always kept in his library, understanding now just how much he had been spared seeing.

Rastead stepped up to Linden. "You had potential, making it a shame that I have to do this. However, an example must be made."

Linden could not speak again, for Rastead sunk his teeth into his neck, biting, pulling. Blood poured down Linden's coat, pooling at his feet. The guards nearest him twitched. Low snarls filled the air. They held in place as Rastead used his teeth to rip Linden's arm from his body.

Holding the arm, he let Linden's limp body fall to the ground. Taking a step back, he examined it, using his free hand to smooth the front of his coat.

His eyes still on the ruined arm, he lifted his voice over the snaps and snarls so that all the guard could hear him again. "While we share the camaraderie of the hunt, and its spoils, not one of you will touch this." He nudged the body with his foot. "You six are to remain here with me. All others are dismissed. Remember what you saw here if any of you find the urge to even *think* about my queen."

Marcelo's chest barely moved with the small breaths he was managing in and out. His effort to remain still and soundless. Nolani clung to him, her face pressed half against his arm, half exposed so that she could see.

Once the other guards cleared the yard, Rastead began feasting on those that he had commanded to stay. Each of the ones that had been in the Coven courtyard. Each of the ones that had gone after Lady McKenna and the others.

Nolani finally turned completely away, shifting to bury her face in the crook of his neck. He felt the way her body convulsed, an effort to expel the horrors she had witnessed.

With each passing second, Marcelo felt himself hardening more and more. It was clear that there was no coming back for his father. That this was Madigan now, and Madigan would die. It was the only way Shianshani and the other realms could remain safe.

Marcelo was going to become king.

Chapter 44

Róisín lay, staring blankly at the ceiling overhead. Her body had wanted to move, to roll her to her side, her hands had wanted to lie over her stomach, her chest, anywhere but at her sides. Yet the pain that speared through her halted her every movement. She had never hurt like this before. Not even when her body had fallen from the sky when she had died.

Perhaps that had been because Caid had gotten to her just in time, her lifeless body crashing into his. At that moment, with the shadows dancing overhead from the way the wind gently blew at the trees outside, she remembered his pain. The way it beat and burned her in a way that stole her breath when he had let her see those moments through his eyes. That searing, blinding fire that ripped her chest apart when their tether had broken.

She would endure whatever pain she could to spare him from ever feeling even the smallest bit of that again.

Róisín took a shallow breath, knowing that was all her bruised chest would allow.

Was this how humans felt after crashes? Fights? *Combat* during war? Their bodies were much slower to heal and recover than witches.

How did they live like this?

She swallowed a moan of pain and squeezed her eyes shut.

The tingles of her magic trying to help her body mend skittered through her every so often, making her shiver and clench her teeth from the assault the shivers wracked all over her battered body.

Monsters. Far worse than anything she had ever faced before. And she and Matthew had been up against many things that were spawned by the nightmares of child witches and untrained magic.

Was Lily okay? Runa? Aja? Cassius?

Would she really stay away from Talista as Jessamyn had asked, no, *instructed* before Lily shifted them away?

Her fingers were almost at the end of a rope over the cliff edge, an abyss beckoning her below. Would she be able to hold on, to climb back up, if she returned to Talista?

Her mind held the echoes of what Lily had said. But what Lily hadn't known was what Róisín's mother had said.

The Goddess had wanted them gone. It had been there, staring her down, laughing at her, since that night. Aoife, rightfully so, but also her mother and herself. Legianne wiped off the map of Covens completely. She failed in Roidon and was given a new task from the Goddess. An impossible task. And now Madigan had returned.

The Goddess still clearly planned for Róisín's end. Still planned to have her locked away in the darkness. Legianne, finally gone. For what purpose, Róisín didn't know. But her gut was holding firm that something was wrong, something was off.

"Who takes care of you?" Caid's sleep roughened voice asked in her ear.

"What?" She blinked away the wetness building in her eyes.

"You asked me that once, not all that long ago," he said.

She turned her head, squinting to see his face in the dim light filtering through the curtains.

"And now, I ask you the same. Who takes care of you when things go to shit? No." He moved some of her hair that had fallen over a cut on her cheek. "I think the question should really be, when will you let someone take care of you?"

"What—" she began, but the word was thick at the back of her mouth. She cleared her throat, wincing at the tightness in her chest. "What do you mean?"

"Stay, Róisín. For the love of God, please stay here. Don't go back."

"I..."

"It's easy, isn't it? When you're the one that can so easily tuck us all into the places you want us, not worrying about any of us getting hurt because those places are the safe ones. Never mind that you're off, without your power, in realms where witches live from Covens that just tried to *kill* you. Leaving us to worry about you more than ever before, because now—" His voice broke. "Now you're coming back bloody and broken."

No. *No*, he was wrong. She *had* worried about him, and endlessly so. Worried about him getting hurt, still, despite the magic that now thrummed deafeningly in his veins. About him with his magic, with it all being so new, and different, and overwhelming, that one day he would find that he didn't want to handle it anymore. And left her behind. That he would no longer find how he felt about her, about them, their future, enough, and leave because all of this...the danger, the risk, was too much.

She had found that small shred of courage and confidence in these last few months, but deep inside was still that little girl that lived in fear. Fear of not being worth love, fear of being abandoned. And at that moment, in the dark of their bedroom, those feelings were reaching for her, grabbing for her, trying to embrace her and drag her under.

But how did she tell him all of that? How did she pull herself open in that way, bearing all to him? And then, would he stay, but only out of pity?

She didn't want his pity. She couldn't bear that. It would be far worse than anything the Goddess, or Madigan, could do to her.

Her throat was tight, and her chest throbbed. She was grateful for the dark at that moment, because it meant that he couldn't see her tears.

Slowly, she rolled to her side to face him, swallowing down the whimper of pain that tried to escape. When she lifted her hand to touch his face, again she found herself thankful for the cover of night because her fingers shook. Shook in a way that vibrated through her hands, to her shoulders, and deep inside, almost to her empty well of magic.

"I'm terrified, Caid. Not just of Madigan and what he is now, or the others." She swallowed hard. That urge to stop, to not say more, beat like a pulse at the base of her throat. "That you were right. What if my mother was wrong, but only because she was lied to?"

The bed shifted, and she felt his arm move, but the feel of his touch upon her never came. "Things have changed since going with Shasta. I don't—" His jaw flexed beneath where her fingers still rested. "Whatever it was, whatever was happening, it's not like that anymore."

"I never thought that your magic was in the dark," she whispered. "But what if all that my mother did was for nothing? What if the Goddess still is going to take me when this is all said and done, and place me in the darkness?"

The warmth of his hand taking hers in it had her gasping in surprise. "Then I go with you."

"What? No."

"What happened in Talista?"

"Madigan, what he's become, the curse, it's..." The blood in her veins began thrashing so loudly that it drowned out the quiet hum of the surrounding house. The tingle started first above her top lip, then surged like a million pinpricks down to her toes.

"Breathe," Caid whispered. "Slow and steady. In, then out. Breathe, Róisín. He can't get you here."

"You don't know that," she managed to say between her chattering teeth. Pain was rioting inside of her, and her body didn't know whether it wanted to tense or curl into the fetal position.

Caid's arm gently slipped around her, and he brought her against his chest. The instant their bodies touched, hers quieted.

Home.

She let his warmth, the smell of bergamot, wood, and musk, wrap around her. "He's found a way to make others like him. And they're..." She trembled. "Caid, they're worse than anything I've ever seen before. I can't even put what I saw into words. We were in a warded section of the castle, the Coven's courtyard. Jessamyn's brother, Runa, along with who I'm assuming is her head guard, Aja, and then one of the Shian-shani guards, Cassius, whom I'm pretty sure is with Prince Anthony given the way they were sitting nearly in one another's lap at our meeting. Sorry, I'm rambling."

"No, details are good. The more we have, the better."

She pressed her hands to his chest, then smoothed them along his skin until they were at his shoulders. Being cocooned by him steadied and grounded her. "Lily had asked if I was okay being there, near Madigan, without my power, and—"

"She knows?"

"Apparently, she's known since we arrived in Baijiola. Jessamyn knows too, and that's why she voiced her concern for my safety there. I think she was handling me with kid gloves at first, because she said something about how she couldn't even keep her own people safe, but in the courtyard..." That crushing weight that had slammed into her with Jessamyn's words found her, and she broke all over again. Instead of anger, this time, it was tears. "Lily grabbed me and brought me home," she said around each painful sob that wracked her body. "Like a grounded teenager."

He stroked a hand along her hair, letting her cry until there was nothing left. Then he hooked his index finger beneath her chin and tipped her face to his. The feel of his lips on her forehead was a balm for her soul. She closed her eyes and let the simple touch soothe.

"Before everything happened, Lily asked why the Goddess, our creator, the most powerful of us all, put all of this into my hands."

His body went completely still next to hers. She no longer even felt his heart at her fingers.

"Caid?"

"What else did she say?" His voice was so quiet, if she were not laying face to face with him, she wouldn't have heard him.

Róisín's voice automatically lowered for her response. "That the Goddess has the Sisters, who know and see everything. And Caid, I can't lie and say to you I haven't questioned it before. Why hasn't she just waved a hand and done these things? Even without Madigan's connection to the Covens, she still had to know something. She knew about the Seer."

The Seer drifts...

"Say something," she pleaded when he remained quiet.

He moved forward, holding her tighter, "I can't. I can't say it out loud. If I do, it puts it out there. Gives it legs to run, to become real."

Which meant he agreed.

"If you go, Róisín, I go with you. That much is true," he said.

"What about Lina? The babies?"

"I don't know. I don't fucking know."

Her body screamed in protest as she clung tighter to him. "I'm scared, Caid. I don't know what to do. This is so much different from before."

"I'm here." He pressed a soft kiss to her forehead again, then her nose, her cheeks. "I'll always be right here."

Then he took her mouth with his, and they were spiraling into their need for one another.

CHAPTER 45

CAID HAD his head under the hood of the old, rusted Jeep Wrangler he had parked on the far side of the cottage property when he heard the crunch of footsteps approaching. Standing back, he wiped his hands on the rag he'd tucked into his back pocket before setting it on the fender.

"Is she still asleep?" he asked Shasta as she neared.

She nodded, her eyes scanning the mismatched panels. "Her face looks better already. That's a good sign. The power is stirring in her enough to help her heal. Why didn't either of you tell me?"

"Wasn't my place to tell anyone." He scratched his jaw and dropped his gaze to his hand that rested on the fender. "And she struggles with reaching out for help. As you well know."

"You can't stay idle, can you?" She nodded toward the Jeep.

"Busy hands, quiet mind."

"Kincaid, I, thank you. For yesterday, I mean. I've been letting my demons win again and get the best of me. I've been an awful person lately."

He shoved his hands into the front pockets of his jeans and leaned against the fender. "Awful seems like a bit of a stretch."

"I haven't been present when we're all needed to be. *That* definitely qualifies me as awful."

He studied her, watching as she chewed on her bottom lip, tugging at a coil of her dark hair. "What's the lumber for in Molennius?"

"I sort of..." She clucked her tongue, then bit her cheek. "Burned my house down."

"You *what*? What happened?"

"Well, I had help. Bren and my wife, Evelyn. They came, and we had quite a celebration."

"Wait." He held his hands, waving them back and forth. "Wait. So, it was intentional?"

"Oh, of course it was." She let out a snort, then covered her mouth. "Ev and I built that thing to withstand anything." Shadows filled her eyes, and her face grew tight. "It was *supposed* to withstand anything."

The realization hit him, and everything about her behavior made sense.

"The only way forward was to get rid of the house." She shrugged. "So, I did."

"I want to help."

She flashed him a wide smile. "I'd be honored to have you there. It's a little different from how you're used to doing it, though. It was a long process to build the first because of the wards and bindings. This time?" She pressed her lips together and swallowed. "This time it's going to be better. Because never again am I going to be trapped in my own damned house."

Caid stepped toward her and held his arms wide. Her brows came together as she eyed him. When he wagged his fingers, gesturing her closer, she seemed to deflate before stepping into the hug.

"Even if it takes a decade to build, I'll be there every day." He squeezed her tight.

"You're a good kid." Her voice was muffled by the fabric of his sweatshirt. "We're lucky to have you."

"I'm lucky to have you." He rubbed his hand over her back, then patted the top of her head lightly. "Mom."

She groaned, but he could hear the amusement in the sound. "I'm not old enough to be a mom."

"You're nearly four hundred, Shasta," Lucius said, approaching where they stood.

"Shh," Shasta said. "Don't you know that you're not supposed to tell a lady's age?"

Lucius looked around, squinting. "I don't see a lady anywhere, so I'm not sure how I could offend one."

Shasta stepped back from Caid and swatted a hand at Lucius, slapping the side of his arm.

"Ow. For someone who'd like to be considered a lady." Lucius lifted his eyes to Caid's. "Don't let her fool you, son. She's probably the fiercest of us all when push comes to shove."

Caid could only nod, unable to find his voice. A burning sensation flared at the center of his chest and there was a flutter in his stomach. How connected and intertwined with these people he had become. He cared for them on the same level in which he had always cared for Lina. Family. He blinked away the sting in his eyes as he looked at Shasta and Lucius.

"Róisín's awake," Lucius said.

"The girls are with her?" Shasta asked.

He nodded. "They've done as much as they could. They could heal the cuts, reduce most of the swelling, and relieve her of pain. They were helping her walk down the stairs when I came out.".

Caid cleared his throat. "I will, shit." He exhaled sharply, the idea coming so quickly it stole his breath. Then he turned to Shasta. "What if I take her to Legianne? I can do the blinky thing with her, right? Where she's a witch too?"

Shasta crossed her arms over her chest and tapped a finger on her chin, her lips pursing as she thought. "It could work, and yes, witches can *shift* with witches. That's how Lily got Róisín back here, and Róisín got Lily to us in Ely somehow despite coming here herself." She winked at him. "How you and Róisín got to my place that first time."

That day had felt like a lifetime ago. Not just months before.

"The Nianti Fields hold great significance to the Byrne family," Lucius said.

"So, like the island was for my ancestors, these fields are for her?" He asked.

"Yes. They settled and lived there for nearly a millennium before migrating to Wurbray. That long in one place is sure to have a significant concentration of power within." Lucius frowned. "To be frank, I don't know why I hadn't thought of that the day she told me."

Shasta rested a hand on his forearm, her voice low, soothing. "We've had a lot going on."

"While that's true, you were a few bottles deep when you thought to take him," Lucius gestured to Caid.

Shasta winced.

"Shasta—"

Caid maneuvered so that he stood between them. Shasta at his back, while he used his height to his advantage to look down at Lucius. "We already talked about it yesterday. It doesn't need to be repeated. We go forward from here."

Lucius's steel-gray eyes bounced as he studied Caid's face. Finally, he nodded. "We only say something, Shasta, because we care."

"I know," Shasta whispered behind him.

"When do you plan to take Róisín to Legianne?" Lucius asked.

Shasta gave Caid's arm a squeeze as she stepped from behind him. "Don't just take her. Ask her. She's edgy after what's happened this week, and I'm sure she's got feelings about how it changes things for her involvement."

Caid nodded, knowing after what Róisín had told him earlier, Shasta was right. "Once she's rested enough."

"We should probably go in." Shasta motioned toward the cottage. "We need to go over everything, and let Ione explain how this spell will work for Matthew. Her magic has been so loud, I'm harboring a migraine over it." She rubbed at her temples.

"She's quite the opposite of Lily," Lucius agreed.

He wanted to take Róisín to Legianne at that moment, but that worry snaked up his legs, winding around his torso, to his chest, where it burrowed a hole to his heart. Once Róisín had her power back to her magic, what was stopping her from throwing herself back into Madigan's path?

And what if that was what their Goddess had wanted?

Chapter 46

Lucius had escaped to the kitchen in need of space. After Lily and Róisín had recounted what had happened in Shianshani, the dream on the creek with Matthew had resurfaced. The air around him had grown heavy, pressing down on him as the walls had inched closer.

He braced his hands on the edge of the sink, focusing on the copse of trees on the far side of the glen through the window. His breathing drowned out the quiet chatter from the others in the living room behind him.

The air behind shifted and a new energy vibrated in the room.

"Jessamyn." He kept his attention forward. "I know things are done differently in Shianshani. However, it's common practice to arrive on the *other* side of the door and knock."

"Ever the diplomat," Jessamyn said with amusement. "I had wholly intended to follow custom. However—" She released a loud, dramatic sigh. "I followed the trace of magic that Lily had left behind, and, unfortunately, our magicks had a rather different plan."

He turned to her. She was dressed in jeans and a simple black tee-shirt that revealed a gray vine-like tattoo twisting up one of her ebony arms. When she noticed him studying her, she looked down.

"Any opportunity to not wear that smothering bullshit I will happily take," she said.

He tipped his head to the side, considering her for a moment. "The Coven didn't have to stand for it, you know."

"Ah, but you know Frederick. He saw an opportunity and seized it. The rest of us had no choice but to follow."

He leaned back against the sink and crossed his arms over his chest. "Why are you here, Jessamyn? What is your plan?"

She took a spot in front of the counter across from him and mirrored his stance. "Well, Lucius McArthur, if you haven't noticed, things have gone awry. And despite my best efforts to get it under control and handled, it appears it's far bigger than even *my* people can manage."

He remained silent, watching.

"I'm not secretly planning to kill you all." Her face fell. "I need my people to be free. Of it all. Not just what Frederick has done to us."

"I apologize if I'm not ready to jump in joy at that."

She released her arms and lifted her hands. "I don't expect you to trust me. I can't say that I blame you. Any of you. I know what he did, the harm he has caused beyond our realm. I didn't expect a warm welcome of hugs and celebration." She placed her hands behind her, gripping the counter top. "Myself, my people, we have to earn your trust. I just hope I'm given the time to do that. Just as I hope you all have the time to earn ours."

Lucius glanced toward the living room. Ione and Shasta's voices had risen in what sounded like an argument. No one had noticed Jessamyn's arrival yet.

"What has Frederick done to the king?" he asked.

"We don't know much," she confessed with a frown. "They all had so many plans to thwart or overthrow their Goddess, it is hard to connect the dots. Aoife, it seems, had several hands at play, and one involved my brother. Knowing what I know now about Madigan and Aoife, it makes it even more interesting. Trouble in paradise? Or was she just that cold of a human being?"

"Aoife was ambitious. Nothing and no one was off limits to her and her goals," Lucius said.

"Not even her granddaughter."

Lucius felt his blood go cold in his veins. "No. Not even."

"Anyway." Jessamyn waved a hand. "I don't know how, but they found a blood curse in an old spell work book that Frederick had found. However, it just appeared they were cursing the Dionomis family. The depth of it all wasn't made clear until we learned Madigan has taken King Rastead's body."

Lucius let Jessamyn's words sink in and he sorted through them, working out his own conclusion. The way the curse served Aoife and Frederick individually. Just how deep everything truly ran in both Aoife and Madigan's quests for ultimate power over them.

"Frederick saw the curse as a way to take full control of the court."

"He did, *and* he certainly did," she said. "The kings, once the curse had settled, were all under his thumb. They were too fearful of being exposed for what they had become after their twenty-fifth birthday, and losing everything. The only way they could hold their shred of power was to do my brother's bidding."

"Jessamyn." Shasta's distaste was obvious in the way she said her name.

Jessamyn and Lucius turned to the doorway where she stood, empty glass in hand.

"Hello, Shasta," Jessamyn said.

"What in the Hells are you doing here?"

Sensing the rise in Shasta's magic, Lucius moved from the sink into the center of the room to intervene. "We all need to talk. There's absolutely no reason that we can't all work together to remedy the situation we currently face," he said. "It affects *all* of us."

"Ever the diplomat." Jessamyn gave him an appreciative nod.

Shasta stared at Jessamyn, her eyes narrowing. "Fine. Let me get some more water and then we'll talk."

After a similarly cold reception from Ione, a curious and watchful one from Caid, Jessamyn relayed the details of what had happened after Lily and Róisín had left Talista.

"How is he making *more*, though?" Ione asked. "Curses, if they're not targeted to one person, stay within a bloodline."

Jessamyn rubbed her temples. "We are just as confused by it as you are. The only reasoning I can think of is buried in the original curse spell work. We're struggling with the translation because it appears to be a mix of several of our Founder languages."

Lucius didn't miss the way Ione's eyes lit up. "Would you let me have a crack at it?" She asked.

"Lily said that you were knowledgeable in the old languages," Jessamyn said. "If you could lend Ten a hand, we would be very grateful."

"What were they saying? The Shianshani guards, I mean," Lily said. "I heard nothing other than that wet, snarly, snapping sound." She glanced at Róisín. "But you, you said they said something."

Róisín nodded and repeated the words, making Lucius gasp.

"What?" Lily asked.

Lucius swallowed hard, then cleared his throat. "They called her their queen."

"Excuse me?" Róisín squeaked out. "Ow." She doubled forward, arms over her stomach. Caid was at her side quickly with water and a small, packed satchel of herbs for the pain from Lily and Ione.

Jessamyn watched them for a moment before adding, "They were saying your blood is pure as queen. A taste will bring them a taste of... There are multiple meanings for the word in Founder Shiini, but the basic is—they get a taste of her blood." She motioned to Róisín. "They will essentially have the best high in all the realms and it allows them to speak with their maker."

Madigan had wanted Róisín that day in the ravine, and Lucius had seen the hunger in which he watched her in Roidon through Frederick's vision in Clarissa's afterworld. Now, that obsession and desire was being bred into monsters. Lucius flexed his hands and paced behind the sofas.

"But their maker is Madigan." Lily's brows were knotted tightly and her face was pale.

"*They* don't seem to know that. I'm not sure what he's telling them." Jessamyn shook her head. "But that is why I made Lily take Róisín out of there. They won't be the only ones hungry for it."

Róisín frowned. "And without my power back."

How could he keep her safe? His eyes found Caid. On the young man's face, he could see in the grim line of his mouth and flexed jaw that he wasn't the only one carrying that thought.

"What do we do?" Lily asked.

"It's going to create a logistical nightmare, but we do everything off-realm. Because you will not want to sit on the sidelines," Jessamyn said to Róisín. "And I refuse to let you back in Shianshani. Even if it's somewhere other than Talista. It's too risky to have you there. For you *and* my people. If I have to create a ward, I will."

Róisín gaped at her. "I can take a hint," she mumbled, before adding quietly, "Everyone seems to know what's best for me."

"You're being fucking stubborn about it, so yes, we do," Caid said.

Lily gave an emphatic nod. "What he said."

Róisín cast narrow eyed glares at both of them.

"I know that you're currently trying to locate your son." Jessamyn turned her attention to Lucius. "In the effort to earn your trust, I would like to offer help with that. I can send some additional Coven members with Ten and Cicile."

"Oh, we've got that already." Ione grinned, her body bouncing on her sofa cushion. "We just need a minute to actually *do* the thing."

Jessamyn scratched her jaw. "Okay. But if you need help beyond that, please, let me know. Where should we create a home base for our work?"

"Ely would be best," Lucius said. "We're already set up there with what we're currently working on. And it's also furthest from Shianshani, so it gives some privacy."

"Wait, the realms are in different places?" Caid asked.

Jessamyn's brows bounced high before coming down as she wrinkled her nose.

"Baby witch." Róisín pointed at Caid.

"Ah. Terrible time to be thrust into all of this." Jessamyn's eyes glittered with amusement.

"Tell me about it," Caid murmured.

"Hold on a second." Róisín straightened. "What about—" She winced when she shifted her weight where she sat. "What about Madigan? Will you all be safe there with him if he's got an army he's making? I saw those things. I saw the way even Aja and Runa struggled against them with the full power of their magic. They're not exactly weak witches or *small*. And if Marcelo and Nolani saw that there were well over one hundred of them now."

"Our goal is to keep the situation as diffused as we can. I met with the king, I mean Madigan, this morning, and as of right now, I have him placated. The more I can continue that, the more time we have," Jessamyn said.

"Which means we can't drag our feet." The walls shifted in on Lucius again, and he struggled to keep his focus on those around him.

"No. But you *do* need to get your son back. I'll have Ten and Cicile in Ely in four days. I think that's all the time we can comfortably agree on," Jessamyn said.

"That should be plenty of time for us to do what we need to do," Lucius said.

"Alright. I will come with them so we can go over everything and cement a plan. Stay safe, everyone." Without another word, she was gone.

"She and Frederick are related?" Caid asked, breaking the silence that had fallen over the room.

"Ah, Frederick didn't like his own people. He thought their skin was dirty, impure, and unworthy. He did many things to his features to change and separate himself from the Shianshani Coven. Drastic measures." Lucius rubbed the back of his neck. "Including using chemicals to whiten his skin when the magic no longer worked."

"The more I learn about the guy, the less I like him," Caid said.

Róisín hummed.

"Thank the Goddess he's gone," Shasta said. "All of them."

Lucius had wanted to agree, but there were moments when he could still feel the stickiness of Frederick's drying blood on his hands. When he still saw the broken, lifeless body at his feet. He was haunted by his actions but couldn't deny that he wouldn't do it again.

CHAPTER 47

MATTHEW HAD been living in another hallucination again. Lily had her arms wrapped around him as they swayed to a song he hummed to her. Their children had grown and started families of their own, and it was just them again. He used the time and space of the quiet, empty nest to soak in every moment with her.

To celebrate their anniversary, he had laid out a meal of all her favorite foods on a blanket in their backyard. But he hadn't been able to think of food first. Instead, he had swept her into his arms, and he had hummed a song that his mother had sung to him as a child. He had no reason to be scared at that moment, holding his heart and soul in his arms, placing a tender kiss on her shoulder. But his heart still thumped heavily in his chest while his lungs squeezed as though something was lurking in the dark.

The burning in his chest was faint at first. As he swung Lily out into a spin, it became fiercer. A ripping, shredding. As though every fiber of his being was pulled apart one by one, by one. When he pulled her into a dip and brushed his lips over hers, it was an inferno that brought him back to the fog fields with a pained gasp.

Everything throbbed. His chest grew tight, squeezing his lungs.

They spasmed, and he coughed. It was a pitiful excuse for a cough and more of a small gasp for air.

He rolled to his side just as bile gathered at the back of his throat.

This was it. These were his final breaths. He had wondered how much longer he had left after he'd taken Mildred's life. The days since had been full of quiet. Even his hallucinations had become soundless. He would never admit to missing Mildred's rasping breath, her taunts and hoarse threats of seeing him in the pits that came from beside him for what felt like months. Yet, he almost did.

How long had it been? Time moved differently in each of the realms. Had it been just days? Weeks?

Matthew didn't know, and feeling his end encroaching, he didn't care.

He prayed to the Goddess that Lily found love someday.

That Lucius found peace.

That Róisín had realized she was strong and capable, and that none of this was her fault.

He squeezed his eyes shut, body tensing as the brutal pain seized every inch of him.

Then he felt it. Something bright and warm inside of him.

It lifted and soared through him, reaching.

When it found what it was seeking, something akin to electricity jolted through him, sending him rolling flat on his back. His bellow toward the sky was more of a hoarse, scraping sound.

Whatever it was, its grasp tightened its hold on something new, something foreign. Then it pulled.

From the depths of him, he found his voice and let out a roar. The sound echoing through the fog around him and beyond.

Lily. The bond.

Somehow, despite being left unfinished, unaccepted, it had come together.

Unless...

His eyes closed, sending tears rolling down his temples into his hair. Of course, they would look for him. Find a way.

But he was in Aunellion. He still hadn't been able to work out how he had gotten there, but he had.

The Goddess forbade access to Aunellion. It had been the most powerful magic used ever in their history to seal it off after Madigan had severed his connection to the coven leaders.

He could feel Lily's magic through the new bond. It moved through him like water moved through a river, filling him. Soothing him. The urge to feel her beneath his hands again, to smell her joy-filled summer scent, hear the quiet melody of her voice beyond what his hallucinations had given him, pulled at him.

The fire and the tightness eased. The roaring in his ears dimmed. When all was settled, the only sounds he heard were the slow, distanced thumps of his heart, and the dry, ragged breaths he could take every few moments.

Lily tugged lightly. He had wanted to tug back, but what would be the point?

No one could reach him here. It would be better for them to believe him gone. They could move on with their lives. At some point, as he had lain there, he had resigned himself to his fate, to his end.

Harsher, more desperate, she pulled again. Before he could stop it, his instincts had him pulling back, just as hard and desperate.

CHAPTER 48

LILY SHRIEKED and doubled over. Róisín caught her before she could fall to her knees and began rubbing soothing circles over Lily's back as the ragged breaths heaved out of her.

"What is it?" Lucius hurried to her other side.

Lily couldn't speak, she could barely breathe. Frantically, she patted her chest, her mouth moving like she was a fish flung ashore. She felt another tug through the new tether inside, and she fell against Róisín. Finally, she could take a breath.

"It—" Lily panted and grasped Róisín tighter. "It worked. The bond. I can feel it. Gah!" She released a quiet whimper just before her knees buckled, but Lucius and Róisín held fast. "But it hurts. Wherever he is, it's not good. *He's* not good."

"Shit." Shasta's mouth set into a grim line. "Can you feel where?"

"I... Hold on." She closed her eyes and moaned in pain. She felt Ione's hands settle on her shoulders. Then the soothing of Ione's magic warmed her, releasing the tension in her muscles. And then the clouds parted, and she saw Matthew. "No," she said, her voice barely a whisper.

"Where?" Lucius asked softly.

Lily looked to Róisín first, then to Ione.

"Oh shit," Róisín said.

"What?" Caid asked from where he had been standing on the other side of the living room at the door, arms crossed, like he was on guard.

Lily used the trio around her to stand and steady herself. "He's in Aunellion," she whispered. "He's in the fields."

Caid's brow knotted. The outlier of the group. He had yet to know what Aunellion was before the Goddess had taken it from all of them.

Lucius's face was tight as he stepped back to let Ione and Róisín lead her to the sofa to sit. Lily's heart hammered, bouncing from one side of her chest to the other. It crashed into a lung, causing her to gasp.

"Before Madigan severed his connection with us, Aunellion was a realm where the Coven led, and the humans hid," Lucius said.

"So, like the reverse of everywhere else." Caid nodded. "Sounds on par with what I've known of Madigan."

"The Milsenetts, their magicks were like none other. Not quite elemental, or mind, or..." He stared unblinking for a moment before shaking his head.

Shasta moved to stand next to him, taking his hand in hers. "They wanted no trespassers, so they created a waypoint of a sort. If you were uninvited to the realm, that's where you automatically went."

"The Fog Fields." Lucius's voice sounded strained, like he had been shouting for days. "But the fog is like a drug. It makes you disoriented, and you hallucinate. Many people have gotten trapped there and perished."

"But Matthew is alive still," Caid said. "If Lily..." He turned his head to look at her. "Right?"

Lily gave him a small nod.

"Can we get him?" Caid asked.

The room was quiet for several long beats. Quiet except for the whirring that was humming in Lily's ears. A weakness had crept into her body, and the effort it was taking to remain upright was taxing her. She needed a bed, a cold shower, *something*.

Ione finally broke the silence. "There could be a way."

"How?" Róisín asked.

"Everything made can be undone," Lucius said.

"Okay, but *how*?" Róisín asked again.

Ione grinned at her and Lily. "Oh, I'll find a way."

Lily wanted to believe her, trust her, but... Not everything could be undone. And this, this was a magic far more powerful than theirs. Even together.

Shasta cursed again.

"What do you two know of the ones coming to work with me from Jessamyn's Coven?" Ione asked.

"They're incredibly gorgeous," Róisín said. Caid cleared his throat, making her sigh. "It's true. You saw Jessamyn."

Lily saw the interest in Ione's eyes and fought the groan building in her throat. "We haven't exactly gotten the chance to get to know them. Given everything that happened in Talista." She chewed her lip and rubbed at the base of her neck.

"This train's been moved around the rails," Róisín said.

"But Jessamyn said that Ten is a linguist, and Cicile is a historian. The energy coming from their magic was very bright," Lily said.

"And noisy. They were quiet during the meeting, but their magic buzzed. Like non-stop chattering," Róisín said. "Kind of like you, right now." She looked across Lily to Ione.

"Are we sure we want to bring them in on this?" Shasta asked.

Lucius rubbed both hands over his face. "I don't think we have a choice."

Shasta licked her lips, then sucked her teeth. "No, we really don't, do we? Ugh, I don't like this, though. We don't know how much what Jessamyn has said and done so far is an act and what's true."

Lucius tipped his head from one side to the other, his eyes steady on Lily's. There was a battle there in the lines of his face, the way his mouth was tight and his eyes swam with the silvers, greens, and white of his magic. She rose from the sofa and went to him, wrapping her arms around his waist.

"We'll follow your lead," she said. "He's yours and you know what to do best out of all of us."

His arms came around her, and he pressed a kiss to the top of her head. "He's yours too, sweetheart. And you know the books the best.

Fortunately for us, our people have been excellent at documenting and recording. You lead, we'll follow."

"I... are you, I don't..." Lily struggled to find the words she wanted. The realms had operated in an autonomous sort of way, but each Coven leader sat on the Council of Covens to work toward keeping order and peace as much as possible among the witches of the realms. Lucius had been the leader of the Council for over two centuries. *He* was a leader, not her. She stepped back and shook her head. "I can't. I don't know how."

"How about being called our point person?" Róisín said. "Leader kind of comes with pressure, and a boatload of stress."

Lily didn't miss the undertones of a scolding in her words, and apparently neither had Lucius. He gave her a small, sheepish smile.

"What do you say?" he asked.

"I think I can do that." She turned to Róisín. She and Ione had risen from the sofa, and Caid now stood behind Róisín. "Does this mean we're for sure scrapping the Covens' plan?"

Róisín nodded. "We've got to get Matthew back, and what's going on in Shianshani taken care of first. The Goddess has an issue with that. She can kiss my ass. We can't put together broken realms, and if she can't see that—" She lifted her hands and shrugged. "Fuck her."

Lily didn't miss the dark shadows that crossed Caid's face. Had Róisín told him about their conversation in the courtyard? Or was it something else?

"Alright, so we've got that settled." Ione clapped her hands, then rubbed them together. "We hit the books, we lean on Jessamyn's Coven for help, and we help them figure the ick out with Madigan. Am I understanding this right?"

"Pretty much," Shasta said. "I'm of no use with Frederick's books, if what Jessamyn said is right. I failed, badly, at learning anything other than our current tongues."

"I can help with that," Lucius said.

"So, Shasta and I with Lily?" Róisín asked. "Because I barely know our languages now. I sort of was, uh, preoccupied being stashed away from an evil grandmother for the first sixty some-odd years of my life and missed that key schooling you all got."

Ione chuckled and Róisín smiled at her.

"And me?" Caid asked. Something about his voice felt heavy and otherworldly when he spoke. Lily studied him for a moment, but she felt nothing different, and despite the tight way he held his body, everything else was normal. Róisín seemed unaffected by it. Had Lily imagined it?

"Ah, you and I still need to work on that magic of yours," Shasta said. "I guess I'll split my time between that and books?" She glanced over to Lily, eyebrow tipped up.

"Uh, sure?" she said. "Everyone okay with our... assignments? Ick, I hate that. I'm not a teacher."

"I don't know, Professor Wallingsford sounds pretty spiffy," Ione said.

"Ione." Lily shot her a glare.

Ione only burst into laughter in response. "See?"

"How am I the younger one?" Lily rolled her eyes.

"Yes, we're okay with where we need to be," Róisín cut in. She stepped to the side, effectively putting herself between the sisters. "We'll check in with one another regularly?"

"Yes. Just as we did before, when you were in Maine," Lucius said with a nod.

Róisín let out a loud exhale. "I like that. I like *this*. It feels more solid and familiar."

"Like we've got this," Shasta said.

Lucius stepped up to Lily's side and offered her his hand. "You, and I, and Ione to Ely?"

"Yes. I know Ione's itching to get to her white board to plan," Lily said.

Ione made a scoffing noise. Then came to Lily's other side and patted her arm. "I may like to stir up trouble, but I am still a Type A personality at my core."

Lily sighed and looked over to where Róisín, Shasta, and Caid stood. "Two days okay? If you keep taking the herbs we made for you, you should be completely healed by then. We'll still be in the timeline of what we agreed with Jessamyn."

"Sounds like a plan," Róisín said.

Lily closed her eyes, trying to quiet the hum that was still growing louder and louder inside of her.

"Ready?" Lucius whispered to her.

Not trusting her voice, she could only nod. Then he whisked them away to Ely.

CHAPTER 49

T HE ROUGHNESS of Aja's palm over her bare hip woke Jessamyn in the pre-dawn hours of the day she was to gather her most trusted Coven members and go to Ely. She opened her eyes slowly, taking in his broad chest, the spray of dark hair there that trailed down the center of his torso.

"Are you sure it's wise to send Runa to Ely?" His voice was deep and clear, an indicator that he had been awake for some time.

"The other choice is you. Would you?" She watched as his eyes narrowed and his jaw flexed tight. "That's what I thought. He can be flighty, yes, but he's always watchful. He notices things that others miss. I need that. Just as much as they do not trust us, they've done nothing to earn our trust yet."

He twisted a lock of her hair around his finger and frowned. "And how often will you be leaving our realm for there?"

"As often as I need to. This is our chance, Aja. Everything we've done is for this moment."

"Should we fail?" He released her hair, then smoothed it away from her face. "What then?"

"We keep going. If we cannot become free, if we cannot tear the wall down and rid us *all* of the abomination it is, what it represents after this, then we keep going until we win."

His index finger traced her jaw, his eyes trailing the movement. "Have you spoken with her? Has she said anything new?"

Aja would already know that Jessamyn's summoning had worked, for it had been he who had found her, collapsed on the floor of her suite's bathroom. Summoning was an entirely different sort of spell work for a witch to perform. Whereas the words amplified parts of the inherited, bodily magic a witch had in wards, some healing spell work, glamours, and summoning took parts of that magic. Drained the well, in a way.

He had brought her to bed immediately, forcing her to rest. Then, she gave in to her weakness and asked him to stay.

"She's been with Sister Future, but no, nothing new. Only that time was close. I don't know if it means we'll succeed, or that we'll fail. Only that our time is running out."

"And what now?"

"Now? We test how ready Marcelo is to lead. All of us."

His nostrils flared with his sharp exhale. "Jes—"

"No, Aja. I know what I've seen, I know what she's told me. He needs to be ready to lead this forward. Especially if I'm to be in Ely. You'll remain here with him and Anthony. You need to be the one to keep the Coven moving forward alongside them."

"You know he doesn't want to lead."

"Right now, he's going to have to. Once this is done, he can set the laws into place that will change it. He wants the wall down just as much as we do. He wants true freedom for the witches. He wants what we all want, Aja." She placed a hand on his chest. "To not hide who we are or who we love."

"Does that mean we no longer have to hide?"

Her breath caught in her throat. At one time, it had been she, Diana, and Aja. Not only had her relationship with Diana been forbidden in their realm, but their relationship together with Aja had been as well. By Shianshani law, both witch and human, a couple was a born man, and a born woman. After Diana had died, it would have been easy for Jessamyn and Aja to no longer hide their relationship, and that moment hadn't been the first he had asked of it. But every time Jessamyn thought about living openly, freely, showing her love for Aja, it felt like she was dishonoring Diana's life and memory.

And she knew it would also place a target on Aja's back for Frederick.

"Someday, Aja," she said softly, leaning into his warmth. Her chest tightened and for a moment, she struggled to breathe as her heart smashed into her lungs with its next few beats. "Someday. I promise."

Jessamyn stood at the entrance to the king's wing. Cassius and Aja at her sides. Aja had been right. Marcelo had balked at his new role at first. Then, he resigned himself to what they were facing, and what he needed to do for the realm.

"To be clear, I'm *not* the king," he had said.

"No." Jessamyn agreed with a nod. "You, Anthony, and Aja are going to work together, as a unit, to keep things here quiet so that we do not stir Madigan or his men when I'm not here. Deflect, sleight of hand, flat out lies. I don't care how it's done. Just do it."

"If he asks about Róisín?" Aja stared down the hall toward the door to the king's main suite.

"It's his fault she's gone again," Jessamyn said. "He's creating these monsters. Spinning some wild tale along the way. If he won't hold himself accountable for it, I will."

"Uh-oh." He chuckled.

"What?" Cassius asked, pulling his attention away from the hall to the pair next to him. "What does that mean?"

"You're familiar with the Granier?" Jessamyn asked.

Cassius' brow came together. "You mean the beast-like thing that no one has seen, but apparently lives in the caves of the North Prindell Province?"

"Not, apparently. They do," Aja said. "Our people used to hunt them."

Cassius's eyes grew wide. "You." He looked from him to Jessamyn.

"It's where our people lived for centuries before migrating south to Talista," Jessamyn said.

"It's so desolate there, though."

"Let that be a reminder of just how resilient the people of the Shian-shani Coven are." Jessamyn hadn't meant for the words to be menacing, only what she had said it to be; a reminder. A reminder of what her people had survived, had overcome, and still remained.

"But what does the Granier have to do with why he laughed?" He pointed to Aja.

She grinned at him. "Because young Cassius, the male Granier, is incredibly territorial. You heard what Marcelo and Nolani said Madigan did to the ones that were in the courtyard, correct?"

He nodded.

"That is what will make this so easy. Granier are known to, literally, eat their own to secure dominance during mating season. Madigan feels a possessiveness over Róisín, and if he thinks that there's more in the ranks wanting her..."

"He'll go after them. Not us."

"Exactly."

"Will it work?" he asked.

"Lady McKenna returned this morning, and was promptly gone after again," she said. "Or at least that's what I'm going to convince our king has just happened."

"Thin the ranks a bit." Aja rolled his shoulders.

Cassius straightened, taking on the stance of a court guard that had been drilled into him since he began academy at ten as all non-noble born within the wall had done. "What do you need us to do?"

"Back me up." She stepped aside so that she no longer stood between him and Aja.

"What—"

Aja swung a fist, connecting with Cassius' jaw.

Cassius stumbled back, bringing a hand to his face, his eyes wild. "Holy Goddess."

Aja widened his stance and braced himself. "Right shoulder and left cheek."

Cassius looked to Jessamyn.

"You two need to look like you just fought with the guard, Cassius," she said.

"Well, shit." He rolled his jaw around and winced. "I'm still beat to Hells after the last one almost a week ago."

"Which he'll notice are old bruises," Jessamyn said.

"Come on." Aja wiggled his fingers, waving Cassius closer. "Anthony can take care of you after. We'll bring a healer in."

Cassius shrugged and let his chin fall to his chest. Then, he charged Aja.

CHAPTER 50

C AID ROLLED over and slipped his arm around Róisín's waist, pulling her close. When he buried his nose in her hair, inhaling the honey and lavender smell of her, she stretched against him, letting out a low hum.

"Morning." Her hair tickled his lips as he spoke. "How do you feel?"

"Like a brand-new woman." She rolled and pressed her face into his chest. "I missed this," she whispered.

"Me too." He stroked a hand over her hair, then down her back. "How do you feel about everything else?"

Her lips were warm against the skin of his chest. "Do you want honesty, or the lie?"

"How about we land somewhere in the middle?"

"I'm angry. More at myself for not being able to do what I needed to do." Her fingers danced along his chest, to his shoulders and back. "I'm so freaking relieved, too."

He tried to rein his body's reaction in. The way his skin lit under her touches. The way his cock rose. "First, tell me why you're relieved. Then I'll tell you why being angry is bullshit."

She tipped her head back. Her turquoise eyes were slivers beneath her lashes. "Oh, you will, will you?"

"I'd think at this point, you knew it was coming."

Róisín lifted a hand, traced a finger along his bottom lip.

"You're trying to distract me so you can deflect." He slipped his tongue through his lips, stroking it along the pad of her finger. "Stop it."

She pouted, then rolled onto her back. "This isn't fair. You see me so completely. I can't hide anything."

Caid brushed his knuckles along her cheek. "I think it's perfectly fair. Because I can't hide shit from you either. You may have said nothing, waiting for me to come to you, but you knew about—"Saying anything again may waken whatever it was, and inside had been blissfully, although worryingly, quiet, for the past few days. "That something was going on with me. Now, cut it out. Tell me why you're relieved. With how adamant you were about throwing yourself on the spit and serving yourself up, I'm sorry if I feel *that's* the lie."

Her lips parted slightly as she inhaled, her bottom lip quivering. "I, this, the plan Lucius and Jessamyn put into place, it's familiar. The outcome may still be uncertain, but this normalcy." She pushed her hand through her hair. "As messed up as that sounds, there's a comfort to it. That hammering anxiety I was feeling, trying to figure everything out, it fell away so quickly."

"It's just like when you all were trying to figure out how to get Madigan before."

"Exactly. I mean, add in Ione, and subtract Nanette." She frowned. "And Matthew. And I *know* this. We don't feel so completely fractured anymore."

Having come into the mix at the tail end of everything, he more witnessed than experienced that togetherness. He could only imagine how it had felt, for all of them, to be so separated these past weeks. "Okay. Now, why are you angry?"

"Ay." She cringed. "Where do I start?"

"First thing that comes to mind."

"Well, that's easy. I'm pissed at myself for failing. Nope." She brought a hand up, covering his mouth. "Let me vent. *You* asked for it. I failed in a way. Because there had to have been a way I could have used my mother's death magic to actually end him. Maybe if I'd kept going, just a little longer. I'm pissed at him, Aoife, all of them for being so

236

selfish and power hungry that they've done this to our people. I'm angry that I can't stop my brain from this ongoing loop of wondering if I've just spent the last five weeks of my life chasing a goal that seemed to only be created for me to either flat out fail, or to lose my mind slowly trying to figure it out until there was nothing left of me."

Caid pulled her hand from his mouth. "What if we can change your fate?"

"Oh, Caid. You sound like my mother now."

"No, really. Would you come with me? I want to see if something works."

"Will you tell me where?" Róisín asked.

He shook his head. "How about you come with me, and we'll call it even for the time you whisked me away to a wheat field, buck ass naked."

Her eyes darted down to his bare chest. "Well, you can't deny that it wasn't a good time."

He burst into laughter and shook his head. "Touché. But really, will you come with me?"

"What was it you said that day?" She nestled against him and nipped at his jaw. "Anywhere."

"This was definitely *not* what I was expecting." Róisín wrapped her arms around herself and shivered as she took in the sprawling Nianti Fields just outside of Wurbray, Legianne's capital. "If you'd said here, I'd at least have swiped one of your sweatshirts. Winter is in full swing here."

Caid scratched the top of his head. "Sorry."

"It's okay. You're still figuring all of this out." She shuffled closer to him. "I'll just rob your body heat while you explain why we're here."

He wrapped his arms around her, letting his magic warm them both. "Well, I figured that if—"

"Oh, shit." Her body tensed against his and she gasped. "Caid, you need to—" She pushed against him, trying to free herself.

"Róisín."

"No," she said through clenched teeth. "Caid, really. Gah!" Her body trembled in his hold. "It's... I don't want to hurt you. I can't—"

Caid was in the air as the explosion of her magic slammed into him. He landed several feet away, dozens of small, lighted insects scurried up from the winter wildflowers and away from him. With a groan, he rolled to his side and pushed to his knees.

Róisín's head tossed back, and a scream tore out of her. Her body wrenched itself into an awkward position as she screamed again. A pulse of magic spread across the field. The hellebore swayed, their happy blooms bending toward the ground.

He needed to get to her. Somehow. Yet, every time he moved forward, another pulse met him head on, pushing him back.

"Róisín!" He lowered into a near crouch, leading with one of his shoulders. The ground beneath his feet rumbled, and he faltered, almost falling.

"Let usssss in."

Caid ground his teeth together and pushed against what felt like a wall. "What a wonderful fucking time to deal with this shit."

"Let ussssss help you."

"No."

"Save herrrrr. It'll consume herrrrr."

Caid twisted, searching for Róisín. She had moved a few feet from where they had shifted to and now stood with her back bowed dramatically and her arms flung out to the side. Her mouth was open in a silent scream, face twisted in pain.

"Fuck." He threw himself against the invisible wall her magic, or some type of magic, had created. "Fuck! Róisín!"

"Let usssss..."

"Fine! Fuck it. Help me." His voice broke as he screamed. "Just help me save her!"

The heat struck him first as his body ignited. His skin tightened as something inside fully woke, stretching and racing to fill every part of him. Then he was moving. His body like a blade cutting through the pulses of magic that echoed from Róisín, trying to knock him back.

When he reached her, he gathered her in his arms, his magic rising alongside hers in what felt like an assault to his senses. The muscles in his arms screamed as her magic pommeled against him. He didn't know what else to do other than to hold her. How was he supposed to save her? What was he supposed to do to stop whatever was happening?

Róisín screamed again. The sound deafening being so close to her.

Then there was silence. His magic had created a cocoon, a barrier of sorts around them. Enough space for it to push back against Róisín's. Pressing, pressing, pressing, until it retreated. Caid felt like his arms were ready to give out at any moment. Every muscle burned with exhaustion from holding her.

Her eyes snapped open, landing on his. They were a storm of reds, yellows, greens, blues, and oranges. They shifted back and forth, as though they were searching.

"Caid?" his name, a quiet, confused whisper from her lips, before her body fell limp in his arms.

"Rest," the voice inside of him said.

Before Caid could question what had just happened, what was inside of him, exhaustion overtook him.

CHAPTER 51

Róisín's mouth felt drier than a desert, and her body felt as though she had just gone a few dozen rounds against Matthew in the training room. With a groan, she forced her eyes open. The pink morning sky of Legianne greeted her.

"What?" She blinked and sat up. The Nianti Fields around her were decimated. It had been among the many places she had never visited in her few visits to Legianne after her mother's death. But the times she had been at Aoife's home in Wurbray, she had seen the rolling field of wildflowers and glowing Nianti from the windows. Now, there was nothing.

Her magic. She remembered the way something inside of her had exploded, and a power like she had never felt before with her magic had been released. And something else... Something else had been there. It had hurt, in a brutal and punishing sort of way. She hadn't been able to move or breathe. For everything she felt returning to her, she felt it leaving her two-fold.

Caid.

Her heart galloped and her throat tightened. Where was Caid?

Shakily, she shifted around so that she was on all fours, not quite trusting her legs yet.

There, something just to her left. She squinted in the dim morning winter light, trying to see more clearly. With a sharp gasp, adrenaline surged through her, and she was up and running.

"Caid!" She slipped and tumbled to the ground. "Caid! No." She patted his cheeks with shaking hands. "No, no, no. Caid! Wake up!"

She reached frantically for their tether and somehow fumbled it.

"No. You have to be okay, you have to be." She shook him. "Caid! Please. I'm so sorry." The tears rolled down her cheeks. "Please."

A groan vibrated from his chest. "Shit." The word was raspy and faint, but it meant he was alive.

Róisín threw herself over his body, grasping at and clutching him.

"Easy." He flinched. "I think I pulled a muscle. Or sixty."

Her laugh was watery. "I'm so sorry."

His hands moved to her shoulders. "You good?"

"I am now."

He cupped her face with his hands. "No, you good? Your power? It's back?"

She pressed her lips together and nodded. "What—" She cleared the thickness in her throat away. "What happened?"

Caid released her face and shuffled up into the sitting position. "Fuck if I know. I think..." He looked around them. "I think something else was here."

She let him pull her into his lap and rest her head against his chest. His heart was a steady thump against her ear. Slowly, ever so slowly, the panic that had bloomed inside of her ebbed. "You felt it too?"

"No, I, it, dammit." He made a noise of frustration and shoved a hand into his hair. "I don't know what it is. Inside of me, I mean. Whatever it is, it knew that something was wrong." He dropped his voice. "It helped me save you from whatever was happening."

"Are you okay? I didn't?"

"I just need about a million of those lidocaine patches, but I'll be fine." He looked away from her to where she had woken up. "Do you know what that was?"

"No. I've never actually been to the Nianti. I've rarely come to Legianne, and when I did, or do, it's never a long stay. With no other witches here aside from Aoife and I, it was the once place I let myself be selfish with my feelings over. I *hate* it here." She shuddered hard enough that her teeth chattered.

His lips fell into a tight line and his eyes darkened with deep browns, forest green, and hints of black. "Then let's get the hell out of here."

Róisín wrapped her arms around his neck. "Can we... Would it be okay if we went back to our house in Maine?"

His eyes cleared, settling back to their natural hazel spray of colors. Hope lit bright in them. "Is that where you want to go?"

She nodded and rested her head against his shoulder. "Ireland was my home, and I thought it could be again. It hasn't felt quite right. Greens Glen, it's just...*that* is home."

"What about Helen?"

"Your place hasn't sold yet, it's still half furnished with a couch and bed..."

He pursed his lips, then nodded. "That sounds pretty perfect, actually."

"Let's go home."

HELEN DIDN'T GO WILLINGLY. SHE HAD FELT RÓISÍN'S energy from the magic the moment Róisín had arrived at the house. There were questions, and most Róisín could not answer because she was still trying to work it out herself. Especially why her magic had felt so different inside of her. Why it felt more *free*.

Caid's body was already healing from the bruises and strained muscles, but Róisín had seen the way he moved slowly, holding himself gingerly. They both needed to rest. They hadn't much time left before Jessamyn returned.

"I promise, once I get a bit of a nap, I'll connect with Shasta," Róisín told Helen in Caid's kitchen.

Helen chewed on her lip. "You better. I know you haven't told me everything. And I don't expect you to. But make sure you do Shasta, okay? She'll be able to help with whatever happened in Legianne."

Róisín placed her hand over her heart. "I promise, Helen. I will talk to Shasta. How are Lina and the babies?"

"They're all doing wonderful. Babies are growing, and healthy sizes for their term mark. She'll be having a scan in a few days for measurements and if she wants to know the sex of them." Helen sighed, shaking her head, then gave Róisín a wide smile. "You kids. All of you. Go. I know you want to be with the boy. Just tell Shasta, okay?"

"I will. Thank you for everything, Helen." She returned Helen's smile, then shifted home.

When she arrived, it was quiet and felt empty. Her heart kicked up a notch. "Caid?" She called from the kitchen.

"Out here," he called through the open patio door.

She nudged it open and stepped into the backyard. Caid sat in a chair, shirtless, with what looked like a large bandage over the left side of his chest. "What—"

"It's a heat pack. Everything else feels good again." He shifted to sit up more and winced. "Just a bit tender there still."

"Oh," she said quietly. "Okay."

He motioned her closer, and after a moment, she went to him. Carefully, she sat so that she was straddling his lap.

"I thought." She placed a hand to her chest, against the frantic beats of her heart. Her magic rose and gently stroked along the organ, soothing it.

Hello, old friend. I've missed you.

Her magic sighed contentedly in response.

"I know." He leaned back, resting his head against the back of the chair, closing his eyes. "That's why I cut you off before you could panic anymore."

She brushed her hand over the fabric, feeling the warmth. "Can I?"

He cracked an eye open. "You want to?"

She took the heat pack away, replacing it with her palm. Her magic danced around inside of her, embracing her in its old, familiar way. Old, yet new. The newness was almost like her magic in an untrained form. As though she were just learning all over again. Sweat at the base of her skull began to form and drip down along her spine.

Caid shifted under her touch. "It tickles."

"Hold still." When she felt the anger in the muscles of his chest settle and relax, she began to pull her hand away.

"Thank you."

She snatched her hand to her chest as if it had been burned. "What in the Hells was *that*?" She lifted her gaze from his chest to find that his hazel eyes were open and steady on her. "Caid?"

"Meet the thing that's been living inside of me since the moment *my* magic woke up."

"That long? Why didn't you say something sooner?" She looked down at her hand, then at his chest.

"It wasn't that bad at first. It was just like a shadow, following me around. Now?" He shrugged. "I feel like Eddie Brock in Venom."

"I have no idea who or what that is."

"Probably a good thing you don't."

"Caid."

"It helped me save you. *Whatever* it is, it knew that something wasn't right." His voice was thick and rough. His expression was dark.

Róisín stroked her thumb over the stubble along his jaw. "We need to figure this out."

"We will."

"But—"

He brought her mouth to his, kissing her softly.

"Kincaid James McGrath, are you trying to distract me?"

He kissed her again, a little harder this time. His tongue licking along her bottom lip. "Is it working?"

"I hate to admit that it is." She moved to sit further up his lap.

He shifted his hips up, rocking against her. "Good."

"We'll just revisit this conversation later." Her eyes fluttered closed. "Because we really need to figure this out."

"Mmhmm." He kissed along her neck, chuckling when she moaned. "Hopefully by then, the gang will be back together, and that asshole Madigan will be dead once and for all."

Róisín leaned back, feeling his length pressing through his jeans against her. "What if David comes?"

"Fuck that little rabbit." He nipped at the skin of her shoulder. "Let's make a deal." He sat back and suddenly she felt chilled in the absence of his warmth. "We dig to the bottom of whatever the hell is in me, and you tell me what you and the bunny talked about the last time we were here."

She had effectively pushed what David had said out of her mind once everything spiraled in Shianshani. Now it crashed down around her. His words to her clamoring against her worries about what the Goddess had truly wanted from her. He had also known that Caid wasn't human from the beginning.

"Hey." Caid's voice was whisper soft. "Where'd you go?"

"It's too much." Her voice shook. "Everything, it's all too much. I can't handle it."

He shook his head. "Then don't. For right now, don't."

"You make it sound so easy."

He moved his hands from her hips, slipping them beneath the waist-band of the joggers that she wore. The roughness of his palms scraped over the skin of her ass. He gave her a light squeeze. "It can be, if you let it."

Her magic hummed inside of her. The vibration of it ignited every fiber of her being. Almost as though it were encouraging her to let go, even for just a moment. Not letting the voice of doubt find its way inside, she took his mouth with hers.

His possessive growl rumbled from his throat as he held her in place, grinding against her.

Róisín took his bottom lip between her teeth and pulled. With a laugh, she released him and slipped back and down. Her mouth trailed along his chest, down his stomach, where she stopped at the button of his jeans.

She slid the silver tab through the hole, then dragged his zipper down. When she looked up at him, he was watching her from lidded eyes, his chest rising and falling rapidly. "Up," she said.

He lifted his hips, and she tugged his jeans down, releasing his swollen cock.

"Róisín," he said roughly when she didn't move.

Róisín stroked the length, bringing her lips closer. She swirled her tongue around the head, squeezing the shaft with her hand at the same time. He hissed out a breath, his hips bucking. Then he was reaching for her, pulling her back up.

"Not today." He tugged at her joggers. "I can't today. I need you."

She pressed a hand to his chest to steady herself as she lifted. She gripped his cock in her other hand, stroking the head along her folds. They both moaned.

"Jesus, Róisín." His breathing had become heavier.

Slowly, she lowered herself onto his him until she was fully seated. Then she rolled her hips slightly. Her walls tightened, and that first burst of ecstasy shot through her, lighting her on fire. The cool breeze of the autumn air along her bare skin heightened the sensation.

Róisín pushed up until just his tip was still inside of her. Then she quickly lowered herself. Electric currents hummed and buzzed at her core, wrapping tightly, and she clenched in delight.

Leaning forward, she hovered above one of his nipples for a moment, before taking it between her teeth, biting softly. He hissed out a curse and dug his fingers into the soft flesh of her hips, pulling her against him tighter. She laved the spot and moved closer to his ear. "Fuck me." She used her tongue to pull his earlobe to her teeth, nipping it lightly. "Please."

He reared up, thrusting hard. She gasped, then released a small whimper as the first tingles set off through her core, spreading over her body.

"It would be *my* pleasure." He grinned at her. He lifted her slightly, then released her at the same time as he thrust upward. Their bodies joined with a loud slap, and Róisín knew she wasn't long for the orgasm.

"Caid." She moaned.

She met every thrust of his with a rock of her own, over and over. Her body no longer felt like it belonged to her. She had given it over to the sensations, letting them dance and race through her, unsure how she was still in one piece.

When she felt as though there wasn't anything left holding her together, her orgasm overtook her. Her body tensing, as Caid kept their pace, urging every drop of bliss from her, before she felt his release inside.

Their movements slowed, and Róisín collapsed against his chest, breathless. Her body felt deliciously spent.

Once they had caught their breaths, and Caid's heart wasn't a racing beat in a rock song's chorus beneath her ear, Róisín asked, "What do we do now?"

"We go shower. Then we should probably eat something. Let Lina know we're here before Helen does. *Sleep*." He let out a sigh. "Then go to Ely to get this show on the road."

"David knew you weren't human. From the start." She wasn't sure why she had chosen that moment to tell him, or why she hadn't also said what David had told her about Sister Future.

His body jerked. "Say what now?"

"David. That's what he told me that day we came to get some of your stuff. When you got here, he told me that my human was here. After I said that he knows you're not human, he told me he always knew."

Caid's breaths were coming out loud, harshly. However, he wouldn't have time to tell her what he was thinking, because that was the moment Lina arrived.

"Ah! Shit! You two are naked! My eyes," Lina cried out.

"Knocking or ringing a doorbell would be nice, Leen," Caid said. Róisín could hear the tightness in the tone trying to drown out the light tone he was using.

"Anyway, I'll just wait in the living room. Go get decent, please. I have questions."

Róisín waited until she heard the patio door close before she pulled back from Caid.

"She has such shit timing." He wiped a hand over his face. "Fuck."

Part of Róisín was relieved for Lina's interruption. Her thoughts had so quickly scattered, then spiraled, she needed a moment to pull herself together before she and Caid talked.

"Hey." He caught one of her hands in his. "Breathe, Róisín. We've figured everything out to this point. This isn't anything new, okay?"

"I'm so tired, Caid. For every answer I get, there's twenty more questions. Each is worse than the ones that came before."

He tucked a lock of her hair behind one of her ears, then kissed the tip of her nose. "Let's go see what my sister wants, so we can kick her out and get some rest. The day is almost over, there's not a lot we can do about any of it right now."

"Easier said than done." She rose from his lap and bent to retrieve her joggers and tee-shirt.

"I know. But we've gotta try." He pulled his jeans on.

She paused at the door, turning back to him. "Together?"

"Always."

CHAPTER 52

T HE BLARING sound of a horn at the intersection near the cafe where Marcelo sat with Nolani on the sidewalk caused him to wince. Angry shouts followed. The person in the crossing mark that the car had almost struck, waving their hands, flashing obscene gestures and shouting even more obscene remarks.

"It's so easy to forget this all exists when you're behind the wall," Marcelo said. "But the quiet, it's unnatural."

"Because," Nolani began, swiping a fry from his plate, "it *is* unnatural. All the realms are in their early and mid-twenties for centuries now. Even *Earth* has finally progressed forward."

He hummed his agreement, eyes trying to follow all the movement around them. He had started venturing outside of the wall when he'd turned twelve. The age the king and queen had both deemed him old enough to do so. It had been a shock at first. The cacophony of noise, sights, and smells.

Once the overwhelm of it all no longer assaulted his senses, he fell in love with everything. He had never liked the wall, how it cut him off from the realm around him, but once he experienced life on the other side, he grew to despise the structure more than ever.

Then Nolani came crashing into his life, literally, when he was sixteen and everything became more.

"Celo." Nolani waved a hand in his face. "Where've you gone on me?"

"Hm?"

"You went somewhere. Was it at least a good memory?"

He gave her a soft smile. "Depends on which set of eyes you're remembering it from."

"Oh, Hells, Celo." Her face flamed red. "Will you ever let me live that down?"

"Never." He leaned his forearms on the table, bending his upper half over it to be closer to her. "Because if you were not such a klutz, we would not be here right now."

Her gaze dropped to where he had rested his hand, palm up, in front of her. She lifted her hand to place it on his, but hesitated, eyes searching the milling crowds of people around them.

"It's time, Nolani," he whispered. "We shatter the walls holding us in."

"Are...are you sure?"

"I've always been sure. There's nothing I want more in my life than you. I want you more than I want that damned wall down. More than I want my brother, Cassius, and others who love like they do, to be able to live openly. More than I want gone the invisible walls that keep your people from being truly free here." Relief filled him when she laid her slender hand over his. "You're my everything, Nolani. I love you."

She danced her fingers in circles along his palm and wrist. "I love you, too, Celo."

"Will you stand at my side as I tear down everything my family has put into place? Will you rewrite Shianshani history with me?" He had wanted to ask her more, but in the days he had spent in the Coven's wing, he'd learned that there was much he didn't know about witches and their customs.

"You can ask, Celo. I may be a witch, yes, but my family has lived with human customs for a few centuries now."

He bit his bottom lip, brows furrowing. "How?"

"I know you. For eight years, I've learned the lines of your face. How different each of your emotions and expressions are as you feel them. I can see there's more you want to say, and after that—" Her breath caught at her last word and that was when he noticed she had a tear rolling down her cheek. "I can safely assume what it is you want to ask me."

"Would you be my partner in life, forever? My wife?"

"There's nothing I want more than forever with you." She gave his hand a tight squeeze.

He frowned at their hands. "But your forever looks different from mine."

"Perhaps." She rose and came to stand next to him. She placed a hand on his cheek and bent closer, her lips brushing his. "Time is what we make it. And we'll make the best of every minute we get."

He stood and swept her into his arms, closing his mouth over hers in a long kiss. Around them, a few passersby whistled, while others shouted for them to get a room. When he heard the whispers questioning if it was the prince, he moved to shield Nolani by turning them away from the people on the sidewalk and moved closer to the building.

"It's okay." She smoothed her hands over his chest.

He placed a hand on the building next to her head. "Is it? Once he's gone and I'm..." The rest of the words became trapped in his throat. He took a breath and tried again. "Until I can undo it all, I have to be—"

"I know. I'm not going anywhere. I'm going to weather all that you have to, because that's what partners do, Celo."

He lay his forehead against hers. "We just have to survive all of it first."

She tapped a finger on his chin. "We'll get to the other side of this. You and Jessamyn will make this realm everything that it is meant to be. Everything the people deserve it to be."

"I never wanted this."

"I know. But you need to remember that it won't be forever. It won't be a crown weighing upon your head. You'll have the power to put the laws into place to end that."

"What about Anthony?"

"He doesn't want to be king either. He is only willing to step up in that role because he knew you didn't want it."

Marcelo sighed. He linked a hand with hers and looked toward the looming wall. "I need to get back inside. Check in with Aja and Anelle. Jessamyn is set to return from Ely this evening with an update from the others."

Nolani leaned into his arm, her free hand coming to his arm. "I'll see you this evening at the Locaw Preserve fundraiser?"

He nodded.

"The king?"

"He'll be there too. Cassius has been called to guard my mother for the evening."

"Madigan wants him in public looking like he's been through a meat grinder? Won't that raise an alarm and cause questions?"

Marcelo shrugged. "To be honest, it beats the Hells out of me. One second, his actions are calculated, easily followed, and explainable. The next? Nothing makes sense, and it's unhinged chaos."

"A desperate man does desperate, dangerous things. He'll want to talk to you soon, I imagine."

Marcelo thought of the whispers just moments before. Word would surely get back to the king. Despite that he hadn't been Rastead for several weeks now, he had still ridden Marcelo about duty and his future as king. Which meant that Marcelo would have to face him, probably sooner rather than later, for the first time since learning that he was someone else.

"Be careful." Nolani squeezed his arm. "Use Jessamyn's guards when he calls for you."

"Aja won't leave my side," he said. "You should be careful as well. You saw what he did in the courtyard with the others. With Jessamyn's plan, and Lady McKenna still off realm, even in his calmest moments, he's wound so tightly."

Nolani inclined her head, then tipped it to the left, her eyes shifting to look across the street. Marcelo followed her gaze and saw at the patio to the bistro there sat three Coven members. "Jessamyn left every base covered."

He felt his body sag, and his lungs loosen. "Good."

She rose to her toes and pressed a kiss to his jaw. "Tonight."

And then she was off, moving with a crowd crossing the street. With heavy feet, he turned to face the wall. He used each step forward to the gates to slip back into his character, pulling his mask on. He only hoped he made it to Aja before he was beckoned to the king.

CHAPTER 53

"*WAKE UP.*" The familiar voice was wispy, faint, when it reached Róisín's ears.

She rolled first to her back, then to her other side. Her body shifting away from Caid's and the heat that was pulsing off him. They had left the windows cracked, forgetting to close them. Exhaustion had dragged them down by the time they had got Lina out of the house. The chilly autumn air that drifted through them wasn't enough to cool Róisín, and she kicked her legs free of the blankets that had tangled around them.

"*Wake up.*" The voice prodded again. "*You always were such a brat.*"

That had been enough for Róisín's eyes to fly open.

"Good. Now we can get this shit sorted so I can be off to my next destination." Aoife's tone was flat and almost hollow.

Róisín sat up, looking around the room.

"Over here."

In the antique wingback chair Lina and she had hauled up the stairs what felt like a lifetime ago, sat Aoife. Or at least Róisín's dreamlike version of her. She wasn't quite corporeal. Her edges fading out into nothing.

Caid thrashed in his sleep next to her, letting out a shout.

"He'll be fine," Aoife said.

Róisín rubbed at her eyes, then pressed the heels of her palms hard against the sockets. "Go away."

"I wish I could." She made a strange noise with her mouth, then a dry laugh echoed around the room.

The scent of death overwhelmed Róisín's senses. She gagged and realized that no, this wasn't a dream.

"I apologize for my appearance." Aoife motioned downward. "The darkness isn't a place where you can remain...orderly."

Róisín had questions. Dozens, perhaps hundreds, more. Yet, she couldn't find the words. Goosebumps crawled along her skin, in a determined march, leaving the hairs along her arms and the back of her neck standing on end. She was dreaming, she had to remind herself. She had to be. There was no way that Aoife could have escaped the Darkness a second time.

Then again, Madigan had returned.

Róisín pinched the inside of her thigh and immediately sucked in a sharp breath.

"This isn't a dream," Aoife said. "And I'm not technically here."

"Then what is going on?" Róisín asked.

"I'm executing the conditions of my temporary release," she said. She lifted one of her hands, waving it back and forth. The motion was a normal speed, yet the hand appeared to move like a stop-time motion film. "Madigan is seeking to restore his magic. You cannot let that happen. If it does, there is no chance to restore the balance among the witches." She rose from the chair and moved around Róisín's bedroom, lifting and inspecting random trinkets as she moved.

"So he *can* get his magic back in King Dionomis's body," Róisín said.

"He can, and if you all dilly dally much longer, he *will*. As the Covens stand right now, with all of us gone, or—" She chuckled. It was a sound of malice and delight. "Powerless, that balance can return before it's too late. She will be unstoppable if you don't."

"Who?"

Aoife's features tightened in annoyance. "Unfortunately, you took so long to wake up, our time is up. He'll be waking soon."

"Wha—"

Caid shot upright with a roar, nearly tackling her. The bounce in the mattress toppled her onto her back. "Are you okay? What happened?" His hands frantically moved over her, checking her. "I was trapped in that fucking floor again—"

"Caid."

"—and I couldn't get out. I wasn't asleep—"

"Caid."

"—but I wasn't awake either."

"Caid!"

He sat back on his calves, eyes round.

"I'm okay." She struggled into the sitting position. "It was Aoife. I don't know exactly, but I'm okay. Are *you* okay?"

"I'm pissed as hell, but I'm fine. How can she be back? Are you sure?"

"She wasn't really back. She was here, but she wasn't. I can't really explain it."

He crawled up the bed and fell panting against the pillows and headboard. "Shit, Róisín."

She took a second to gather herself, her thoughts racing with trying to piece together what Aoife had said. The abruptness of her arrival, the strange way she spoke, the cryptic message she left with.

"Is she trying to fuck with me?" Róisín asked aloud, shoving her hands into her hair.

"What did she say?"

"Something about the balance with the witches," Róisín said.

"Okay, so that's on par with what the Goddess said, right? Unite the Covens or whatever it was? That'd be balancing things back out." Caid shifted so that his back was against the headboard and stretched his legs out before him.

"I don't know. It took my brain forever to clear that sleep fog. I was convinced it was a dream at first, but then I could smell the rot inside of her, that death. At that point, she had already started saying things."

"Do you think the Goddess sent her?"

"I mean, who else? A reminder of what she wants from me."

Caid reached forward, his hands coming to her waist, and he pulled her back against him. "Given the return of Madigan and what he is now, you'd think that'd be a pass on any deadline she imposed on this whole thing."

"But she didn't give me a—oh, shit. Madigan." She spun, her hair spinning around her head and into her face. She pushed it away to look at him. "Aoife said he's trying to get his magic restored."

"How? Can he do that? I thought humans couldn't? She just wanted to scare you."

"I don't think she was saying it to scare me. I think she knows somehow that he can truly get it back." She squeezed her eyes closed and pinched the bridge of her nose, trying to remember what else Aoife had said. "*Madigan is seeking to restore his magic. You cannot let that happen. If it does, there is no chance to restore the balance among the witches.* That's what she said, word for word."

Silence fell over them, Róisín's mind churning in overtime at the possibilities. Just as everything had righted itself and come together after being tipped to its side and scattered for so long, just as the ground beneath her feet had finally felt solid again, it was all gone.

It brought Róisín back to her first conclusion about her fate.

"I can do this," she said. "I can fucking do this."

"Talk it out," Caid said.

Which meant it was time to tell him what David had said. "I asked David who had sent him to watch over and help me. He said that it was Sister Future that had done so. He is her charge first, and the Goddess's second. Given that Goddess is our creator, is a puzzle in itself. Then he made that remark about having always known you weren't human."

"Your mother, she said that it was Sister Future that came to her both times," Caid said. "It was her that told your mother about what the Goddess wanted to do."

Róisín pulled her bottom lip between her fingers. "Was it her that told my mother about our bond, though? Or at least my bond with *someone* in your family?"

"I'd bet my life savings on it," he said.

"Okay, so that could explain that. Which, I hope it does, because, fuck, I can't take this feeling that I've been living with for the past month and a half. I am exhausted trying to keep myself together because every day it feels like my skin wants to scatter leaving the rest of me to fall to bits."

"That sounds a lot like anxiety, babe."

"Whatever it is, I hate it. It's distracting me and I can't help but feel I'm being *made* to feel this way. If I'm scattered, disoriented, and unorganized it makes me distracted. Then, I'm an easy target." Her heart raced, and her lungs began squeezing and loosening far too quickly. "It isn't lost on me that once I begin to find order in the chaos, and level ground again, that Aoife shows up with a cryptic message and my body's first reaction is to vibrate so hard I fall to pieces on the floor."

He brought his arms tight around her. "I won't let that happen."

She leaned into him, laying her head on his chest. "I know you will do your best to try to not let it. But we're facing our creator, Caid. None of us are powerful enough to go against her. Look at what's happened to everyone who has tried."

"She will be unstoppable if you don't."

"Who is the 'she' that she was talking about, though?" Róisín asked. "She said if we didn't stop Madigan from his magic, we couldn't restore the balance among us, and *she* would be unstoppable."

"Jessamyn?" Caid offered.

"Maybe?" She shook her head. "I don't think it's her. Amid all the chaos in Talista when we were there, I could see beyond that mask she wears. She's scared, Caid. Scared for her people, herself even."

He pressed a kiss to the top of her head. "I guess the question is, what do we do?"

"What's always worked best before," she said. "We go to the others with what happened, and we work together to figure it out and find a solution. If the Goddess is trying to shake me back up, she won't do it. If I'm going to the darkness, I'm not going without a fight."

"That's my girl."

CHAPTER 54

"U NITING OUR Covens?" The lines that had appeared between Jessamyn's brows moments earlier deepened.

Róisín hadn't been able to find Shasta, but Lucius had been in his living room with Jessamyn when she and Caid had arrived in Ely. She had wanted them all together, like before. Instead, the moment she saw Lucius, everything spilled out of her.

Caid had paced along the wall of windows, their tether frequently vibrating and rumbling from his unspoken emotions when the subject touched that protective part of him. Lucius and Jessamyn had been silent, sitting, watching her.

Róisín let out an uneasy breath. "That night in Roidon, the Goddess told me I needed to bring everyone together. Something was happening and we could only face it as one." She sat up straighter and cleared her throat. "I said nothing the day of our meeting, because after talking with Lily, I agreed it was best to shelve it for now. Not just because of learning of Madigan's return, but I've spent weeks feeling I was a second away from clawing my face off and scratching my skin bloody while basically pretending to know what I was doing."

She shrugged, feeling her face heat. Caid moved away from the windows and lowered himself onto a cushion next to her. His nearness

259

gave her courage to say her next words. "It was time for me to admit that I had no clue what I was doing at *all*. With any of it." Her gaze landed on Lucius. "I'm sorry. I should have—"

"That's enough." Lucius's voice was like a whip cracking, making both Jessamyn and Róisín flinch. Next to her, Caid's body tightened like a coil, ready to spring.

The silence that fell over the room was deafening.

"Not only can not *one* of us say we knew what we were doing then, or now, but to expect you to know any better than us would do you a disservice." Lucius's voice had an edge to it that Róisín had never heard before. His eyes were no longer steel-gray, but a deeper, fathomless color. The energy from his magic filled the room with a hot, heavy air. "We will never know why it was you who was set on this path." The room seemed to breathe a sigh of relief as Lucius brought the magic back within. "But I am grateful, enormously, that it is with us you are with on it. You will not apologize. For any of it, Róisín. It could be any of us in your position."

Róisín knew that he had said the words to comfort her, but she couldn't help feeling as though he said them to give himself the same.

Where had everything gone wrong? Where had everything spiraled?

When the Goddess had given you the impossible to do, and your family couldn't bear to let you do it alone, a quiet voice said inside.

Caid's voice was low when he spoke. "What about what's happening with my magic?"

Róisín's head swiveled to him in surprise. He had been so guarded about what was happening, even with her. For him to so casually bring it up now... She reached for his hand that rested on his thigh. He turned it palm up, letting her tuck her fingers between his. Then he folded his fingers over hers, gently squeezing.

Jessamyn leaned forward, curiosity shining bright on her face. "The baby witch, correct?"

Caid nodded. "I believe in more means than new to this magic thing, yes."

Her brows knotted.

"I'm only forty," he said. "You're all... older."

Jessamyn's laugh was full and hearty. "I like you."

"What has been happening, Kincaid?" Lucius asked.

"It's, since it woke up, it's—" He faltered, his chin falling to his chest.

Róisín let her magic lift, then fill her, warm her. When she felt full to bursting, it danced down her arm to their joined hands. His head jerked up, eyes a stormy sea of the colors of his own magic that had welcomed and danced with hers. She smiled at him, her thumb stroking the back of his hand.

It had been meant to be a reminder that whatever it was, maybe it wasn't truly bad if it had helped save her in Legianne.

His shoulders came up and back, then he looked at Lucius. "It, uh, it started that day, in the ravine behind the house. I guess I should say that night? Whenever it was that we got to Molennius after..."

Lucius nodded in understanding. No one in the room had wanted to voice Róisín's death. Not even her.

"What happened in at the ravine?" Jessamyn looked from each of them. Her eyes settled on Lucius and she nodded.

Róisín shifted her gaze to Lucius. His eyes were a dance of colors as he stared at Jessamyn. Was he telling her what had happened? Showing her? Róisín watched a silver tear streak down Lucius's cheek, giving her the answer to her questions.

Jessamyn released a shaking breath that echoed loudly in the quiet room.

Róisín bit the corner of her lip and cast her eyes down. She knew she shouldn't feel shame for what had happened. None of them had known that Madigan and Aoife had children together, tying Róisín, distantly to him. However, it didn't stop her from wishing she had been just a little stronger. Been able to hold on just a little longer.

When the fog cleared her mind, Caid's voice was still strong and steady next to her.

"I can't explain it. It just said that it would consume her, and I"—his chest heaved with his breath—"I was fucking scared."

Jessamyn and Lucius exchanged a look. Róisín couldn't help but notice how quickly the two had not bonded but had developed some sort of relationship. Was it age? Mutual respect? Common end goal? Róisín wondered, studying the pair.

"It's not uncommon for witches to speak, and I mean truly speak, with their magic," Jessamyn said. "It's not any different from those of our people who say that their magic is them and they move together as one. Like a fingerprint, not one of us truly holds magic in quite the same way. Similarly, yes, but never wholly the same."

"So, mine is, what, more symbiotic?" Caid asked.

"No, it's still innate, just as all magic is at its core," she said. "Yours just has a little pizzaz to it, that's all. Like mine." She grinned at him. "My brother's is that way as well. Once, as a child, his magic told him that he could fly. We caught him on the roof of the home we lived in, ready to test it out."

"Why's mine so..." Caid lifted his free hand and moved it in a rolling motion. "Angry, though?"

"You have to remember, Kincaid, while it may feel like a long time has passed, it's only been a few months. It is freshly awoken power, after forty years of dormancy in you," Lucius said.

"Oh." The air raced out of Róisín's lungs, leaving behind a throbbing and burning sensation. "Oh, shit. Even if it's been dormant all this time—" She shifted so that she sat sideways, her knee slamming into Caid's with the movement. "*All* of it?"

"Given Lina showed no signs of it," Lucius said. "Unfortunately, yes."

Róisín brought her hand to her mouth, her eyes filling instantly. She remembered the pain that ripped through her after Aoife had died when the entire Legianne Coven's well of magic came to her. It was a feeling that she would never forget. To know that Caid had amassed an entire Coven's worth of magic at the same time that his own had come to power...

"I'm so sorry," she whispered to him.

He lifted their joined hands and pressed a kiss to her knuckles. "It would have happened eventually, whether you fell from the sky or not."

"How has it been since you've traveled to your Coven's source spring?" Jessamyn asked.

"Not as intense. I think that's because it feels like I have more control over it," he said. "And since Legianne, the feeling still sort of creeps in, but it isn't talking to me anymore. Or, at least, not right now."

Lucius and Jessamyn both nodded.

"It's because you and your magic worked together. You vocalized your acceptance of it in its state," Jessamyn said. "That doesn't mean it will not pop up and say 'hey' once in a while, though."

"Just as with your power"—Lucius gave Róisín a pointed stare—"I wish you'd come to me sooner about this. Even without what is happening around us, there was no sense in allowing an unnecessary stressor into the mix if you needn't do so."

Caid shrugged. "There's sort of been a lot going on these past few weeks."

Róisín and Jessamyn hummed in agreement.

"What now?" Róisín asked.

"That's a damned good question," Lucius said. "It would seem that we're stuck in a pattern of never quite being able to grasp something solid to hold on to."

Róisín understood that feeling all too well. It had chased her most of her life, and somehow it had finally caught her.

CHAPTER 55

C AID SAT at the far end of the counter at the small local diner, waiting. He had slept like shit. His head throbbed. He wanted off this rollercoaster ride, but he wasn't doing it without Róisín.

There were days when he felt closer to that possibility than others. But right now he felt like he was a million miles away from it.

He had seen it settle on her features, that determination of hers. This new, jarring turn in the track of this ride had brought them back to a straight stretch where they could stare down what it was they faced as they raced toward it. And he worried she would try to race ahead of them to get there first.

"Hey," Wyatt's voice said. "You'd think you'd be tanner," he added, lowering himself onto the stool next to Caid.

"Tanner?" Caid pushed his cup of coffee across the countertop, the smell making his stomach churn.

"Yeah. People come back from vacation, especially one that was almost a month long, typically tan, dude." He waved to the server behind the counter, then held up two fingers to signal his usual order. "You're whiter than you were when you left. Did you have fun at least?"

"If you can call hanging around pompous rich folks fighting over who gets to hang some piece of history that should've remained buried in the sand wherever, fun."

Wyatt tipped a brow up. "Why'd you stay gone so long, then?"

Needing to keep his hands busy and calm his racing thoughts, Caid reached for his cup and a packet of sugar. "Trying to find the right time to propose."

Wyatt drew in a shocked breath so quickly he coughed. "Holy shit, McGrath, proposing already?" he asked between coughs.

"Here ya go, honey." The server placed a rounded plate of pancakes and sausage in front of Wyatt. "And this." She handed him a cup of water.

"Thanks Marilyn," Wyatt said. "Appreciate it." After he'd drank half of the glass, he turned back to Caid. "Well? Don't keep me in suspense. What'd she say?"

"Yes, obviously," Caid said.

"I'll be damned." He propped his chin on his fist. "Our favorite grumpy bear is going to get married. Oh! I get to plan the bachelor party. We'll go down to Portland."

"I don't need a bachelor party," he said.

"Sure ya do. Everyone needs one. You know Lina will plan a bachelorette for Róisín. So why not?"

He couldn't help but wonder how Róisín had done it. Juggling it all. The different realms and the way their time moved. Who knew who she was and who didn't. Almost like a double life, but not. At least, at that moment to him it certainly felt like he was living a double life.

He handled stress well. Or, he liked to think he did. But this constant state of uncertainty he found himself in day after day. He had thought Róisín's power being returned would be enough to ebb that feeling, but he still couldn't shake it.

Probably because everything about their future was uncertain.

"No strippers." Caid took a long drink from his coffee. He hadn't been paying attention to how much sugar he had added to it, and the sickly sweet taste made his eyes water.

"Nah, man, that's not my thing either. But!" His hand shot into the air, one finger raised. "A Sox game! Wait." He spun the stool with too much energy, sending himself fully around. That, and the goofy grin on

Wyatt's face when he caught the counter edge, loosened Caid's chest enough for the laughter to trickle out. "Do you two have a date yet?"

"No." Caid shook his head. "But it's not like the baseball season isn't like seven months long."

"True, true." Wyatt bobbed his head up and down. "What's the plan for coming back to work? I've got the Carneys deck done. You've got Bud's shed for his wife, and that bathroom gut for the Stanfords on the calendar."

"And a dozen calls of people wanting estimates," Caid added. The same guilt that had filled him when he'd played the messages on his old phone resurfaced. He should have planned better; he should have been more responsible.

His brain shouted at him that everything had happened so fast, that they had still been trying to piece everything, piece *themselves*, back together.

"Quite a few new folks in town." Wyatt took a pancake and wrapped it around one of the sausage links. After he dipped it into the syrup, he shoved the whole thing into his mouth. "Probably a few years' worth of work, easy," he said around a full mouth.

Caid side-eyed him, fighting the urge to laugh again. "You're gross, you know that?"

Wyatt shrugged. "You're the one that picked me as your best friend. Not like you didn't know what you were getting into."

Caid's eyes fell to his now empty cup. Best friend. Wyatt had been more than that in Caid's eyes. Wyatt's family had been there for him in a way his own hadn't. They had also extended that support to Lina many times over the years. Wyatt was family. His first family.

He watched Wyatt clear the rest of his breakfast from his plate, listened to the way he happily hummed along to the song playing from the speakers overhead.

Caid trusted Wyatt with his life, but what would Wyatt do when he found out who Caid really was?

CHAPTER 56

THE SOUND of ticking tapped at Lily's ear. Time. She had seen, as she worked alongside Ione, Ten, and Cicile, buried under books, why Róisín always seemed to be under the unbearable pressure of time.

The clock in Lucius's living room, on the other side of the manor, so far away that she shouldn't be able to hear it, tick-tocked, tick-tocked, clamoring in her brain.

She had been so selfish before. Lily could admit that now. Not that she hadn't been aware of what was going on, or what it could mean for her life. She had disassociated from it. Had dug into book after book, doing what she loved most; researching and learning.

Even after Matthew had tagged along to help, her days became peppered with his awful jokes, sarcasm, and endless conversations with himself.

As she grew closer to him. Laughing at those awful jokes, most times only because of the way his green eyes glittered, and the corners crinkled from his grin when she did. Looking forward to when he would move his self-talk outward and include her.

Her magic stroked along their tether. She hadn't touched it since that day. Since she had felt that soul-crushing pain in his pull back.

Looking around the room, she checked to see if any eyes were on her. Then she gave the tether a gentle tug.

When no response came, her heart tumbled down her chest and into her stomach. She hadn't known how they had worked, the tethers of those bonded. How would one know if there was someone still at the other end? Her eyes had caught Róisín's attention, and she was just digging up the courage to nod toward the door, hoping Róisín would understand it meant she needed to talk in private—when Matthew faintly tugged back.

She wondered what expression she wore when his response had come, because Róisín's eyes filled with tears, and her chin quivered as she pressed her lips together.

Lily blinked and focused on keeping her breath steady in and out.

"Are you okay?" Róisín mouthed across the table to her.

Lily gave her a slight nod, feeling her face heat with the embarrassment that had quickly flooded her. She shouldn't have done it while she was around everyone. She should have found a quiet space.

"Oh! Hey, wait a sec," Ione broke the silence.

Everyone's heads whipped in her direction. She was almost nose to the paper of the book before her, her finger tracing along the page and her mouth moving silently as she read the words.

"Care to share with the crowd, Ione?" Róisín asked.

"Sh. Gimme a sec." She waved her other hand as though to shoo Róisín away. "I need to make sure I'm getting this right."

Ten and Cicile exchanged a quick look before turning their attention back to Ione.

"Ah! I was *right*." She shoved her chair back to stand, crashing into the side of the chair Runa had been sitting in, flipping through a magazine that looked a few decades old. "Oops. Shit. Sorry, babe."

"Babe?" Ten asked.

Now it was Lily and Róisín who exchanged a look. One of curiosity, eyebrows high and eyes wide.

"Babe? What's up with that?" Róisín mouthed.

Lily shrugged. She had noticed the way Runa had followed Ione around the past few days, like a lost puppy dog. However, she hadn't known that they'd taken any time together, alone.

"Alright, so!" Ione pointed down to the book. "This is Founder Nulion. I think the reason it threw us off at first is, well, because Founder Nulion *is* a blend of like nine different languages, including many of the founding languages of the realms."

"Hold on." Lily fought the urge to cover her ears, the ticking growing so loud that it was a roar. She needed it to stop so she could focus. "Founder Nulion? That's Aunellion."

"Exactly." Ione spun the book around and slid it across the table to her. "Look at the last page."

Lily shifted through the book carefully. The pages were made of a thin, tissue-like paper. "What about it? It's..." She drew her finger along the words, her brain slowly processing each word and translating it. "The moon cycles?"

"Yes and no," Ione said. "It's a spell work for an autumn harvest, which tracks the moon cycles."

"What's this have to do with anything?" Lily, puzzled, read over the page again. At the bottom, she noticed two dates listed.

"The moon doesn't affect the curse," Cicile said. They scratched their jaw, blinking for a moment. "Yeah, no. The kings since the installation of the curse have just been driven more by the hunger of whatever the curse does to them."

"Ione, I can hear your brain from over here. You've already worked it out. The rest of us don't operate on the same wavelength," Róisín said.

Ten leaned back in her chair, her head bouncing up and down in an emphatic nod. "*My* brain never stops, but even it can't keep up with hers."

"The spell work tracks the green moon of Aunellion. There are only"—she glanced down to Cicile—"two? In recorded history?"

Cicile straightened. "Yes. Only two. The first was nearly nine hundred years ago. And the most recent," their hand shot to their mouth, barely stifling their gasp.

"Well?" Runa tossed his magazine on the table.

Cicile spoke from behind their hands. "A little more than a century ago."

Róisín looked from the book to Ione, her attention resting on Cicile last. "You two are saying that this is Madigan's book?"

Ione cleared her throat. "I don't know."

"Is there a way we can tell?" Lily asked. "There are dates here." She pointed.

"And I can feel remnants of energy around it," Ione said, "from magic."

"I'm the only one in the room that has been around Madigan while he's had his magic." Róisín's voice was barely a whisper, and her face had drained of color.

"Are you okay to..." Lily motioned to the book.

Róisín stared at it, unblinking.

"We could call Shasta or Lucius in," Lily offered.

"No." She leaned forward. "I can do it."

They all fell silent as Lily slid the book over to Róisín, and she picked it up. Her eyes closed and her body tensed. Lily was sure it was a sign that the assumption it was Madigan's was true.

"I don't feel any of his magic around it. There is magic, yes, but it's not his," Róisín said.

"Frederick's, clearly," Cicile said. "And probably Diana's. She is the one he made translate it for him. We worked so closely with Diana for many years, and with Frederick being the Coven leader for so long, it would make sense that their energies being tied to that book went unnoticed by us."

"Where's Diana now? Maybe she could help with how Frederick got his hands on this," Lily said.

"Uh..." Ten looked over at Runa, her expression filled with unease.

"Frederick killed Diana after she translated it for him." Runa's tone was flat, emotionless, but his deep maroon eyes had lit with bright reds and golds from his magic rising in response to an emotion the death clearly elicited.

Lily had to wonder if Diana had been his partner.

"Alright, so the book is from Aunellion. We can deduce that much. It wasn't Madigan's, we can also deduce that." Róisín frowned. "How did Frederick get it, and when?"

"He could have gotten it before Aunellion was sealed," Lily said.

"But if the Milsenetts didn't invite him..." Róisín chewed on a fingernail. "It's doubtful they ever invited anyone."

"When was the curse enacted?" Ione walked over to the whiteboard. She wrote the date in which the realm had been sealed by the Goddess on the middle left side. Just above it, she wrote the rough date of the green moon.

Runa's voice was quiet when he responded. Ione turned to him, marker tapping against her thumb. He repeated himself, only slightly louder this time. It must have been enough for Ione to have heard, because her brow wrinkled.

"That's not... unless he had the book from before?" She pressed the marker to her chin. "No."

It was at that moment, the trio from Shianshani said, "Shit."

"Exactly," Ione said. Then she shook her head. "What? Why shit?"

If they weren't facing a monster, and what now felt like the impossible, Lily would have laughed at her sister. She knew that within Ione's head, there were at least thirty conversations bouncing back and forth, sorting through information.

Róisín rose from her seat and went to her, taking the marker from her hands. "The curse has been in place for three generations of Dionomis rulers." The marker squeaked as she wrote the details on the board. "Either our dear pal Freddie had the book for a while, planning to use maybe another spell or something in it. Then—" She scribbled down Aoife's name. "My sweet, innocent grandmother comes along and suggests doing this thing." She wrote 'curse my shitty cheating bonded's new family' down. "And then boom, we have a curse that creates a blood thirsty, flesh-eating monster once the dude turns—" She looked over her shoulder at Cicile.

"Twenty-five," they said.

"Twenty-five." Róisín squeaked the marker across the board. Then she stepped back and looked at the board. "But something doesn't add up."

"That's because he figured out how to get to Aunellion," Runa said.

"How to get by the Fog Fields?" Lily asked. She studied the board and what Róisín had written. It made sense, yet Róisín was right, something was missing.

"No. How to get past whatever it was the Goddess did. How to get there after, when no one was there," he said. He was staring at the board so intently, Lily wouldn't be surprised to see it burst into flames.

Róisín offered him the marker. "You know something, or have a theory, and you need to explain it."

"It's not a theory." He stalked around the table and snatched the marker from Róisín. Lily didn't miss the way his other hand stretched, and his fingers brushed Ione's outstretched fingers when he passed by her on his way to the board. After he finished writing, he stepped aside. Ten's gasp was more of a squeak, and Cicile's was a clear sound of doom.

"Sunlan Westrill," Ione read the name on the board aloud.

"I was hoping you shitted over something else," Ten said.

"I was hoping you *both* shitted over something else." Cicile covered their face with their hands and let out a low groan.

"What is Sunlan Westrill?" Lily asked.

"Not what, *who*," Ten said. "Sunlan went missing roughly eighty-five or ninety years ago. He was last seen with Frederick, heading off-realm."

"Of-fucking-course." Róisín groaned and threw her hands up in frustration.

"How does it connect him to this?" Lily used her index finger to draw a circle around the board from where she sat.

"Aoife had already come to Talista, several times. Starting just a few years before Madigan made his split," Runa said. He capped the marker and handed it to Ione. Giving her a wink, he walked back to his seat. "The rumors about what they were doing, naturally given both of their ambitious states, were all tied to the Goddess. But Jes, she and Di—" He pressed his lips together. "Frederick wanted control of the court entirely. Not just what his position as Coven leader entitled him to."

"You mean High Mage," Lily said.

"Ah, no. Coven Leader. That High Mage shit didn't come into play until *after* the curse and the wall." Runa folded his arms over his chest. "They managed to, amid their scheming, learn of a spell work book of curses."

Lily caught Róisín rolling her eyes and pinching the bridge of her nose.

"This feels like the movies, for fuck's sake." Róisín made a grumbling noise.

Lily hadn't seen many movies, but couldn't deny that the entire thing, from what happened in Molennius at Shasta's to what they faced now, was that level of surreal. If only they hadn't actually experienced it. Which made it on some level to Lily feel worse.

"You think Frederick used Sunlan to get to Aunellion somehow?" Cicile asked the question the rest of them had been asking in their heads.

"That, or Sunlan knew how to get there and after he told Fred how —" Runa drew a line with his index finger along his throat.

"Shit," they all said.

"The dates in that book." Cicile nodded toward Lily. "They match the recorded moons."

"We should bring in Lucius and Jessamyn," Róisín said.

"I'll go find Lucius." Lily pushed to her feet. She needed air, she needed space. Everything felt too bright and too loud. The urge to pull on the tether was overwhelming. Hope and fear wrestled with one another in her chest, her heart screeching in pain when they crashed into it.

There was a chance they could get Matthew home.

CHAPTER 57

JESSAMYN FOUND herself in Lucius's company again. There was a quiet steadiness in his presence. A sense of calm despite the chaos. She at first reasoned that it was something that had come with age, his centuries of experience leading his people, and sitting at the head of the council for so long.

But then memories of Frederick, only a half-century Lucius's junior, would slip past the barrier she had created inside of herself. His selfishness, his maliciousness. The black pulsing power inside of him that would even make the more fearsome creatures of the night recoil in fear.

No, it was just who Lucius was as a person.

"So...since I have my power back," Róisín began.

"No," Lucius and Jessamyn said in unison.

"What?" she squeaked out. "But why?" She scowled at them. "When do *I* get to make a choice for myself? When does everyone else stop making them for me?"

A heavy silence fell over them. Jessamyn studied the woman sitting before her. The defeated slump of her shoulders. Lines bracketing her mouth, lips tipped down into a frown. *The Hidden Child* is what Frederick had called her. Brenna had found a way to conceal her from Aoife, from all of them. It was a feat that Jessamyn had always marveled at. The skill, the magic it would take to create such a cloaking spell and ward... But she understood, too, Róisín's feelings. From her birth, her life had always been decided for her. Even when she hadn't known it.

"Well." Jessamyn sucked her teeth and tipped her head to the side. "I hate to say it, Lucius, but I will need her to make an appearance at a gala in three nights' time."

"Absolutely not," he said.

Róisín glanced nervously between them, then lifted her hand. "Just curious, and probably dumb question, but, again, *why*? But this time, the reason is that my gut feels like the acid's going to bubble up my throat and I'm going to throw up all over this beautiful rug at my feet." She rubbed her bare toes across the plush gray rug. "In my head, going sounds like a good idea, because up there, I *am* a badass. However"— she brought her hands to her stomach and her face turned an ash color —"the rest of me is admittedly terrified."

"Just like the rest of us." Jessamyn had to fight the way her body wanted to flinch at her own admission. It left her feeling exposed, raw. She had only ever let those vulnerable parts of her be shown to those she held close.

Lucius leaned back against his desk. "What is happening in Talista right now, Jessamyn?"

She felt barely a foot tall beneath his stare. A downside to their time together. For all she had picked up about Lucius's personality, intents, relationships with the others—he had clearly done the same with her.

"I currently have Madigan set to unknowingly lend us a hand in culling his creatures." She shrugged, hoping her tone sounded as casual as she forced it to be. "Once I learned of how he disposed of those from the courtyard, knowing the only chance we would have should he be able to gather them and act..." She buried her face in her hands. "I'm no better than my brother for what I'm doing, but at least I'm doing it to protect my people. To protect you." She glanced at Róisín. "All of us."

"They're truly that powerful?" Lucius asked.

"They're astonishingly so. Their strength is like I've never seen before," Jessamyn said. "My brother and Aja, they're not only my top guards for the Coven, but they're incredibly powerful and skilled with their magic. They were struggling to keep up with them. Marcelo said that there were easily over one hundred with Madigan the day he and Nolani saw them. My Coven is barely two hundred strong at the moment. The other witches of Shianshani that could help won't risk their positions in the Senate or at court."

Lucius ran a hand over his mouth, his sigh sounding more like a growl than an expelling of air.

"My purpose at this gala?" Róisín asked.

"He's approached Anelle, trying to locate you. He believes you've returned one more time, and another attack from his men ensued." At Lucius's questioning look to Róisín, Jessamyn stood from where she had been sitting. "It was staged. She hasn't been back since Lily brought her home. I was..." She tugged her ponytail loose, trying to keep herself busy. "I was testing a theory. Aja and Cassius scuffed one another up a bit and I had them come to my meeting with the king."

"And did he..." Lucius spread his arms out.

"He did. Nine men."

Róisín let out a low whistle. "Not only is he a monster now, but he's even more psychotic than before. *Great.*"

"Which is why you're staying put," Lucius said tightly.

"Jessamyn?" Cicile popped their head through the cracked door. They lifted a book, waving it slightly.

"What is it?" Jessamyn read the title of the book, wondering if it was supposed to mean something to her.

"Runa has just returned with some books from the archives." Cicile slipped a folded sheet of paper from behind the cover. "And we found this."

Jessamyn was instantly overwhelmed by the smell, even as faint as it was, that drifted from the paper. "Have you?" she asked, reaching out with a shaking hand. Her heart thundered in her ears and her vision blurred.

"The second it slipped out, Runa, he"—Cicile blinked quickly at the dampness there—"said to bring it to you."

Jessamyn carefully unfolded the paper until the slightly faded ink in a familiar scrawl greeted her. Her free hand came to her mouth just as the sob had broken free from her throat. "Diana."

Róisín approached her on one side, and Cicile moved to her other. Together, they guided her to a chair, helping her lower into it.

"Is she going to be okay?" Róisín whispered over her head to Cicile.

"I think so?" They took the mass of Jessamyn's emerald hair and quickly braided it, then placed a hand on her shoulder. "Jes?"

"I, I just need a second." With the paper pressed to her chest, she focused on her magic, using it to calm and center her. When she placed it back into her lap, the words staring back at her, her heart and mind threatened to fall apart again. Until the words Diana had written began jumping out at her. "What the?"

Róisín and Cicile sat on the armrests of the chair.

"My love, I wish I had more time to spend with you, but I fear with his behavior my time is running far shorter than I believed it to be. There is a book that he has learned of, a very dark book of spell works belonging to Cronan Milsenett. Sunlan, much to the misfortune of not just he and I, but all of us, has found it, still in Aunellion. I had hoped that would be the end. No one can get there, no one can exist there. Not anymore. But, my love, he has found a way. Of course he has found a way. He has forced me to translate it for him, and now, on the morrow, he and Sunlan leave. Only he shall return, as that is the price paid to enter the realm. He will return. He will return. *When he does, my time has run out. I don't know if you will ever find this. I have a candle before me, and this parchment will find its way to the flame once I'm done. But I needed to get the words out. I love you, and I always will. Never forget that or our moments together. Tell Aja he will always have my heart as well. In another life, we could have loved outside of the shadows. Perhaps in—"*

Jessamyn turned the paper over, then back again. "She must have been interrupted and tucked it into the nearest book." She stroked a hand over the words. Her fingers paused over the blotches of ink that had clearly been Diana's teardrops landing on the page. Emotions and memories of the past threatened to pull her down. Instead, she focused on what they all needed most at that moment. She could grieve again later, when she was alone.

She turned to look up at Cicile. "Has Ione made progress in translating the book?"

"She's about halfway through. If your brother would leave her alone, she would probably get more done," Cicile said.

"My brother?" Róisín's quiet snort on her other side had her spinning. "What do you two know?"

Róisín held up her hands in surrender. "I'm not a tattletale."

Jessamyn glanced over her shoulder. "Cicile?"

They hopped off the armrest and quickly made their way to the door. "Sorry!" they called out before slipping into the hall.

Róisín ignored the glare Jessamyn shot her. "At least we know there is a way to get to Aunellion," she said with a cheer that was an obvious lie. Jessamyn could see the pinched lines around her eyes and the tightness in her jaw.

Lucius rubbed his chin. The smell of his magic, a sweet floral and musk, and just a touch of earth and wheat, filled the room. His voice was gravelly when he spoke finally. "It seems there is. At a cost."

Jessamyn could say, with every fiber of her being, that she didn't like the way Róisín's magic flared next to her in response. Beneath the girl's stubbornness and her battle with her self-worth, Jessamyn could see clear as a cloudless day just how loyal she was to those she loved.

What would she have to do to keep Róisín from being the one to sacrifice herself to get Matthew home? She couldn't bear the thought of another summoning. The last took so much from her body. Yet, the heat that now radiated from Róisín's body, causing sweat to bead along Jessamyn's spine...

No. This cannot be what she meant. This cannot be. I need the Legianne witch.

Jessamyn's fingers twitched in reflex, wanting to crumple the paper in her hand. Diana's words. She forced her hand to flex, pushing her fingers out, and quietly muttered, "Shit."

CHAPTER 58

EMBARRASSMENT AND shame had driven Shasta to Molennius and into hiding. She knew the others needed her, but for just a moment, she needed to slink home with her tail between her legs. With her home cleared away and preparations beginning for the new, she had secured a penthouse in the city center.

It was there she sat upon a plush, red suede sofa with her knees drawn to her chest, a soft throw across her legs, staring into a cup of steaming tea as if it held all the answers she sought.

Ione was translating the book that stunk of rot that Jessamyn and the others claimed had been Frederick's, swearing the curse was within the odd leather-bound covers. Shasta had believed it. It was an ominous thing, and it hummed with whispered, harsh voices promising destruction.

She shuddered and pulled her legs in tighter.

And, Róisín had her power returned. She could access all her magic again. That was certainly different. It felt louder than before. Róisín also seemed more vibrant. Her skin was a rosy flush and her eyes bright.

Both things had given Shasta the perfect opportunity to slip away. She had felt Lucius's tugs on the line they shared as Coven leaders and knew it had been him checking in on her as best as he could, with the limitations the thin tether allowed. Yet, she couldn't bear more than a slight tug back, just to let him know she lived, still.

A drunk, I became a drunk to run from my problems. Again. She frowned into the cup.

"If you stare at that any harder, it just may explode," Brenna said.

Shasta startled at the interruption, nearly spilling the tea in her lap. She blinked at her friend, then searched the room. "Where's Ev?"

Brenna lowered next to her and grimaced. "She couldn't make it, Shasta," she whispered.

"What?"

"She..." Brenna wiped her palms along her thighs. "We both tried, but she couldn't cross. I went back through nearly a dozen times and we tried over and over. It was like a wall held her in."

"Has Stephen learned something?"

"He's learned lots of things." She rolled her eyes. "He apparently didn't pay much attention to me when we were together and I tried to explain or show him."

"Oh, he paid attention plenty, Brenna," Shasta said, making her chuckle. "Can others still cross through the veil?"

"Some haven't been able to cross for months," Brenna said.

Shasta tugged at one of her earlobes. "Have you been able to figure out when it all started? When people began having trouble? Ev was late, but she had still been able to cross until today." When Brenna remained silent, looking down at where her hands were wrung together, knuckles white, in her lap, Shasta shifted her mug into one hand and reached for her with the other. She hooked a finger beneath Brenna's chin and gently turned her head to face her. "Bren, what's happening?"

"Stephen said that so far, the furthest back he's learned of has been roughly around the time that Aoife passed."

Shasta gasped. "Do you think?"

"I don't know. Why would the Goddess do that to the afterworld, knowing Aoife was going to the darkness?"

"When does anything she does make sense to us?" Shasta shot back.

Brenna buried her face in her hands. "I'm worried, Shasta. I'm worried about what's happening there. What's happening here that you won't tell me about? Róisín's in trouble, isn't she? What I did...it was for nothing, wasn't it?"

Shasta covered Brenna's hands and said, "You need to go to her to talk about that. It's not my place. But she's okay now. Kincaid, he takes care of her. He's a good one, Bren."

Brenna's entire body slumped, and she closed her eyes.

"That's not all." Brenna released her hands, then turned them so that she was now holding Shasta's. "Stephen found someone. He said they seemed lost, almost frantic. They were looking for someone and Stephen wanted to help him."

"Who?"

"Shasta, he said that he was Clarissa's brother."

Shasta's brows came down, knotting so deeply that she could see the dark hair of her eyebrows.

"I saw him. Stephen brought him to us."

"And?" The room around them grew hot and spots danced along the edge of her vision.

"He looks just like Clarissa."

It was impossible. Clarissa didn't have any siblings. She and Brenna had known her for centuries before she passed. They would have known, wouldn't they? Lucius. She had to find and go to Lucius. This had to be a mistake.

CHAPTER 59

E XHAUSTION REACHED its heavy hands for Matthew, grabbing him by the ankles, trying to anchor him. Once Lily's pain raced down their line after his body had reacted, responding to her first desperate pulls, he managed enough energy to move from where he had lain. Slowly. Sometimes he crawled, other times he did his best to scoot along on his stomach.

"It eats your brain, you know," a gruff voice said to him on his left.

His fingers curled into the dirt beneath him, his head dropping, causing his shoulders to hunch. His lungs burned from exertion. Every breath made his body quiver in pain.

"The fog was a natural thing, but Cronan Milsenett was ever the opportunist," the voice continued. There was something familiar about it, despite the way it sounded more like the wind. Faint, moving. "The Aunellion, they were a different breed of witch. I think how the realm looks is a testament to that. You're lucky, you know." The voice was nearer now.

Matthew lifted his head and realized he'd made it to a park bench. Aoife sat, legs crossed, reclined with her arms along the back of the bench. He hadn't stumbled into a hallucination since the bond with Lily had snapped into place. A part of him had hoped that it had meant his time was nearing its end. However, seeing Aoife before him, peering down her narrow nose at him with curiosity, killed every ounce of that hope.

"It's a shame Clarissa hadn't been able to do more," Aoife said. "She and Lucius were determined enough. Although, I don't think they quite understood the truth of it." She snorted. "They just thought she was meddling. *Bored*. They didn't know the truth. No one does."

"Wh-what are you talking about?" He managed the rasping words somehow.

Ignoring him, she drew her attention up, staring into the distance. "Anyway, where was I? Ah, yes. Cronan hated us all. The Aunellion were far superior in his mind. Came by it naturally, you know. His father and mother before him, theirs before them. All the way down the line. Pompous and sadistic. What a pair of traits." She snorted.

He wasn't sure how much longer he could last. Hunger pains had been gnawing at him, making him constantly dizzy. His body quaking with each movement he forced from it. He certainly didn't want to spend his last moments trapped in a hallucination with Aoife, of all people. Lily... He'd give anything to have her there with him as the heart in his chest slowed to ceasing.

"The Milsenetts didn't pass down gems or jewels, no, they had a delicious little book filled with spell work that our kind would never, ever dare to use. None of us were daring enough to pay the price of it. Cronan was a ballsy, wicked man. He dared. And that, son, is how this place became so accursed."

"What in"—he pulled himself closer—"the Hells are you talking about?"

She shrugged casually. "Among many things, I'm only merely explaining how the fog became what it is now. Disorienting, eating away at your brain while you die a slow, cruel death."

"You'd know about cruelty, wouldn't you?"

"I have...done things. But I would never do this."

Matthew grasped the end of the bench. Struggling to pull himself upright, he studied her. "You murdered your entire coven."

"Everyone always made me out to be the evil one." She tsked. "Did I want power? Of course I did. I wanted everything she had, and more.

But I never would have made people suffer the way the Milsenetts did. Our well source had a..." She snorted, then coughed. "Sedative to help with that."

He leaned against the bench and cradled his head in his hands. His head throbbed so heavily that it was blurring his vision. "This sounds a lot like the potatoes to po-tah-toes argument."

"Oh, Matthew." Her laughter was like a faint gust of wind. "So young, so naïve. You'll learn the truth of it all. Soon enough. I'd love to divulge, however, that's beyond my—" She sucked her teeth. "Conditions of release. I've already said too much." She appeared to shudder. The sound of a ragged, shaking exhale escaped her.

With the last effort he could muster, he practically flopped himself ungracefully upon the bench next to her. "Usually, my hallucinations are happy or sad. You're my first angry hallucination," he mused.

"Who said I'm a hallucination?"

Extending his arm, he reached his hand through her middle. "See? Hallucination."

"Maybe I'm a ghost."

"An angry ghost, then."

"It's almost time," she replied, ignoring him.

"Thank the Goddess for that. I don't know how much more of pitiful Aoife I can take." He lifted a hand to rub his chest.

Aoife burst into laughter, so hard it caused her to snort. "You're all fools."

Slouching against the back of the bench, he tried to focus on her. "What are the conditions of your 'release?'"

"To tell you to restore the balance. With all of us gone, it can be done."

He waited for her to explain more, but her jaw had tightened and her back had straightened. "Something comes."

Before he could ask what, she vanished.

Unlike the other hallucinations, where he came back to a foggy awareness, he still sat on the bench, his chest now heaving as he tried to breathe. Head pounding, and slight shaking in his hands.

Maybe Aoife hadn't been a hallucination. Perhaps she had been an apparition telling him his time was up. He folded himself over his legs, lifting his hands to press them to his ears, trying to block out the roaring sound building around him.

It was then that he heard it, just moments before covering his ears. A soft tapping sound at the core of the roaring he heard. Movement across asphalt.

Aoife had been right, something was coming.

CHAPTER 60

Caid walked into the kitchen, heading straight to the refrigerator for water colder than he'd get from the tap. He'd been spending his weeks swinging ancient weaponry, ducking and dodging incoming blows while he trained with Brent, so to feel so sweat slicked, sore, and thirsty after just one day back on a job site, had been surprising.

It also felt good. It was familiar, and it had settled something inside of him. Róisín was in Ely with the others until that night. Yet, despite the distance, he hadn't felt that same incessant prodding of panic and worry that he had before. She had her power back, everyone was working together again, the last piece of whatever puzzle this was he sat before, it had been picking a hammer back up.

If he could just remedy the rest of it, working out what the Goddess's intentions were. Or, if maybe it were Sister Future behind it all. Maybe it wasn't any of them, but someone else...

He rubbed a hand over his face and pulled open the refrigerator. He had just reached for a bottle of water when he saw the figure sitting on the back patio. Cautiously, he moved toward the door, unscrewing the cap to the bottle. His magic automatically began to rise and move through him.

"Stand down, son." Lucius didn't take his attention away from the tree line. "It's just me."

Caid noted the four empty beer bottles on the small table next to him. Things couldn't be good if *Lucius* was drinking.

Lucius waved his hand, motioning for him to join him. "It's not usually like this. Our life. This chaotic spiraling that it currently is. It'll pass."

Caid eased himself into the chair next to him. "You good, Lucius?"

His gaze followed Caid's to the bottles and chuckled softly. "It takes far more than that to get me tossed, son. Far more. No." He shook his head, the corners of his mouth turning down. "This"—he waved his hand before his face—"is what happens when you have one kid facing a demon that will not die, and another trapped in a realm where the only way out is for the spilling of another's blood over the well source."

Caid shot forward in his chair, coughing out his mouthful of water all over the patio stones before him and himself. He wiped the back of his hand over his mouth and pulled the fabric of his now wet shirt away from his chest. "What?"

"They learned Frederick did indeed go to Aunellion after it had been locked away from us. There's always a way, just as I told Róisín when she came to me asking if it were possible Madigan had been able to get there to draw more power to his magic. There's always a way."

Slowly, as if on its own accord, Caid's body fell back into his chair. "How?"

"It works as an exchange. Two people go, one leaves."

He said it so casually that it took a few extra seconds to process in Caid's mind. "And this was figured out how?" He needn't worry about panic. His magic did it for him, quickly tugging on his tether with Róisín. She pulled back immediately, sending happy sparks of her magic, like sunshine glimmers, down the line.

"A letter from Jessamyn's partner, the one who translated often for Frederick, tipped us off. Ione and Ten worked double-time to figure out just how it worked."

Caid's mouth fell open, but no words came. "Are we talking a lot of blood, or? No. You said two go, one leaves. Does it *have* to come to that?"

"Unfortunately, yes. Ione could translate from one of the old founder languages just how Frederick did it. Sunlan, one of the most intelligent Shianshani witches I've ever had the pleasure of meeting, was the one that learned of the way." He snorted. "It was all right there, in the Alleyette archives."

The shudder rolled through Caid's body, unbidden, at the thought of Alleyette. "And the curse?"

"The book it is in is nearly translated. Ione isn't fluent in Founder Nulion, so she's had to take the languages it's derived from and place them together. Much like a puzzle with tiny pieces, it makes it a little more complicated."

Caid rubbed a hand over his jaw and studied Lucius. There was no need for magic of the mind to know exactly what the man was thinking, or planning. He could see it in the hard set of his eyes, the way he held his shoulders high. He swallowed before he put his voice to the question in his head. "What do we do now?"

Lucius turned to look at him. "I get my boy back where he belongs. Home."

The words froze Caid. He knew, but it hadn't changed the way they hit him.

"I know I don't need to tell you, because we've been in the shit enough lately to see how you never leave her side, but she'll need you, Kincaid. After I'm—" Lucius's breath caught. "After I'm gone. Make sure you take care of her."

"I will, sir," Caid said. There was a tightness in his throat that had him fighting a wince. An unfamiliar pain there in the way it squeezed.

"There you are," Shasta said, exasperated, when she appeared before them. She eyed Lucius and the bottles. "Are you drunk? After all the shit I, rightfully, caught for self-medicating, and now you...you hypocrite!"

Lucius sighed and closed his eyes. "I'm not drunk. I don't know how you all drink that garbage. It tastes like the bottom of a lake."

Shasta leaned closer to him and sniffed a few times, loudly. "Alright, I believe you. The last time I saw you drunk, it was seeping out of your pores. You smell like regular Lucius to me."

"Happy to have passed your roadside exam, Officer," Lucius

mumbled. He pinched the bridge of his nose, then tipped his head back to look at her. "You were looking for me?"

"Brenna came." Her eyes darted toward where Caid sat. Then she looked at Lucius, an unspoken question in her eyes.

"He's a part of this, Shasta," Lucius said.

She bit her bottom lip. "Alright. People are getting stuck on the other side of the veil. Ev had trouble a few weeks back, and that's why she was late. This time, she couldn't cross at all. She's not the only one either. Stephen's been doing some digging around, seeing what he can stir up, and it's most of the people he's talked to."

Lucius pushed his hands through his hair. "Shit. How long? Do we know?"

"That's the thing, it so far, unless they're able to find out otherwise, all started around the time that Aoife died," Shasta said.

Lucius's hands fell to his lap.

"Was it to keep her there?" Caid asked.

Shasta sat on a small table facing them. "No. Where Aoife was, there is no getting out. Which makes how she got out all the more peculiar."

Lucius tipped his head to one side, his face turned thoughtful for a moment before he tilted his head enough to look over at Caid. "What are the odds Aoife said something about that to Róisín when she came?"

"That night in Roidon?" Shasta asked.

Lucius slid his eyes toward her. "This is why I've been tugging and yanking, Miss Fiero. I'm not sure where you've been that's been so—"

"Dammit, Lucius," she said.

He shook his head. "This is all hands on deck. You're not the only one with things going on, or the only one to have gone through shit, Shasta. There is not one of us right now that is in the best head *or* heart-space at the present time. But we have to fucking deal with it, because life goes on."

Caid felt himself sinking deeper and deeper into the chair, wondering if he could convince his magic to let the wood absorb him as it had been in his nightmare nights before.

"You haven't a clue what in the Hells you're talking about." Shasta spat the words as she spoke them.

Lucius lurched to his feet, the muscles of his jaw rippling as he stared down at Shasta.

Parents fighting, Caid realized. This had to be what it felt like to be in the room when parents were arguing over something, anything. As much as he'd wished for family in his life, *this* was the part he would wish away.

"I do. You lost Evelyn in one of the great wars of Earth, then you lost Brenna. The one thing you had left that brought you comfort and security, your home, locked you in. But guess what? Evelyn, until recently, has been able to cross the veil regularly. You are now able to see Brenna again. The house can be rebuilt, new, better. Cut"—he lifted his hand—"the"—his index finger jabbed toward her—"shit."

Caid sucked in a breath, pressing his lips together in fear of the noise the whoosh would make if he let it out. He couldn't recall hearing Lucius curse, ever. Once, at most? Maybe twice? Caid shook the thought from his head so he could focus on him and Shasta.

"How *dare* you." Shasta lifted her voice higher and was shouting.

Lucius scoffed and shook his head. "How dare I? How dare I *what*, Shasta? How dare I be the one here with everyone while we work to break this curse? How dare I be the one that's here for Róisín to bring her worries, her fears to? The one she comes to when her power has faltered and she doesn't know what to do? Or how dare I stay awake all night long, worrying about my son, and that no sooner than I will get him back, I have to say goodbye to him?"

"What—" Shasta blinked. "What are you talking about?"

Lucius only shook his head. "You weren't here. With *us*."

Shasta looked at Caid, who didn't dare to utter a word. "This isn't fair."

"*Life* isn't fair, Shasta. You need to realize that. Because if you don't, you'll open your eyes one day, and you'll find yourself alone. There's only so many times you can be absent in times of need before people turn their backs. Or worse, it's too late because they're gone." The silence that fell over them was defeating. Lucius's voice was broken, cracking when he spoke next. "She needed you, Shasta. We both did."

Shasta's eyes shone with the tears that had built there.

Oh, shit, Caid couldn't stop his body from flinching as though he'd been hit. Shasta hadn't been there when Clarissa had been sick, or it was that she hadn't been there in her last days. This was a decades-long lid-blower unfolding before him.

"The only difference between then, and now," he began softly, his shoulders loosening slightly, "is that there's still time. It's not too late with Róisín. Or Matthew."

"What about you?" she asked.

"It's already too late for me, Shasta. And you missed that, too." He turned to Caid. "Back to the topic at hand, Aoife?"

Caid quickly sat up straight, scrambling to gather his thoughts and the quick change in the subject. "No, no, she didn't. Shit, but there was something from before."

"Before?" Lucius released a small groan and rolled his eyes skyward. "You two. First her magic, then yours. Now?"

Caid kept his attention on Lucius, unable to, *afraid* to look at Shasta and see her expression. "Róisín said that David told her it was Future that had sent him to watch over her, that he was a charge of Future, and not the Goddess."

"The Sisters are known to often use animals as a more clear vision to help them read fate, and adjust as needed." He made a snipping motion with his fingers, making Caid's stomach drop like a brick to his feet.

"Future was also the one to come to Brenna," Shasta said.

"Both times she was visited?" Lucius asked.

"I... She only said who came that first time." Shasta frowned, looking down at her feet.

"When she came to Róisín and I, she said it was Future both times. Future was the one that told her that the Goddess had wanted to bring Róisín to the darkness after Madigan. The fear of the whole power being too much and Róisín turning bad thing." Caid's tone was light, but the anger inside of him was smoldering.

"And this is exactly what I mean." Lucius gave him a narrow-eyed stare. "When were you two going to mention *this*? This is why she's been hovering in my study with Jessamyn and I as late instead of with the others in the library, isn't it?"

Caid rubbed the back of his neck, feeling his face flame. "Probably? She's more of the mind that the Goddess still wants her in the darkness.

That what Brenna did wasn't enough, and that Róisín is the one that has been given these things to do despite the Goddess's power to end it all herself, to fail, and go to the—" He stopped, unable to say it again. He swallowed hard. "What if this entire thing is not the Goddess? What if it's Future?"

Lucius's laughter was quiet at first. As it built, his body shook with it. Caid and Shasta exchanged an uneasy look with one another. Slightly bent over, Lucius brought an arm over his stomach. "No. Son. Unfortunately, you're wrong. It's not Future," he said between his breaths of roaring laughter. "It's *always* Gea."

Gea? Who the fuck was Gea?

CHAPTER 61

Róisín moved from room to room of the cottage, calling out to Caid. When she hadn't gotten a response, she tugged down their line, receiving distracted pulls back. He was there, but where? Why couldn't he just call out to her? Frustrated, she stomped toward the front door and threw it open.

There, on the far side of the yard, the upper half of his body was folded over the fender of a—

She squinted, watching for a moment. What *was* that? A Jeep?

As if he felt her eyes on him, he righted himself, knocking his head on the propped hood. Cursing, he rubbed furiously at the spot he hit and turned around.

"Where in the Hells did that come from?" she asked.

He looked down at the Jeep, wiping his hands on a rag. "The neighbor."

Her eyebrows raced up her forehead. "Caid, our closest neighbor is a good ten kilometers away."

"I was really bored." He shoved the rag into his back pocket and made his way toward her. "You're all off saving the realms, and I was, well, you know."

"Does it run?" She eyed it curiously.

"Was a little touch and go at first. He held his arms out, looking down at the stains on his clothes. "But as you can see from my stately appearance, I gave it a tune-up."

"Parts?" She lifted a brow. "How long has this been out here? How have I not noticed it until now?"

"It's been a few weeks, and—" Caid scratched at his jaw, flashing her a boyish grin. "That, uh, blinky thing is pretty fucking handy."

"We call it shifting." She swallowed, fighting down the chuckle that had wanted to escape.

"So Shasta says. Blinking"—he lifted a hand—"shifting"—he lifted his other. "All the same."

Róisín only stared back at him, unable to speak or even blink as she processed the scene before her. Had she been so deep in trying to figure the Covens out she had not only become physically separated from everyone, so separated from *him*, but had become separated in other ways? And Caid, when he had been abruptly thrown into all of this...

She tried to keep her steps steady, slow, as she walked down the steps and toward him. She wanted to race to him, throw herself at him, and beg forgiveness.

The instant his arms came around her, her body nearly melted against him. Pressing her face against the middle of his chest, she drew in the smell of him, let it surround her. Let it ground her. "I'm sorry."

"For?"

"Anything and everything. All of it."

His big hands rubbed over her back, up and down, then in circles. "It's not like you made all of this happen, Róisín."

"I know. But you're only here because of me. In this massive, awful mess, because of me. So yes, I'm sorry." She clung tighter to him, buried her face deeper. His chuckle was a rumble against her nose, eyes, and mouth. She pulled back and eyed him. "What?"

"Nothing."

She shook her head and pulled from his embrace. "No." She drew the word out. "It's something."

Caid lifted his shoulder briefly, then dropped it. "Just thinking of all the times I've wanted to tell *you* that *I'm* sorry."

"For what?" She winced at the way her voice cracked, then pitched high.

"All the times I've been shit at this and couldn't help you. I don't know all of these languages." He flung an arm out, shaking his head. "And I know fuck all about history. I did well in school and was honors society and all, but I've spent the last almost twenty-three years of my adult life swinging a hammer, crunching numbers. It's really fucking Goddamn easy to forget."

Róisín took a step toward him but stopped.

"I'm the fixer, Róisín. I'm the one that makes everything better, makes it right. Everything with you, it..." The arm that was still extended fell to his side, slapping against his thigh.

"Caid," she said softly, going to him again. "I don't need all of that from you, and I don't want that. That's *never* what I wanted."

"But—"

"No." She pressed a finger to his lips. "You said yours, now I say mine." She lifted to her toes and brushed a kiss across his lips. "I was an unmoored ship, drifting. I didn't care about my future, because I never thought about it. Yes, I had Lucius." Her heart gave a sharp thump in her chest. "And Matthew. Clarissa for a time, and before, I had my mother, father, and Shasta. Evelyn too, even if I don't quite remember her still. Nothing ever anchored me. Nothing ever pushed the clouds away so that I could see the sun, see the hope."

Her thumbs stroked over his cheeks, and she smiled at him. "I didn't care about what happened with Madigan before, because I couldn't see past him and that moment. I had no future. Until you. You fixed my ship's anchor and cleared my skies. I've never wanted anything more than you as you are. I don't care about all the rest. And this?" She tipped her head toward the cottage where they were all to meet, one last time before Lucius... Tears stung the back of her eyes. "Bumps in the road to get there. You take the wheel on the things *I* can't do. I'll take the wheel when it's something I can, and you can't."

He dropped his forehead to hers. "Together."

"Always." She pulled him closer, running her hands through his hair. "I love you."

"I love you." He crushed her to his chest, holding her tightly. "Wanna take a spin? We can go top down."

Her laugh was watery and shook their bodies. "Caid, it doesn't *have* a top."

Releasing her, Caid held out his hand to her, waving his fingers to motion her closer. "It's not like it's raining, and I can always get one later." He went to the passenger side first, opening her door. "My lady." He tipped at the waist in a mock bow. "Your chariot."

With a giggle, Róisín hoisted herself in, immediately groaning. "This seat is like a wood block."

"I shall add that to my blinky grocery list." He rounded the hood to the driver's side. "Did you get the photos Lina sent? Those black and white streaked things?"

Her laugh this time was more of a snort. Shaking her head, she faced him. "Those are ultrasound photos."

"Ultra-what? Are the babies going to be Superman's enemies?"

"No." She playfully pushed his shoulder.

His gaze turned thoughtful as he started the engine. "So there were babies in those photos?"

"You didn't see the *hands*?"

He placed his hand on the back of her seat, looking over his shoulder as he reversed. "Uh, maybe?" He drummed his fingers on the seat as he maneuvered the Jeep around. Then he confessed, "No. No, I didn't."

"Oh, Kincaid James McGrath." She sighed, putting her hand on his thigh.

The Jeep came to an abrupt stop, sending her body rocking against the seat. His pupils had grown wide when he looked at her. "Say that again."

"Kincaid..." She stroked a finger along his thigh. "James." Her hand moved to the inside of his leg. "McGrath." Her hand inched upward and stomach tightened at the sound of his sharp intake of breath and the flutter of his magic down their tether.

"Fuck." He shoved the shifter into neutral and set the park brake. "Raincheck on the ride of the four-wheel kind. Come here." He reached for her.

Without hesitation, she swung herself over him. "We don't have long before everyone is here."

"Then stop talking." He palmed one of her breasts. "So we can get busy." He brought his other hand to the back of her head to pull her mouth to his, cutting off her giggles.

Róisín's skin tightened and heat built in her core in that euphoric way it always did at his touch. When his teeth grazed along her neck, she released a soft sigh. His fingers dug into her hips, pulling her closer to him. She rocked gently, satisfaction filling her at the sound of the groan rumbling from his chest.

Fumbling with the lever on the side of the seat, Caid used his legs to shove it away from the steering wheel so that they had more room. Róisín reached for the hem of her shirt, pausing when she saw his eyes on them, watching, waiting.

"You're killing me, Róisín." His voice hoarse, he reached for her shirt. She closed a hand over his, stopping him. After a moment, feeling that wave of heat mixed with impatience rush down their tether, she flashed him a grin, then yanked the shirt over her head. He grabbed it from her and tossed it into the passenger seat.

"Jesus," he whispered before leaning forward to close his mouth over one of her breasts.

The feel of his tongue on her nipple through the fabric of her bra sent a jolt of ecstasy through her, and she instinctively moved her hips.

"Caid." She rolled her hips more frantically. Her head dropped to his shoulder. "Can I take your pants off now?" she asked against his neck, causing him to laugh.

"You do mine, I do yours?"

"Sounds like a plan." She pressed a soft kiss to the side of his neck before letting her tongue trail along toward his chin, tasting the salt on his skin. Her hands skimmed down his chest to the button of his jeans.

His head fell back against the seat and her name was a plea from his lips, fueling the fire already raging inside of her. "Do you know"—her fingers found their way under the waistband of his boxers—"I've never done this in a car?"

He brought his head up and cracked an eye open. "Are you serious? Aren't you like a hundred years old? Not even a Model T?"

She flashed him her most mischievous grin before moving away from him to lower herself to the floorboard. "No planes, trains, or automobiles."

Before he could make a remark, she was gripping his jeans and boxers with both hands, telling him to lift his hips so that she could pull them down.

When she took him in her mouth, he let out a shout that echoed through the air. He gripped the back of her head, meeting her rhythm with his hips. One of her hands followed her mouth as she hollowed her cheeks, drawing to his tip and back, her tongue circling him while her hand squeezed and stroked.

"I'm gonna come, Róisín," he rasped.

She let the tip of her tongue trace along the seam at the head of his cock, then lifted her head. "And?"

"Get up here," he said, "take your pants off."

Something about the demand, his tone, had her stomach rippling and her walls clenching tighter.

There was no hesitation as she wriggled free of her pants. His hands were at her panties, snapping the fabric on the sides. He brought one hand between her legs, his fingers stroking her, while the other shucked her panties out of the Jeep.

"Some animal may eat those."

"Not my problem right now." He rested a hand at her hip, fingers flexing into her soft skin as she lowered onto him. His thumb drew circles and danced over her clit.

"Caid." Her body began to tumble toward orgasm.

Caid lifted her off him slightly, then as he brought her back down, he drove his hips up, thrusting himself into her. She cried out his name, her fingers gripping his shoulders. He reared up into her again, setting a brutal pace that had them both panting with each slap of their bodies as they joined.

"Caid, I'm going to..." She whimpered. Everything inside of her grew tight, squeezing him, while her skin ignited from head to toe. A weightlessness carrying her away, over the edge.

Róisín angled back slightly, just as he reached for the second lever on the side of the seat, bringing the back of the seat flat. The angle they created was just enough.

Release exploded inside of her, making her scream his name. Her body rocked frantically, wringing out every bit of the orgasm it could. Her knees squeezed his sides, and her body exploded with a flood of sensations.

"Róisín." Her name was hoarse from his lips as he pumped his own release into her.

With a sigh, she slumped over him, nestling against his sweat slicked chest. "I can't believe I waited one hundred years for that."

He brought his arms around her, laughter filling him. "I take that as you requesting a repeat performance?"

"That, sir," she began, propping herself up on his chest with one arm. "Is a request for many repeat performances."

He brushed his knuckles over her cheek. "You've got a deal."

The walls that she had carefully constructed that morning to block out the reality of that day arriving, regardless of how much she had willed it to stop, suddenly tipped toward her. Before she could gather herself, stop them, they tumbled.

"Hey." Caid pushed the hair from her face. "Hey." His tone was soothing as he brought her against him. "What is it? What's wrong?"

"I—" She couldn't stop the sob from coming. Or the next, and the next. She curled against him, the breeze drifting over her bare back.

Their bodies jostled as he fumbled with the seat levers, sitting them upright, and again as he scrambled for their shirts. "Ah, fuck it." He cursed and shifted them both into their bedroom. He pulled her over his lap and yanked a blanket over her, tucking it around her shoulders.

"I can't, I can't lose him, Caid." She said around her cries. "I lost one father. I can't lose another. How do I stop it? How do I make it all stop?" She felt his body shudder and quake against hers. Placing a hand on his chest, feeling his heart thunder against her palm, she looked up to see the tears streaming down his face.

"I wish I knew, Róisín, I wish I knew," he managed.

CHAPTER 62

MATTHEW GROUND his molars together, struggling to pull himself forward. He had sat on the bench for only a mere moment after the ghostly apparition of Aoife had faded and his mind had cleared. It was ungraceful, and even if he had an audience, he wouldn't have cared. The sounds of footsteps nearing had driven him to his rolling, slumping dismount, and subsequent crash to the ground in his attempt to flee.

However, the footsteps followed him. Now, shining black loafers appeared in his blurred line of sight. He couldn't muster any remaining energy before firm hands gripped his arms and pulled him to his feet.

"Up we go, son."

Matthew's heart stopped, his legs buckling. Unlike with Aoife in her non-corporeal state, these hands were very real, not a hallucination.

"Come on, let's get you over to this bench."

For just a moment, Matthew leaned into the touch and its warmth, letting it surge through his tired body and ground him. Then pulled away so quickly, he stumbled, nearly falling.

"I'm here, Matthew." Lucius caught him. "This is real. This isn't the fog."s

Matthew licked his dry, cracked lips. "Dad?" he croaked.

"I've got you." Lucius brought his arm around his shoulders, tucking him against his side.

"But how?"

"A team effort, you could say. I wish we had found a way sooner."

"I can't..." Matthew was breathless, dropping heavily on the bench. "Madigan? Lily? What happened?" He grew dizzy as the words rushed from him. "Róisín?"

"You'll be brought up to speed soon enough," Lucius said. "Right now—" He reached into the pocket of his suit jacket and pulled out a small pouch. "You need to take this."

Matthew eyed the pouch suspiciously.

"Lily and Ione put it together. It will help with the fact it's been two months without food."

"Ione?" Matthew's hands shook as he grasped the pouch.

"She and Lily have been staying at the manor. Ione has been helping us to get you back home."

"Nanette? Shasta?"

"Nanette is dealing with some things with her Coven. Shasta has..." He cleared his throat. "She's been around helping as she can. Working mostly with Caid on his skills."

"And Róisín?" He took a pinch of the contents of the pouch and brought them to his nose, hissing at the rancid smell of them.

"She's well," was all Lucius said.

Matthew fought the urge to gag as he chewed and swallowed the first pinch, going for a second once he swallowed it down. Immediately, his magic warmed his body. His skin, having grown used to the cold as his magic had become mere scraps in his days there, broke out into a sweat.

Lucius lowered to the bench next to him and squinted into the fog around them. "It's taken over."

"What do you mean?" he asked, getting a third pinch down.

"This is far beyond the castle." Lucius lifted a hand, his finger pointing in one direction. "We're in the city square. The clock tower and fountain are just there." He moved his hand just to the left of them.

"You've been here." The realization shouldn't have been a shock to

Matthew. Between Lucius's age, and the time he's spent at the head of the Council, clearly he had been to Aunellion before.

"Many times." His eyes took on a distant look briefly before clearing. "You forget, it wasn't long ago that this"—he gestured to their surroundings—"happened."

The fatigue that had settled into Matthew's muscles had faded, and his eyes no longer burned. His blurry sight was sharpening.

Lucius's mouth pressed into a thin line. "How are you feeling?"

Matthew studied him for a moment. Something in the tight way that Lucius held his body, and the way the lines at the corners of his eyes and around his mouth seemed deeper, more pronounced. Movement behind Lucius drew his attention. "Uh, dad?"

Lucius shifted to look at him. "What?"

"I've been in this shit hole for Goddess knows how long, two months or whatever." He pointed over Lucius's shoulder. "I can't say I've ever seen the fog take the shape of a soldier before."

Spinning to look, Lucius cursed under his breath.

"I take it that means that it's *not* a hallucination," Matthew said.

"No, son. This is a divine intervention to our own intervention."

"Excuse me?" He watched as Lucius rose and undid the buttons on his jacket, then set it on the back of the bench with care. "Care to explain?"

Lucius looked down at him, and suddenly all Matthew could see painted on his face was deep sorrow. "How are you feeling?"

"*Why*? Dammit, dad, what the Hells is going on?" Matthew shot to his feet, the rising anger and frustration inside of him not allowing him the room for him to marvel at easily it felt to move again.

Rolling the sleeves to his shirt, Lucius turned to him. "I'm not to return to the other realms, Matthew. It was the sacrifice that had to be made to get you back."

Matthew sucked in a breath so sharp, his lungs smarted from the sensation of a million needles piercing them. Lucius held up a hand to stop him from speaking, shaking his head.

"It was an easy choice, Matthew. One I did not hesitate to make. I did have to fight Róisín. She was ready. But you both are young, your lives ahead of you after all of this... This shit is taken care of. Any parent would do the same for their children."

"There has to be another way we can do this." An urgency in Matthew took the place of the anger and frustration he felt only moments before. He was not standing here, saying goodbye, forever, to his father.

"We've looked, Matthew. Time was running out. This is it. This is what we have."

"No," he replied firmly.

Lucius turned back to the fog, squaring his shoulders. "It's time you know the truth."

Matthew's attention was split between the growing numbers of soldiers approaching them and the cryptic words Lucius was saying. The way his face had hardened as he said them. He had thought he had seen Lucius angry before. He realized at that moment it was nothing compared to the rage that settled over his face, tightening his lips, darkening his eyes.

The ground rumbled beneath their feet, and Lucius's face shifted to something else, something more pain than rage. "I'm your father, Matthew."

"As I've said before, you're my father in all the ways that count." He stepped up beside Lucius. "All the ways that matter."

"We won't have time for it all." He placed a hand on his shoulder, meeting his eyes. "You'll find all of it in my office. The false drawer in the back of the blue cabinet. But this much I can tell you now." He gave his shoulder a firm squeeze.

"Dad?"

"Your mother and I met and came together as the fall of Aunellion was approaching. Her family was trying to flee to a safer place, and I was taking refugees in Ely. Giving them shelter, and helping them settle either there, or elsewhere that proved to be safer for them. Clarissa quickly became an incredible asset to the cause with her compassion and intelligence. It isn't surprising that we had become more than united by the cause as we spent more time together."

"What..." Matthew's breaths came faster.

"She stayed for almost seventy-five years, but her family, they still weren't safe. They had to make a choice, and they made the one that any would have. They fled to the farthest realm they could. Clarissa went with them briefly. But she, of course, didn't stay away long. Just a few months." His features softened and his eyes lit up. "She was pregnant with you when she returned."

"You're—" Matthew covered his mouth with a hand. "You're really my father. You're actually, *truly*, my dad."

"I am. We should have told you sooner. We should have never let others say what they did, but..." The dark shadows filled Lucius's face again. "You'll understand once you look."

Matthew went to sit again, but turned in a circle instead, trying to catch his breath and slow his heart that was now racing with each breath. "We need more time. This can't be it."

Lucius's face twisted, and his eyes filled. "I'd hoped we had more time, you and I. I'd wanted to be the one to tell you everything. To be there for you after you learned it all. Face what's next together. Unfortunately, the scissors are in hand, and Present and Future have decided."

"I hate this." He drove his hands into his hair and tipped his head back. "I hate this!" he shouted into the sky. Emotion clogged his throat when he looked back at Lucius. He would not be reconnected with his father, blood or not, just to be torn away again. He wasn't. But he didn't know what he could do. How could he fight the Sisters? How could he fight the hand that they had been dealt?

The sound of clanking armor neared, and Lucius's body coiled, ready for action.

Lucius's voice was rough when he spoke, "Just remember, even after, I love you, Matthew. If I had to do it over again, I would do it the same, every time. For you."

Matthew struggled to find his voice. He tried swallowing the thickness down first, then clearing it. Time was running out; the soldiers were almost upon them. Near enough now, he could make out their faces. Their skeletal faces with gaping eye sockets. The way their armor glinted despite the lack of sunlight there.

He drew in a ragged breath, then pushed out the broken words. "I love you, Dad. No matter what, I will always love you."

Then the melee began.

Chapter 63

"And?"

The one word cut through Future's skin, rattling her bones. She swallowed down the shriek that wanted to explode past her lips. Turning, she faced the hooded figure.

"What are you doing here?" Future hissed the words, her belly tightening into a knot. Her sisters had already retired to their rooms, and thankfully, their mother hadn't graced them with their presence that day. Yet. There were still three hours left before the new day began.

"Consider me impatient at this point." The figure lifted a milk-white hand and reached their fingers toward Future's loom. Their long, slim fingers with cracked skin almost brushed the threads before they were jerked back and tucked into the folds of the cloak. "Time is running out."

Future lifted a hand to her chest. "What? No. We need more time."

"We cannot risk them being apart again. There is too much at stake. They are the strongest together. She *will* scatter them again."

Future bit her lip, tasting the bitter copper tang against her tongue. "But Aoife—"

"Are you sure? You were so sure last time. Look what happened."

Sighing, Future turned back to the loom. She felt the figure step up next to her. There was no warmth in their presence. The room seemed nearly frigid, and darker somehow.

"Aoife reconsidered. She has followed through." Future's heart squeezed tight, her vision blurring at the memory of what she had to do in Aoife's cell.

The hood moved as the figure turned their head. She could feel eyes burning on her, into her. "You better hope that it will be enough."

Then Future was alone in the small living room of the cottage. Heat quickly filled the room, leaving her lightheaded and overwhelmed by it. She dropped onto her seat and covered her face with her hands, trying to steady her breaths.

Would it be enough? Would any of what she had done be enough?

She had risked everything. Had betrayed her sisters. Their mother. She had shown her true face and used the darkest part of her magic for her own purpose.

It had to be enough.

CHAPTER 64

Róisín shuffled her way into the kitchen, rubbing at her puffy, bleary eyes. They had stayed at the cottage for a day after Matthew's return before Róisín had wanted to give him and Lily space and privacy. She closed the keys in Lily's hand, telling her to take the time they needed there. It was theirs for always if they wanted it.

Matthew had appeared in the hallway just outside of the living room at the cottage, hours after Lucius had left. His body, thin and marked with fresh wounds from what looked to be a vicious battle, crumpled to the floor immediately.

Then his shouts for Lucius began. A desperate, frantic plea that shattered her heart more and more each time his voice cracked his name out. They echoed in her mind still.

Caid had brought Matthew to the room Róisín had set up for him, trying to create it to be a space that he had once had at the cottage when they were younger so that he would have some semblance of comfort when he woke again.

Then they had waited.

Shasta paced and made herbal blends with Lily to put on his wounds to stave off infection, while his magic worked through his worn and broken body to heal it.

Lily stayed vigilantly by his side, never straying far.

Ione gave them an update on the translation progress and to check in, but Lily quickly shooed her away.

Then Shasta left for Ely to help where she could. And exhausted, Róisín asked Caid to take her home.

An arm snaked around her waist, pulling her back from the refrigerator and making her yelp in surprise. When she hit the hard wall of Caid's body, her hammering heart eased.

"You good?" he asked against her throat.

"I managed a few hours, finally." She leaned into him and closed her eyes, drawing on his strength for support. "You?"

He spun her to face him. "I'll get by."

She tipped a brow up. "You'll get by? What kind of answer is that?"

"The one you're getting right now." He brushed his nose against hers then kissed her lightly. "Will you be okay here for a few hours? We've got a load of lumber coming to the site this morning that I'll need to sign for."

For just a moment, standing in her kitchen with him talking about going to work made it easy to brush aside everything else. To pretend that nothing had changed and it was just as it had been before for them.

"I'll be okay. If I remember right, Lina said she would be by on Monday so I could help her finish the registry for the party in a few months. And it's..." She peered around him at the wall calendar he had hung to help him keep track of the time on Earth as he adjusted to the various speed time passed on the other realms. "Actually Monday."

"If you need me..." He gave their line a gentle tug.

In response, she gave a harder, firm tug that had his body jerking a step closer to her.

"Maybe not that hard. I'll be with Wyatt." He bent his head and took her mouth with his. She sunk into the kiss, taking his bottom lip between her teeth, making him groan. His mouth chased after hers when she broke then kiss. "I could be a few minutes late, I suppose."

She laughed and stepped away from him. "No. Your sister's coming and after last time..."

"I'm gonna tell Wyatt," he said abruptly. His hazel eyes melted into a swirling, storming sea of color as his magic rose.

Róisín lifted a hand to his cheek. "Are you sure?"

"It's only right he knows. I'm pretty sure he'll be fine about it, but if he's not—" He swallowed audibly.

"We'll figure it out if that happens. I don't think you need to worry about it with him. You two are practically family."

He nodded, his jaw ticking and nostrils flaring.

"It'll be okay," she whispered. "Navigating it has its hard moments, but it'll always be okay. Because you have me."

A corner of his mouth lifted. "You and me against the realms, right?"

"That's the idea of it." She rose to her toes to give him another kiss. "Now go." She gave him a light shove. "Before I rip your clothes off and we give this kitchen table another run for its money."

"You say that like it's a bad thing," he said as he walked backward toward the front door.

The door opened before he reached it and Lina came inside. "What's a bad thing?"

Caid winked at Róisín.

"Being back here and dealing with someone who doesn't under-stand manners," Caid said to Lina. "*Knock* for fuck's sake."

"You two are decent," Lina said, before adding under her breath, "This time."

He rolled his eyes and yanked the door open wider. "I'll be home around three," he called.

"Where's he going?" Lina asked after the screen door slammed shut.

"He's gone back to work now that we're here again."

"Oh? So, these aren't just visits?" Lina bit her bottom lip.

"No. Ireland was my home for a long time, and being back there, it does something to my heart, yes." She looked around the kitchen, taking in everything. "This is my home now. This settles inside of me in a way that Ireland doesn't anymore."

Lina danced in place, clapping her hands for a second before rushing Róisín and throwing her arms around her. "Thank God! I thought I was going to have to resort to begging. And I mean begging Shasta to show me a way to make some herbal spell to put on you two to get you to come back."

Róisín laughed into her friend's hair, squeezing her tightly.

"I mean, you two can go wherever and do whatever. But having you in particular here it's"—she sniffed—"it's the best."

It was the best, and Róisín could admit that. Her friendship with Lina had opened a door within her, showing her a world that she hadn't known could exist. Before, Matthew had been the only friend she'd had. The only connection beyond surface level she'd had. And never had she been able to show her true self to a human until Lina.

She was sure that what had grown between them had helped her with getting the seeds planted for a friendship between her and Lily.

Friends. Róisín had *friends*.

The idea both warmed her and left her feeling suddenly heavy as she thought of Matthew in Ireland with Lily.

"Alright." Lina nudged Róisín toward the table. "You sit down and I'll scrounge up something to make you." She glanced at the clock. "A late breakfast. Nuh-uh." She pointed at Róisín. "You look like you just rolled out of bed, and not because my horny brother couldn't keep his hands off you. Something's unwell; your spirit, soul, heart. Let me take care of you, get my mom practice in. You can tell me if you want, otherwise, we'll sit here and try to figure out why the three different cribs I picked for the babies are so drastically different in price when they look to be the same thing."

Róisín could only smile at her and concede. "He really is horny, isn't he?" Róisín said quietly, settling back into the chair, then quickly doubled over, laying across her legs, holding her stomach with how hard the fit of giggles hit her.

"Oh, no! No, no, don't make me laugh that hard. I'll pee myself! I can't—" Lina gripped the counter with one hand and her stomach in the other. "Ah! Why'd you do that to me?"

Róisín dabbed at her damp eyes, body still shaking with laughter. "I'm so sorry, Lina. I couldn't help it." She coughed. "It just came out. My head, it's not in a good place right now. I just lost someone who was like a father to me and—" She let out a painful breath.

"Shit." Lina sobered. She stared at Róisín, unblinking, for a long moment. "You know, he's only been like that for you. Caid, I mean. Not even back when he used to sneak out there." She inclined her head toward the backyard and the woods.

"The day I told him who I was, what I was, the trees told me he kissed a girl out there," Róisín said. The jealousy that crept along her skin, seeking entry into her heart that day, was absent now.

"Carrie Longwood probably. She was a year older and got it in her head that Caid would be an *excellent* way to make her quarterback boyfriend jealous." She made a face of disgust. "I'm so happy it back-fired on her."

"She used him?"

"Oh, Caid totally knew." Lina waved a hand and rolled her eyes. "He was kind of interested in her. He was the same then as he is now, but he's always had his limits. She told him at lunch one day to meet her, and he sent the quarterback in his place. To which, the quarterback called it off for good. Said they weren't getting back together after her stunt. He and Caid became pretty good friends after."

Something about hearing about Caid's youth settled her some. Her breathing had leveled and the throb that had begun in her head had calmed.

"He's always been more worried about taking care of me than anything for himself, though," Lina said softly. "Until you. He was such a goner for you the moment he laid eyes on you in the gym." She grinned. "But! Remember, you were mine first."

"I'll always be yours, Lina." And Róisín meant it.

"Alright. Enough sappy, sappy, and really, please *don't* make me laugh anymore. Two babies on the bladder is brutal. Let's see if you've got the goods to make a fall soup. That's perfect for a day like this."

CHAPTER 65

L ILY GREW more unsure with each passing day that her heart would ever be the same. Matthew's clothing in tatters when he'd arrived at the cottage. His body bleeding and broken. His rough screams and shouts for Lucius echoed through her mind, following her into her dreams at night.

New pain bloomed right there at the center of her chest with each beat of the organ every time she gently cleaned the wounds that littered his body, praying quietly to the Goddess to please still her hands so they shook less and didn't hurt him.

Was she still praying to the Goddess? She paused her movements. The blood-stained rag she was wringing in her hands hovered over the bowl of red tinged water.

Was she giving her hopes, her devotion, to a being so powerful that they could have ended this long ago, but chose not to? Instead, let people suffer. What was this all accomplishing? What was the realm shattering revelation this was to bring?

Matthew's low moan of pain drew her back to the room.

Lucius would have the answers. He would have the reasonings, the rationales to make this all make sense.

But he was gone. And he wasn't coming back.

She pressed a damp hand to her chest, pushing harder and harder. Her heart slammed against her palm in protest as though it were shouting at her, *"Just let me hurt. Let it hurt."*

A familiar tug came down her Coven line and her pain shifted into anger. A red, hot thing that burned her veins. Her grandmother.

Instinct had her wanting to tug back, to reach through the line and connect with her to see what it was she needed. But she struggled against it, focusing back on her task of cleaning the remnants of the gash on one of Matthew's forearms.

His body was healing slower than it typically did with witches, and at first, it had caused her to worry. It had been Shasta and Róisín that had soothed her worries, reminding her about what he had most likely endured in Aunellion. How he would get stronger. He was healing, and that was what mattered.

"Lily," Ione whispered from the doorway of the room.

She turned to her sister, drawing her brows together. "What are you doing here? You're supposed to be in Ely with Shasta and the others."

"I wanted to check in on you. See how you were doing. With Matthew." She glanced at his prone form, then back to her. "And I wanted to ask you something."

"She reached out to you too, didn't she?"

Ione nodded.

"Give me a second to finish cleaning this one. I'll meet you in the kitchen."

With a quiet click, Lily was alone with Matthew again. She frowned as his face shifted, his features tightening, brows pinching, and his mouth set into a grimace. She had used a mix of herbs and flowers in the water to help aid the pain, but she knew there was a pain that she couldn't soothe. With spell work or her magic.

Standing, she leaned over the bed and brushed a lock of his red hair from his face. She nearly pressed a kiss to his cheek but hesitated. How things were the night they had been separated, and how things were between them now, despite their bond, could be different. She could wait until he was awake, until they could talk. Until she could know that he still hoped for them the same as she had.

Ione was in the kitchen poking the buttons of Caid's beloved coffee maker when Lily entered.

"How in the Hells do you turn this thing on? I've been dying for a cup of that delicious creamy stuff Róisín made the last time I was here."

Lily rolled her eyes and walked over to the machine and tapped the button marked Brew with a little added flare. "Maybe you need to get some sleep when you aren't working on the book instead of rolling around your bed sheets with Runa."

Ione's face turned tomato red. "I am not."

Lily chuckled. "You've called him babe or baby at least forty times just when I've been in earshot, Ione. You are."

Ione sighed and shifted her attention back to the coffeemaker. "I really like him, Lily. He's…"

Lily waited for her to finish, but Ione frowned instead.

"I can't go back to Roidon. Even before, but now, with Runa." She shook her head. "It's not fair to him."

"You could go to Shianshani with him," Lily said.

"Shianshani," Ione began, but was interrupted by the beeping of the machine, signaling it was finished. She pulled the cup from the tray and blinked down at it. "Now what do I do?"

Lily opened the refrigerator, taking out a sweet cream. From the cupboard, she pulled down a container of mocha flavored syrup. "Hand me that." She pointed to a small device next to the machine. She put all the ingredients in the drink, then turned the small drink mixer on. Handing the cup back to Ione, she said, "Shianshani what?"

"It's not a good place for people like us either. It's worse than Roidon, Lily. The humans and witches alike. They, oh, Hells, this is so good." She closed her eyes, reveling in the drink's taste. "I need one of these for myself."

"You have to learn how to make the drink properly too," Lily said. She waved a hand in a circular motion at Ione.

"Shit, Lily, it's depressing to talk about. Especially when I have this." She lifted the cup. When Lily only stared back at her, she sighed heavily. "They don't just shun queer people in Shianshani, Lily. They execute them. It's *illegal* to be with anyone that is not the opposite of your sex. Your born sex," she added as what seemed like an afterthought.

And then it clicked for Lily about what Ione was saying. *People like us. Your born sex.*

Runa hadn't been born male. How had she not known? She shook her head. It wasn't her business to know. It was for Runa to decide who knew and who didn't.

"Then you two stay in Ely," Lily said.

Ione gave her a soft smile. "Oh, Lily. Ely is yours, with Matthew. But don't worry, we'll find a place. I know we will."

"You really like him, don't you?"

Her eyes were bright over the top of the cup when she lifted them to Lily. "My heart is saying that I love him, Lily."

Lily took the cup from her and placed it on the counter. She wrapped her sister in her arms, holding her tightly while they rocked back and forth.

"This is really going to chap Grandmother's ass, isn't it?" Ione asked.

"What do you think she wants?"

Ione shrugged. "I haven't a clue. I can't remember the last time she reached down my Coven line, though."

"Should we be worried? When Shasta returned from seeing her, she said that grandmother told her that the council was voting on whether she should retain her status as leader, or if the Wallingsfords were to be removed from the position."

Ione leaned against the countertop and scratched the side of her head. "Think they voted her out and now she's tucked tail, looking for a place to stay?"

"They may have voted her out, but no, I don't think she'd come to us for somewhere to go. She's far too proud for that. I hate to say it, Ione, but we're going to have to talk to her again at some point."

"Key word being *some* point." Ione took the cup back up into her hands. "I'll get out of your hair so you can take care of Matthew. And I'm taking this with me."

"Róisín will want her cup back."

"If I can remember to, I'll bring it back." She lifted it in a silent cheer, then shifted away.

Lily looked around the kitchen of the cottage, trying to organize her thoughts. About what they faced with Madigan in Shianshani and that life around it all hadn't stopped. Her sister and Runa. Her grandmother. Matthew.

She wasn't alone in dealing with a multitude of things. She knew her situation wasn't unique. How were any of them supposed to breathe? How were any of them supposed to get through each day with it all? Somehow, they were doing it.

Needing something to distract her, she went back to Matthew's room and eyed the tall bookshelf in there. The books were tucked haphazardly. Some stacked, and some lined the shelves neatly. Knowing it was exactly what she needed to quiet the extra noise in her head, she walked over to it and began shuffling the books around and organizing them.

The more she worked, the more relaxed she became. A song from a dream filtered into her head and she hummed it, lining the books by height and color before her.

"How do you know that song?" Matthew's voice rasped from the bed behind her and her body froze.

CHAPTER 66

MATTHEW BLINKED up at the familiar ceiling. His eyes felt dry and gritty, just as they often did after he had spent the day rolling around on one of the beaches that his mother and Brenna dragged him and Róisín to.

Around the burning of his chest as he drew in a breath, he half expected the smell Brenna's fluffy pancakes to greet his nose. Instead, it was the smell of summer and an array of blooms from around the realms that met his senses.

The happy, fluffy memories fled in an instant, making room for the painful ones to wash over him.

Lucius.

Then he remembered what Madigan had done to Róisín's childhood home.

He was hallucinating.

He'd never gotten away from Aunellion.

His father had sacrificed himself for nothing.

Matthew's body screamed at him in protest as he pushed himself up and back as much as he could manage on the bed. From his new, slightly inclined view, he could see the differences between this room, and the one Brenna had turned into a bedroom for him all those decades ago.

"You're getting too old to sleep on the floor in a bag, Matthew. And, as much as I love and adore you—I'd much rather not have you share a bed with Róisín," Brenna said to him.

She had led him down the hall to a closed door that he had known once was Stephen's office. When she had opened the door, revealing the bed, a wardrobe, and a bookshelf with some books that she later told him his mother had brought to make it feel more comfortable, he had looked at Brenna, confused, asking if she was sure.

"You're like my own. There's no one else I'd rather have in this space. I know Stephen would agree."

To lighten the heaviness of the mood, Matthew had told her, "Of course he'd agree. What father wants his teenage daughter, sharing a bed with a twenty-year-old?"

It worked. Brenna had burst into a fit of laughter, snorting and holding her stomach.

This room was not that room. Róisín had rebuilt. Of course she had, he thought.

He *was* home. He *had* made it.

As his racing heart calmed, he heard the faint humming of a familiar song. Turning his head to the right, he saw Lily standing before a bookshelf, rearranging books.

But that song she was humming. She couldn't know that song. It had been a song that his mother had made up on a whim one night when he was a small child. There had been a wicked, thrashing storm in Cascadia one night, and it left him awake and terrified.

His mother had come in to soothe him, to sit with him, hoping to help him fall asleep. When the usual songs had failed, she had come up with a new one about a brave boy who battled the storm monsters. It became their song.

A soft melody meant to soothe and relax.

"How do you know that song?" His voice sounded foreign to his ears when he spoke. It was rough and dry. It cracked on some words, and others faded to whispers.

Lily shrieked and spun around, clutching a book to her chest. "Matthew!" She blindly shoved the book onto the shelf and raced toward the bed. "You're awake. How do you feel? Can I get you anything? Water? Something to eat? I can make—"

"Answer my question."

"What? Oh, I heard it in one of my dreams not that long ago." Her cheeks turned pink, and she cast her eyes down. "We were dancing."

When he said nothing, she lifted her eyes back to him.

"Matthew?"

"What else—" He coughed, his throat begging him to stop speaking. "What else from that dream?"

"It's foolish, really." She waved him off. The pink creeped down her neck and caused her chest to flush as well.

"I'd like to know, please."

She brought her hands together in front of her, lacing her fingers. "We were older. Our children were grown and flown, as they say. It was just a sweet moment in a dream, that's all."

No. It wasn't. But how did he tell her? How did he tell her he saw the same moment? Except for him... Maybe it wasn't, though. How much of what unfolded in his mind was hallucinations, or something else? And how could they have shared the same dream?

"It was our anniversary. We were dancing in our yard and I was humming it to you," he said.

Her hands came apart, swinging around to her sides. "We were in a kitchen in one. I think it was ours, making cupcakes for something. I was..."

"Pregnant." He learned if he kept his voice to a whisper, it hurt less to speak. "With our second. The cupcakes were for our first daughter's birthday."

"How?"

He tried again to push up further in the bed. Grimacing from the pain lancing through him, he got himself to sit against the small headboard. "I don't know. I thought I was losing my mind and they were all just hallucinations."

Had Lucius dreamed of fishing at the creek? What of the little boy that was there?

"Lily," he said her name softly. "Are you scared of me? Is that why you're standing all the way down there?"

It must have been the right words because relief washed over her, loosening her body and she came to the side of the bed, carefully lowering herself onto it.

"Do you... do you need anything? You've been asleep for a few days, and I—"

"Lily, stop." He reached for her, something lightening inside of him when she took his hand. He would work out what the shared dreams meant later. And when he was alone, he would take the time and space he needed to grieve his father. Right now, having Lily's hand in his, truly being in the present with her, was all he wanted to think about. He made to move closer to her but was halted by his still healing body.

"You're going to have to come a little closer," he said.

With a shy smile, she scooted onto the bed so that she was sitting next to him. He let his fingers dance through the red, gold, and white strands of her hair. His body warmed, and he fought the urge to groan as that part of his body woke with fervor.

That, too, could wait until later. He was no good for her right now. He already struggled to keep his movements gentle. The urge to grasp hold of and possess her was strong.

Instead, he moved his fingers to cup her nape, bringing her closer to him. "My breath probably smells awful, but I'd really like to kiss you right now, if that's okay."

"I don't care what your breath smells like." Her words were warm and tickled his lips as she spoke.

His mouth closed over hers, soft and gentle at first. His fingers flexed, moving to grip her hair as his body rioted, demanding more.

While he was fighting it, Lily took control of the kiss, pressing him back against the pillows and moving slightly over him. Her lips pressed harder against his, her tongue seeking entry of his mouth.

When he let her in, feeling her tongue against his, tasting her, he couldn't hold back the groan of pleasure, or stop his hips from rolling, seeking hers.

He reached up and took her face in his hands, diving deeper into the kiss for just one moment longer before breaking their connection. His body was a mix of searing pain and tingles of euphoria.

"Lily," he said, his voice gruff. "I can't be gentle with you, not yet, and I need to be. I want to be. That first time with you needs to be slow and gentle, because that's what you deserve."

She blinked down at him, biting the corner of her lip.

"Okay?"

Lily gave him a small nod. "Did I hurt you?"

"No." He brushed his lips over hers, using every ounce of what little energy he had to keep it just a light touch. "You could never hurt me."

"I should go make you something to eat."

"Will you stay? Lay with me for a bit?"

"Are you sure?"

His emotions surged despite his want for them to stay weighed down somewhere inside of him. Not trusting his voice, he nodded, then moved his arm out, a gesture he hoped she understood he wanted her against him.

Once she settled at his side, her head on his chest, he broke. He couldn't stop the tears from rolling down his face, or the sobs breaking free. His body shook from them and the pain each one caused to burst through his body.

Lily's arms came around him, holding him tightly. "I'm so sorry. I'm so sorry," she whispered against his chest.

Matthew had no words, only cries as he held her back, letting his emotions wring him dry.

CHAPTER 67

CAID SWUNG himself up onto Wyatt's lowered tailgate. His weight settling next to Wyatt made the truck bounce, and Wyatt extended the hand that held his open can of soda out so that it wouldn't spill.

"So..." He took a long drink from the can, making a satisfied 'ah' sound after he swallowed. "I've been thinking about the bachelor party."

Caid groaned. "We haven't even set a date. Maybe pump the brakes a bit."

"Ah, come on man, live a little." He swung his dangling legs back and forth. "I've gotta say, I think she's the best thing that's ever happened to you."

Caid's head whipped around.

"What? It's true. I remember what it was like with Kate. You were so fucking unhappy. We could all see it. Everyone except you." He shrugged. "Sure, you went places with her. But you two never went far or for long. You always came back down. Like a doom cloud chased you home, and it'd take days to shake off. Now?" He laughed big and hearty. "You take off for almost a month to God knows where and come back engaged. Engaged! That's not the Kincaid McGrath I know." He eyed Caid from the corner of his eye. "Which means, it's gotta be *big* love."

Caid nodded. "Very, very big fucking love."

Wyatt grinned at him. "Would you look at us, all grown up and doing adult shit, getting into relationships and—"

"Hold up." Caid straightened and set his soda down. "You're dating?"

Wyatt rubbed the back of his neck. "Only a few weeks now. Met through one of those apps."

"Where's she from?"

"New Hampshire, but her family owns some inns and whatnot. They bought one earlier this year over in Moosehead, and she's the one running it for them."

Caid scratched his jaw. "Well... shit. It's serious?"

"Got pretty serious, pretty quick. She's got two boys and they go with their dad on the weekends. So we switch weekends at each others' places. You and Róisín should come over for dinner this Saturday, meet her."

The sign blinking over the open door couldn't have been any more clear to Caid at that moment. "I'll check with Róisín, make sure she's gonna be around." He rubbed his sweat soaked palms on his thighs. "Hey, Wyatt, I uh, well, fuck, I don't really know how to bring this up but..." He stretched out his arm and lifted his hand, letting the tips of his fingers ignite like he had the day he had told Thomas and Lina he was a witch.

"Woah." Wyatt's head swiveled from Caid's hand to his face and back. His eyes grew wider. "How?"

Caid folded his fingers in against his palm, then opened his hand, revealing a baseball sized round of packed earth. "Uh, it's a kind of long and fucked up story, but, I've got, I guess I'm—"

"A warlock?"

"I don't know if they use that term. I've only ever heard them say witches."

Wyatt reached out and seized the ball from Caid. He turned it this way and that, bringing it closer to his eyes so he could inspect it. Letting out a low whistle, he tossed it from hand to hand. "They?"

"Róisín and her family. Sort of family, I mean. Her mom and dad passed away a while ago. But she's got people she's close with. Like family."

"Is that why she always has this sort of"—he tossed the dirt ball up, catching it with ease when it came back down—"glow sometimes?"

"Yeah. It's the way the magic fills the body, the energy it burns."

Wyatt nodded, and they fell silent for several minutes. "Quick question, don't get pissed or anything, alright?"

Every muscle in Caid's body tensed. This was it. This was where he lost his best friend. "Okay," he said slowly.

Wyatt looked over his shoulder to where they had set up staging and their sawhorses for the site. Part of the bathroom remodel for the Stanfords included a large bay window. "Why are we doing this by hand? I mean, if you have magic, can't you just"—he wiggled his fingers—"and be done with it?"

Caid wanted to fall off the tailgate and throw himself on the ground with shame. Even Róisín had said that Wyatt would be alright with it. Why had he doubted? There wasn't anyone he knew that couldn't care less than Wyatt for who someone was.

"Given I've only had this for a few months, I don't know the full extent yet of what I can and can't do. And it'd draw an awful lot of attention if I was out waving my hands around and *poofing* additions and shit on houses."

Wyatt pursed his lips and nodded several times. "True, true. I guess we still have to do it the old-fashioned way."

"Well, I wouldn't exactly call it old-fashioned." He hopped from the tailgate, their lunch break nearing its end. "We've got pneumatic tools and battery-operated shit now. We don't have to mill our own wood." He reached for his tool belt, slinging it around his waist. "Or make our nails."

"Yeah, yeah." Wyatt waved a hand at him like he was a mosquito buzzing in his ear. "I get it. You've got magic and all, but you're still the same sarcastic, hard ass as always."

"Can't help the way I was born," Caid called over his shoulder, walking toward where he had his chop saw set up.

Their steady work rhythm had returned quickly, not missing a beat.

Caid had reasoned that it was because although the time elsewhere may have been several weeks; there, it had yet to even be a full month.

Wyatt stopped a few times to ask questions, wondering how the magic worked, and how Caid had learned he had it. Then Caid watched in amusement for nearly a half hour while Wyatt tried to make a dandelion grow in Mrs. Stanford's mum pot.

As they packed it up and called it a day, Caid couldn't wait to get home to take Róisín in his arms and just sit with her. Take this moment, this time. Whatever they could, because for all they knew, instead of waking up for a regular day tomorrow, they could be plummeted into chaos.

How had Róisín done it before? There were times he had seen her slightly rough around her edges, like that day she had left for Ely, being gone nearly the entire day. The same day that he had decided that he was going to wait for her to come back, that he was going to tell her how he felt about her. But mostly, she seemed so focused and steady, taking it a day at a time. Not like someone who was staring at a bomb counting down and no clear way on how to diffuse it.

Just like they were now.

He rounded the corner leading into the cul-de-sac of her house, *their* house now he needed to remind himself. On the corner by the stop sign, the Collins kids, James and Zack, had a small flower stand set up, filled with bouquets of late season blooms. He pulled his truck to a stop in front of them and wound his window down. Their mother, Melissa, walked over with a smile on her face, shielding her eyes from the sun.

"Heard you and your lady were back from your trip," she said. "You two have a good time?"

"It was good to get away, but it's better to be back. How much for two?" He nodded toward the flowers.

She looked back at her boys. "Oh, where it's the end of the day and I need to get them in and cleaned up for dinner, we could do a twofer. How about fifteen?"

The boys pulled two bouquets from the tin canister they had been tucked in and brought them over to her. Caid handed her a twenty-dollar bill. "Keep the change, and don't spend it all on ice cream." He winked at Zack next to Melissa.

"What do you say to Mr. McGrath, boys?" she asked.

"Thank you, Mr. McGrath!" They said in unison.

Caid tapped two fingers to his forehead in salute to them and turned into the cul-de-sac. When he pulled into the drive, Róisín and Lina were sitting on the porch with thick books opened over their legs. The sound of his engine, and the music from the radio, had their heads lifting.

He locked eyes with Róisín and mouthed along to the song blaring from the speakers "*I was made for lovin' you baby, you were made for lovin' me...*"

Lina's eyes grew round and she jumped to her feet as Caid cut the engine, silence falling over the yard.

"I'll take that as my cue to skedaddle," Lina said, louder than she needed.

Caid hopped out of his truck as she neared.

"You're so gross." She playfully slapped his shoulder.

"I mean, boys *do* have cooties." He gave her an exaggerated shrug.

"Ugh. I hate you, but I love you. Be extra sweet to her. Maybe you can have some luck pushing that sad, black cloud over her head away so the sun comes back." Lina brushed a kiss over his cheek, then climbed into her SUV.

"How was work?" Róisín called over to him.

"We built shit," he said. He rounded the hood of his truck and reached through the open window on the passenger side, grabbing the flowers.

"Those are pretty," Róisín said when she saw them.

"Not as pretty as you."

She laughed, her eyes steady on him as he approached where she sat on the stairs. "So corny."

"Yeah." He set the flowers next to her, then took both of her hands, pulling her to her feet. "But that's part of my charm."

Looping her arms around his neck, she kissed his chin. "You've got charm in spades, Kincaid McGrath."

Bringing his arms around her, he swept her up into a kiss. He playfully dipped her backward, moving his lips from hers to her neck. Then he brought her upright and tucked a strand of her wayward hair behind her ear.

She released a soft, contented sigh. "You're everything I need, and exactly what I want."

"Guess we're even in that aspect then." He stroked his knuckles over her cheeks. "I told Wyatt. You were right, he was totally okay with it. Just another day on the job site."

Róisín leaned against him, her arms around her waist and her hands smoothing across his back. "Told you. I also get it, though. It's hard because there's always that little sliver of doubt that prods at you and makes you scared."

"Was it like that with me?"

"I was one hundred percent convinced you were going to run away from me." She bit her lip and her cheeks blazed red.

"Never." Her hair was soft around his fingers as he dug them into it, cradling her head in his hands. "Remember when I said I didn't care if you sprouted horns? I don't care. I'll love you no matter what."

"I know." She smiled in the way her entire face lit, and her eyes crinkled at the corners. "I love you."

Before he could kiss her again, she leaped up against him, jumping so that her legs wrapped around his waist. He quickly braced himself to steady them and brought his hands to her ass to hold her.

"Gross. Get a room, you two," a familiar, but raspy, voice said from the porch.

Startled, Róisín yanked away from Caid, and together, their eyes found the waiting figure sitting next to Róisín's flowers.

Matthew.

CHAPTER 68

JESSAMYN SAT atop her desk, rubbing furiously at her temples, trying to push away the throbbing that beat there. Everyone's voices bounced around her, some elevating as the argument at hand became heated.

"Enough!" Jessamyn's shout made the room flinch collectively.

"Jes—"

"No." She lifted a hand to silence Aja. "I said enough and I fucking mean it!"

His jaw ticked as he stared at her.

"First, yes, his numbers are down. But is it *enough*? Even with Róisín having the full power of her magic back, is it *enough*? If you"—she looked at Runa—"and you"—she gave a pointed glare to Aja—"struggled against them and not only are you magically strong, but you're both far more physically stronger than I, Róisín, or Anelle. We have no other witches with the skills in their magic, nor the power behind it. What then?"

Runa looked down at his foot, scuffing it on the floor.

"Exactly," Jessamyn said. "I will not lose any more of our Coven than we have already. Nor will I risk any from another. We are *better* than this. We are better than Frederick. Our chance to show that is now."

"Then what do we do?" Aja asked.

"There's been two more reports of missing people in the last seventy-two hours," Anthony said. "Not staff either. Which means either he or *they* are moving beyond the wall."

"How many more of *our* people do we need to risk? If we're going to talk about that, we need to consider human casualties," Marcelo said. "While he may have culled some of his own, he's slipping further and further into the madness that the monster inside of him is pulling him into."

Jessamyn ran a hand over her face and moved off of her desk. "How has it come to this? Such a fucking mess!" She threw her hands up and spun around. Inside, she grasped harder at that rope, holding on for all that she had. She couldn't lose her grip on this. It had been too long. She had given too much to this already.

Anelle cleared her throat. "Why don't we pause things here and go back to the beginning? What we know, what we've seen, etcetera. Maybe it can help us successfully get something of a plan in place because—" She took an audible breath. "I agree with Aja. If the king sees even just a glimpse of Róisín, it could put him into action against the rest of his men. We need to face the reality that we may need to take action against him before we make progress on breaking the curse."

"Ione will break the curse," Runa said tightly. "She has the book mostly translated."

Jessamyn had heard the possessiveness in his tone and turned her head to eye him, lifting a brow.

"Then what?" Anelle asked. "We have to hope when Jes locates which of them is the curse that we're able to quickly figure how to undo the thing."

"And if we can't..." Anthony chewed on his bottom lip.

"We have to do what we have to do for our people," Marcelo said. "*All* our people."

Jessamyn hung her head. The world around them was growing uglier and darker by the moment. "Alright." She spun around to face them. "Let's start with what we know."

"He's bolder than the last three kings have been," Runa said.

Anthony snorted a laugh. "That's because it's a sadistic witch from the most vile realm ever."

Jessamyn pinched the bridge of her nose. "While I agree that you're not wrong about that sentiment, let's keep it simple. Please."

"Have we been able to determine if it's him or his men leaving the bodies out in the orchards?" Marcelo asked, looking at Aja.

"He seems to continue to be discreet in that aspect, despite his boldness in other areas," Aja said. "The marks on the bodies show they struggled and fled to an extent. Given the aggressiveness of the men in our courtyard that day, it wouldn't shock me to find they're making a sport of this."

"He has to know. Which means he condones it," Marcelo said.

"Maybe he's letting them do it because it's conditioning them?" Anelle blinked when they all looked at her. "Just tossing out ideas. None of us know what in the Hells he is planning. It must be something, because why else would he be making more like him?"

"She has a point," Jessamyn said. "And the question that remains is *how is he passing this on?*"

Runa shifted his weight and scratched his jaw. "Just, uh, tossing this out there but, what if he's cursing them? No, no." He wagged a finger at her. "Let me talk this out and you'll see, it makes sense. Ione has said that the book is Founder Nulion, and Diana's note confirms that it was in fact Cronan's. Perhaps our king knows exactly what curse was placed on him. And he knows how to place it. Just not how to break it."

Jessamyn chewed on her cheek, her thoughts churning. Could it be that simple? "No. He doesn't know. In our interactions, he is increasingly frustrated by our lack of being able to locate it to break it. With how he's acted since coming to me, I can say that if he knew the curse, then he would have brought it to me to undo it."

Aja moved from the windows, further into the room. "Why does he want it broken, though? He appears to delight in the chaos being a true monster causes."

"I think he fears what he'll do to Róisín," Jessamyn said. "The fear I saw in his eyes was very real that day I went to him when she first left.

He had begun to change in front of her, and I think he's concerned he won't be able to control it."

"Which circles us back to Lady McKenna," Marcelo said.

Jessamyn looked over to where the two princes sat on her sofa. "You're away from the pomp and circumstance, Marcelo. No need for those formalities here. Hopefully, we see a day soon when things return to what they once were and the days of yore are done with."

"A day we will all celebrate," Anthony murmured.

"But yes, it brings us back to Róisín, doesn't it?" Her shoulders slumped in defeat. "Dammit. We need to make sure whatever plan we put into place when she's here for the gala is sound. Any sign of trouble, and we're out. *All of us.* I don't give a shit what fuss it may cause. There will be no more losses. Unless it is one of Madigan's men. Understood?"

They all nodded.

"Alright. I need to get back to Ely to check with everyone there. See what progress has been made. I know with the recent loss"—she rubbed the sudden ache at her chest—"it's been more like trudging through sludge, which is understandable."

"I'll head back now." Runa shifted away before she could tell him otherwise. They would have to have words at some point. Something was brewing between him and Ione, or something was already happening. He would tell her not to worry, he was fine. But she *would* worry. She would always worry about him. His happiness, his safety. All of it. He may have closed off that life from before, but *she* remembered. Sheltered by their parents, or not, she had witness the hurt of those years he had felt trapped inside of the wrong body.

Did Ione know? Would she love him the same when she found out?

"I'll get a team assembled to lay a plan in place," Anelle said. She waved to Anthony and gestured toward the door. "You and Cassius are now one of us. Let's go. Grab him and meet me in the training hall in thirty minutes."

Anthony rose and looked at Marcelo.

"You and Cassius know the perimeter far better than I," he told Anthony with a wink. Once Anthony had left, Marcelo stood. "What do you need from me?"

"How comfortable do you feel about stoking his fire?" Jessamyn asked.

"In public? Reasonably decent about it. He's still set on appearances. In private? Hells no."

"Well, lucky for us, it would definitely be public. However, I'll need to speak with both you and Nolani together. She needs to be on board with this."

Marcelo eyed her with curiosity. "Are you?"

"Oh, Marcelo." Her laugh was light. "How many times have you proposed to her?" The laugh grew deeper when his face reddened. "Everyone loves Nolani. You would have the support from both sides of the realm, human and witch alike. I'm not asking you to do anything you don't already want to do. You've only just let your father dictate your future for you."

"But—"

"No, Marcelo. You will, however brief it may be once this is all settled, be wearing that crown. I know your plans to dismantle the court, and I wholly support that. However, it's time for you to act like that king you will be. If you don't have that courage, then..." She lifted her hands, moving her arms out. "We are absolutely fucked."

His jaw flexed with the clench of his teeth. "We what, step out into the public's eye as a couple? It's that simple, really?"

"When was the last time the king told you of the approved ladies for marrying?" she asked.

"Two days before Lady, I mean Róisín, arrived."

"Which means, despite him no longer being Rastead, he still holds the same values and expectations for you as the future king of the realm, Marcelo. Yes, it is that simple. The Fatomes are a well-standing family, even welcome at court. However, in his eyes, they're still a refugee family."

"Wait." Marcelo suddenly paled. "Nolani said her family was from Aunellion. Does he?"

"To be honest, I would be surprised if Madigan knew them. The Milsenetts rarely interacted with their own Coven. They made the laws and held them with a firm hand. As long as you marched in line, you were safe from ever crossing paths with them."

"But the Coven line?" Aja asked, startling her. She had forgotten that he remained with them in the room.

"Was severed when Madigan cast his connection with the leaders aside. And I'm sure his first death and subsequent loss of magic would have sealed that deal," Jessamyn said.

Marcelo let out a loud breath. "Okay. I'll speak with Nolani. When do you leave for Ely?"

"I'll go in the morning to give us time to talk."

Once he was gone, Aja turned to Jessamyn. "It gets more complicated each day."

"Messier," she mumbled. "And I'm questioning if I can clean this up before we're totally buried in it."

He stepped up to her and took her in his arms, smoothing his hand down her back. "If she hasn't come to you again to tell you otherwise, you have to hold on to that hope that you're doing the right thing."

Jessamyn lifted her hands, placing them on his chest. The hardness of the muscles beneath her hands grounded her. They had only briefly talked about Diana's letter. The matters at hand not giving them more time. Would they have it after? When things settled? Would she be there, with him, then?

"But is it the right thing? We're putting Róisín in the line of danger. Even with her magic..."

"We'll just need to make sure there's no chance for failure." He pressed a kiss to the top of her head. "We can't go against him if he still has several dozen like him to stand next to him. They'll tear us apart."

She slid her hands up and around, clasping them behind his neck. "I know. I don't like any of this, but I know."

He bent slightly to swing her up into his arms. "Come on, let's rest a bit before you and the prince get to scheming."

She couldn't help the snort that shot out of her. "Rest?"

He used his booted foot to shove open her bedroom door. "Mm. It's been nearly three days since I last had a taste of you." He kissed her hungrily before tossing her onto the bed.

CHAPTER 69

"WHAT HAPPENS now?" Nolani asked from where she perched on the window seat of Marcelo's room.

Marcelo glanced up from his sketchpad and the lines and curves that were taking shape to form her figure. "We don't die?"

She slammed her book closed and turned, her legs dangling. She wiggled her toes, then sighed. "Dammit, Celo."

"What?" He blinked at her.

Pushing her hands through her hair, she rose and crossed to him. Gently, she pulled the sketchpad from his hands, then the charcoal pencil, and placed them on his desk. She climbed onto his lap, straddling his legs, and took his face between her hands. Lowering her face so that they were almost nose to nose, she squinted at him. "What is going on in there?"

"You don't really want to know. Trust me." He felt the bile rise in his throat at the thoughts that pounded against one another in his head.

"No, I really do." Her voice was soft, but her touch was softer when she moved her hands into his hair, stroking.

He closed his eyes and leaned into her touch. "We were supposed to run away. Just you and I. Leave this realm and settle somewhere *else* so that we could live our lives how we wanted to. Now look at us, getting ready to become king and queen of a realm neither of us wants."

"Sometimes—" She brushed her lips over his forehead. "We have to do the hard stuff before we get to the good stuff."

His hands had settled at her waist. He flexed his fingers, letting the feel of her soft skin beneath the pads anchor him. "But we've done all of that. Secret meetings, dark hallways, disguises in hotels around Shianshani. We've paid our dues."

"Just a little longer, Celo. We're almost free of it." She bent her head and nipped his chin, then gave him a soft kiss.

"Are you sure you're alright with this?"

"I've already told you yes, Celo. When you asked me to be your wife the other day, and now. This changes nothing. I only ask that you speak with my father first."

He watched his finger draw along her jaw, stopping at her chin. Hooking his finger, he tipped her face up to his. "He's going to tell me no."

"He's going to ask what you plan to do to keep me safe from Rastead and the rules of court, but no, he won't tell you no."

"How can you be sure? There's so much at risk for your family, too. Not just what the new king brings." He hadn't been able to bring himself to say Madigan's name aloud.

"There you are," Anthony panted the words when he burst into the room.

Marcelo groaned, letting his head fall back against his chair. "What is it?"

"We need to talk," he said.

"I'll get my things," Nolani said. She slid off Marcelo's lap. He halted her from moving away from him, grasping one of her hands.

"Stay," he whispered. "Please." He turned his head to look at Anthony. "About?"

"You *are* staying to take the role of king after—" He cleared his throat.

"Isn't that what we discussed yesterday with Jessamyn and the Coven?"

Anthony lifted his hands and shrugged. "I just, I know how you've felt about this your entire life, and now it's here. You have to do it."

Nolani quietly slipped from Marcelo's side and returned to the window seat.

"Look, Ant, I know you—"

"No. No, no." Anthony rubbed a hand over his face, making a sound of frustration. "I don't. Shit, no, I definitely don't."

"But I thought?"

Anthony let out a small, nervous laugh. "So did I. I really did. I wanted to take that crown and make this realm everything bright, happy, and *free*. It was all such grand ideas I had."

"Are you alright?" Marcelo rose. When he glanced at Nolani, the worry and unease he saw in her eyes mirrored his own feelings.

"I think—" He blew out a breath and pinched the bridge of his nose. "Woo, I think this is what we call a, uh"—he waved his other hand in a flapping motion—"I'm going to be sick."

Nolani darted into the bathroom and returned with a trash can. Marcelo guided him to a chair and helped him lower into it. Nolani shoved the trashcan between Anthony's legs and stepped clear.

"Are you on something?" Marcelo asked.

"Reality. A very heavy dose of it. *That* is what I'm on." Anthony bent over and placed his head between his knees. "It hit me like a brick wall this morning. Rather alarming if you ask me. Going along, doo-doo-doo, and *wham*."

"Alright." Marcelo rubbed the back of his neck. He was unsure of what to say or do for his brother. He looked at Nolani for help, but she was staring at Anthony's bent body, a look of sympathy painted on her face.

Anthony's body wretched as he heaved and emptied the contents of his lunch into the trash can. "Ugh. I've been to war already. I've killed other men, for Goddess's sake. But this?" He sat upright quickly, then squeezed his eyes closed, groaning. "Why does this feel so much different?"

Marcelo had wondered the same thing. How his position now, nearing the end of his prince-hood, the clock ticking down to the placing of the crown he'd fought his whole life against, felt different.

Why he found himself actually ready instead of filled with the dread he had carried for most of his twenty-four years.

"Because this is a different enemy we face," Nolani answered for them.

Anthony snorted. "It's more than that."

"The reality of it, succeeding the king so soon," Marcelo said.

"I think that's what it is." Anthony pointed a finger at him. "I realized if you didn't do it, I'd have to do it and no, Hells no, I really actually don't want that. I don't have a clue about politics. That was a slap in the face." He scoffed. "I want to change these things, but how would I do it? The Senate would walk all over me. I'd be a shit ruler and never find a way to dismantle the throne." His head lolled to the side so he could see Marcelo better from his slumped position. "You know what you're doing. There's a real chance for change with you on the throne."

Marcelo wanted to laugh at him. Did he understand the political game of it all? Yes. As much as he hated to admit it, he did. While he doodled on notepads in meetings, or while he and Rastead had sat in the high loft overlooking the senate floor, he had actually been paying attention. Absorbing the volleying of the parties as they argued. Which tactics one party used to get their way over another. He'd learned how Rastead had played the game, getting the senate to do his bidding while thinking it had been their own idea.

He hated it. Every time he was free of them, he would spend an eternity under the hot spray of his shower, scrubbing his skin raw as though he could scrub the filth of that game from himself.

But no, he didn't know what he was doing. And he sure as Hells didn't know how he was going to make the changes in their realm that they all hoped for.

"I just need to get Lady Fatome here to accept my proposal." Marcelo tried to lighten the heaviness that had settled in the room.

"What?" Anthony seemed to be shocked free of the ailments of just a moment ago. He jolted upright, his head swiveling to Nolani. "But you love him!"

Nolani rolled her eyes skyward. "I've already accepted the buffoons' proposal."

Anthony's head now quickly spun to face Marcelo, his brows pinched.

"She wants me to talk to her father. Tell him my intentions."

"And?" Anthony arched his brow. "Wait. Do you think *he'll* say no?"

"No," Nolani said as Marcelo said, "Yes."

Anthony's mouth rounded into an O shape.

Marcelo pushed a hand through his hair. "I'm going to go talk with Aja. Perhaps if I arrive at the Fatome manor with Coven guards, my proposal, and a promise for safety..."

"He'll say yes," Nolani said. The assurance in her tone gave him some strength to face this next task. He only hoped it was enough.

CHAPTER 70

S HASTA STOOD at Lucius's sink. She had her head hung between her shoulders, eyes squeezed closed as she battled the simultaneous crashing waves of grief and guilt.

They'd had their goodbye, she and Lucius. They'd said their apologies. Hugged. Expressed their love for one another. But she couldn't shake that feeling of shame and guilt.

She had disappointed Lucius. Again.

The promise she had made to him to do better, to find help, someone to talk to, so that she *stopped* running and hiding when things got hard, hung around her in faint echoes.

She had come to Ely after Ione's visit to Ireland to check on Lily and Matthew. While she didn't know any of the Founder languages, she knew history. With Lily's need to be with Matthew, Shasta took her place at Cicile's side.

It had been interesting to see the dynamic between Ten and Cicile. How fluidly they worked together. One was an extension of the other. They were dry witted and kind.

Runa seemed to be more wall than a person, unless Ione was around. She heard their shared laughs, saw the way he was always watching her. She couldn't help but wonder how much their Coven had suffered under Frederick. Runa and Jessamyn the most. Not just as his siblings. That would have been difficult enough. To be his siblings and be the very beings Frederick was incredibly vocal in his distaste of.

Jessamyn was clearly protective of Runa, but who protected her? Aja was never far, his ever-watchful eyes on her—

"Why are you at Lucius's? Where's Róisín? I don't have long. I can feel the veil already pulling me back."

Shasta jumped, pulled from her thoughts. She whirled around, finding Brenna standing on the other side of the kitchen island. Her hair was a wild, red tangled mass of curls and her chest heaved with her false quickened breaths.

"Bren? What's happening?"

"No, you need to tell me what's going on *here*," Brenna said. "Shit, where's Stephen?" She spun around, her eyes wide when she faced Shasta again. "He crossed with me."

Shasta moved around the island slowly, hands up. "Calm down. He's probably just in another room."

"Uh, this guy just appeared." Ione stood in the doorway next to Stephen, who looked just as shell-shocked at Brenna. "Oh, hey, Brenna."

Brenna wasn't looking at Ione, or Stephen. Her eyes were on the dark giant standing behind the pair, body tense and ready. Runa.

"Why is Jessamyn's brother here?" Brenna asked. "What in the Hells is going on?"

Ione looked at Shasta nervously.

"You two go back in with Ten and Cicile. It'll be alright." Shasta waved them on.

"Are you sure?" Ione was side-eying a silent Stephen.

"That's Róisín father," Shasta said. "It's good."

"Wait. A human can cross the veil?" Ione's nose crinkled. "I think I want to stay for this."

Shasta sighed. "Fine. Sit down, now. All of you."

"Not until you tell me why I can't find Róisín," Brenna said. Her voice was tight, the anger in her words thicker than molasses.

"She's in Earth's realm with Caid, Lily, and Matthew." Shasta pointed to the table. "Now, sit. You said you have little time and you wouldn't be here if you didn't have news. Where's Ev?"

The question brought Brenna down from her anger, and her face fell. "It happened again. We tried over and over. I don't even know how we got here." She gestured to Stephen. "No one can cross, Shasta."

Ione gasped.

Shasta gripped the back of the chair she stood near. Her nails dug into the soft wood. "What do you mean, no one?"

Stephen answered when Brenna remained quiet. "No one has been able to cross through for days now."

"And the creatures from the darkness have been spotted in the afterworld." Brenna's words were a fearful, quiet whisper.

"But how? They're *locked* into the depths," Ione said. Her face had paled and her eyes were glassy. "The Goddess makes it so."

"No one I've talked to seems to know." Stephen put his hands on Brenna's shoulders and tucked her against his chest. "I've been making my rounds down there, seemingly the only one that can move a little easier through the different afterworlds. The people I've talked to have all met a wall when trying to cross at some point."

"Can you not move through the worlds anymore?" Shasta asked Brenna.

"I'm stuck in Ev's." She lifted a hand to cover one of Stephen's. "We haven't been there long enough to build our own. So that's my only conclusion about why I can stay with her. I've not been able to move from it since our last visit, though."

"Shit." Shasta put her hands on her hips. "What about the creatures?"

"They have not done anything to anyone, yet. But, Shasta, they just roam freely. There's nothing limiting them. What if they cross the veil?"

"Could they? Cross the veil?" Runa asked.

Brenna's attention flicked to him, then to Shasta.

"We don't have time for that right now, Bren," Shasta said. "If the veil is pulling you, we need to know everything about what's happening there. Then we'll talk about the rest."

"This is way more important than the crap going on here," Ione said. "Especially on the chance they *can* cross."

"Evelyn seems to think that if they've been able to move from the darkness to the afterworld that it's a real possibility that they can move through the veil." Brenna's face contorted and her body shuddered. Behind her, Stephen's edges had already faded. "What were you able to find out about Clarissa's family from Lucius?"

Shit. She had been so caught up in their argument that day, after she mentioned what was happening in the afterworld, she had forgotten. A tightness grew in her chest.

"No. We, uh..." Shasta swallowed, trying to push away the pain that had grown at the back of her throat. "We got lost in trying to work out what was happening with the veil."

It was only partly a lie. Thankfully, one Brenna appeared to accept.

Stephen grimaced, pulling Brenna tighter against him.

"You two need to go back, you can't keep fighting the call. It'll rip you to shreds if you do." Shasta eased closer to Brenna. She stopped a step away, just far enough that she could hide the tells Brenna would see. Just far enough to hide her guilt.

"You'll tell Róisín that I love her? That we love her? If we can't—" Brenna's words caught.

"I will. You two be careful. Especially you." She narrowed her eyes at Stephen. "I know the moment you return, you're going back out into the worlds. Stay safe. We don't know what's going on, and the darkness's creatures have no bounds or morals."

Stephen gave her a nod. "I only hope we can return with news that helps us get answers."

"Me too," Shasta whispered as they faded.

Ione exploded once they were alone. "When were you going to tell us *that* was happening?"

Shasta hung her head. "I'd only just found out not even a week ago. I went to Lucius first, but...we ended up fighting about stupid things because I hide from things when they're tough. And—" She let out a shaking breath. "He was leaving. Now he's gone, Matthew's back and a mess, and I'm here trying to keep my shit together long enough to be of use and helpful because I promised Lucius I'd be a better person. Is that good enough of an answer for you?"

Ione blinked rapidly. "Yup," she said at length, letting the *p* pop loudly. "Now the question is, what do we do about it?"

How would Lucius handle it? What would his next step be? He was such a natural leader and always just knew which step was the best to take.

"Keep our focus on Madigan. We need to get that book finished and figure out which one was the curse's root. We're too close to shift our focus now." Shasta reached behind her to where her still full glass of water waited. Taking it, she made her way back to the library.

CHAPTER 71

AFTER RÓISÍN and Caid greeted Matthew, Róisín watched as Caid slid back into his truck and disappeared, saying he would be at Lina's so she could have time with Matthew.

He had looked better in just a few days than he had when he had made it back to them, but he was still too thin, and his eyes were haunted, shadows clinging there.

"Are you just going to stare at me all night?" he asked.

She leaned close to him, taking his face between her hands and squishing it forward, making his lips pout. "I can't help it. I've missed this dumb, handsome face."

"I've missed your dumb, beautiful face, too. But"—he tugged her hands away—"don't do that again. I'll be forced to wrestle you and you know I always win."

"Ah, dammit." She swung her arm in a defeated, *shucks* movement. "I can't believe Lily let you out of her sight."

"She didn't."

Róisín eyebrows shot up. "Matthew! Did you sneak off on her? You're going to give the poor woman a heart attack."

"She's tied up with Ione at the moment. That chatter." His body shuddered and his eyes drooped. "I can't. It's too much right now."

344

She pressed her lips together to stave off the slight quiver of her jaw. "Being here gossiping with me isn't?"

He looked around her living room. "It's quieter here. And—" His voice dropped to a whisper. "It doesn't have the memories that even the rebuilt cottage does."

"Oh, Matthew." She moved closer so that she was snuggled against his side. "I'm so sorry. I didn't even think when I told Lily that you two could stay."

"It's okay." He patted her arm. "If you'd asked me, I'd have probably said yes thinking that I could handle it. But..." His head fell back against the cushion, and he pushed a hand into his hair. "Shit, Róisín, this is fucking really hard. I feel so... lost." His chest stuttered with his staggering breaths. "Mildred was right there with me. I could have. But I didn't. He could still be here with us."

She eased off him and moved to the coffee table in front of the sofa so that she could face him. "You didn't know Matthew. None of us knew. We don't even want to know how many lives from the Shianshani Coven were the price that Frederick *happily* paid to get that information. You can't blame yourself for any of this."

Just like she wished Caid would stop blaming himself for what happened with Matthew. He hadn't spoken of it in a while, but she knew that the demon still chased him.

"It's easier said than done. He's my real father, you know," Matthew said.

"Lucius? He? I thought he and Clarissa?"

"I don't know the whole, but yeah, Lucius was really my father. I didn't care either way. He was the one that raised me. Taught me everything I knew. He was—" His throat bobbed with his swallow. "He was my best friend." He swiped at his eyes in a jerking movement.

"Aoife was there," he said abruptly. "In Aunellion."

"What?" Her hands released his when her body straightened and she moved back.

"She told me how the Milsenetts created the Fog Fields in some weird rambling monologue where she tried to play off that she wasn't as bad as Madigan and his family were."

Róisín barked out a sharp laugh. "Says the woman that killed off almost her entire Coven."

"That's what I said."

Recalling the night Aoife came to her, she took her bottom lip between her fingers and rolled it back and forth. "Did she say anything else?"

"Something about how, with all of them gone, we can restore the balance. I don't know who she meant or what she meant. She didn't bother to elaborate, and the next thing I knew, Lucius was there, and the fog was suddenly filled with a creepy skeleton army that wanted to cut our heads off."

Róisín tugged on her ear. "She came to me not that long ago. Um..." She dropped her gaze to her lap. "For this to make sense, I need to tell you something. But first, how are you feeling?"

Matthew leaned his elbows on his thighs so that their faces were inches apart. "Not a very good lead in, Róisín. You should have asked how I felt *first*. Tell me what's going on. Lily dodges it, and there's a reason Ione is at the cottage right now with an update"—he wiggled his index fingers in the air, miming quotation marks—"on something."

When she opened her mouth, the only sound that came out was a small squeak, and she quickly closed it.

"Róisín."

"Madigan's not dead." She said the words so quickly, they ran together as one and she jumped up from the table, darting backward as Matthew shot to his feet.

"What?" The word burst out of him like a slap.

"I killed him in Roidon. He and Aoife both. But something happened. His spirit or soul or whatever is inside the body of King Dionomis in Shianshani's realm. That's not all. He's some type of people eating fucking monster. I've been banned from Shianshani, which is killing me because it's my fault, somehow, I'm sure of it, that he is still alive. I didn't have my magic for a really long time after that night because apparently there *is* a limit to our magic, so Jessamyn sent me home because it wasn't safe and it felt like being yanked out of the game at the most important part of it so..." She buried her face in her hands and let out a scream of frustration.

Matthew covered his face with one hand and held up the other. "Hold on. I need to process all of that because I get the impression that you said it a million miles an hour hoping to slip something by me, thinking I wouldn't notice."

She used the wall to brace herself up and bit her lip, watching as Matthew stood in the middle of her living room, frozen.

"Madigan has his magic?"

"No."

"Who in the Hells is Jessamyn?"

"You don't remember Frederick's sister?"

His hand fell from his face, revealing his shock.

"She's nothing like him. *None* of them are. He was just as awful to them as he was to everyone else. I can guarantee there was a celebration in the Coven's courtyard when Jessamyn received his magic and they knew he was gone."

"Who?"

"Lucius," she whispered. "He was in Clarissa's afterworld, being all Frederick-like and..."

"Shit."

"Shit," she agreed.

"What about your magic now?"

"It's back and better than ever. Caid learned a little party trick about well sources for our magic wherever our Coven originates from."

He lifted a brow. "Nanette?"

"Ah, no. Shasta. Nanette's sort of indisposed at the moment. Some council stuff on Roidon she's trying to handle." Lily could tell him what she felt comfortable with him knowing. That wasn't Róisín's place to fill him in.

Matthew lifted his hands, fingers out, and started ticking items off a mental list. "Okay, Madigan, alive. Frederick, dead. Your magic, gone but back. Jessamyn, I want to trust your word, but... What do you mean by monster?"

She lifted her hands, crooking her fingers near her mouth and widening her eyes. "Like a real-life monster. And he's made an army of them."

"Wait. A"—he mimicked her—"monster? Like Vlad, the Dracula guy?"

"No? Yes? I'd say you have to see it to know, but Hells." She shuddered.

"And what are we doing about all of this?"

"Trying to break the curse so we can lop off his head."

Matthew coughed. "Excuse me?"

"Aoife told me he can't get his power back or he'll be unstoppable, which given how near indestructible he is *now*?" She flinched at the memory of the fight in the courtyard. "Apparently, he's trying to do so. Good thing is, we were already trying to figure out the curse. That's why Ione's here. She's working with some of the Shianshani Coven with a book they found that Frederick had. Once she gets it translated, hopefully we can figure out how to undo it. Then I cut off his head. Maybe I need to burn his body, too."

"That's not a little twisted," he murmured.

"You didn't see him, Matthew. I don't know if stabbing him or cutting his head off is enough."

He let his body fall back onto the sofa, sinking into the cushions. "Is this our new normal now?"

"I hope not. But it's a mess and I can't help but worry that the quiet and calm is only going to come in stolen moments. Like this," she said, sitting next to him.

"One more question. What in the Hells were you doing in Shianshani to begin with?"

"Trying to figure out a plan with Lily to unite the Covens."

He shifted and looked down at her. "Why?"

"Because the Goddess told me after I got out of the Seer's house that I had to. Something's coming, Matthew."

CHAPTER 72

LILY SAT in an overstuffed chair with her legs tucked beneath her. There was a book open in her lap, but she struggled to focus on the words. When Ione had left and she'd gone back to the bedroom, Matthew had been gone.

The light scuff of footsteps had her lifting her head and seeing Matthew enter the room.

"I'm sorry," they said in unison.

"Wait." Matthew looked down at her; his brows drew together tightly. "What are you sorry for?"

"I should have gone outside when Ione came. I didn't even think until after she left and I went to check on you, only to find you gone as well. The noise." She frowned. "I'm sorry."

"I'm sorry for leaving and not saying anything."

"You're a grown man, Matthew. You don't have to let me know you're going." She closed her book. "I wish you'd mentioned it so I could have gone too, in case something happened." She looked him over, noting that the color had returned to his face and the wounds he had returned home with were only faint marks on his skin. "You look well, so it is what it is."

"Well, *that's* not any sign you've been spending too much time with

Róisín." He rolled his eyes. "At all. That was a classic Róisín deflection, sweetheart."

She held his eyes with hers as he lowered to his knees before the chair.

"I can let it go for now, because we have bigger things to worry about." He took the book from her hand, and she opened her mouth to protest. "No. It's okay. I get it. If she wasn't bottled up like a soda that's sat in the hot sun all day, I don't think she'd have told me either. At least not yet. Hells, Lily." His sigh was heavy. "It's a fucking mess."

"It's not so bad." When he only stared in response, she closed her eyes and her body crumpled in the chair. "Okay, fine. I'm absolutely terrified. It was so much easier before, when I was just the book girl, reading all day and deciphering things to see if it would be useful for the others. I'm..." She swallowed hard, her pulse dancing at the side of her throat. "*In* it this time. I couldn't sit back while Róisín was trying to figure out the Coven thing, and you were gone. My grandmother—no, not right now, she doesn't get this space or me anymore."

"What happened?" He asked in a whisper.

"Some other time." She lifted her hand and pushed her fingers into his silken red locks. He leaned into her touch and his eyes fell closed, so she kept stroking her fingers through his hair. After a moment, his eyes flew open. His pupils were blown wide, nearly swallowing the green of his irises.

She felt her breath catch and her heart slow as he moved closer, leaning over her. "Lily." His breath was warm against her mouth.

"Y-yes?"

"I'm going to do my best to be gentle with you." His words tickled her face. "I may have a moment where I lose that battle, but—" He captured her mouth with his.

The kiss was possessiveness, need, and want. She leaned into it, opening for him, letting his tongue dance alongside hers. Her body responded immediately. Her core tightened around the fire that was growing there. The skin at her nape and at her side where his hands rested tingled.

Matthew tore his mouth away from hers, his breaths ragged.

"Is everything—Oh! I can walk. Matthew, put me down. You're still hurt."

"I just need you to keep feeding me, Lily. Otherwise, I'm fine now." He adjusted his grip on her and walked down the hall toward his room. He laid her on the bed, a smirk tipping one corner of his mouth up. "You're not going to run from me, are you?"

Her face grew hot. She covered it and groaned. Laughing, he pulled her hands away.

"I'm sorry. It was such a knee jerk reaction. No one has ever looked my way, let alone wanted to kiss *me*," she said.

"Oh, Lily." He climbed onto the bed and pressed a warm kiss to her stomach where her shirt had lifted and exposed an expanse of skin. "I want to do far more than just kiss you." He used his nose to nudge the hem of her shirt up, tracing his lips and tongue along the skin he exposed. "I want to taste you." He nipped at one of her breasts. "I want to feel you." A calloused hand skimmed up her side, leaving a trail of goosebumps in its wake. "Here." He cupped a breast and stroked a thumb over the nipple, making her breath catch in her throat. "And here." He moved his hand between her legs. His fingers stroked along the seam of her joggers, and she whimpered at the touch.

"I'm not running," she whispered, feeling breathless.

"Good." He untied the joggers, letting his knuckles graze over her skin. She watched the way the muscles in her stomach quivered at his touch. Watched as he moved his hand beneath the waistband, beneath her panties.

"Matthew."

"Hm?" His fingers found her most sensitive spot and stroked lightly. She cried out and her hips jerked. "Did you need something?" He stroked again, looking at her with a wicked grin splitting his face.

She reached for him, her hand finding his arm, nails digging into his skin. "It doesn't, oh!" she cried again, rocking harder against his hand. "It doesn't have to be gentle."

Matthew moved his fingers along her folds, finding and teasing along her entrance. "Was I your first kiss, Lily?"

Before she could answer, he slipped a finger into her. Her back arched, and she moaned loudly.

"What was that? I didn't quite catch your answer." He added a finger, pressing deeper before curling his fingers just so, making her moan.

"No." She tipped her hips up against his hand. "Just because they didn't want *me* necessarily, doesn't mean they still didn't have me. What —" When his fingers abruptly left her, her eyes flew open, and she looked down her body at him.

"Lily." The tender way he said her name had her eyes stinging and her nose burning.

"It's okay. The life of the shy, dorky girl."

"No." The word was sharp and firm. "No, it's not okay."

"Matthew—"

He pressed his fingers back into her and shook his head before moving lower. He used his other hand to tug down the joggers and panties. His mouth kissed along her hip bone before finding her clit.

"You're an amazing, fucking smart, and beautiful woman, Lily."

Just the feel of his breath on her as he spoke pushed her closer to her peak.

"You deserve to be loved and worshiped." He circled his tongue around her. "And I intend to spend the rest of my life doing both."

Lily was thankful he couldn't see her, or the tears that spilled from her eyes.

Matthew's mouth closed over her and he sucked her clit, laving it with his tongue. The sensation it aroused within her, along with the pumping of his fingers, made her shatter.

She writhed and gripped the sheets. Her vision blurring and her body becoming an explosion of feeling as she tried to keep her thighs from clenching on him. He hummed against her, and she couldn't help herself. Her legs became a vise, and she rocked against his face and hands until she was wrung out.

Matthew sat back on his heels and placed his fingers in his mouth. The fingers that had been in her. His eyes were bright on hers as he drew them back out with a satisfied hum.

"I think I found my new favorite flavor," he said wickedly.

Feeling emboldened by his emotions toward her, she sat up and crushed her mouth to his, tasting herself on his lips, his tongue. She leaned against him, pushing him onto his back, and swung one of her legs over him. His hands came to her ass, squeezing hard. The sensation relit her body.

"I need you, Matthew," she whispered. She kissed his jaw, his neck. Her hands reached down, grasping the bottom of his shirt, tugging frantically. He sat up, taking her with him, and yanked the shirt over his head. "I want you," she panted the words. "I want all those things we had in our dreams. A life with you, a family with you, your love. I know it'll take time, but—"

"Lily, shh. You're overthinking it." He laid her down and then rose to kick off his pants. "What I feel in here?" He patted a hand on his chest. "It's all for you. Nonstop, and it's *big*. This isn't desire for you, or even the bond, Lily. We've spent enough time together, in those books you love so much, that I know exactly what it is." He moved over her, settling between her legs and bracing his arms on either side of her head. "This is love, Lily. Time's already done its thing."

"I love you, Matthew. I love you so much."

He thumbed away her fresh tears and brushed a kiss over the tip of her nose. "Perfect." He reached down between them and brought the tip of his cock to her entrance, nudging it in slightly. "Because I love you, too." Then he drove himself into her. She cried out, fingers grasping at his back as emotions filled her, splashing against the wave of sensation being full with him brought her.

He brought her to her first orgasm gently with his mouth and fingers, but this time, as her hips met each of his thrusts, it was coming hard and brutal. Her cries were more like shouts as she rose, rose, rose. His name was a scream torn from her lips as she tumbled down, her body on fire, shuddering and clenching. Stars exploded behind her eyes from the intensity of how hard it hit her. Matthew came tumbling just after her, and now, as his movements slowed, he dropped his sweating forehead to hers.

"Thank goodness we got to have this here, and not the dreams," she said.

"Goddess." He burst into laughter. "Ah, shit, Lily." He flopped next to her, his body quaking with his laughs. "You're fucking perfect."

CHAPTER 73

"FOR THE record, I *did* knock," Lina said when Caid side-eyed her. He had been standing at the counter trying to assemble *something* that looked like dinner to eat when the bag of groceries plopped next to him and Lina appeared.

"Tapping it with your finger doesn't count, Leen."

She huffed and began unpacking the bag. "Scoot. What *is* what?"

"Food." He lifted his bowl.

Picking up the package that sat near the sink, her eyes bounced back and forth as she read. "This is disgusting, Caid. You can't eat this! Put that down." She pointed to the counter. "Right now."

He spun his fork in the noodles, lifting the bowl slightly while dipping his head closer to it. Slowly, he opened his mouth.

"Kincaid James McGrath!" She lunged for him.

He hopped back a step and shoved the forkful into his mouth.

"Give me." She snapped her fingers, then motioned for the bowl.

He forked in another bite. When she reached for the bowl again, he said, "Ah-ah," and wagged the fork at her. "You should be polite in the presence of company."

"What?" She halted, brows knotting.

Caid turned his head toward the kitchen table, where Matthew sat wearing a bemused grin. He waved to Lina, and she winced, her face flaring red.

"Oh, uh, hi. You must be Matthew," she said. In a stage whisper to Caid, she asked, "How long has he been there?"

Caid chuckled and shook his head. "Only a few seconds."

Lina took the distraction as the opportunity to swipe the bowl from him and dump its contents in the trash. "So! Matthew," she began cheerily, "you're Róisín's cousin?"

Matthew's eyes darted to Caid. "I, yeah, you could say that."

"Nope." Caid took her by the shoulders, then turned her toward the living room, guiding her toward the door. "Save your questions for another day. This is guy time."

"Oh! So you two can bond and whatever, since you and Róisín are engaged, and he's going to be your cousin."

"What?" Matthew's voice squeaked high.

Caid tipped his head back and groaned. "Fuck, *Leeeeeen*, come on."

"What?" She batted her lashes at him. "You said *fiancée*, and that's not a word you toss around like candy at a parade, Kincaid. Not to mention, Wyatt acted really weird at the grocery store earlier when I saw him. Gigglier than a teenage girl with her eyes locked on her crush and speaking in like, code or something, like I'm supposed to be in on it."

"I'll tell you what, scram now, and I'll pay for you to have foot massages the rest of your pregnancy," Caid said.

She chewed her cheek, staring at him. "Make it that, plus three months of postpartum and you've got a deal."

"*Fiiiiine*. Just go." He gave her a gentle nudge.

"It was nice meeting you, Matthew!" she called over her shoulder as she ducked through the door.

"Engaged, huh?" Matthew asked with a smirk. "When's the wedding?"

Caid scratched his head. "We haven't exactly gotten past the asking and her saying yes part. Things sort of went to super shit right after."

"Hope you don't mind, but I tinkered with the Jeep a bit this morning. I saw it sitting tucked off to the side and"—he spread his hands out before him—"fuck, I'm so bored."

"How do you think I ended up with the Jeep?"

"The difference is," he said, resting his elbows on the table and pointed a finger to Caid, "even if you'd gotten your magic when we all do, you're what? Forty? You'd still be training and learning how to use that magic. Me?" He fell back in the chair with a huff. "It's like what Róisín said the other day. Except I got benched at the half. I didn't get to play *any* of the second."

Caid drummed on the counter, willing his heart to calm down. "I'm sorry I fucked up."

"What? You think? Shit." He shoved both of his hands into his hair, gripping it. "Shit, Caid. No. That was all me. And I wasn't thinking it all the way through when I did it. I realized what she was talking about and just...jumped."

"If I'd been able to do more..." He lifted his hands, looking at them. "She would have never left that room."

"Mildred was almost six centuries old. We were fucked the minute she got involved." He tipped his head to the side. "What happened after?"

"Depends on what you want to know."

"All of it."

Caid studied him for a moment. The way he held his body casually, but his posture belied the tightness of his face, the shadows there. With a nod, Caid told him about the days and the weeks after. Leaving nothing out. Róisín's loss of power. What had happened with her and Lily in Shianshani. Even the voices and the darkness that gnawed at his insides.

"That's normal. Mine talks to me all the time," Matthew said casually. "Except more often than not, mine wants me to go sit my ass on a beach somewhere in the realms with a fruity beverage. The kind that comes with an umbrella. However"—he ruffled his red hair—"beaches and I don't get along."

"Yeah, well, it'd have been nice if that'd come in the handbook." He rose and went to the refrigerator. "I've got nothing that pairs well with an umbrella, but want a beer? Water? Whatever the hell this shit is." He pulled a bottle from a shelf and lifted it. The contents were cloudy with something thick floating at the top. "This has to be from Lina."

"I've got a better idea." Matthew stood and stretched. "We've both

356

got some shit to work out, and I know an excellent way to let off that steam."

The way Matthew's eyes glinted with mischief, Caid hesitated to agree.

"Oh, come on. We'll be back before Róisín or Lily. It's all good." He held out his hand.

"I'm gonna regret this," Caid muttered, but took Matthew's hand anyway.

CHAPTER 74

"WHAT IN the fuck is that thing?" Caid asked from behind Matthew.

He tipped his head back, looking up, up, up, the front of the massive, horned beast they stood before. "That, my apparently soon-to-be brother-in-law, is a Krogor."

Caid's response came as an incredulous shout. "What?"

Matthew spun around to him, his grin so wide it made his cheeks ache. "It's just a baby one. *Mostly* harmless."

His eyes were glued to the beast. "Mostly harmless. Yeah, I'm not buying that. You know, Matthew, if you wanna just go right ahead and toss me over a cliff and get it over with, I'll go willingly." His eyes caught Matthew's. "Just don't say I didn't warn you about Róisín when she finds out. But really—" He faced the beast again. "I'd rather *not* go out being gnashed to death by teeth."

Matthew walked over to him and put a hand on his shoulder. "I don't want you dead. Quite the opposite, in fact."

"Could've fooled me. This looks *nothing* like what Róisín said when I asked what a Krogor was. They seemed...smaller, by her description." He held his hands roughly two feet apart.

"That's surprising. She hates these things." Matthew studied the

Krogor. Its thick, rough coat was like the quills of a porcupine. As it moved toward them, the coat chattered ominously. From its back and shoulders, long, serrated spikes jutted out. Both feet and hands were long and twisting claws. Matthew knew they were sharp, having not been fast enough a time or two to dodge an incoming blow.

It chose that moment to release a ground rattling roar, exposing teeth long enough to puncture a man clean through with ease.

"You've probably been training with Shasta where Nanette is out, right?"

Caid nodded, keeping his eyes locked on the monster. Matthew could hear the thunder of his heart from where he stood.

"And given you're a bit more jacked than you were a few weeks ago, Brent's been giving you the rounds."

Caid nodded again.

"Consider this"—he spun away from Caid and back to the Krogor —"real life training. And therapy."

Caid snorted. "Therapy?"

"Yeah. Pretty easy to see that you and I are a lot alike in that aspect." Matthew winced as the ground shook beneath their feet again. The Krogor had moved closer to them, the rattling from its tongue growing louder in warning. "You've got some shit to work out that beating the piss out of yourself against Brent isn't helping with."

Caid dropped his hands to his sides, pressing his lips tightly together. It was all the proof Matthew needed to know that he'd hit the nail on the head. He didn't need to know what Caid was kicking his own ass over, but knowing he was, was enough.

Standing at the edge of the Dead Forest that night, the unspoken words that passed between them had shifted something in their relationship. It had made the minutes, the hours, in Alleyette more bearable.

A friend. A brother.

"Its weak spots are its blind spots," Matthew said.

"And those are?"

"There." Matthew pointed to the side of its face, just in front of a set of horns. "Same on the other side. And there." He pointed lower to an area just below an arm. "But only that side."

"That's it?!"

"Yup."

Caid let out a loud breath. "Alright. Let's fucking do this."

And together, they charged forward.

THE PEAS ON MATTHEW'S FACE WERE ONLY MAKING HIM FEEL colder. Nothing eased the pain that throbbed around his left eye. He was also pretty sure he had broken his nose. From across the living room, Caid let out a low groan.

"That was a hell of a shot, by the way," Matthew said from beneath his half-thawed peas.

"I still missed," Caid said.

"By barely an inch." But he knew the response was pointless. He had seen, quickly, in the way Caid fought with a different vigor than he had in Alleyette. Róisín's death chased them all, but he saw how it nipped at Caid's heels more viciously. And with Madigan's return...

"If it hadn't been for you ripping that horn off." Caid's words trailed off into a hiss. "Shit."

Matthew had felt the Krogor that morning. Few witches had been sent out to deal with the monsters and beasts that new, untrained magic created. It had been something that he and Róisín had been trained by Brent for.

Their skills with their magic proved of worth to be on the hunt, while other witches located the new magic and worked with the child and family in training. That had been Lucius's push when he'd taken the position as the head of the Coven Council. No one was left behind anymore.

Lucius.

The ache from the way his chest tightened wasn't from the new bruises blooming there. Nor was the burn that began just behind his eyes. That he hadn't received Lucius's magic yet...

"What in the Hells you two? Are you fucking kidding me?" Róisín's raised voice made him wince and groan.

"No, shh, quieter babe, please," Caid pleaded. "No noise."

Matthew couldn't stop the watery chuckle, grimacing as it rocked his body. "You should see the other guy."

"I've got ointment and stuff in the upstairs bath, Lily, can you go grab it *all*, please?" she said.

Matthew shot upright. The thawing peas landing in his lap right on a forming bruise along the top of his thigh making him wince. He caught sight of Lily's feet darting up the stairs. Then he saw the way Róisín was glaring at him. He pointed to Caid. "He threw the first punch."

Her eyes narrowed on him and her nostrils flared.

"It was him." Caid groaned. "I was just defending myself."

Silence fell over the room. The only noise in the house was the sound of Lily upstairs pulling first aid supplies from the bathroom closet.

Then Caid and Matthew's childlike giggles split the air.

"Ah, fuck, that hurts," Caid managed between his chuckles. "Shit, shit."

"Stop making me laugh." Matthew tried to sound serious, which only made them laugh harder.

"Are they alright?" Lily asked.

"I say we leave them here to suffer, and go to Lina's," Róisín said.

"Please don't. She'll drag you back over here." Caid reached for Róisín. "She's gone into mother mode and it's awful."

"She tried to steal his dinner," Matthew added.

Caid pointed in Matthew's direction. "Yeah, that."

Róisín covered her face with her hands and shook her head.

"I'll get this one out of your hair." Lily moved around the coffee table toward Matthew. "So you can tend to that one."

When she bent to loop his arm around her shoulder, Matthew waved her away. "I can stand."

She hesitated but took a step back to give him room.

Matthew slipped his hand into Lily's. "Sorry for beating up your fiancé." He winked at Róisín. Before she could respond, he shifted himself and Lily back to the cottage.

Lily lifted a hand and traced along the cut that split his eyebrow. "Do you feel better at least?"

The weight on his shoulders fell off, and he brought her against him, kissing the top of her head. She saw right through him.

"How'd you know?"

"What? That you and Caid wouldn't actually beat the Hells out of one another?" She pressed her face against his chest. "I can feel everything here." She placed a hand over his heart. "And here." She pulled back slightly and took his face in her hands. "It pulses down our line sometimes. I wish you'd talk to me about it, but if this works right now, then..." She shrugged.

He smoothed her hair back, then kissed her forehead softly. "I'll get there, Lily. I just need to find the words for it all first."

"Promise?"

"Promise."

CHAPTER 75

Róisín WINCED at the same time as Caid did when she rubbed the lidocaine cream over his back. The bruises there were big, black, deep purple, and angry.

"Sorry," Caid mumbled into the pillow his face was buried in. "I didn't mean to."

This time, when she applied more lotion, she sent a wave of warmth down their line before the pain hit and he yanked out of reflex.

"I don't see why you won't let me heal you," she said.

"I'm a big boy, I can handle—" He hissed. "I take it back. Do your thing. Make the magic."

She tossed the bottle onto the bed next to him, then placed her hands on his skin. Moments later, the remnants of the bruises, a fading yellow, were all that remained. "Better?"

He rolled onto his back. "A million times better."

"Since I know you two didn't have a round of fisticuffs in the backyard, want to tell me what really happened?"

"Bonding."

She snorted and lifted a brow. "You're dead serious, aren't you?"

"Only kind of." He pushed himself into the sitting position.

"Oh, Caid." She sighed heavily. "Old habits are hard to break, aren't they?" She shifted and settled carefully next to him.

"You lied, you know."

"Lied?" She jerked her head up. There was a new gleam in his eyes, a brightness in the hazel that hadn't been there in a while. Something about seeing it had her settling back against him.

"Yeah. That Krogor thing? One hundred percent *not* what you said it was."

She was moving again, hopping up and off the bed. "You two found a Krogor? Of *course* you did. And he thought it was a good idea to bring you along? Nope. Never mind." She spun on a heel and stomped into the bathroom. She needed a shower. Her fraying nerves began to pull apart in Ely as Lily and she waited for Ione to finish translating the last page of the book, causing her to nearly sweat through her shirt.

As she had felt something *other* hovering in the atmosphere between Ione, Runa, and Shasta. Something heavy and new. It had made it hard to focus on what Ione said. What Jessamyn said.

She cranked the hot water all the way over, her muscles tightening as the water came out cold at first, pelting her like ice. Slowly it warmed and she let her head hang between her shoulders under it.

Caid's lips pressed against her skin between her shoulder blades. "I'm sorry."

She squeezed her eyes shut. "No, I'm sorry. It's so stupid of me to be mad at you."

His hands went to her shoulders, and he turned her to him. "Wanna talk about it?"

"Ione finished translating the book." Róisín swore he stopped breathing.

"And?"

"Nothing, yet. Jessamyn is reading it now. She knows the most about the curse, so she would be the one to catch anything on the pages that would stand out as the one they used."

"What happens now? More waiting? Christ, I don't know how you all do it."

She let her body fall against his. "We don't exactly have a choice.

There's so many moving parts in all of this. I just want to... Ugh, dammit. *I* want to go kick the shit out of a Krogor."

"Matthew said you hated them."

"I *do*. Doing something is better than doing nothing."

He backed her against the wall. "I can think of something we can do that's certainly not nothing."

She bit back her giggle as she remembered Lina's and her conversation about him. "Did you at least have fun?"

His tongue traced her collarbone, and he hummed. "Mm. Good times. We gossiped; braided each other's hair.."

When his teeth grazed the front of her throat, her body lit like a freshly struck match. Her core grew tight and hot with anticipation. "And you feel better?" She had hoped that some type of conversation happened between the men about their time in Alleyette.

He tugged her earlobe into his mouth, the stubble along his cheek rubbing against hers. "Mostly." He brushed his lips over her cheek, soothing the slight burn there from the chafe. "I don't think that broken part of me will ever change."

She nudged him back, noticing the way his eyes had darkened. "Caid—"

"I'm going to do my damned best, Róisín. Everything these past few weeks, and earlier with the Krogor, it's all been so that I can be *better*. Better for the next time."

Her throat grew tight. "Hells, Caid. You looked like you found your way into a wood chipper barely an hour ago." Matthew too. Her chest stung with pain.

How had they all ended up so broken? More than ever before. She wasn't sure they could ever be whole again, or at least as whole as they had once been.

"It's the being able to keep going. Getting back up after getting the shit kicked out of me, Róisín. This is nothing like I've ever known before. Getting slammed into by a ball of fucking *air* and tossed into a wall, that's a lot different from a fist to the face."

She shivered, the water coming from the shower head slowly losing its heat as the hot water began to run out. He stepped closer, caging her with his body, his heat.

"When I said together, this is what I meant," he said. "You're not facing him alone again. I'm not losing you *again*, and he's not winning, again. This ends with us."

He brought his mouth to hers, leaving her unable to respond. His magic lifted around them, warming the space, and she pushed her worries aside, leaned into his surety. Let him pull her deeper into the kiss.

"Lift your hands," he said. "Please," he added, nuzzling her neck.

Obediently, she lifted both arms, laying them back on the cool tile of the wall.

"Don't move." He nipped at her shoulder, then made his way down her body, caressing and kissing a map across her skin. He hummed in delight when his fingers moved between her legs. "I'll never get enough of this." He stroked along her seam before teasing her entrance with a finger.

She couldn't stop the way her hips automatically moved toward him, chasing his touch.

He nipped her hip, and her core fluttered in response. "I said don't move, Róisín."

"I can't help it," she panted the words.

His tongue traced along the line of her hip, down her thigh. With his mouth hovering before her, so close to where her body ached for him the most, he lifted his gaze to her.

"Caid." His name was a plea from her lips.

Holding her eyes with his, he moved closer, his tongue darting out. Her hips rocked. "Róisín." It was a deep rumble from his chest, and a warmth against her most sensitive place when he was near. Her legs weakened, and she wanted to fall against him. "Don't move."

She drew a shaking breath in, bracing for the feel of him.

He shifted his hands over her. One flat against her stomach, making her muscles quiver at his touch. The other, he used to spread her further apart before he laved her clit. If he had felt the slight way she tipped her hips closer, he said nothing. He circled her with his tongue, then pulled her into his mouth, sucking.

Róisín's arms started to fall away from the wall, but she caught herself before they dove into his hair and placed them back overhead.

The inability to grip his head and grind against the delicious things he was doing with his tongue brought her to the edge. Her body erupted and her breaths quickened.

Caid brought his hand away from her stomach, slipping one finger, then another, inside of her. Their slow rhythm of in and out was enough. Her body tightened for just a moment before she shattered.

Before she could slide her limp body down the wall, Caid was lifting her, bringing her legs around his waist.

His hand back at her stomach between them, he spread his fingers. "I can feel it here. The way you almost—" He kissed her jaw. "Shake first, then you tighten." He bent his head, hovering over a breast. "Then your whole body sort of rolls." He closed his mouth over her nipple, drawing into his mouth. "It's amazing."

She could feel his cock nudging her and shifted her hips back. "It *feels* amazing." She tilted her hips forward, the tip of him slipping in. Slowly, they moved together to close the gap.

"Róisín." His breath was warm against her mouth. "I love you. Fuck, do I love you. The things I don't think, but *know* I'd do for you. It's, shit, I can't—" His mouth crashed into hers. His kiss was hard, desperate.

She clung to him, returning the emotions.

She shoved her hands into his hair, gripping tightly. "I'd burn the realms for you, Kincaid McGrath."

His eyes flared with greens, browns, and reds.

"Forever." She rocked against him, then circled her hips. "Always."

"Fates be damned." He pressed her harder against the tiles and rocked into her, over and over. The words she wanted to say were stolen by the breaths that escaped in pants, and her cries as she returned to her edge, tumbling over with him following closely behind.

Could the fate the Sisters had seen for her be changed?

Chapter 76

Jessamyn leaned back against Lucius's desk and held her gaze on Runa's. "I'm leaving you in charge here for the next few days. I need to be present in Talista for the gala and planning Róisín's arrival to the very *t.*"

Runa stretched his legs before him and crossed them at the ankles. "How's that any different from what I've been doing here already?"

"Considering I too have been here nearly as much as you?" She lifted a brow. "Do you love her?"

He had brought his hands behind his head, clasping them, and had just closed his eyes. But they flew open now. Despite the dark of his skin, she could see how his cheeks deepened with color. "Excuse me?"

She smirked at him. "Oh, Runa Irinell Lunestran." She let out a hearty chuckle. "You act like I don't know you nearly as well as I know myself. You know exactly what I'm talking about."

Runa was sitting up straight on the sofa now, hands folded in his lap. He cast his eyes downward. "Can I? After this short while? It's been just a few weeks."

Jessamyn thought about Diana, how quickly they had fallen for one another. Aja had been a slower, burning kind of love. "What does your heart tell you?"

"Absolutely yes. Hells, Jes, I've never..." He shook his head. Pushing quickly to his feet, he began pacing. He rubbed a hand over his bare head. "She knows. She knows who I was, and she still loves me. Says it doesn't matter."

Jessamyn's heart gave a happy flutter against her ribs. "Because it doesn't matter."

"What do I do? What do *we* do? We'll never be accepted anywhere," he said.

"The laws will change in Shianshani."

He snorted a cruel laugh. "Laws and how people are, Jes, are two completely different things. You can't change the minds of people."

Her future pressed against her chest, and for a moment, it stole her breath. "Runa, promise me, no matter what happens, you—" She swallowed, trying to clear her throat, but it was too tight, emotions too thick. Her next words were broken. "Stay with Róisín. You and Ione. Wherever she goes, you stay with her. It's the only way I know you two can be completely safe."

Runa stopped pacing and spun to face her. "What do you know, Jes? What *have* you known this whole time and haven't said?"

"Don't worry about it. Please, just promise me." The edges of her vision blurred as the pressure within her chest grew.

He stood in front of her, his large palms on her cheeks. "Jes," he whispered. "No. *NO*. Does Aja know?"

Closing her eyes to hide the tears building there, she gave a slight nod.

Runa's sob was more of a gasp before he crushed her to his chest. "There has to be something else, another way."

She wrapped her arms around his shaking body. "Just promise me, Runa. Promise me."

His chest heaved a breath against her. "I prom—"

The door burst open, Ten and Ione rushing in.

"What is it?" Jessamyn asked.

"We can't." Ten shook her head, then hunched over, hands on her knees, trying to catch her breath.

"There's nothing we can do with the curse to reverse it," Ione said.

"But how?" Jessamyn's ears buzzed. "All spell work is written in such a way it can be disassembled and reversed."

"*None* of the spell work in this book can be," Ten said. "It's something else. I can't explain it. The words are bound to their order, like a ward has been placed on each of them. It's held in place, we can't."

"Shit." Jessamyn ground her teeth together. She should have known. Everything to this point had been as complicated as possible. Why would this be any different?

"What do we do?" Ione asked quietly.

"You go to your sister and get Róisín. We need to, all of us, sit down and re-plan how these next few days are going to go. You"—she looked at Runa—"go to Anelle and Aja. Get Marcelo, Anthony, and Cassius too." She lifted a hand to halt him mid-step. "And Nolani. We meet here, not the Coven suites, as a precautionary. Every move we make now gets planned *here*."

CHAPTER 77

"WHAT IS—" Lily gagged. "This?" She lifted the bottle, its thick contents swirling.

Róisín's hand flew to her mouth. "Oh, no, no, just throw the whole thing away. Don't open it. That's *supposed* to be lemonade. That I made before..."

Lily walked over to the trash can, popped the lid, and let the bottle drop with a thud. Róisín had been doing what she called 'panic cleaning' when Lily's frantic knocks sounded that morning. She had gone to see Ione, and when she returned, Matthew was gone, again. Róisín had been home when Matthew had arrived, convincing Caid to let him tag along to the job site with him. She had made both men promise that was where they were going, and not looking for trouble.

Now Lily joined Róisín in the cleaning. They scrubbed every surface to a shine, even the nooks and crannies.

"How do you do it?" Lily fell back onto her bottom and tossed her scrubbing brush into the bucket of cleaner.

Róisín lifted the rag she held, placed it on the wall she was washing, and moved it in circles.

"No." Lily waved a hand at her. "This." She spread her arms out.

"Lily, why do you think I'm practically scrubbing the paint off of my walls?"

She pushed her jaw off to the side slightly and aggressively chewed her bottom lip.

Róisín climbed down from the small ladder she was on. Setting her cleaning supplies on the table in the living room, she walked over and dropped next to Lily.

"The first time I truly felt helpless is when I walked through that door right there." She tipped her head to the front door. "Sure, I had Matthew and Lucius, but it was the first time I was very much alone. I didn't know what to do. I was crap at most of my magic, and I questioned every day if that would be the day I screwed up. Screwed up for myself, for all of us, and Madigan found out I wasn't some girl who dabbled with spell work. To be honest, I'm surprised at myself for how far I made it. I wasn't exactly—" She released a small laugh. "Equipped properly. My mother meant well, but she never really showed me more than the basics with my magic."

"Why?"

"I think it really exhausted her own magic keeping herself and I hidden the way she did. It was a lot of energy to put out there too, which was a risk in itself. For me to use the full power of my magic, that would have been a beacon." Róisín crossed her legs. "And we have a good idea of what Aoife's plan was. Those first few weeks here, just trying to find my place in all of this. Trying to figure out who I was while also dealing with everything else. I wanted to disappear so badly."

Lily swirled the brush in the water. "Why didn't you?"

"Everyone started coming together. Nanette and Lucius worked with me. Shasta and I reconnected after whatever wall it was in my mind came down, and I remembered our history. Matthew came. You started helping us. It became like a family. The one that I chose. I couldn't abandon any of you, not when you all were risking everything to help me. And I learned a *lot* about myself. I stopped doubting myself *as* much. I mean..." She made a raspberry noise with her lips. "I still doubt at least once a day that I can do this."

She rested her elbows on her knees, then laid her chin on a fist. "I'm doing it right now, actually. Back then, I had my mother's books to read through when I needed the distraction to find some focus. Now? I don't have that, so I clean. Everything. Because thinking about just sitting there and waiting makes my skin crawl."

"I may have alphabetized all the bookshelves in the cottage," Lily said.

"It's hard being on the sidelines."

"I hate it."

Róisín pat Lily's knee. "Me too. I thought a few times of us going back out there and trying to figure out this Coven thing, but I can't give that the time right now. Not with Madigan here."

"Not to mention, mostly, aside from Baijiola and Trifoa, we *are* united. Think about it for a second." Lily lifted a hand, fingers against her palm. "You have Ione and I, sorry *Grandmother*, but we count as Roidon." She lifted a finger. "Matthew is Ely." Another finger. "Shasta, Molennius." A third finger. "Jessamyn is absolutely in." A fourth. "You," she wiggled all her fingers.

Lily was right, Róisín realized. They were more than halfway united. Once Madigan was done, gone for good. Her heart skipped in her chest.

"Róisín? I just saw Caid, and he said you were home." Lina's voice called from the other side of the screen door.

"In here!" Róisín called back. She rose to her feet and offered her hand to Lily. "You should probably stand when you meet Lina. Everything Caid is? She's the exact opposite. And you'll love her."

"Why does it smell like a hosp—Oh, you have company? I can come back." Lina jabbed a thumb toward the door.

"No, stay. This is Lily." Róisín motioned to her. "Lily, this is Lina. Caid's sister."

Lina winced as she held out her hand. "Do I have to admit to him?"

Róisín rolled her eyes. "Pretty sure he asks the same about you."

"Oh, he loves me." Lina shook Lily's hand. Her eyes roamed the living room, her nose scrunching as she sniffed. "It smells like a hospital in here. With a splash of citrus."

"Giving it a seasonal scrub," Róisín said. "Wanna help?"

"What are you using? Helen said I need to be careful around chemical stuff."

Róisín handed her the bottle of solution. "No bleach, all-natural stuff."

"Gimme a rag." Lina held out both hands, motioning with her fingers. "If I wash anything in my house one more time, Thomas is going to glue my hands together. He wouldn't really," she added when Lily gasped. "I'd glue his ass to a chair first."

Róisín looked at Lily who was watching Lina with eyes wide. "Told you. Exactly the opposite."

"Oh, for sure. For every one word Caid says, I say twenty to make up for it." Lina giggled.

Lily only blinked, making Róisín burst into laughter.

Róisín picked her own rag back up. "Hey, Lina?" She turned. "Did you steal my rabbit?"

"Uh..." Lina's eyes darted around the room, looking everywhere but at her. "I can go grab him?"

Róisín sighed.

"What? It was really fucking lonely here without you and Caid. Helen's great and all, but when Thomas is gone." She pouted. "David's been keeping me company. Giving me updates."

"Updates?" Róisín felt her brows crawl upward. It had been David to tell Lina that Madigan was Stewart Munson, the businessman in Greens Glen that's factory was poisoning the town.

All Lina said was, "Yeah."

"Lina." Róisín moved closer to her. "What has David been telling you?"

She wrung the rag in her hands. "Just a little about where we're from."

The blood rushed to Róisín's head, and she licked her lips. Pounding on the screen door had them all jumping and whirling.

"Lily? Róisín?" Ione's voice rang out.

Róisín and Lily locked eyes.

"Come in!" Róisín shouted.

Ione appeared a second later. Her gaze landed instantly on Lina.

"Caid's sister, Lina." Róisín waved toward her. "Lina, this is Lily's sister, Ione."

"Hi, nice to meet you, but I need to steal my sister and Róisín," Ione said. To Lily and Róisín, she said, "We need you in Ely. Now."

"Caid?" Róisín asked.

"He'll need to be brought up to speed." Ione nodded. "But he should stay with Matthew. I know he knows what's going on, but the risk is too much."

"He'll say otherwise and be pissed he was left behind," Lily said. "They both will."

"We'll deal with that later. Right now, we need to go. *Now*," Ione replied firmly.

Róisín frowned. She had so many questions for Lina that she needed the answers to, but this... this was important, too. "Dammit," she mumbled. She felt a hand lightly touch her forearm and found Lina watching her with sad eyes.

"I'll get all this taken care of," she told Róisín. "And I can tell Caid when he gets home. Maybe by the time you come back from whatever..." She lowered her voice. "I'll find the courage to tell you what David has told me. I'll at least try my best."

Róisín gave her a tight hug. Then, with Lina standing with her unused rag in hand, wearing a frown and her eyes glittering with coming tears, Róisín, Lily, and Ione shifted away to Ely.

CHAPTER 78

"ABSOLUTELY FUCKING not," Caid said as he struggled to keep his barely contained rage in check.

Róisín's nostrils flared wide on her exhale. "Caid—"

"I said no." He folded his arms over his chest and squared his shoulders. His eyes never left Jessamyn's, despite Róisín's interruption.

He had come home from work, an exhausted and worn Matthew in tow, to find his sister waiting for him. Not Róisín. After Lina had told him about Ione's arrival, and where Róisín had gone, he paced the house like a caged animal. Waiting.

He knew Róisín. Knew exactly what she would say if they asked her. What she would give of herself without question.

Despite Jessamyn sending Róisín away from Shianshani, and keeping her away, he still didn't trust her.

He especially didn't trust her not to offer Róisín as the sacrificial lamb to Madigan to save herself and the Shianshani Coven.

Shasta, she was there; he knew. She had stepped in for Lily so she could stay with Matthew. But, since her argument with Lucius, she had been unreadable and more withdrawn. He hadn't noticed her drinking again in the times he had seen her, but she wasn't someone he felt he could trust at the moment to stand in front of Róisín's self-destructing train. And Lily, as much as he'd come to love her as family, would be steamrolled by Róisín.

A low growl of frustration emanated from his throat.

Matthew had sat on the loveseat in the living room with one knee bouncing. His other knee was still, but he drummed his fingers rapidly against it.

Lina had said for them to wait, Róisín would have news about whatever it had been when she returned. It wouldn't be news. She'd return with a decision made.

"Fuck it. We're not waiting." Caid snapped his fingers and pointed to the ceiling. "We're going, now."

"Thank Goddess." Matthew lurched to his feet. "And it's more that way," he added, pointing toward the left and slightly down. "We'll get you a map of them. You can hang it by the calendar."

It wasn't long after they arrived in Ely that the arguing had begun.

"It won't be for long, and she'll remain under heavy Coven guard." Jessamyn mirrored his position. Except, she tipped her head to one side, as if welcoming the challenge.

Shasta stood along a far wall, chewing on her lip, not looking at anyone in the room. She hadn't said a word as Jessamyn laid out her intentions with the gala and the shouting had begun.

The curse couldn't be broken.

Whatever Madigan was, even without magic, was bad enough that *all* of Jessamyn's most Coven members, along with the princes, were present in the large sitting room at Lucius's manor with streams of fear radiating from each of them. It was enough to finish pushing Caid over the edge. It had been a close enough call the day Róisín and Lily had come to the cottage hurt.

He glanced at his side where Matthew stood behind Lily and caught his eye. The set of Matthew's jaw and the tight nod he gave Caid was the sign that he felt the same as Caid about Róisín and Lily going back to Shianshani.

"Can we"—Róisín gestured to the door—"for just a moment."

Jessamyn nodded and moved to join Aja and Anelle. As Caid passed them, he felt that sludge rise inside of him. The tickles of smoke stroking along his veins. It had been so long since that side of his magic had risen, that the feel of it now sent his heart to his throat.

"What in the Hells, Caid," Róisín hissed and shoved him back against the wall in the hallway. "Since when are you a caveman?"

"It's not being a caveman, Róisín. It's called using my fucking head." He took her by her shoulders, swapping their positions. He placed a hand next to her head and leaned in close, bringing his eyes level with hers. "You'll see an opportunity while you're there. I know you. Shit." He pushed away. "I can even see it in my head how it would play out. Somehow, you'd wind up with him, *alone*, and you'd try to do it yourself. Spare everyone, right?"

She cast her eyes down and remained silent.

"There has to be a different way. *Has to be.*" He paced away to the other side of the hall. "Using you as a stick to poke the monster." He shook his head. "No. It's too dangerous."

"It's the only way. He's the only one strong enough to take care of the others like him. We have to do something. We don't know if he's close to getting his magic back, or not. There's too much risk."

He stalked back to her, placing his forearms on the wall on either side of her. "I don't care about a goddamn soul in that room Róisín. You're the only one that matters to me, and you're not a risk I want to take."

She finally lifted her eyes to his. They were a storm of deep grays, blues, and streaks of green. "Do you think I want this? Do you think I don't still *feel* him all over me, in me? To know he's still here, and that he still..." Her breath caught.

His molars groaned from the pressure as he ground them together at the memory of what she had shown him from that day in the ravine. "Then give me my chance at him."

"No." Her response was quick and firm. "Look, we're all on this weird, forced trust thing here with the Shianshani Coven, and they, us. This isn't self-serving of Jessamyn. She wants to keep her people safe. We want him gone. If we all do this thing together, we have a chance. *I* have a chance."

Caid dropped his forehead to hers. "You shouldn't have said that."

"What?" He felt her forehead wrinkle against his.

"*You* have a chance," he whispered.

"Like you wouldn't say the same. Like you wouldn't be making the same argument I am right now if our roles were reversed."

He cupped her cheek, stroking his thumb along her cheekbone. The warmth of her hand over his hand had him opening his eyes. "I can't let you go, Róisín. What if you don't come back?"

"I'll come back."

"We both know how quick it all changes." He moved his hand to her chin. "I know I'm not going to win this. You'll go regardless, and I can't let it happen when you're angry at me. We can't end like that."

"Caid—"

"If you're not back by the end of the window Jessamyn said, I'm coming to you, Róisín. I can't stop you, and you can't stop me. Got it?"

She nodded, her eyes shining with tears. He lowered his mouth to hers. The kiss started softly, but quickly became more as desperation and fear pushed their mouths together, tongues seeking, teeth colliding.

Róisín's hand gripped the back of his shirt, clinging. He held her face in his hands just as desperately. Their magic wrapped around them, caging them in.

"Don't leave me behind," she said against his mouth.

"I'll come for you," he promised.

CHAPTER 79

JESSAMYN WOVE her way through the milling crowds along the edge of the dance floor. She had two tasks to fulfill that evening. The first, making sure all her Coven were in place, ready for Róisín's arrival at the gala. Everything had been planned down to the very finite details, and gone over so many times, their voices were raw.

"It all lies with the last witch of Legianne..." the voice teased her ear as she searched for the king.

Her second task was standing tall and proud near the throne at the head of the room. Or at least, that was how he appeared to those around him. In the two days Jessamyn had been in Talista full time, she had seen the way his facade had crumbled.

The men stepped out of his control. Had given into the monster, the hunger.

Róisín not having returned.

His lack of magic to go to her himself.

Cracks were there in the tick of his jaw. The way he held his lips in a tight line. The skin of his face shuddered as he fought back the change. Even without his magic, the man that stood at the head of the room was the most dangerous man in all the realms.

And she was about to feed Róisín to him.

She prayed quietly to her Goddess that this was the right thing to do.

At that moment, Madigan's eyes locked on hers. She inclined her head, acknowledging him. Then she tipped it to the side toward a set of arches that would create a space of privacy for them. He tapped one finger to his cheek, signaling he would meet her in one minute. A gesture that she had seen from Rastead to her brother many times since he took the throne fifteen years before.

Were parts of Rastead still there? If there was, she had to question if there was any valid reason to not proceed with their plan. Rastead had upheld the laws of the realm that they had all so desperately wanted to be free of.

Reaching through her Coven line, she found both Aja and Runa. Her four quick tugs let them know she was moving forward. Their two, in return, acknowledged they were on standby.

Róisín was to enter the gala while Madigan was with Jessamyn. A plan that Róisín wasn't on board with at first, and Caid wasn't at all. Róisín had wanted Madigan to see her enter, to see her return and use that to draw him out. It was rash, and Jessamyn couldn't deny that she didn't understand the woman's urge to go at it head on. However, they all needed to remain levelheaded and cautious.

Too much was at stake.

Madigan still had too many men carrying the same blood curse around him, devoted to *him* for them to find any success in defeating him. His men needed to see Róisín first. As a guest of the court, Róisín could not refuse any dances that they asked her hand for.

"He's driven by his jealousy," Jessamyn told her. "We need him to help us. Albeit he'll be doing it unknowingly, but the more men he sees even casting their eyes in your direction, the better. It will mark them."

Caid had pulled Jessamyn aside, threatening her life should something happen to Róisín, and she didn't make it home.

"On my life, she'll come back," Jessamyn promised him.

"You have news." The king's voice was low at her side.

She had to fight off the shiver that tried to dance along her skin. "We found the spell work for the curse within a book that Frederick retrieved from Aunellion." She waited to see if he reacted to her words. His face remained passive, but there was something that flashed in his eyes, his pupils changing. "It took me some time to locate a linguist I could trust within the Coven to translate it."

Out of the corner of her eyes, she saw the grand doors open. Runa's head appeared over the crowd. Róisín was there.

Madigan straightened, his nostrils flaring wide. He made to turn toward the crowd, but Jessamyn reached out to touch his arm, bringing his attention back to her.

"Your Highness, there's an issue with the spell work." She kept her voice low and her tone concerned.

He grimaced, the skin around his eyes rippling. "An issue? It should be as simple as reworking the words to reverse it, should it not?"

Cautiously, she placed a hand on the back of his shoulder, guiding him further beneath the arches. Further away from Róisín. "That is how it *should* work, yes. However, it would seem there is a ward on the words. Once we try to shift them, they lose their power."

"That bastard," he muttered.

"Pardon?" She leaned closer.

"Can you break the ward? Overpower it?" His voice had become deeper, darker.

Shit. What if he lost control right there, around everyone? They had been so focused on getting Róisín in and out that she hadn't placed a contingency plan to keep everyone else as safe as they could be.

His head tipped to one side, appearing to stretch his neck, but the curl of his lip into a snarl indicated otherwise.

"Who is the witch that translated it?" He ground out.

"Ten Tretap," she said. "I can bring you to her and she can explain it better."

"Excellent." His hand dropped to her lower back. He extended his other toward the door at the far end of the row of arches. "Let's go."

Relief flooded her, loosening her lungs and limbs. She had gambled on him and the desire he held for Róisín. The concern that he could harm her as long as he still had the curse within. Luckily, it had paid off. This time.

CHAPTER 80

Róisín dipped into a slight bow. "Thank you, Lord Dostie, for the dance. It was wonderful and I hope your horses prove successful on the track next month."

Lord Dostie took one of her hands in his, lifting it to his mouth. "The pleasure was truly mine, Lady McKenna."

Once he disappeared toward the refreshment table, Aja was at her side, book ending her with Runa who had been dancing with one of the ladies next to her as she danced with Lord Dostie.

"It's time." Aja's words rumbled through her.

"Perfect, because I'm hungry and not for anything they're serving here. Sorry, but your food is gross." She made a face of disgust. "Lily?"

"Just near the door with Anelle and Enon," Aja said.

She had just let him take her hand in his, when a voice said behind them, "If I may have this dance, Lady McKenna, I would be honored far more than this crown atop my head gives me honor."

The trio froze. Róisín lifted her eyes to Runa, then shifted them to Aja. Aja's body had tensed next to her, the heat and energy from his magic rising, making the hairs on the back of her neck rise.

So close.

She swallowed hard and fixed a smile on her face, then turned to face the king. To face Madigan. She stepped one foot forward, then dipped to a bow. "Of course, Your Highness. But it is I who would be honored."

Letting him take her hand, she clumsily reached out to Aja with her mind, lightly tapping. When she felt him open for her, she said, *"One dance and then get me the Hells out of here."*

"I'll have people in place to create a diversion. Be ready when the song ends."

She looked over her shoulder at him, giving him a small nod. While he walked away to take care of the new plan, Runa slipped out onto the dance floor, stealing a lady from a lord in mid-step. He swung her around with flare, then lowered her into a low dip, sending her into a fit of giggles. Then, they settled into the dance near where Madigan and she followed the steps to the music.

"I'm so happy to see you have not been driven away by the animals who call themselves my guard," Madigan said. He stepped closer to her and kept his voice low. "I have made sure that they have been handled for their indiscretions."

"I..." She struggled around the gasp still lodged in her throat. "Thank you, my love. I should not have doubted that you would take care of me."

He spun her out with grace, her dress swishing around her legs. When he brought her back against him, he brought his nose down to her neck. "I can't say that it doesn't pain me you thought I would let others mistreat you without consequence."

His nose grazed along the skin of her neck, and she closed her eyes, swallowing hard. The urge to flee pounding within her. The magic hummed inside of her, begging her to let go and go.

"I understand it will take time for me to earn your trust. But I'm willing to do whatever." His hand skirted lower down her back, his palm at the base of her spine.

"You say that, but how long until your patience runs out? Aoife made me promises too after my mother died." There had been so many promises Aoife had made, each one just another lie to keep Róisín at her side, to keep the secrets she held buried.

His hand moved lower and Róisín's lungs stopped pulling in air. Her body screamed in alarm. In her hazing vision, she saw Runa edging closer with his dance partner. Aja was on the floor dancing near them as well.

"Aoife was a selfish woman," Madigan said.

"And you're not a selfish man?" She made a show of looking up at the crown that sat atop his head. *Breathe, Róisín. Just a little longer. You can do this.*

"I may sit as the king of a realm, Róisín, but trust me when I say that everything I've done is for far more than my gain."

She let him spin her out again. When he brought her back, his hand was no longer on her back. One hand cupped one of her ass cheeks. His thumb stroked along the fabric of her dress. "You said you wanted to rule with me at your side. How is that not self-gain?"

"Do I want that? Yes." He bent his head to meet her cheek, pressing his to it. His lips were at her ear now. "That is just part of it. Perhaps—" His tongue traced the shell of her ear. "The best part. However, I want what she took from my family."

"You want Aunellion back."

"No. I want my family whole again."

"Wh-what do you mean?"

He pressed closer to her and her body tensed. His cock pressed against her stomach and bile rose, burning her throat and making her eyes water.

"She stole my parent. One day, she just swept in and took them from us. Bound them to that house for eternity."

"Who?" she asked.

"My father, naturally, slowly declined. He turned inside of himself, leaving Bernard and I to our own defenses," he continued as though he hadn't heard her. "I made the vow to make it right. To bring them back to us. Unfortunately, she's a powerful woman."

He pulled back enough that the space that was suddenly between them left Róisín off balance and she stumbled her steps. "Who?"

"Gea de Oro." The vicious way he spat the words of the name made her shudder.

"I don't..." She shook her head.

"You do, my love. Unfortunately, we all know her." This time, when he spun her out and around, it was the longest seconds of her life. "She's the one all the fools call their Goddess."

CHAPTER 81

LUCIUS TRAILED his fingers over the photo in the house he had stepped into in Aunellion. He had wanted to laugh when he had seen it after getting the door open. It would be how the Sister Present, and the Sister Future's looms wove it.

There was a shining mischief and determination in the young girl's bright green eyes. Her crooked grin with one front tooth missing. The man and woman standing on either side of her looking down at her as though she were the sunrise and moonset of their lives.

The throb at his side had grown more intense as he shuffled his way up the road, wandering, until he had felt called to this home.

He had reached for Matthew's line and given it a small pull, hoping to learn if he had made it to the others, but there had been nothing. Clinging to the hope that he was okay, that he was with Róisín and the others, he had pressed on, his hand at his side, fingers sticky from the blood that seeped from the blade wound.

Blood shed at the well source. That had been the exchange. A life for a life, and blood spilled. Of course, it would be in the very center of the realm's capital. A realm ruled by witches *would* center on its source of magic.

Lucius wished he'd had the time to tell Matthew everything. Tell him more. But he knew the important part now. That he was his father. Regret settled into his bones over the rest. They should have told him. They shouldn't have kept it all from him.

"Well, isn't this a pitiful sight?" a light, feminine voice said.

"Are you fucking kidding me?" Lucius muttered and pinched the bridge of his nose.

"Did you really think I was going to miss *this*? I'd thought Matthew was my treat. A way to get under your skin just a little more." Her laughter was hollow sounding. "Apparently, that was only a teaser."

Lucius pressed his hand to his side harder and lowered himself into the chair near the bookshelf the photo had been on. His body sighed, and he sank into the cushions. The pain in his body beginning to ebb, fading to a numbness. His magic burned inside of him, screaming to reach the wound. Begging to heal it. He grit his teeth, pressing his will harder against it and in response, it threw itself against the barrier he had created.

"There will be sacrifices."

He wondered if Clarissa had known it would be him that made it. Not Matthew, nor Róisín.

"What are you here for?" Lucius's voice cracked, his lungs wheezing in protest.

The woman walked around the room, touching the items she passed by, picking up some, knocking over others. "Well, Lucius, my love," she began, her back to him, "you're the end of it all. You"—she faced him— "were the last to know of me. And once I find Brenna and that pitiful human of hers, place them back where they belong..."

"You told Róisín—"

"I know what I told Róisín," she shouted. "My little issue proved useful in keeping her at my side, so of course I said it was me. But I'll find her, find out how, and then..." The Cheshire Cat smile she flashed him let him see just how much the past year had slipped beneath her skin.

His laugh was quiet at first. As he sunk deeper into the chair, his lungs clutching, his laughter grew. Once he caught his breath, what he had left of it, he said, "Madigan is still alive."

Her eyes flared wide. "Lying won't keep you alive, Lucius."

"I don't give a shit. I made my choice." He coughed, flinching forward. Bringing his hand to his mouth, he wiped his lips, knowing before he even saw his hand that it would be blood. "He's in Talista. Shianshani."

She was quiet for a moment, watching him as he struggled to right himself in the chair. His body was growing weaker with each passing second. The echo of his heart in his ears slowing and growing faint.

"You're not lying. How?" she demanded.

"I'm quite sure he has his own motivations."

"It's impossible. Róisín killed him. Drew his very last living ember from his body."

Lucius let out a snort that sent him into another coughing fit. Blood spattered on the floor in front of him. "Oh, Gea." He shook his head. "You underestimated us all. We all may have had different reasons, wanted different outcomes, but in the end, you underestimated us all."

"What have you done, Lucius?" Her voice was like venom.

"I just wanted my wife to live. I wanted my family to stay whole until she and I were old and gray. Then leave it all to our children. *You* made the choice for all of us. Damned us all with your actions. I only wish I learned the truth about you before I lost her." He motioned toward the door. "You should probably go. I hear your realms are collapsing around you."

Flames sparked in her pupils and a sound between a scream and a growl tore from her before she shifted away.

He took a moment, letting the stillness of the house envelop him. Leaning forward, he gripped the armrest and struggled to his feet. With one hand clutching along the shelves, he made his way to the photo he had first held. Holding it to his chest, he returned to the chair, letting the cushion embrace him.

The Sisters would have him find his way here. To give him something familiar as he passed on beyond the veil. A wave of gratefulness crashed over him.

"I'm coming, my love," he whispered between heavy breaths. "My heart."

His vision edged black, his heart slowed more, more, more. His eyelids grew heavy and he let them drift closed.

The last thing he thought as he drew his last breath was that he was finally going back to Clarissa.

CHAPTER 82

C AID TRIED to keep his eyes from the tall clock in the corner that ticked loudly as its pendulum swung back and forth. It proved to be the longest hour of his life.

Shasta, Ten, Cicile, and Ione had returned to the library in one more hopeful attempt at learning some way to undo the curse. Matthew remained in the room with him, and now sat with his elbows on his knees and head in his hands. The twenty-seven minutes since Róisín and Lily had left had been filled with silence.

Caid needed to occupy the time remaining. "Shasta told me we couldn't shift with humans."

Matthew lifted his head, nose scrunched and brows knotted. "What? Shifting with humans?" He said, blinking. "No, we can't. Well, I thought we couldn't. But the princes being here before they all left for the gala proved that wrong, didn't it?"

"*Are* they human, though?" Caid brought one of his legs up and rested his ankle on his knee.

"The curse wouldn't change that. The humanity of a cursed person remains intact, regardless of what that curse does to them. So it would seem that we can shift with humans."

Caid rubbed his jaw. "Is it because they were a sort of rogue Coven?"

Matthew shook his head and sat back. "Yesterday was the first time I've met Jessamyn, but she's..." He lifted his hands palm up and moved them side to side. "She's incredibly intelligent, and I'm sure having Frederick as a brother pushed her to test the limits of her own magic. Along the way, she most likely made some discoveries, which—" He paused as though he were working his theory out in his mind first. "The people in that room were definitely a part of it. A movement perhaps? Even the humans."

Caid had felt a familiarity in the conversation at that moment. If he closed his eyes, blocking the image of Matthew out, it would feel as though he were sitting with Lucius once more. His chest grew tight.

He cleared his throat, and with effort reigned his emotions in. "You got all that from being around them for just a few hours?"

Matthew shrugged. "You'll do it too, after a time. Learn the distinct smells of magic. The way others look when they're letting their minds be opened to another witch. It's a lot of body language and how people speak but knowing the other two open doors to reading people with no need to be here." He tapped his temple.

The tug came quick and sharp, doubling Caid over and making him gasp so harshly, he was sent into a coughing fit. Matthew was on his feet and at his side in a second.

"What is it? Róisín? Are they okay?"

Caid blindly reached for the armrest of the chair. "We need to go, now."

"Fuck. We're not going unarmed."

Caid rolled off the chair, hitting the floor hard when the second tug came more as a yank. He willed his magic to rise, to help him. He needed to be up and moving, not rolling around the floor in the fetal position. Róisín was reaching for him. She needed him.

He got to his feet, his skin humming with magic, clawing to be released.

Matthew was in the doorway, shouting for the others. He looked back and saw Caid standing and jerked his head toward the training room. "Let's go stock up and get the Hells to Shianshani."

He took two steps towards the room and crumpled.

"Matthew!" Caid shouted, leaping over the table between Matthew and him.

"What happened?" Ione asked, appearing in the doorway across the hall.

Matthew's eyes rolled into the back of his head, his mouth moving with silent words.

"Matt!" Caid shook his shoulders.

Ione dropped to her knees, her eyes on where his pulse visibly hammered at his throat. "Matthew! Matt!" She patted his cheeks. "Matt, breathe!"

CHAPTER 83

MATTHEW COULDN'T catch his breath as two very different types of pain tore through him. The new magic coming to his body burned like acid through his every fiber. Raced like lava through his veins. Filling him. His body whipped backward, his back arching, and he let out a bellow that bounced around the room, slamming against the walls.

"Matt!" Caid's voice was sharp, strong, at his side.

"Gah!" he cried out, folding forward. He ground his teeth, his breath seething through them.

His heart knew. It knew if this magic was coming to him, then Lucius was—

No, he wouldn't think about it. He couldn't think about it. Not right now. Not when Lily needed him. When he needed to be there for the others.

But he couldn't stop it. His heart raced, pounding harder and harder as the first wave of grief hit him. His lungs were equally unforgiving, squeezing tighter and tighter.

"What's happening?" Ione's voice wavered. "Is he okay?"

"I—" Matthew squeezed his eyes tight, the tears streaming down his face. "Fuck!"

"Let's get him up and to the chair," Caid said.

"What's—that's..." The rest of Shasta's words went unspoken.

"What do we do, Shasta?" Ione demanded. "You're the adult here. Don't just stand there!"

"Fuck," Shasta said. "Alright. Um, this is him inheriting."

"Inheriting?" Caid asked.

"Oh, shit," Ione said with a gasp. "*No*. I'd hoped. Shit."

Caid raised his voice. "Someone fill me in?"

"Stop shouting," Matthew ground out. "You're all so fucking loud."

His body was at war with itself and overwhelmed. He couldn't move. Even his eyelids didn't want to move, remaining slammed shut.

"Inheriting is what happens when a family member, or a Coven member if there is no family and you are the leader, comes to you," Shasta explained to Caid.

"Shit," Caid whispered, understanding.

"I can't breathe." Matthew frantically grasped at his chest. His chest heaved with the effort but failed to bring in air. Behind his eyelids, everything was flashes and bursts of light.

"Get him up," Shasta said. "Ione, go grab water."

Caid's strong arms hooked around Matthew under his arms from behind.

"We've got weapons," Ten announced when she entered the room.

"Set them on the table right there for now," Shasta said.

"What now?" The vibration of Caid's voice against his back made Matthew whimper. The sensation of it sent his already over sensitive body into shock. "Matt, tell me what to do, how to help you."

Bring my father back, is what he had wanted to say. Instead, he told Caid, "I need dark, quiet. Just for a minute. *Please.*"

"Alright," Caid said. "Be right back," he added.

Matthew felt his feet shuffling over the floor. One of Caid's arms banded around his back, Matthew's arm slung over his shoulder. "You can just toss me over your shoulder, man."

"I didn't think you wanted the damsel routine," he said.

It made Matthew want to laugh. The effort to lighten the heaviness of the mood was appreciated, but he couldn't. Not with his broken mind, soul, and body. Not right now.

"Just pick me up," Matthew mumbled.

They stopped, and then Matthew felt the spinning sensation of one of the rides that Róisín had dragged him on several years earlier at something she called a festival when they had visited California on a trip. Round and round they had gone, faster and faster, until Matthew had been sure his brain was going to shoot out of his ears. He had loved it. They'd ridden the ride several more times, then stuffed their faces with all the greasy fair food. They had repeated that experience every year after.

It took Matthew a second to realize he was surrounded by silence. The voices of the others were not even a faint whisper through the walls. His breaths were harsh and labored, but he could breathe.

Then he forced his eyes open. The room they were in, even in the pitch black of it, he knew it. It was his room at the manor.

The room that his parents had spent hours in reading him bedtime stories at night. Where Clarissa had sung him lullabies. Lucius gave his long, winding, the-point-will-get-there sometime that day, talks. And he was currently on his bed.

What should have hurt, soothed. Slowly, ever so slowly, everything came back to Matthew. The burning and pressure eased. Then his lungs stretched, causing him to gasp as he could draw in his first full breath. Although his heart still hurt, it had no longer thrashed in his chest.

"Lucius is gone," he whispered, feeling Caid's presence on the other side of the room. "I want to... I-I don't know what I want. But it's not to feel like this."

The bed dipped next to him, and he felt Caid's arm come around his shoulder.

"I've lost them both, and I don't know what to do." His voice broke.

"We can just sit here for a second." Caid squeezed his shoulder. "Take a second to just... I don't know. Something."

"But—"

"Take it, Matthew. For fuck's sake, you just lost your father. I don't know what went down before you came back from that place, but I can guess it wasn't good. It made how your face looked after the Krogor look good. I'm guessing it was something you two faced together. So"—

he pat his back lightly—"take the fucking second. Then we'll go fight the monsters."

Matthew heard the unspoken words. The real and figurative monsters they'd fight. He dropped his chin to his chest, his eyes burning with the sting of new tears. "Alright."

CHAPTER 84

PANDEMONIUM HAD broken out in the grand hall that the gala was being held in. Aja, Runa, and Anelle stood in the center of the room, arguing amid the fleeing guests. Jessamyn's anger became a white heat inside of her and she pushed through the throngs of people toward them.

"What happened?" she demanded.

"They were dancing. We were right there, Jes. Róisín screamed, and they were gone," Runa said.

She rubbed at her temples. "They shifted? Is that what you're trying to tell me?"

Aja and Runa nodded.

"That's impossible, he doesn't—" She spun to face Anelle.

"No. To appease him earlier this week, I tossed a few herbal things at him, lit some candles, and..." She shrugged. "Intentionally failed. He had to have found other witches to help him."

"Are we sure it wasn't Róisín that shifted, and he went with her?" Jessamyn asked.

"He started the shift. He was fading first," Aja said. "The music stopped and everyone panicked."

She counted three breaths before responding. "Find them," she said to Runa and Aja. She pointed to Anelle and said, "Get me Marcelo and Nolani."

The trio before her vanished, leaving her amidst the screaming crowd. She tipped her head back, taking in the massive, jeweled chandelier overhead.

"I should have known," she whispered. A single tear escaped her eye and rolled down her temple into her hair. "I should have known. You should have known. To give me this task would be to fail. I failed."

"Jes! Jes!" Anelle shouted from one of the side entrances where she stood with Nolani and Marcelo.

This was her one last chance.

Renewed and determined to bear the weight that had been placed upon her shoulders, she began pushing people out of her way.

She held her hand out to Nolani. "I need you to trust me."

"I-I don't know how much help I can be, but—" She licked her lips and nodded.

Jessamyn took her hand, and her magic danced up through her body, down her arm and into Nolani's. There, at the center, Jessamyn found Nolani's magic, and the broken tether to Aunellion. Amidst the noise around them, she heard Nolani let out a small gasp.

"Nolani," Marcelo's panicked voice exclaimed.

"Just, just another second," Jessamyn pleaded. "There." Yes, Madigan had found his magic again, and with it, the very faint tie to any remaining Coven members. She released Nolani's hand and opened her eyes in time to see the young woman collapse against Marcelo.

"Did you find them?" she asked Jessamyn.

"Yes. You two get out of here. Find your brother and Cassius and go. Anelle, I need you with me."

Marcelo hesitated, and Jessamyn shook her head. "But I can fight if you need me to."

"Get everyone on the other side of the wall, Marcelo. That's what I need of you right now. Leave him and the others to the Coven."

He pressed his lips into a thin line, warring with staying and going.

"This is where you lead, Marcelo," Jessamyn said before shifting away with Anelle.

CHAPTER 85

Róisín's knees hit the stones of the castle roof hard, making her cry out in pain. Her magic scrambled to the spot, soothing. Then hands were pulling her to her feet before she could stand on her own.

"You'll have to forgive me, my love." Madigan ran his hands down her arms and gave her a soft smile. "I've only just gotten it back and in this body"—he looked down—"it appears there's a learning curve. I didn't mean to hurt you."

No. No, she couldn't do this again. Her skin crawled, and she wanted to shiver, shake, *something*. She couldn't fill her thoughts with Caid while standing before this monster. Once had been all she could bear. Before she could change her mind, she gripped her tether to Caid and pulled with all her might.

Madigan traced a finger along her jaw. "Now that we have some peace away from that silly little party..."

She pulled the tether again. Caid would come with Matthew and Shasta. Hopefully Ione, Ten, and Cicile as well. With the Coven already there, maybe it would be enough against them.

She took that sliver of hope and held it tight.

The wind whipped around them, twisting her dress around her legs and throwing her hair in her face. She pulled it away from her mouth, watching Madigan.

"You said." Her teeth chattered with the words. From the cold, from the fear that skittered up and down her spine. "The Goddess *stole* the Seer?"

He took the crown in his hands and threw it across the stones. "She tried to take me, too. Other Aunellions who shared ancestry with my parent. Anyone who had any inkling of sight."

Róisín wrapped her arms around herself. The cold of the night air was seeping into her bones. She wouldn't use her magic to warm herself. She would hold on to every drop, so when she needed it, she had it.

"Wh-what happened?"

"You saw what happened. My parent, locked for eternity in a house not even in their realm. All for what? Because they could see. They knew all her secrets and she needed that control over them so she could rule you all."

The anger was a palpable thing that pulsed from him.

Keep him talking, Róisín, a voice whispered to her.

"The Go—" She closed her mouth and swallowed hard when he shot her a look dark and rage filled. "Gea de..."

"Gea de Oro." His tone was rich with annoyance. "Rather, *Hydrangea* de Oro."

"Is just, what, one of us?"

He nodded.

"What of the Sisters, though? Are they really her daughters?"

"Unfortunately, yes. The girls had the poor misfortune of being born to her. It's really where it all started. Her quest for power and control over all of us." He waved a hand dismissively. "Enough about her. She will not take any further space in our lives." He prowled toward her, a hungry look in his eyes.

"Róisín!" Jessamyn called out from the entrance to the roof. "Get out of here!"

"She'll be going nowhere, Lady Lunestran," Madigan said. "She and I are working out our terms of marriage, aren't we, my love?" He was close enough now to take a lock of her hair between his fingers.

"Apologies, Your Highness, but I believe Queen Marsenna may have an issue with that. Given divorce is illegal here in Shianshani," Jessamyn said.

Róisín caught sight of Anelle's shadow moving along the parapet behind Madigan and quickly brought her attention back to Jessamyn.

"Then I'll just have to create a law that says it's allowed"—his thumb stroked the lock of hair—"in dire circumstances."

"And is this? I mean, a dire circumstance, Your Highness." Jessamyn was nearer to them now.

"I feel that being unhappily wed is certainly dire. Don't you?" He lifted his eyes from where he had been watching his thumb's movement to Jessamyn.

"So this law would apply just to the crown?" Her nod was so slight, Róisín almost missed it.

The groan Madigan released made him sound more like a petulant teen than the monster he really was. When his body turned away from Róisín, it had been the signal Anelle had been waiting for. Her shadow sprinted silently across the stones. Jessamyn adjusted her stance, readying for his reaction.

Thick coils crawled from Jessamyn's arms. "Róisín, go!"

Róisín didn't hesitate. She took the small space that Madigan's moving had given her and fled.

CHAPTER 86

THEY HAD shifted into chaos. People dressed in finery ran by them, screaming and shouting. Monsters with deformed jaws, glinting teeth, and enormous onyx eyes snatched at them. Some were covered in blood so badly it dripped from them. Mutilated bodies littered the ground.

Caid spun his sword around, panting. To buy himself a moment, he shot a ball of flame at one of the guards. No. *Monster.* These were monsters. There was nothing person-like about them at all. He followed it with ice spikes. The monster went down, snarling and snapping.

How long had they been at it? Why had for every one they felled, three more appeared from thin air? The monster moved to advance on Caid, but was halted when Ione shifted behind, her dagger glinting in the light of the fires that had erupted around them, as she drew it across his neck.

"It feels like we're extras cast in the wrong movie," Ione shouted to him.

He looked down at his blood-stained jeans and work boots. "If only it were a movie."

"Right?" She tossed one of her daggers over his shoulders, then pumped a fist. It landed in one of the monsters with a squelch. "Gosh, that felt fucking great, though."

"Caid!" Róisín's voice rang out. From where, he couldn't tell, and it made his breath catch in his chest as he spun around, searching. He had felt her tug moments ago but had still yet to find her. Or any of the others. He heard Matthew's rage-filled shout across the courtyard. Then the clang of swords.

The rumble behind him, the smell of rot engulfing him, had him spinning with his sword out, slashing as he swung the spiked mace he held in his other hand. It landed with a squishing, thudding sound against the face of another monster. It laughed at him, its long, snake-like tongue flicking out to lap up its own blood.

Jessamyn had been right. The strength these monsters held was unnatural.

He ducked the incoming blow, flipping the mace and ramming it into its kneecap. The monster bellowed and fell to its knees. Rearing back his sword arm, Caid used all his strength to bring it down, severing the monster's head.

Ione was back at his side, using her magic and her remaining Katana to fend off another.

"We need to find the others," Caid shouted.

"No shit. We were also *supposed* to stay together!"

He ducked again, lowering himself into a roll just in time to avoid a foot to his midsection. The move caused Shasta, who was quickly approaching them, to nearly trip over him.

"She's on the roof!" She pointed frantically.

"Who?" He and Ione asked.

"Róisín. The prince, he's at the wall gate. He said Jessamyn and Anelle went to the roof to get Róisín." Her face paled.

A sound from above pierced the air. It wasn't until Runa and Aja raced through the cluster of battling witches and guards, their roars deafening, that Caid realized what he was seeing.

Jessamyn tumbled through the air. Her body was motionless as she raced for the stone courtyard below.

"Shift!" Both Aja and Runa shouted at her. The pain in their tones made their voices sound raw.

But it was too late. Silence, for that one moment, fell over them, punctuated by the sound of her body crashing through a market stall.

Aja exploded, his yell ringing off the stone of the castle and the wall.

"Runa." Ione's voice was teary next to Caid. "I need to..." She patted herself down, then pulled a small knife from her waistband. "I have to help." Then she was off, leaving him and Shasta.

"Caid!" Róisín's voice was behind him, closer to the gate. He whirled, scanning the faces, letting his magic reach out and search for her.

"I need to find Lily," Shasta shouted over the noise.

Caid flipped his sword and held it out with the handle pointing at her. "Take this." She took the sword and began to turn away. "Hey, Mom? Don't die. Got it?"

Shasta blinked down at the sword. "Okay," she said finally. "You don't die too, okay?"

Giving her a quick nod, he used the mace to make his way through the crowd toward where he felt Róisín. He wanted to call to her, but something inside of him told him to move quietly through the crowd.

By the time he reached her, she was hurling a fist sized rock at one monster's head, while elbowing another in the throat. When the one that had taken the rock to the face advanced on her again, Caid drew back the mace, like he was readying to hit a home run. With a growl, he swung. The sound of bones shattering in its face could be heard over the noise around them.

The monster stumbled, falling. As it tried to gather itself, Caid gripped the handle in both hands, bringing it overhead. After all his years of chopping wood, the movement was muscle reflex as he came down on the monster's face.

"Duck!" he shouted at Róisín, immediately coming up and swinging out into the one she had elbowed in the throat. Its hands came to its face just as she spun, kicking her foot into its midsection.

"Caid." She threw her arms around him, peppering his face with kisses.

"Jessamyn," he said thickly.

"I know. I—" She looked to the spot of the parapet where Jessamyn had fallen. "I shouldn't have listened to her. I should have stayed up there."

"She made her choice, Róisín. She knew what she was up against with him. If she told you to go, she made her choice." He looped an arm around her waist and moved her aside. Lifting his leg, he kicked his foot against the chest of another monster. It tried to grab Caid's ankle, snapping its teeth at him. "What the fuck are these things?"

She stilled, her eyes swirling with a rainbow of colors. The air grew thin and hot. Caid felt his own magic rise around him, giving him a reprieve so he could breathe. Suddenly, the monster crumpled into dust. Róisín swayed slightly, and Caid brought her against him.

"Maybe don't use that one right now, okay?" He pressed a kiss to the side of her head. "And thank you for *not* trying to do this alone."

She placed a hand on his cheek. "I couldn't do this by myself. I realized that up there with him that I needed you."

"Ah." He lifted a brow. "So you only called me because you needed me." He flexed his pec muscles. "Just the hired muscle, right?"

Sighing heavily, she lightly shoved him. "No. You said together. So —" She turned to face the chaos in front of them. "Together."

CHAPTER 87

"MARCELO!" RUNA hollered, tossing something that resembled a massive hammer in his direction.

Marcelo had to leap into the air to catch it and nearly dropped it. The weight of it wasn't much, but it was unbalanced. He had gotten Nolani clear of the wall with his mother and as many of the guests and staff as he had been able to. In seconds, inside the wall had come to resemble a battlefield.

The Coven were doing their best with weapons and magic to take down as many as they could, and from where he stood, Marcelo couldn't tell who was winning. He could only pray that it was his side.

He didn't want to imagine what would come next if they didn't at least gain the upper hand in this.

Marcelo dodged an incoming blow that was followed by the sound of teeth snapping together. His heart stopped when he saw the creature's face barely inches from his.

This is what they were facing. He had only seen his father's face in profile, but seeing it now, head on... His body and mind became a riot of wants warring with one another.

Flee. Fight. Scream. Cry. Vomit.

Instead, he steeled himself, ducking again, driving the hammer's head into the monster's stomach. Before he could deliver another blow, Marcelo's back slammed into the side of the wall next to the gate, stealing the air from his lungs and igniting his body with pain.

"You fight well, for a human," the man who wore his father's face said, his nose only inches from Marcelo's.

He ducked just as Madigan swung at his head again.

"Quick too. Are we sure that none of my magic was inherited down the lines?" He threw his head back and cackled. "That would be quite rich. Now, where's my queen, son?"

Marcelo struggled against his grip, causing Madigan to press his forearm against his windpipe harder. His vision danced with spots as his lungs tried to gasp in as much air as they could. "Mother cleared the wall with the others."

"I don't care about that whore," he spat. "Róisín. Where is Róisín?"

"She's not your queen." He slumped down the wall slightly, his legs struggling to keep him upright.

"Ah, that's where you're wrong."

Marcelo's head throbbed. "She won't be your queen if you kill all her friends."

"My boy." Madigan leaned close, the first row of his teeth grazing Marcelo's earlobe. "This was all her idea."

"No," Marcelo said firmly.

"She was performing for you all. I knew every step you all took because she's mine. Wholly."

"No," he repeated.

"You'll see. When she dons the crown and stands at my side, you'll see her for who she truly is."

Madigan turned, leaving so quickly that Marcelo could not get his feet under himself, and he collapsed to the ground. His chest heaved with his heavy breaths, his vision blurred, his head pounding with fresh fear.

"Marcelo!" It sounded like Lily was calling him from below the water's surface. "Marcelo! Matthew, help him up."

Arms came around him from behind, pulling him to his feet. Lily checked him over, while Matthew stood before them, back-to fighting off a monster that took advantage of Madigan's absence to advance on them.

Finding a semblance of strength, he straightened and turned to Lily. A foreign feeling filled him. It was dark, venomous. *Potent.* "Where's Róisín?"

Matthew was suddenly at his side. "I heard what he told you, and I suggest you rein it in." His hand clasped Marcelo's shoulder, fingers digging into his muscles and tendons, making him wince from the pain. "This isn't our first dance with him, but it is *yours.* You can either stand united with us, which includes Róisín, against it. Or you'll find yourself on the other side. And I can say this"—he leaned closer, his voice a storm in Marcelo's ear—"you'd best hope that it is I that kills you before Caid finds you. You'll go roughly, but far more gently by my hand, than his."

Marcelo whipped his head around to face him.

"Do you trust Jessamyn?" Lily asked quietly.

"Undoubtedly." Marcelo's answer came quickly.

"And she trusted Róisín. Wanted to protect her, keep her safe," Lily said. "You know what he did to her, but you're not the one that was there after. Those nights that he haunted her dreams." Lily's eyes filled with tears. "You didn't hear the things she called out in her sleep. The way she screamed at her own body to do something. He thralled her that day, Marcelo. She couldn't do anything to save herself. And she *died* that day. Think about it. Before you go back out there." She pointed out to the battle going on outside of their temporary reprieve.

She and Matthew stepped away from him. Rage painted on Matthew's features, his eyebrows harsh lines over his narrowed eyes. Disappointment filled Lily's.

"Wait!" Marcelo called to them. "He's looking for her. He said she's going to be his queen. We need to find her before he can."

"Then that's where we're going." Lily stepped between him and Matthew.

Matthew reached out and grabbed Marcelo's shoulder again. His tone was a low warning. "I meant exactly what I said earlier. If it's not me, it *will* be Caid."

Marcelo had to admit he understood. If it had been Nolani, he would feel the same way. Absolutely murderous and without mercy.

Chapter 88

THE SEPARATION started gradually. Róisín and Caid had been tag teaming their way through the marketplace and across the massive courtyard, but slowly the gap formed, pushing them further and further apart.

Her lungs ached, and her muscles were heavy and sore with exhaustion. She couldn't go on like this. All the things she had gone against, all her training, this one moment in Shianshani had been far beyond. These monsters felt impossible and never-ending.

They had found success. The bodies of Madigan's men were spread all over. Some were decapitated. Others had their heads pommeled in the absence of something to remove it.

Róisín panted, wiping the back of her hand across her mouth. The sweat that rolled down her face stinging the cut on her top lip. She lifted the short sword she had found just as a monster brought a cutlass swinging down on her. The impact made her wince.

Then, the monster's head was gone.

"You'll stay away from my queen or your lives will be forfeit," Madigan told the headless body as it crumpled. Then he lifted his head, his eyes dark and locked on her. "We should leave. It's far too dangerous for you here."

Róisín took a deep breath, her magic swimming through her, around her. "No. I'm not going anywhere with you."

His eyebrows shot up. "My love—"

She loosed the blade at her side, spinning it in her hand. Gripping her short sword, she took her fighting stance before him. "I'm not your love, Madigan. I never have been and could never be. Not after what you did to me."

He blinked at her, confused.

"You call me your love, but you violated me when you took my choice away. Maybe," she said, her grip on the sword hand tightened, the leather groaning from the pressure, "I'd have been a more willing participant if you hadn't thralled me."

"Ah." He nodded, finally understanding. "*That*. I needed to see your intentions, sweet Róisín. I needed a peek inside to see who you truly were. You wouldn't have allowed that if I had just knocked on your door and asked politely, now would you?"

"Of course not."

He sighed. "You're really going to make me do this?"

"This is how it should have been in Roidon."

Tipping his head to one side, he grinned at her. "Oh, that smell was delicious." He licked his lips. "You say you were not a willing participant, but—" He took his bottom lip between his teeth, his eyes grazing every inch of her. "That was very real."

Of course it was, just not for you.

He took a slight step forward. "Perhaps we can start there and—"

She lunged at him, her blade plunging into his ribs as she spun away.

He roared and yanked it free. When his eyes found her, they were black. "With my magic returned, I can keep the beast within at bay, but, do not"—his body shuddered—"make me release it. It *will* be the end of you."

He was wiping his blood from the blade when she saw her opportunity. Recalling the day she watched Caid and Wyatt horsing around on their lunch break when they were working on her house, she ran at Madigan.

Dropping her shoulder, she connected with his midsection and wrapped her arms around him, following him down. His body landed, and the air exploded out of him. She drew her fist back and slammed it into his face. The sound of his cheekbone shattering filled her with satisfaction.

"I can give you eternity," he snarled at her.

She punched him again. "I don't give a shit about that. Why would I want forever with someone who won't let me make my own choices?"

He caught her fist in his hand before she could hit him again. "You forget, my love." He grinned up at her. His face was caught in his change, making the grin part monstrous with his rows of sharp teeth, and part devil with his bloodstained human teeth. "I am a siphon."

Her magic, as if on impulse, reached for her as it was pulled from her grasp. He flipped them so that he was on top of her. Róisín struggled to get her knee between them. She let out a scream, trying to use that feeling of sound bursting from her to propel herself forward. The skin around his eyes rippled, and he leaned closer to her.

"You may find eternity worth giving up a few things." He was trying to whisper, but the monster was overtaking him, making the words more guttural.

She reached for her magic, yet even when she dug to the very bottom of her depths, it was still empty. There was nothing. He was getting closer to her face with each press of his body. And she was growing weaker.

This is it. This is my end.

Madigan jerked back with a howl. A look of surprise flashed over his face.

"Run!" Caid shouted at her from behind him. "Run, Róisín, now!"

"No." She squared her stance, reaching for her magic again.

There. Something was right there.

His eyes were hard on hers over Madigan's shoulder. "I love you."

"Caid—" Her stomach dropped.

Caid had pulled his magic up, his body becoming pure fire. Wind whipped around them, sealing them off from reach. The flames wrapped around Madigan as the pair struggled against one another.

"Go!" Caid said, his voice deep and rough.

She squeezed her eyes closed. *Just a drop of anything,* she begged. *Anything.*

"*Caid!*" Shasta's voice rang out, desperate, from across the plaza. She was sprinting toward them with a long, silver sword in her hand. Throwing it in the air, she called out again, "Caid!"

Róisín felt her magic surge up within and immediately called it forth. She opened her eyes, death on her fingertips, just as Caid effortlessly caught the sword and Madigan spun free. Caid raised the sword. The sound of metal rang through the air from the force of his swing. Madigan dodged and spun behind Caid, latching himself to Caid's neck.

"No!" Róisín screamed, death pulsing forward in snaking black wisps of smoke from her body. It was nothing like that night in Roidon. Compared to what moved through her now, that had been quieter, muted almost.

This was freedom. This was *power*.

Madigan's spine snapped straight, eyes going wide. The skin of Caid's neck between his teeth, his blood bright red rivers dripping down his chin.

Róisín pressed forward. The wisps crept up his body, wrapping around him. His mouth opened and shut soundlessly, the wisps slipping inside.

When she spoke to him, her voice was guttural, otherworldly. Each word she spoke reverberated around them. "I will always find you, Madigan Milsenett. I will end you every single time. You can never hide from me. *I will haunt you*. You'll never escape me. This, I promise you."

Behind Madigan's body stilled by her magic pulling, pulling, pulling, the life from him, Caid moved shakily on his feet. With one hand pressed to his neck, he gripped the sword Shasta had thrown him in the other. He flipped the handle for a better grip before drawing his arm up, swinging down.

The cut was clean, sending Madigan's head tumbling. His body slumped to the ground with a soft thud before it shattered into millions of tiny little pieces.

"Róisín..." Caid staggered toward her a step.

She rushed to his side. Shasta was on her heels, breathing heavy from her sprint across the castle grounds. Together, they brought their arms around his middle and the trio slowly lowered themselves to the ground.

"It's going to be okay," Róisín whispered. Her heart thundered in her ears as her vision edged black. "It's going to be okay. I can fix this. I can fix you."

Caid's body clenched and she could hear his teeth grinding.

Shasta took one of his hands in hers. "Don't you dare, Kincaid James McGrath. Don't you dare."

"I must be in deep shit," Caid managed faintly. "Mom used my full name."

Shasta's lips spread into a small, shaking smile. Her eyes glimmered with the tears that had built there. "You'll only be in trouble if you let go."

Róisín looked away from her, focusing her everything on his neck. Her magic reached deeper into him, panic rocking through her when she still had yet to feel anything to grab hold of, anything to bring together. She pressed her hands, sticky from his blood, over the gaping wound at his neck. His pulse waned, his breaths became fainter.

Then she felt it. Slowly, their tether unraveled and began to fade. "No." She ground her teeth together, dredging up more power, reaching, reaching. "No, no, no, no. Caid, please," she choked out between the rising sobs. "No. Don't take him."

Shasta's gasping sob sounded from where she held his other hand.

Róisín moved closer and carefully placed his head in her lap. "Caid," she whispered. Then, her head fell back, the gray clouds overhead filling her vision. She screamed. A fire so hot, so intense, ripping through her as though she was being incinerated by the suns of all the realms at once.

Her lungs and heart seized, and it felt as though her chest were being ripped open, the organs torn from her chest without care. She wanted to scream again, but there was nothing there. No air, no voice. It had all been torn from her as the tether between them frayed. Thread by thread, pulled to its limit until it snapped.

Then...it was gone.

The rage, the anger that took the place of the pain was so sudden, it made her gasp. It filled her, clinging tightly to every fiber of her being. It hummed along her skin; beat with her heart. Moved with each breath in, and each breath out that her lungs gasped for.

Róisín had defeated Madigan again. She had brought almost all the Covens together. Had lost her mother. Had lost Lucius.

Now, Caid.

For what?

Her magic flared hot, knowing before she grasped what it had wanted. What it was doing for her.

"Róisín," Shasta said quietly. "Whatever you're thinking..."

"No." Her voice would have startled her if she had any feeling left inside. It was deep, vicious. Like it had teeth. "No more. This ends *here*."

"Róisín, don't." She reached for her but stopped.

"I love you, Shasta. Tell the others I love them. I can't." She shook her head sadly. "I can't anymore. They've taken too much from me."

"I love you," Shasta whispered. She gave her a tearful smile. "Please be safe. Take care of yourself and be safe."

Róisín let her magic wrap around Caid. She stroked his hair from his face with a shaking hand. From the corner of her eye, she could see the others making their way closer, nearly there. Her eyes found Matthew's in the melee.

He halted, his eyes growing round.

She had just gotten him back. The smallest piece of her heart that remained gave a sharp beat.

"I love you," she mouthed to him, then let her magic take her and Caid away.

CHAPTER 89

THE CLOCK chimed a new hour; the sound cutting through the silence of the room and making Matthew flinch. He had made his way back to Ely after they had gotten everything handled in Shianshani.

Once Madigan had died, his men had become disoriented and confused. They had lost their leader and were driven solely by their hunger after.

It made taking care of them easier.

But the damage had been done.

They had learned Jessamyn hadn't been able to shift; Madigan had driven a blade into her chest before pushing her from the roof. There had been other Shianshani Coven casualties, but they had thankfully been few.

As for the motley crew of himself, Lily, Ione, and Shasta, their losses had been devastating.

Matthew covered his face as the first sob wrenched free. The broken look on Róisín's face as she held Caid's body. He saw it every time he closed his eyes. His sister. His *brother*.

It had felt like it had been just moments before that he and Caid had been sitting on his bed. Caid urging him to take a second and let himself feel that grief. Now he was gone. And all that he felt was suffocating grief.

The moment Róisín's eyes locked on his. He knew. She was going and he couldn't stop her.

It hadn't been the end. She had severed her connection with Coven leaders, and the connection that had been created when they had first faced Madigan.

Shasta had felt it moments after Róisín disappeared. Then it hit Matthew. Almost like she had hesitated with theirs.

The blue cabinet at the center of the wall of bookshelves caught his attention, and he quickly rose from the chair. When he reached it, he paused with his hand on the handle of the middle drawer. Above it was a tall cupboard where he knew Lucius kept his secret stash of candy and Irish whisky. Below, more drawers. He'd start here in his search for the hidden one Lucius had spoken of in Aunellion.

Slowly, he pulled it out, swallowing hard. Turning his hand palm up, he felt along the top of the drawer. Nothing.

He moved to the next drawer and had the same result.

The third drawer, all the way in the back, along the wall, he felt the small seam. There wasn't a handle or a knob, so he tried pushing against it. With a click, the square popped out enough for him to grasp with his fingertips.

Holding the square in one hand; he reached with his other and pulled out notebook after notebook and several files.

Sitting on the floor, he opened the first file to find his birth certificate.

"Lily!" he shouted, jumping to his feet, spilling the notebooks and other files all over the floor. "Lily!"

A second later, she was bursting into the room. "What? What is it?"

With a shaking hand, he held the paper out to her. "Tell me I'm not reading that wrong."

She squinted her eyes and scanned the page. "Matthew," she said his name on an inhale.

He snatched the paper back from her, his eyes back on the line where *Mother* was filled in. The name Clarissa Burke McArthur in print on one side, and his mother's beautiful, scrawling letters on the other.

The Burkes in his hallucinations in Aunellion had been real. And they were family.

His eyes dropped to where it listed his mother's Coven name and birth realm. Typed neatly in both spaces—Aunellion.

Epilogue

FUTURE BRUSHED her fingers over the loom, her eyes damp with tears, her throat swollen with the sob she desperately tried to hold inside.

She had failed.

The thought hammered at her behind her wet eyes, and now a headache had built into a full percussion section, beating away.

She had failed.

They were damned, and it was her fault.

The tips of her fingers paused at the start of the loom where the tattered ends of a brilliant gold and green woven thread protruded. Kincaid James McGrath's line. The mysterious line that had appeared on Future's loom, and only her loom just as she had been promised it would centuries before.

Their secret. Their hope.

They had been waiting for that line to appear. For so long. So long that Future had lost hope that she had been right.

Where did I go wrong? The fury of her mistake burning in the tears that rolled down her cheeks.

So many regrets filled her now as she rose from the loom. With a heavy sigh, she gave the large wooden frame a nudge to roll it to the side. Her lids were weighted with grief, her bed was beckoning her.

Just over the threshold of her bedroom, the frame jerked to a stop. Something catching its wheel. Confused, Future eyed the floor that led into her room. Moving her loom with her was a ritual she performed every night and had done so for nearly six centuries. Never had the loom caught during the trek.

The board just to the left of the wide plank that created the threshold was raised just enough to create resistance for the small wheels of the loom's frame.

Frowning, Future walked to it, pressing down on the corner with her slippered foot. The board creaked as she depressed it. When she removed her foot, the corner rose.

How odd.

She tipped her head to the side, then dropped to her knees for a closer look. She studied the board with the same scrutiny a teacher would on a failing student's test that had no wrong answers present. The nails were still present, and the board did not appear to be rotted.

She traced a finger along the lifted edge, feeling the slightly worn grooves of a board frequently shifting. Lifting her head, she glanced back into the main room. It remained empty; their mother having left hours before. Present and Past had retired with their looms to their rooms not long after.

Nudging the loom back into the main room, she slipped into her bedroom and searched for something sturdy, yet thin, that could pry the board loose. Settling for a letter opener, she crawled across her bedroom floor and set to work lifting the board.

When she peered into the discovered space beneath the floor, a small gasp escaped. It wasn't fear she felt. It was a new terror that had Future rocking back, falling on her bottom, hand covering her mouth.

No, that can't be.

Scrambling back to her knees, she looked again. The long line of a brilliant gold and green thread that had once been woven across her loom sat haphazardly balled before her. Its end tattered, as though it had been yanked from her tightly woven loom abruptly.

On shaking legs, she rose to her feet. The discovery made her next decision for her. She needed to flee. She was no longer safe in her own home.

ACKNOWLEDGMENTS

First and foremost, thank you reader. To all of the readers who have stepped into this world with me, and have become invested. There were many times I almost walked away from this (because this is hard!), but the support helped me find that courage to keep moving forward and tell more of this story.

I'm also forever grateful to my editor, Brit. She had not only given me the feedback to help me grow as an author, but she's given me the tools to help me as well. With her in my corner, I don't know as though this story would have the depth and dimension that has shaped it into what it is. Or the em-dashes and feelings.

Justin, my sounding board and number one supporter. Even when whatever is coming out of my mouth doesn't make any sense at all, but I just need to get it out.

My son, who wants to give everyone he knows a copy of my book, and tells anyone who will listen that his mom is an author. To see the pride in his eyes, and hear it in his voice, over something *I've* done has been such an incredible thing that leaves me with those BIG feels.

Lauren, do you read this part? I hope so. From Insta friends, to Beta reader, to "want to be my positivity reader" you have been such an amazing human from the start. I'm so grateful for you.

To my loved ones who have passed on. Bringing you back to life on these pages in bits and pieces through these characters has given me a chance to be with you, just one more time. That makes every tear shed, every frustrated yank of the hair, or teeth-gritting moment worth it. If I can no longer have those moments with you in real life, I will embrace them on the pages.

My paternal grandfather, Bert Sr. My storyteller and poet. You'll always be the first one I think of when I sit down to write.

And of course, my parents, and my sisters.

About the Author

H.S. Sullivan comes from a long line of storytellers and poets, so it is of no surprise she has been scratching down stories of her own since she was a small child.

She holds a B.A. in Journalism and is an award winning journalist for feature writing and photography. Writing professionally for 16 years, she often moonlights as a ghost writer for fitness blogs and magazines.

Sullivan was born and raised on the northern New England coast, where she currently lives with her husband, son, and their rescued heeler mix. When she's not writing or reading, she is training for her next Masters weightlifting meet, tending to her gardens, or swimming in the Atlantic.

The Unraveling of Covens is Sullivan's second novel. Her debut was Daughters of Legianne, the first in the Realms of Covens series.

To stay up-to-date on the Realms of Covens series and other upcoming works, visit hssullivan.com or follow on Instagram at @themothermermaid.

www.ingramcontent.com/pod-product-compliance
Lightning Source LLC
Chambersburg PA
CBHW072019020726
47501CB00006B/1868